Volume 12

Satisfy your desire for more.

Good Girl Gone Bad

by Dominique Sinclair

Reagan's dreams are finally within reach. Setting out to do research for an article, nothing could have prepared her for Luke, or his offer to teach her everything she needs to know about sex. Licentious pleasures, forbidden desires… inspiring the best writing she's ever done.

Aphrodite's Passion

by Jess Michaels

When Selena flees Victorian London before her evil stepchildren can institutionalize her for hysteria, Gavin is asked to bring her back home. But when he finds her living on the island of Cyprus, his need to have her begins to block out every other impulse.

White Heat

by Leigh Wyndfield

Raine is hiding in an icehouse in the middle of nowhere from one of the scariest men in the universes. Walker escaped from a burning prison. Imagine their surprise when they find out they have the same man to blame for their miseries. Passion, revenge and love are in their future.

Summer Lightning

by Saskia Walker

Sculptress Sally is enjoying an idyllic getaway on a secluded cove when she spots a gorgeous man walking naked on the beach. When Julian finds an attractive woman shacked up in his cove, he has to check her out. But what will he do when he finds she's secretly been using him as a model?

***Romantic Times BOOKclub* 4½ Stars—Fantastic Keeper**

Reviews from Secrets Volume 1

"Four very romantic, very sexy novellas in very different styles and settings. ... The settings are quite diverse taking the reader from Regency England to a remote and mysterious fantasy land, to an Arabian nights type setting, and finally to a contemporary urban setting. All stories are explicit, and Hamre and Landon stories sizzle. ... If you like erotic romance you will love ***Secrets***."

— *Romantic Readers* review

"Overall, for a fan of erotica, these are unlike anything you've encountered before. For those romance fans who turn down the pages of the "good parts" for later repeat consumption (and you know who you are) these books are a wonderful way to explore the better side of the erotica market. ... ***Secrets*** is a worthy exploration for the adventurous reader with the promise for better things yet to come."

— Liz Montgomery

Reviews from Secrets Volume 2

Winner of the Fallot Literary Award for Fiction

"***Secrets, Volume 2***, a new anthology published by Red Sage Publishing, is hot! I mean ***red hot!*** ... The sensuality in each story will make you blush—from head to toe and everywhere else in-between. ... The true success behind ***Secrets, Volume 2*** is the combination of different tastes—both in subgenres of romance and levels of sensuality. ***I highly recommend this book***."

— Dawn A. Long, *America Online* review

"I think it is a fine anthology and Red Sage should be applauded for providing an outlet for women who want to write sensual romance."

— Adrienne Benedicks,
Erotic Readers Association review

Reviews from Secrets Volume 3

Winner of the 1997 Under the Cover Readers Favorite Award

"An unabashed celebration of sex. Highly arousing! Highly recommended!"

— Virginia Henley, *New York Times* Best Selling Author

"***Secrets, Volume 3*** leaves the reader breathless. Each of these tributes to exotic and erotic fiction offers a world of sensual pleasure and moral rewards. A delicious confection of sensuous treats awaits the reader on each turn of the page. Sexy, funny, thrilling, and luscious, Secrets entertains, enlightens, and fuels the fires of fantasy."

— Kathee Card, *Romancing the Web*

Reviews from Secrets Volume 4

"***Secrets, Volume 4***, has something to satisfy every erotic fantasy… simply sexsational!"

— Virginia Henley, *New York Times* Best Selling Author

"Provocative…seductive…a must read!" **4 Stars**

— *Romantic Times*

"These are the kind of stories that romance readers that 'want a little more' have been looking for all their lives without crossing over into the adult genre. Keep these stories coming, Red Sage, the world needs them!"

— Lani Roberts, *Affaire de Coeur*

"If you're interested in exploring erotica, or reading farther than the sexual passages of your favorite steamy reads, the ***Secret*** series is well worth checking out."

— *Writers Club Romance Group* on AOL

Reviews from Secrets Volume 5

"***Secrets, Volume 5***, is a collage of lucious sensuality. Any woman who reads ***Secrets*** is in for an awakening!"

— **Virginia Henley,** *New York Times* Best Selling Author

"Hot, hot, hot! Not for the faint-hearted!"

— *Romantic Times*

"As you make your way through the stories, you will find yourself becoming hotter and hotter. ***Secrets*** just keeps getting better and better."

— *Affaire de Coeur*

Reviews from Secrets Volume 6

"***Secrets, Volume 6*** satisfies every female fantasy: the Bodyguard, the Tutor, the Werewolf, and the Vampire. I give it Six Stars!"

— Virginia Henley, *New York Times* Best Selling Author

"***Secrets, Volume 6*** is the best of ***Secrets*** yet. …four of the most erotic stories in one volume than this reader has yet to see anywhere else. … These stories are full of erotica at its best and you'll definitely want to keep it handy for lots of re-reading!"

— *Affaire de Coeur*

Reviews from Secrets Volume 7

Winner of the Venus Book Club Best Book of the Year

"…sensual, sexy, steamy fun. A perfect read!"

— Virginia Henley, *New York Times* Best Selling Author

"Intensely provocative and disarmingly romantic, Secrets Volume 7 is a romance reader's paradise that will take you beyond your wildest dreams!"

— *Ballston Book House* Review

"Erotic romance is at the sensual core of Red Sage's latest collection of short, red hot novels, ***Secrets, Volume 7***."

— *Writers Club Romance Group* on AOL

Reviews from Secrets Volume 8

Winner of the Venus Book Club Best Book of the Year

"***Secrets Volume 8*** is simply sensational!"

— Virginia Henley, *New York Times* Best Selling Author

"***Secrets Volume 8*** is an amazing compilation of sexy stories discovering a wide range of subjects, all designed to titillate the senses."

— Lani Roberts, *Affaire de Coeur*

"All four tales are well written and fun to read because even the sexiest scenes are not written for shock value, but interwoven smoothly and realistically into the plots. This quartet contains strong storylines and solid lead characters, but then again what else would one expect from the no longer ***Secrets*** anthologies."

— Harriet Klausner

"Once again, Red Sage Publishing takes you on a journey of sexual delight, teasing and pleasing the reader with a bit of something to appeal to everyone."

— Michelle Houston, *Courtesy Sensual Romance*

"In this sizzling volume, four authors offer short stories in four different sub-genres: contemporary, paranormal, historical, and futuristic. These ladies' assignments are to dazzle, tantalize, amaze, and entice. Your assignment, as the reader, is to sit back and enjoy. Just have a fan and some ice water at your side."

— Amy Cunningham

Reviews from Secrets Volume 9

"Everyone should expect only the most erotic stories in a ***Secrets*** book. ...if you like your stories full of hot sexual scenes, then this is for you!"

— Donna Doyle, *Romance Reviews*

"***Secrets 9***...is sinfully delicious, highly arousing, and hotter than hot as the pages practically burn up as you turn them."

— Suzanne Coleburn, *Reader To Reader Reviews/ Belles & Beaux of Romance*

"Treat yourself to well-written fictionthat's hot, hotter, and hottest!"

— Virginia Henley, *New York Times* Best Selling Author

Reviews from Secrets Volume 10

"***Secrets Volume 10***, an erotic dance through medieval castles, sultan's palaces, the English countryside and expensive hotel suites, explodes with passion-filled pages."

— *Romantic Times BOOKclub*

"Having read the previous nine volumes, this one fulfills the expectations of what is expected in a ***Secrets*** book: romance and eroticism at its best!!"

— *Fallen Angel Reviews*

"All are hot steamy romances so if you enjoy erotica romance, you are sure to enjoy ***Secrets, Volume 10***. All this reviewer can say is WOW!!"

— *The Best Reviews*

Reviews from Secrets Volume 11

"***Secrets Volume 11*** delivers once again with storylines that include erotic masquerades, ancient curses, modern-day betrayal and a prince charming looking for a kiss. Scorching tales filled with humor, passion and love." **4 Stars**

— *Romantic Times BOOKclub*

"The ***Secrets*** books published by Red Sage Publishing are well known for their excellent writing and highly erotic stories and ***Secrets, Volume 11*** will not disappoint. "

— *The Road to Romance*

"***Secrets 11*** quite honestly is my favorite anthology from Red Sage so far. All four novellas had me glued to their stories until the very end. I was just disappointed that these talented ladies novellas weren't longer."

— *The Best Reviews*

"Indulge yourself with this erotic treat and join the thousands of readers who just can't get enough. Be forewarned that ***Secrets 11*** will wet your appetite for more, but will offer you the ultimate in pleasurable erotic literature."

—*Ballston Book House Review*

Reviews from Secrets Volume 12

"***Secrets Volume 12***, turns on the heat with a seductive encounter inside a bookstore, a temple of naughty and sensual delight, a galactic inferno that thaws ice, and a lightening storm that lights up the English shoreline. Tales of looking for love in all the right places with a heat rating out the charts." **4½ Stars**"

— *Romantic Times BOOKclub*

"I really liked these stories.You want great escapism? Read ***Secrets, Volume 12***."

— *Romance Reviews*

Satisfy Your Desire for More... with Secrets!

Did you miss any of the other volumes of the sexy **Secrets** ***series? At the back of this book is an order form for all the available volumes. Order your*** **Secrets** ***today! See our order form at the back of this book or visit Waldenbooks or Borders.***

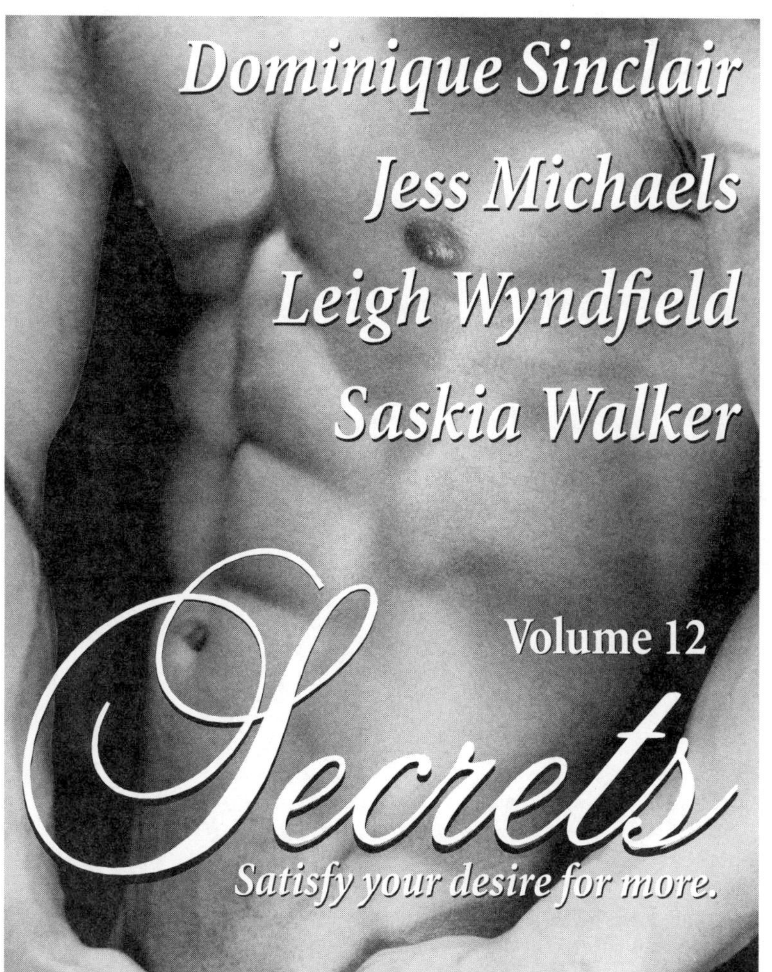
Dominique Sinclair
Jess Michaels
Leigh Wyndfield
Saskia Walker
Volume 12
Secrets
Satisfy your desire for more.

SECRETS Volume 12
This is an original publication of Red Sage Publishing and each individual story herein has never before appeared in print. These stories are a collection of fiction and any similarity to actual persons or events is purely coincidental.

Red Sage Publishing, Inc.
P.O. Box 4844
Seminole, FL 33775
727-391-3847
www.redsagepub.com

SECRETS Volume 12
A Red Sage Publishing book

ISBN 0-9754516-2-6

Published by arrangement with the authors and copyright holders of the individual works as follows:

Photographs:
Cover © 2005 by Tara Kearney; www.tarakearney.com
Cover Models: Chayne Jones
Setback cover © 2000 by Greg P. Willis; email: GgnYbr@aol.com

Printed in the U.S.A.

Book typesetting by:

Quill & Mouse Studios, Inc.
www.quillandmouse.com

Contents

Good Girl Gone Bad

by Dominique Sinclair

To My Reader:

When a man comes along who makes you want, makes you crave… When a man comes along who is everything you secretly desire, everything you secretly need… When a man comes along, go. Willingly, wantonly. Let there be no regret. Let there be seduction. Let there be love.

Chapter One

"One shot, Reagan," Paxton Anderson, the senior editor of *Glimmer Magazine,* said looking over the top of her black rimmed glasses with her piercing green eyes. "Blow it and you're filing paperwork for the rest of your days here. I need a continuous piece, fifteen hundred word per segment, four issues."

Reagan scrawled notes on a flip notepad as fast as she could, trying to stamp down the elation building inside her like a helium balloon. An unfortunate Aspen skiing trip had ended with the broken right arm and leg of the writer originally assigned to the piece, leaving no one but Reagan available to turn out the continuous article on relationships for the independent woman.

"First installment on my desk by Friday; we're chasing a deadline. Questions? Good. Get to work." Paxton swiveled her chair and yanked out a file drawer.

Reagan closed her notepad. "Thank you, Ms. Anderson, you won't regret assigning me—"

"Are you still here?"

"No, ma'am, I'm-a-going. Gone. Thank you." She back stepped to the door and reached blindly for the handle. "I'm so grateful for your belief in me—"

"Shut the door behind you."

Reagan nodded, stepped into the hallway and softly closed the door. Then jumped up and down, barely concealing a delightful scream. She had spent a year working for *Glimmer* as a staff writer. But her duties rarely went beyond refilling coffee cups and line editing other writers' pieces. Oh, she had submitted idea after idea of her own, hoping to have an article published and her by-line shinning back at her like a beacon to a full time writing career. All had been rejected.

Now she could visualize herself answering fan mail. Offers would come flooding in from magazines across the country to steal her away from *Glimmer* with the promise of more money, more exposure, more fame. Ah, she was on her way to being the new, savvy, voice of today's women. All her hard work had finally paid off.

A little niggling douse of guilt tried to interject that she shouldn't be so happy at the expense of another's trip down a mountain head over heels, but darn it! She deserved this opportunity, no matter how it came about.

She fairly skipped back to her cubical. She even ignored a few requests for coffee refills, saying, "Sorry, deadline to meet."

She sat at her desk, deadheaded a dried flower from the African violet her mother gave her, then pulled out a fresh pad and sharp pencil and scrawled across the center RELATIONSHIP-INDEPENDENT-WOMAN and circled it. She tapped her pencil on the pad, biting her lower lip, waiting for brainstorm release.

Nothing came.

Nada. Zip. Blank.

The little niggling of doubt began filtering through her happiness like a gray mist.

She opened her drawer, pulled out the file containing her already rejected article ideas and scanned through them, hoping to find something worthy of re-working into a masterpiece.

The gray mist turned to a big, black rain cloud. She wrote about topics like skin care and choosing a reliable nanny—topics she felt were of interest to the modern woman—topics Paxton said over and over *Glimmer's* readers weren't interested in.

Maybe Reagan was trying too hard, maybe she just needed to relax and allow ideas to freely come. Maybe she should just admit she wasn't the type of writer *Glimmer* was looking for—

An arm wrapped around her shoulder. "Um, um, um, sweet thing. Heard you got an assignment. Whaddya say we hit the town tonight, paint it purple?"

Reagan sniffed and glanced up at Michaelo. Today he wore a zebra stripped satin shirt unbuttoned to the naval, tight leather pants and four inch boots. She tried to smile, but her bottom lip trembled.

He knelt down at eye level with her, swiped a tendril of hair behind her ear. "Oh, pooh, something has my Reggie upset. Tell Michaelo about it."

She shoved the file back in the drawer, not caring she didn't return it to its alphabetical position. "I'm never going to be a writer! Why did I ever think I could do this? Everyone was right, I should just find myself a nice husband and have babies."

"Whoa. What's happening here? Five minutes ago you looked like you could fly as you sailed past me in the hallway. Now you've got tears in your eyes."

"Paxton wants me to do the article on relationships for the independent woman. In three days!" She buried her hands in her palms.

Michaelo rubbed her back. "Now, now. It can't be that bad."

"Yes, it can! I've just been fooling myself. I can't do this. I know nothing about men, or relationships, or being independent. I still take my laundry to my mother's every Sunday for heaven's sake!"

He spun her chair, tilted her chin to look at him. "You're forgetting one thing, Reggie."

"Yeah? What's that?"

"You're a writer. Research is what you do best. Okay, so you are a bit of a *Little House on the Prairie* type of girl, but you can learn about women that go *va-va-voom*."

"How?"

"I'll take you out on the town. We'll go to all my hotspots; you can interview some *real* women."

Reagan couldn't help but laugh through the hiccups of despair. "Are you trying to get me fired, Michaelo?"

"Just wanted to see you smile. All you have to do, *suga*, is what you do best. Observe. Research. Read." He reached under her desk, pulled out her purse and tucked it under her arm. "Michaelo says, go!"

Reagan smiled and stood. "Thank you, Michaelo."

"Hey, what are friends for? Oh, would you mind if I borrow that strawberry gloss again? Got a lunch date."

"Top drawer. See you later."

Michaelo waved goodbye with the end of his scarf.

Reagan browsed the bookstore for over an hour and compiled a stack of research materials including a Cosmo magazine, some of the new Chic Lit books that were all the rage and a guide to being an assertive woman. Nothing sparked a topic. She was no closer to an article than before.

She glanced around the bookstore in one last hope at inspiration. A man sat at one of the tables, cup of coffee and newspaper in hand. Maybe that's what she needed to do. Get a latte—double the whip cream and chocolate sprinkles—sit and take a deep breath, let the ideas come freely, naturally.

The man lowered the paper.

Reagan tripped over her feet.

She darted into an aisle, books crushed to her chest. She blew out a long, slow breath. *Calm down, Reagan, act natural.* She peeked around the corner and sighed. She hadn't seen him since this past summer, when for two glorious weeks she had taken her three year old niece for swim lessons at the city pool. Fourteen marvelous days when Reagan handed Josie over to his outstretched, muscular, tanned arms and wished it were she he took by the waist and gently lowered into the water.

Every day while Josie splashed in the pool under his careful supervision, Reagan had waited on an empty bench in various *please-please-please* notice me positions. Draping her arm over the back of the bench and crossing her legs, one sandaled foot swinging. Sideways, knees bent and head tipped back to glory in the sun. Elbows on knees, her forearms pushing what little breasts she had together, feet vee'd outward.

Two torturous weeks and Reagan finally resigned herself to the fact she wasn't the type of woman who attracted tanned, buff summer boys. Never had been, never would be.

What would she have done with a man like him anyway?

What would they have had in common?

What would her mother say if she were to bring a man like that to a family dinner?

Only, the man sitting across the bookstore seemed completely different than the golden boy of summer past. The blonde highlights had faded, leaving his hair dark. His once smooth face with chiseled features now had a day's growth of beard. He wore reading glasses, of all things, and a beige cable knit sweater taut over muscles. He was dark and sexy and edgy and dangerous and handsome. And, *oh my…*

Who was she kidding, anyway? She couldn't even muster the courage to say hello. The "good girl next door, meant to marry, have kids, bake cookies," everything her mother wanted in a daughter summed up Reagan to a tee. Well, almost. She could never be as perfect as her mother wished.

She glanced down at her pile of books. No use continuing to fool herself. *Glimmer* had been her dream job, but dreams had to come to an end. Paxton would simply have to hire out a freelancer, and she'd be fired.

Reagan set down her pile of books on the lip of the shelf, then happened to scan a title on a bookspine: *Time Tested Secrets of Seducing Mr. Right.* And the next: *365 Nights of Passion.* And *The Karma Sutra. The Joy of Sex. Make Love to Your Man. Learn to Pleasure Yourself.*

Good heavens. Reagan took a small step back. She heard of books like these, but good girls like her never would dare...

She glanced over her shoulder left and then right, then slid out a book titled *Learn to be a Bad Girl and Get the Man You Want.*

She opened the book to a full color picture and quickly slammed it shut. She swallowed thickly. Women did that? With another glance around, she slowly opened the book again.

Before long Reagan had a book tucked under her arm, a *must buy* pile of three on the floor, and her nose in another. According to the books, even *she* possessed the potential to be a sexual vixen, to attract the man of her dreams and become the type of woman men fantasized about.

She stepped back and leaned against the bookshelf behind her, the book crushed against her chest. She closed her eyes, allowing the pleasure of fantasy, of imagining herself a brazen woman she'd never be in true life. A woman Luke would respond to, want, need.

If she were that woman, Reagan would tousle her hair, lick her lips and saunter toward him, slide onto the table and put one leg on either side of his chair. Her skirt would be short and tight instead of the ankle length floral she wore now, and it would hike up to her panty line—no she would be wearing no panties at all. She would slip the top button of her blouse while her eyes smoldered her desire.

"Reagan," he would growl as he took off his reading glasses.

She would run her hands through his hair while he gazed at her with dark, hungry eyes. His hands would slide up her calves, around to her knees and gently open her legs further—

Reagan swallowed, didn't dare allow herself to continue on with the fantasy. Already her breasts ached in the confines of her sensible bra. Her sex pulsed in her lightweight control top undies. How quickly her brief fantasy aroused her, how quickly she succumbed to her licentious desires.

Reagan bit her bottom lip and nearly whimpered. What she wouldn't do for the brazenness to walk over to his table and act out her fantasy. She peeked around the shelf one more time.

He was gone.

"Excuse me."

Reagan moved her foot to slide the pile of books out of the way with her sensible flat sandal. "Sorry," she said, glancing over her shoulder.

Oh. My. God.

She swallowed hard and slowly turned around, hiding the manual on multiple orgasms behind her back. "Luke."

Luke studied her a moment. "Josie's aunt, right?"

Heat swarmed like hungry butterflies from her head to her toes. She felt faint, lightheaded. He remembered her. *Wow.* "Um, yeah. Reagan. My name. It's Reagan."

He leaned his hip against the shelf, nodded at the book behind her back, cocking an eyebrow. "Find anything good to read?"

She glanced down to the couple posed seductively on the scarlet red cover of the top book by her feet. *Oh god, oh god, oh god.* She shrugged as she slid the stack further out of the way. She could absolutely die. "Oh, you know, just browsing."

Luke smiled, stepped forward, reaching around and taking hold of the book. His hard body pressed against her breasts; his mouth hovered just above her. "Let's take a look."

Reagan clutched the book as Luke tugged. His hot breath caressed her nape. Dizzy from the masculine scent of him and the seductiveness of his rich, deep voice, she involuntarily loosened her fingers.

He slid the book from her hand. "Interesting."

She closed her eyes in nothing short of complete embarrassment, then peeked one eye open to assess the damage as he flipped through the pages. He paused to study an illustration; she could only imagine what he thought of her.

"It's, ah—for work." She grabbed for the book. "May I have it back now?"

Luke swung it above her head, a smile tugging at the corner of his mouth. "Work, huh?" He lowered the book and held it in one hand, seemingly taunting her to try for it again.

Of all her imagined fantasies about Luke, being caught reading about sex had never come into her thoughts. "I…it's…"

If she were going to be an honest to goodness writer, she needed to act like one. She raised her chin a notch and looked him squarely in the eye. "Research," she said.

He set the book down, braced his hand on the top shelf above Reagan's head and leaned closer. "What exactly is it you want to learn from these books, Reagan?"

Little vibrations hummed through her body from the way he said her name, deep, rich chords, almost a whisper. She dropped her chin and glanced away. "I—I don't know, exactly."

He captured her chin with two fingers, lifting her gaze to meet his for several long moments that held Reagan's breath. "Tell me."

"I…" She moistened her bottom lip, craving for him to lean down and kiss her.

He lowered his gaze to her damp lips as he lightly traced his fingers from her chin down her throat to cover her wildly beating pulse. "Don't you know what's in those books, Reagan?"

Luke's words swirled over her mouth in a moist caress. Reagan breathed the faint taste of coffee and sugar. How she wanted his firm mouth to press against hers, to kiss her, to ravish her. Slowly she shook her head, biting her lower lip.

His fingers left her pulse; his hand moved down over the ruffle of her blouse and skimmed across the fabric to the swell of her breast, cupping it so softly Reagan nearly cried out. She contained herself, knowing someone would come to investigate if she made a noise. For now, their corner of the bookstore was empty.

"Look at me."

She sucked in a breath and slowly returned her gaze, fearing she would find him amused. Instead he rewarded her with a look of satisfaction, and his hand pressing harder against her breast, lifting upward and squeezing her nipple between his thumb and forefinger.

Reagan fought against a twinge of pain and unexpected pleasure, tensed against the warmth radiating between her legs.

"Do you want to know what's in those books, Reagan?"

She never knew her body could feel like this, tight and aching, yearning and alive. If those books could teach her how to have this again and again…

"Yes, Luke. I want to know." She barely recognized her tone. She sounded ragged, out of breath. *Seductive.*

Luke lowered his mouth and suckled her bottom lip, nipping it before moving to her throat. The stubble of his beard scraped against her skin, sensitizing her flesh. Reagan dropped her head back, fingers digging into the wood shelf behind her for support.

"Do you want me to show you what's in those books?"

"Y-yes."

He trailed his tongue up her neck and kissed behind her ear, turning her body molten gold, ready for his molding. His hand left her breast and teased down her stomach, the lightest of touch and yet her body shivered.

"I'll need you to be a very good girl." His erection, taut against his jeans, pressed against her hip. "Do everything I say." He bunched the fabric of her skirt, pulling it slowly up her thigh. "I need you to say yes, Reagan. Tell me you'll obey."

Reagan arched as he reached up her skirt and palmed her heated juncture. Her head thrashed to the side. She adjusted the width of her legs, opening wantonly for his touch. "Yes. Anything."

Luke slid a finger beneath her damp panties, parted her swollen folds and pressed against her nubbin. Nothing had ever felt so good as being touched by Luke. A flood of pure pleasure washed through her, weakening her knees. Her body slid down the bookshelf.

He edged her bottom onto his thigh, supporting her as he slowly began to stroke the engorged pleasure point as he kissed her.

Heat built with each stroke, her breasts swelled and ached. The back of her throat went dry. She both wanted to end the orgiastic sensations and stay suspended in the intensity of it, die of the pleasure.

"Tell me again." He sought her channel, the pad of his finger pressing just at the opening and she knew the fulfillment she needed wouldn't come until she offered complete abandonment.

"Anything, anything you ask. Just please—"

He thrust his finger deep inside her, his thumb pressing against her nubbin. She cried out against his shoulder, biting as her internal muscles tightened around him, drawing him further in as she climaxed.

When she finally relaxed against him, he said, "I'm sure you will." Luke slid his finger from her, rounding his hand to her bottom. "We'll start soon."

Reagan's legs still trembled an hour later when she returned to work. She sat at her desk, dropped her head back in her chair. *What did she just allow to happen?* She placed her hand over the flutters in her stomach and went over every touch, every kiss, and tried to hate herself for her licentious behavior. Only she found her body responding to the memory. Even now with the sounds of phones ringing, faxes humming, copy machines spitting out paper, her body felt damp, dewed with wanting, anticipation.

"Soon..." she heard Luke echo.

Good heavens, in one encounter she'd gone from being a good girl to very, very bad. And yet she knew if Luke wanted her again, she wouldn't hesitate. Bad had been very, *very* good.

Reagan leaned forward in her chair, turned to a fresh page in her notepad, and scrawled in bold letters: *Good Girl Gone Bad* and circled it. She tapped her bottom lip with the pencil several times then began filling the page with words associated to what she'd just experienced and knew, thanks to Luke, she had the topic for her article.

Chapter Two

Good Girl Gone Bad, segment one, hit Paxton's desk first thing Friday morning, and Reagan spent the day with damp palms and her heart beating like a hummingbird waiting for her summons. It finally came at four o'clock. Feeling like she could throw up at any moment, she left her cubicle and walked toward the lion's den. She knocked on Paxton's door.

"Enter."

Reagan drew in a deep breath and placed her hand on the door handle. A hand wrapped around her stomach. She nearly jumped out of her skin. "Don't worry, baby doll, you're gonna rock," Michaelo said, his baby soft face buried just behind her ear.

Reagan turned around. "What if she hates it?"

"Honey, I got hot reading it. When you're through with him, I'll take him."

She shook her head, eyes wide. "It-I-uh—it wasn't me!"

Michaelo sucked in his cheeks, which if she wasn't mistaken had a sheen of glitter today, and struck a pose. "Uh-huh, and I'm wearing men's underwear. Your secret's safe with me."

"But-but-but-"

He reached around her and opened the door. "TTFN."

Reagan swiped her palms on the back of her skirt and stepped into Paxton's office. She took one glance at Paxton, perched behind the large desk, glasses on, shaking her head as she read over her pages, and Reagan wanted to run.

"You wanted to see me?" Her voice sounded barely louder than a mouse.

"Sit."

Reagan moved to the padded leather chair and perched on the edge, a sinking feeling in her stomach. There was no need to get comfortable. She folded her hands in her lap, unfolded them, folded them again while Paxton flipped page after page.

"*Good Girl Gone Bad*. Did I not make it clear the article was on relationships for the independent woman?" Paxton didn't bother to look up.

"I-uh..."

"How many articles have you submitted to me in the past year?"

"Over fifty?"

Paxton set the pages down, leaned back in her chair and took off her glasses. "And how many did I accept?"

Reagan felt herself shrinking into the chair. "Er, none."

"None. So why did you think submitting a piece off-topic would be acceptable?"

"Well..."

Paxton leaned forward, peering down her long, straight hawk-like nose. "Let me make one thing clear. I don't like my chain yanked. When I ask for something, I get it. You newbie writers think you can come in here and run the show. That's my job. I say what goes into print, nobody else. Do I make myself clear?"

Tears brimmed in Reagan's eyes. She nodded and stood. "Yes. I'm sorry to waste your time."

"Did I excuse you?"

Reagan shook her head.

"Sit."

She complied like a scolded puppy. There was no need for a tortured rejection, a simple "No thanks" would have sufficed. Clearly Paxton had a point to hammer home.

She picked up the article. "Is this piece fiction?"

"No-no-no. Of course not. It's the, um, actual experience of the, er, subject. Names have been changed, as noted." As well as the city and their physical descriptions.

"And you can follow this up with three more segments?"

Reagan's mouth dropped open. She gulped. This wasn't a rejection. *Oh my god, oh my god, ohmygod!* She nodded her head repeatedly.

Paxton lifted the cover page and read aloud again, "*Good Girl Gone Bad*. All I can say, Reagan, is good goddamn work. It's sexy. It's sensual. It's every woman's fantasy. Congratulations."

Congratulations. Reagan could have cried. Any doubts over writing about her experience with Luke floated away. She leapt to her feet, reached her hand over the desk to shake Paxton's hand. "Thank you, Ms. Anderson. Thank you so much."

Paxton simply raised a brow. "Make sure the other pieces are as good. You could be looking at a regular column. And bonuses."

Oh. My. God. *Her own column? Bonuses?* "They will be, I promise. Thank you, thank you, thank you," she kept repeating until she was out the door. She jumped up and down in the hallway and squealed, then rushed to find Michaelo.

She found him by the water cooler and flung her arms around him. "I did it! I did it! Paxton's accepted the article. She might give me a column! I get bonuses!"

Michaelo swung her around, then set her on her feet. "Hot damn, you're on your way, Reggie. Feel good?"

She dropped her head back and closed her eyes. "Awesome. It feels totally awesome." Now that she experienced being a bad girl, she could turn out three more articles. No problem.

Reagan's elation climbed to a higher level when she listened to the message on her home phone. She'd tried not to dwell on the fact she hadn't heard from Luke since their first encounter, instead she'd focused on writing the article. But in the back of her mind a little voice niggled constantly, saying she'd never see him again. She wasn't good enough, or bad enough, or whatever it took enough to hold a man's interest.

"Tomorrow. Six o'clock. I'll pick you up," Luke's smooth voice said on the recording.

The little voice of doubt was finally silent.

Reagan danced in a circle. "I did it, I did it, I did it!" Excitement and anxiety and a thousand more emotions flowed through her. She had energy to burn.

Knowing the next twenty-four hours would pass with excruciating slowness if she didn't do something to occupy her mind, she suddenly beamed. There was work to be done. Grabbing her purse and keys, she headed for the bookstore way across town to pick up the titles she'd left behind at the other store, where she'd never dare enter again for fear an employee had seen her and Luke.

Paxton would be impressed when she turned in the next segment of *Good Girl Gone Bad* early and in the process, she'd have a jump-start on Luke's next *lesson*.

Six hours later, Reagan sat at her kitchen table and slashed her pen across the words she'd written, ripped the sheet out of her pad, wadded it and tossed it into the growing pile on the floor. The books only made her crave Luke, and she'd found no direction for the second article.

Slapping down the pen, she bowed her head into her palms. Three more articles, *hah*. She couldn't write one. Dumping the books in the trash, she went to bed, only to sleep fitfully. She tossed and turned, considering and dismissing topic ideas. Slipped in and out of sleep, dreaming briefly of Luke touching her, kissing her. Of standing on top of a table in the bookstore reading her article word for word for everyone to hear. Of Paxton sitting behind her desk, eyes growing huge behind her glasses, her mouth moving but no words coming out.

Reagan woke feeling as if she barely slept. She laid in bed staring at the ceiling, mourning the loss of her column and bonus, possibly her entire career. If not for Luke she would never have written the article Paxton loved so much.

She smiled. *If not for Luke.*

If not for Luke indeed.

He was picking her up tonight for the next lesson. If Luke delivered anything even close to what he showed her in the bookstore, Reagan would have all the inspiration she needed for the next segment. Just a different kind of research, something she'd never find in a book or on a website.

It's not like Luke would ever know. She'd used a pseudonym and changed their names and physical descriptions. He'd never read a women's magazine. She'd already featured their first encounter. One more couldn't hurt.

Besides, she may be a good girl, but she wasn't naïve. Luke wouldn't show up with a bunch of daisies and a box of chocolates and take her on a real date. No, he'd take what he wanted from her while giving her one heck of a lesson.

And during the process, she'd do some research for her next article.

Mutually beneficial for everyone.

Research never promised to be so fun.

At six o'clock the doorbell rang. Reagan's heart thudded to her stomach. She took in a deep breath and counted to ten. She crossed the room slowly, smoothed her sweater, and opened the door. Luke leaned against the doorjamb. A tailored black suit molded his broad shoulders, a white dress shirt setting off his golden tan. He still had the shadow of beard giving him a dangerous, sexy edge. A tug pulled at the corner of his mouth as his gaze lingered over her body.

She closed her eyes and inhaled the scent of him, a combination of earthy spice and clean soap as he stepped inside. She shut the door and leaned against the wall for support. "I, um, didn't know how to dress." She waved a slightly trembling hand to her typical ankle length skirt and sweater set. "You didn't say where we were going."

Luke lifted a shopping bag. "Brought what you need."

She eyed the package, a little *humm* of pleasure vibrating through her. Imagine, him taking the time to pick something out for her, his hands selecting it. She took a hesitant step forward, then stopped, her earlier thoughts of this not being a proper date coming to mind. "Thank you, but really, you shouldn't have."

He set the bag on the floor by her floral print sofa, turned and leaned against the back. "Take off your clothes."

Reagan gulped. He couldn't be serious. "Here?" *Now*? Her two-bedroom house sat on a quiet street with hedges obscuring the view inside if someone should pass by. *Still!* She never even walked around in her bathrobe without closing the curtains.

"Yes." He stuffed his hands in his pockets and crossed his long, powerful legs at the ankles. "If you want to learn, Reagan, you must obey."

The table lamps were shining bright. There were no shadows to conceal her body from him, no way to hide the heat flaming her cheeks. The one and only lover she had, a boyfriend she dated all four years of college, use to call her a prude when she'd insist he turn off the lights before she would dash nude from the bathroom and jump under the covers.

"Could I dim the lights, maybe light a candle?"

Luke shook his head.

Reagan wished she'd thought to create a romantic atmosphere before he showed up. Light a few candles, turn off the lights. Now it was too late. She'd agreed to do anything he asked. She needed this experience for her next article. No, she needed to experience this for herself… Her trembling fingers went to the top pearl button of her soft gray sweater and slipped it through. She gazed downward as she worked on the next, gathering courage to see this through.

"Look at me, Reagan." His tone was soft, yet commanding.

She bit the inside of her bottom lip and slowly lifted her gaze, only she focused on the Monet print hanging on the wall just beyond his shoulder.

"You have beautiful eyes. Has anyone ever told you that before?"

She looked at him then, into the warmth of his gaze, and shook her head. "No," she whispered, nearing the last button.

"That's a shame. You're a very pretty woman."

She lowered her lashes, savoring his seductive tone as she slid her arms out of the sweater, folded it and held it against her stomach.

"But you don't believe that, do you?"

"I think, I mean, I know I'm attractive, but I'm not—I'm not sexy." Nothing felt sexy about standing in her white cotton bra and plain skirt.

Luke moved toward her, his sensual eyes moving languidly the length of her body. He took the sweater from her and tossed it aside. Reagan's mouth parted. She could hardly breathe.

He walked behind her, barely touched her shoulder. "Sexy isn't something you're born with." The warmth of his words swirled her shoulder. A shudder coursed through her, her nipples budded. He skimmed a finger down her spine. "Sexy is something you feel when you're confident, know what you want and aren't afraid to get it." He unfastened her bra.

Reagan crossed her arms to hold it in place, unsure what to do, what to say. She wasn't confident. Always second guessed herself and changed her mind about what she wanted from one moment to the next. Except for this. She wanted Luke and all he promised to teach her.

He lifted her hair and kissed her nape. "You need to trust yourself, Reagan. Stop denying what you want, who you want to be."

Reagan leaned against the hard planes of his body. Her body slowly caught fire as his mouth traveled to just behind her ear to the spot she'd dabbed with perfume. Heavens, she could scarcely breath. She wanted Luke to take her, end the madness of his slow caress. She closed her eyes and let go of the bra.

"Tell me what you want." The deep cords of his voice vibrated through her, deliciously awakening more craving.

"I don't know. I—"

"Let go and trust yourself. Your body knows what it wants, listen to it."

She turned her head to nuzzle her lips under his jaw. "I want you to touch me."

He braided his fingers in hers and lifted her hand to her breast, pressed her palm to her nipple, squeezing his hand over hers. She rolled her head into the hollow of his shoulder, her back arching.

He kissed her shoulder lightly. "Your body was made for touch."

Sensations swirled and danced in a sultry rhythm as she rotated her bottom against Luke. He hardened against her. "Make love to me."

He lifted his mouth to her ear, nipping her lobe. "You're nowhere ready for that. You wanted to know what's in those books. You're going to learn, slowly, one torturous step at a time."

One step at a time? Reagan could barely handle Luke's touch. Luke's kiss. How could she survive this drawn out game?

He pressed his erection against her. A moan rumbled deep in his chest, the pads of his fingers dug deeper into her breast. "And it has nothing to do with love. Finish undressing." He swatted her bottom as he moved away.

Reagan watched him return to the sofa, her bottom stinging, and knew she wouldn't deny him anything. Luke was her teacher of carnal delights; she would accept all he offered and ask nothing more. She stepped out of her shoes, slid down her skirt and panties and looked to look him for guidance.

"Turn around."

She obeyed, watching over her shoulder as Luke's gaze languidly roamed her body. When she faced him again, it took every bit of strength to stand with her head high and not attempt to cover her body or shy away.

He took a pair of strappy black high-heeled sandals out of the bag and walked over to her. He knelt on one knee, whispering a hand down the side of her breast, her ribcage, smoothing over her hip and down her leg. Goosebumps prickled in his wake, delicious shivers radiating through her.

"You have a beautiful body, Reagan. You have soft curves and contours that don't belong hidden." He lifted her foot and slid on the shoe.

Reagan placed her hand on his shoulder for balance as he buckled the strap at the ankle. He moved to the other foot, pausing to kiss the inside of her knee. Liquid honey flowed from the spot, heating as it spread.

A good three inches taller, Reagan adjusted to both the height and the womanly power wearing high heels and nothing else gave her. Her breasts lifted upward, her calves were taut. Luke stood, took her hand, and led her toward the sofa.

She caught her reflection in the gilded mirror over the fireplace, and for a moment barely recognized herself. Her cinnamon hair was tousled, her green eyes wild. Luke sat her down and eased her backward. He took her sandaled foot and set it on the coffee table, her knee bent high, then repeated the process with the other.

She gazed at him questioningly as he moved away and discarded his jacket. She dared not move, though her legs were spread open, her pelvis titled. Revealed. Bare. Aroused.

He walked behind the couch and ran his hands over her shoulders, squeezed gently. "Touch your breasts, Reagan."

Her first instinct to his command was to refuse, but as his hands massaged, she closed her eyes and leaned her head back against the cushion. "Trust yourself, Reagan. Become one with your body's pleasure."

She cupped her breasts, lifting slightly. Her toes curled. "You've got perfect breasts, just the right size," he said and Reagan opened her eyes to watch his hands slide over her shoulders to the tips of her breasts. He squeezed both nipples, keeping the pressure just shy of pain.

Reagan cried out as her womb contracted in one fierce spasm, and her womanly juncture pulsed, readying for his touch. Silver heat moistened her depths, and tracers of light flashed around her vision. Her body arched for him, silently begging, wanting the complete fullness of him now.

Luke leaned down, his breath hot against her lobe. "Tell me, are so easily aroused by every man who touches you?" He pinched her nipples harder.

Yet her body responded. Her sexual response heightened to a new level. "No. No man has aroused me the way just looking at you does."

He released and gently soothed her nipples with the lightest touch, then took her right hand and guided it downward. "I want you to come for me." He ran his tongue down the length of her neck, kissed her collarbone.

Reagan was too lost in the sensation of his mouth and his hand on her nipple to realize where he was taking her other hand until her fingers touched the soft, dewy hair on her mound.

"Open your legs wider. Touch yourself for me."

"I've never," Reagan began, but found herself obeying his command. She could deny him nothing. Her body wouldn't allow her.

She spread her thighs further apart and dropped her knees outward as she slid her hand around the curve of her womanly juncture, parting her folds with her middle finger. She pressed against the throbbing nubbin; her breath hitched as another spasm shot through her center.

Luke's breath became shallow, hot against her temple as he pressed her breasts flat, the pads of his fingers digging in. "Come for me, Reagan. Come for me," he whispered, his breath ragged.

Reagan entered her sheath, surprised to discover how wet and hot her channel had become. She withdrew and caressed her nubbin with the moisture of her sex, at first slowly, in little circles and then with more pressure, dipping into her well to slicken her touch. Her body began to tighten from head to toe. Heat filtered through her like a sauna. The air thick and fragrant with her desire.

"Luke," she cried as his hands began to work her nipples in rhythm with her own touch.

"Let yourself go, Reagan." He pinched her nipples again, harder.

Her hips began to rotate, her hand moved quicker, fiercer until the breath stole from her lungs. Her muscles bunched and shivered. Suddenly a white-hot paroxysm of iridescent glow exploded from her core, blinding her of all but sheer, glorious sensations ebbing and flowing.

She slid her finger deep into the flow of molten release and gripped her thighs together. She arched her back, thrashed her head to the side and sought Luke's mouth, bit his lower lip, her cries drowning in his throat. Knocking over a bowl of potpourri, she gulped in the scent of lavender and held herself tight, climax pulsing.

When her body began to relax, and her ragged breathing calmed, Luke released her breasts and kissed her tenderly, suckling as if to soothe her scattered senses, bring calm to the storm that tossed her body with undeniable pleasure.

"Good girl," he said, against her mouth and stood.

Sated, exhausted, Reagan slid her hand from between her legs and realized her knees trembled. She never knew how erotic it could be to have a man watch her, guide her through such tortuous pleasure. It was beyond the realm of anything she ever experienced or fantasized.

The muscles flexed across Luke's broad back, stretching his white shirt as he took something black out of the shopping bag. Reagan's body stirred again, little pulses of begging want. She wanted Luke inside her, to feel the power of her pleasure while touching him, kissing him.

Luke returned to her, pulled her to her feet and raised her arms, her tender breasts thrust high. Floating on an orgasmic cloud, Reagan dropped her head as he bound her wrists with one of his large hands and lowered his hot mouth to her nipple and breathed.

A moan slipped from her swollen mouth as he soothed an aching nipple with his tongue, moistening and laving away the pain he deliciously inflicted. He then moved to heal the other nipple and then kissed his way down her stomach, releasing her hands as his tongue glided through her damp, curly hair.

She dropped her arms and gripped his shoulders when he parted her swollen folds with his tongue. She gazed down through half-mast lids as he suckled her nubbin. "Luke," she breathed, knees wobbling.

He stood and kissed her with the flavor of her passion and raised her arms again. He draped a silky black dress over her body, smoothing it out over her hips, her bottom, and then turned her around to zip it. "We're late." He nipped her shoulder with soft teeth.

Reagan leaned against his frame, reached around and held his hips. "Hmm, late?"

He groaned and pressed hard against her, his mouth nuzzling behind her ear. "Go put your hair up, but don't touch your makeup. You have that just-fucked-look that drives men crazy."

She bit her bottom lip, turned around and linked her arms around his neck, pressing her sensitized body to his hard planes and gazed into his dark eyes. "Does it drive you crazy?"

"More than you could ever know." He nudged her nose with his. "Now hurry up."

"Just let me find my underclothes."

"You'll go how you are."

Chapter Three

A college professor? Reagan tucked a wayward strand of hair behind her ear and smiled at the stodgy old man who just revealed Luke's occupation, hoping her surprise didn't show.

"How did you two meet?" he asked, puffing on a sweet-scented cigar and swirling a tumbler of cognac.

"Um, I—we," she glanced across the dark, smoke filled room where Luke stood with a group of men, his hands in his pockets. "Actually, my niece took swim lessons from Luke this past summer."

The man next to her let out a deep, belly filled laugh. "Luke still doing that, huh? Son of a bitch, he's got more stamina than I ever had. I look forward to quiet, peaceful summer breaks, and he goes out and works with youth groups. One summer it was some big brother program, another year he coached a basketball team for gangsters."

Reagan sipped her wine, trying to absorb this new, unexpected twist on who she thought Luke to be. Instead of some golden summer boy who lived for girls in bikinis, he was a college professor, saint for troubled kids, preschool swim instructor extraordinaire and teacher of seduction and sexual discovery. And the main topic of her article in *Glimmer Magazine*, circulation nationwide. Reagan inwardly groaned. What had she done? If anyone discovered it was Luke she had written about—she gulped down another swig of wine—his job and obvious stellar standing in the community were in jeopardy.

She glanced over to him again and found him watching her. Instantly she forgot about the article. His dark gaze languidly traveled her body. Heat flamed her cheeks knowing he was seeing her as she'd been earlier, naked and lusty for him, and how she was now, bare underneath the silk, her womanly body still slick and fragrant.

"It was nice meeting you, Reagan," the man said with a nod and stepped away.

"Ah, you, too." She bit her bottom lip, wondering what to do now that she'd been left alone.

There were plenty of women at the party, mingling or talking in groups. Reagan normally had no problem meeting new people, or simply blending in a crowd if she didn't feel like socializing. Tonight was different.

For the first time in her life, she stood out from the crowd. In the little black dress, high heels, hair swept off her nape carelessly, lips swollen and red, Reagan looked like a vixen. Since the moment she'd walked into the party on Luke's arm, the women had eyed her as if she were the enemy, as if she intended to steal their husbands and corrupt their morals. God, what would Mother think?

Luke made her this way with his words, his touch, the way he guided her to a culmination of passions never before explored. Just thinking about it stirred a longing in her to be alone with Luke again. Her body was ready for him.

She loved the way he transformed her. She didn't recognize herself when she was with him, and yet somehow she seemed to be the person she always craved inwardly to be.

Reagan touched her wine glass to her chest to cool her heating body, and swept her gaze upward beneath her lashes to watch Luke again. He looked at her, a tug playing the corner of his mouth. She melted into a moment where Luke seduced her with nothing more than his gaze and silent desires.

Everyone in the room faded out, leaving only Reagan exposed and raw under Luke's visual seduction. Her breath turned shallow, tingles of heat spread through her. She moistened her bottom lip. She wanted Luke to come to her, touch her. He raised an eyebrow, turned back to the group of his colleagues and excused himself.

Reagan waited a moment, then followed him through a set of double doors leading to a terrace. She slipped into the crisp early autumn air tinged with the taste of salt and sea. A breeze whisked off the ocean and pressed the silk fabric of her dress against her body and lifted loose strands of hair to dance in ribbons. She smiled at Luke, who was standing with his hands on the balustrade, staring out to the black vastness of the Puget Sound. The midnight blue sky melded with the ocean in the distance, the lights from ships and the stars almost mirroring each other as they passed silently in the night.

She wrapped her arms around him, attempting to steal his warmth. "What are you thinking about?" she asked, running her hands over the hard muscles rippling his stomach beneath his crisp white shirt.

"You." His voice, smooth and deep, drifted on the billows of fog rolling in off the ocean like dunes of cotton.

"Hmmm. Me, huh?" She snuggled further against him, her nipples budding, chills coursing her arms and legs. She braved a hand under the waistband of his trousers.

His body stiffened, shoulders to toes. "Don't."

Reagan smiled, stroked the length of him, feeling him swell and lengthen in her palm. "Why not?" Knowing she could make him respond made her feel a touch of the power he possessed over her. Knowing his colleagues were just inside while she touched him made her feel naughty. Wicked. Sinful. "Afraid someone will find us out here like this?" She gripped him low at the shaft and squeezed softly.

He sucked in a breath and let out a long growl. "Damn it, Reagan." He took her hand and withdrew it, turned around and glowered down at her, his eyes onyx in the darkness. His jaw tensed.

He didn't scare her. She straddled his leg, pressing her heated juncture against the hard muscle of his thigh and rode him with little glides, her hand cupping his balls over his slacks. "I want you, Luke."

He crushed his mouth to hers in a searing kiss, hauling her off her feet and backing her until she rammed against a trellis climbing the weather beaten stone wall. His teeth sank into the pulse at her throat as she tore at the button of his slacks. He freed his erection and hiked her skirt, slid two fingers deep into her.

"Are you sure, Reagan?" he asked against her mouth, delving his tongue deep into the hallows. His thumb worked her nubbin, fingers pressing deeper into her.

Reagan clenched her fingers around the rungs of the trellis as she fought against an orgasm. She thrashed her head to the side. "Yes, Luke. Now." If she didn't have him inside her, now, she would surely die.

Withdrawing his hand, Luke wrapped her legs around his waist and gripped the trellis on either side of her head. He rammed inside her until his full length was buried deep to her core, stretching her walls. Instantly an orgasm shattered. Luke held taut as red petals from a crushed Clematis fell onto her shoulder.

When the pulses eased and her body relaxed, Luke withdrew and entered into her again and again with excruciating slowness. Each thrust was so intense, her body cried out in pain and pleasure. She feared she could take no more. She couldn't breathe. Couldn't not.

Reagan abandoned the trellis to dig her nails in Luke's back, wanting him deeper inside her, wanting to be closer still. The scent of the crushed Clematis petals, the scent of her passion swirled as she cried out against his shoulder, begging him to stop…to never stop. In answer to her plea, he began to thrust harder, deeper. She hurt, she wanted. Her knees trembled as they locked tighter around his waist.

He covered her mouth with his, and in one final thrust, his hot semen filled her in union with another climax of her own, raking her with a searing and delicious release. She sobbed his name, then went limp in his arms.

Despite her protests, Luke carried Reagan from his Jaguar, into the parking garage elevator and to his First Avenue penthouse, where he gently sat her on a chair in his bedroom. He removed her shoes, then gently pulled her dress over her head.

"I'm sorry for embarrassing you," she whispered.

He shushed her apology with the tip of his finger to her swollen mouth, followed by his mouth.

She didn't know what had overcome her. One moment she was in the throws of orgiastic pleasure, the next she was being carried out of the party in Luke's arms, his colleagues watching with wide-eyed expressions, the wives gasping.

Luke left Reagan naked, slipped through a door and moments later she heard water turn on. She didn't regret for one moment giving her body to Luke. After tonight, she would never be the same. She had experienced the rawest element of man and woman, found pleasure she hadn't known could exist.

Luke returned to her, swept her hair back and kissed her forehead before scooping her into his arms and carrying her into the hunter green bathroom. The lights were off and he'd lit vanilla scented candles peppered on the counters and edge of a Jacuzzi tub. He lowered her into the pool of warm, circling water, soaking the sleeves of his shirt.

"Are you okay?" he asked, tone deep and soft and caring.

Reagan nodded, the water soothing. "Yes, thank you. I'm sorry—"

He pressed his finger to her lips again. "Shh." Lowered his head and kissed her softly as if she were made of delicate glass. "Rest now." He stood, dried off his hands and left her alone.

She closed her eyes, dipped back her head to drench her hair. How could any man be so tender and yet so fiercely passionate? Never did she believe a man like him existed. Never did she believe a man like Luke would want her. Never in her wildest dreams did she believe she could experience such passion.

Whatever he was willing to give, to show her, to teach her, she would accept and ask for no more. He'd already given her more than a good girl like her could hope for, and she'd die remembering every vivid detail of their time together.

Luke returned sometime later with a big, white fluffy towel, offered his hand to help her from the tub then dried her, taking care to soak up every droplet of water shoulder to toe, then wrapped the towel around her middle, tucking the end above her breast.

He swiped a wet locket of hair behind her ear, cupped his hands on each side of her head and gazed deep into her eyes. "Better?"

She nodded and parted her lips for his kiss. His tongue glided under the tender lining of her upper lip. Then he softly nipped her bottom lobe before taking her hand and leading her through the bedroom and into the living room, where a fire burned in the black stoned hearth, and soft music played in the background.

He knelt on an ivory bearskin rug by the fire, smoothed his hands up her calves, under her towel to cup her bottom. Reagan gazed down at him, the fire casting hues of burnt sienna across his handsome face. He bunched the towel in his hands and tugged until it fell away. Taking her hands, he lowered her to kneel before him.

Without breaking the magnetic gaze he held her in, she reached for the button of his shirt, worked it through the tiny hole, moved to the next and the next, her gaze finally dropping to the sight of his chest. She reached the last button, smoothed her hands under the flaps, rounded his shoulders and shed the shirt. Lightly she traced her fingers back up his arms, ran her palms over his pecks, pressing her right hand to feel the beat of his heart.

"Thank you," she whispered.

He cupped her cheek, pulled his thumb across her mouth. "For what?"

She glanced away, suddenly feeling shy. "For showing me what it can be like."

"I've only just begun."

The words reached in and soothed away Reagan's worry that he'd taken what he wanted and would be done with her now. "What more is there?"

He lowered his hand to cup the underside of her breasts and lifted them for his mouth to softly take one dusky peak after the other. Reagan shivered and melted, heated and quaked.

"You'll have to wait and see," he said and guided her to lie on her stomach.

The fur soft beneath her, the fire warm on her naked flesh, she closed her eyes as Luke spread out on his side beside her and smoothed his strong hands over her back. "I didn't mean to hurt you," he said, lowering his mouth to the back of her shoulder, circling his tongue.

"Hmmm, I wouldn't have changed a thing." She burrowed deeper into the fur, snuggling in like a cozy kitten.

"It's not like me to lose control like that."

"I enjoyed knowing you wanted me so much." No one had ever lost control like that with her. Because of her.

His hand slid over the arch of her bottom, between her legs to the heat of her juncture and pressed against her nubbin. "I want you still." He moved behind her to kneel between her legs, held her hips and pulled her upward and back.

"Take me." She held herself on her forearms, tilting her pelvis by instinct for him. Thick and hard, he entered her, slowly, pushing to the honeyed core of her, the pads of his fingers digging into her hips, thumbs rotating. His legs trembled as he rotated his pelvis against her, eased out and delved deep inside her again. He moaned her name, then a rumbling curse as he began to pump, ramming the sweet insides of her with delicious thrusts.

Reagan woke Sunday morning and found herself lying on the couch between Luke's legs, her head on his chest, a throw blanket tangled around her hips. A slice of morning hazed through the window, brushing Luke's sleeping face with a touch of sunshine. She smiled up at him, brushed a soft kiss to the underside of his jaw and slipped her fingers through the soft hair on his chest, over the sculpts of his pecs to play with a dark nipple. She'd never woke to a day feeling more alive, more wanted, more satisfied.

She only wished the enchanting discoveries Luke gifted upon her were equally poetic for him. Oh, she knew he desired her, lost his control for her, but she wouldn't be foolish enough to believe she'd been the only one. Trying not to think about the other women before, the other women he'd shown such pleasure to, she closed her eyes and simply felt him breathe beneath her.

His hand came up and tangled in her hair. "Morning," he rumbled, pressing his lips to her crown.

A glow spread through her as his hand slid down her neck to tightened around her back, possessing her, claiming her, if only for the moment. "Luke?"

"Hmm?"

"I just want to let you know," she began, knowing she needed to be the first to say the words, for she couldn't bear to hear them from him, "I understand how this works. I don't expect anything of you because of last night."

He opened his eyes, angled his head to look at her. "Then maybe I should let you know you're the first woman I've allowed to stay."

Her heart gave a little lurch, then she realized although he'd allowed her to stay, but he hadn't taken her to his bed. "Why me?"

"Because you're sweet and sexy and beautiful. At my touch, you abandon your innocence and you give me your complete trust without question. You feel with every part of your body and mind." He positioned her atop of him, her knees sinking into the cushions at his sides, and he guided her down the hard length of him. His eyes closed on a sharp intake of breath. "Because I don't know if I can ever get enough of you."

After a morning, afternoon and evening of sex in varying degrees, hot and wild, slow and excruciating, Reagan wondered if Luke would get enough of her.

Heaven help her, she hoped not.

Chapter Four

Reagan wore her dark Marilyn Monroe style sunglasses to work Monday morning, afraid if anyone looked into her eyes they'd see the sinful secrets she kept. She went straight to her cubicle, forgoing coffee in the break room, and sat down at her desk. Her chin and cheeks were chapped from Luke's beard stubble despite the cream she'd laved on. Actually, her entire body was tender and sore, delightfully so. Every inch of her was branded with the memory of her time with Luke.

She took off her glasses and spotted the weekly addition of *Glimmer*, all shiny and new, sitting on her desk, the side bar in bold pink letters: *Good Girl Gone Bad.*

"Oh my god," she breathed, staring at the cover. During the weekend, beneath Luke's hands, his kiss, his body, she had forgotten the magazine hit the newsstands Sunday morning. She ran her finger over the words, then quickly flipped to the article.

Wow. The article looked even more fabulous than she could ever have imagined. And the picture. *Double wow.* Paxton had used a full color photo of a woman in the throes of passion, sex book in hand as she leaned against a bookshelf, and a man, cover model gorgeous, with his hand up her skirt.

Heavens, is that how she had looked?

Reagan traced the bold letters across the top, *Good Girl Gone Bad* and italicized underneath, *The true story of a woman's journey to discovering her wild side.*

How very true the title was. Luke had opened a door for Reagan, invited her to step inside a realm she never dreamed existed. Though she'd stood scared and unsure, it was Luke who had guided her across the threshold, took her hand and led her on her journey.

His words returned to her, *"I don't know if I can ever get enough of you."* Reagan couldn't suppress the delightful spread of tingles coursing her skin.

Reagan read the article three times, elation climbing inside her almost as delicious as her time with Luke. She couldn't believe she'd accomplished her goal. She'd published an article. And it was just the first rung on her ladder to success.

Ready to climb, she fished out a clean tablet and began to outline the next segment, writing until her hand cramped and the smell of heavy perfume brought her out of her licentious world. She glanced up to see Michaelo standing at the cubicle entrance. He wore a black net shirt she knew to be his "lucky" one.

"Hot date tonight?" she asked with a smile, feeling enough joy to share with the world.

He cocked out his hip, planted a hand on it and tapped his foot. "Would you mind checking your email? The Internet guy is saying you went way over your quota for the week just this morning alone. The servers keep shutting down."

"What?" Reagan reached for her mouse and clicked open her email. Sure enough, her inbox was flooded, with more email popping up every second. "Oh. My. God. Michaelo, look at this!"

He grinned and knelt beside her. He took control of the mouse, opened an email at random and read the letter:

"Dear Ms. Smith," Michaelo looked at her, rolled his eyes. "Not very original."

"Yeah, yeah, just read." She closed her eyes and braced herself for the words.

He cleared his throat.

"Dear Ms. Smith, I just wanted to say thank you for writing Good Girl Gone Bad. I've always fantasized about doing something naughty in a public place. Your writing truly made me feel as if I were Roxanne in the bookstore with Logan, I could barely breathe as I read and reread. Thank you for sharing this experience with me. I'll remember it forever. P.S. Hurry with the next installment, pleeeeeasssse."

Reagan opened her eyes and plucked a tissue out of the Kleenex box. "I'm going to cry. I've dreamed of this day forever. It seems almost too good to be true!"

Michaelo opened another email.

"Dear Ms. Smith,

"I'm writing to let you know that your article in Glimmer magazine has saved my marriage. My husband and I have been together for fourteen years and over the past few years the spontaneity and passion has fizzled from our relationship.

"No more! After reading your article, I took my husband to the

bookstore and we reenacted the scene in Good Girl Gone Bad. It was the most amazing sex we've ever had, and we can't wait to read about Roxanne and Logan's next encounter (I should have my DH bailed out of jail by then—he got so carried away in the bookstore, he screamed out my name when he climaxed and knocked over the shelf, which toppled several others like dominos. He didn't have time to pull up his pants before the manager came running over—but believe you me, it was well worth it!)."

Reagan and Michaelo stared at each other for a long moment, then burst out in laughter. "Oh. My. God." She clamped a hand over her mouth. "Someone got arrested because of my article!"

"Don't worry, toots, sounds like it was the most exciting day for them in a really long time. Bet he'll ask to keep the handcuffs as souvenirs."

They went through dozens more emails, printing off the ones Reagan wanted to keep. She'd start a memory book—she had all the supplies from her sister's scrap booking party last spring.

"Oh, no!" Reagan grabbed her purse and jumped from her chair. "I forgot I was suppose to meet my sister and mom for dinner."

Reagan rushed into the Italian restaurant twenty minutes late. She spotted her mother and sister at their usual table by the window overlooking Elliot Bay. She slung her purse strap up her shoulder, took in a deep breath and crossed the restaurant, ready for the guilt trip.

"Sorry I'm late," she said, forever apologizing to her mother while her perfect sister with her perfect hair, makeup and clothes sat perfectly straight and had undoubtedly arrived ten minutes early.

"I took the liberty of ordering for you," Mother said, lifting a glass of ice tea, three ice cubes, a lemon wedge and sprig of peppermint—as always.

Reagan's sister rubbed her slightly protruding belly. "I really wish you'd be considerate, Reagan. Mother is very busy this evening. Even in my delicate condition I was able to make it on time."

Reagan snapped open her red linen napkin and draped it over her lap. Oh, how much she wanted to tell her do-all-good sister she was late because she wrote her first article and was reading fan mail. That she had a deadline to meet and really shouldn't be taking this dinner break at all.

Instead, Reagan reached for patience. "Since Mother ordered for me, I don't see that I've really caused much of a delay, now have I?"

"That's not the point—"

"Girls," Mother said in the tone that reprimanded more than words or threats ever could.

Reagan and Catherine put on fake little smiles and let a would-be argument go. *Again.* Sometimes Reagan wished they could just pull out the claws and tell each other exactly how they felt, instead of walking on eggshells and pretending to be the best of friends.

Since they had been little girls, it'd always been that way. Blonde and blue eyed like Mother, Catherine was the princess of the house who lived up to all Mother's expectations of the perfect daughter. Prima ballerina, honor roll, social graces matching the Queen of Britain. Catherine had married a wonderful husband, lived in a lovely house and had a beautiful daughter with another grandchild on the way.

While Reagan, with her father's features, had buried her nose in novels from the age of six, achieved average grades in high school, went to college and wanted a career before family. Mother never asked how Reagan's work was going. Instead she would inquire if Reagan had met a nice young man who wanted to settle down, followed by a *"And just why not? You'll be too old to get a decent husband if you wait much longer."*

Reagan sighed.

"Something wrong, dear?" Mother asked.

"No, work has just been busy."

"That's nice. Have you met any nice young men lately? You know Mrs. Bollox from the garden club mentioned her son is coming home from *Harvard* for Thanksgiving break. How about we throw a nice little dinner party and you two can…"

Mother droned on. Reagan remembered being in the back of the car on the way to private school. Every day, Mother would deliver one of her *"Now remember, you're a good girl. Boys only want one thing,"* lectures despite the fact there were no boys to give *it* to at the all girl school.

These days Mother had a radar three counties wide for single, eligible, suitable men in the hope her daughter would do the respectable thing: marry, have kids, and join the garden club.

Reagan was tired of apologizing for wanting a different path than her mother and sister, and decided from that moment on, she wouldn't.

The waiter came to the table and laid a single stemmed red rose in front of Reagan. "From the gentleman at the bar."

Surprised, Reagan looked across the room and saw Luke. Dressed in a pair of worn denims, loafers and a soft button up navy blue shirt, he was leaning against the bar, talking to another man. Her heart skipped a few beats as she picked up the rose and inhaled the sweet fragrance. Luke turned to look at her, meeting her gaze, holding it in a long, slow seduction of secret pleasures they shared. Warmth spread deep and low in her stomach, her breath turned shallow.

"Yummy," Catherine said, shocking Reagan. She didn't think her sister had a raging hormone in her entire body.

"Who is *that*?" Mother asked.

"A friend." Reagan stood. "I'll be right back."

"*Humph*. Looks like trouble to me," Mother said with her notorious air of superiority.

Reagan stared down her mother. "It's what he looks like to me that matters."

The waiter appeared with their order and set down a plate of spinach lasagna at Reagan's place setting.

"This isn't what I want. Take it away. Bring me the biggest piece of chocolate cake you have, two scoops of vanilla ice cream—make that French vanilla, and a cup of coffee, please. I've had a long day."

The waiter nodded and backed away, looking at Reagan as if she were completely insane.

No, not crazy, she thought. *Liberated*. She wove through the tables, leaving her mother and Catherine in their wide-eyed, speechless state, and headed to the bar.

She took the hand Luke held out for her, grateful to have something to clutch. Never had she stood up to dear old mum. "Fancy meeting you here," she said, forcing the tremor from her voice.

He pulled her against the length of his hard body. "Do you remember Reagan, from the party?" he asked the man next to him.

"Dean Nelson's house. How could I forget," the man said with a wink.

Oh, heavens, no. *The Dean's house*? She gulped and offered her hand. Bad enough when she thought she was at a party with Luke's colleagues, but she'd—they'd ruined the Dean's Clematis vine! "N-Nice to see you again. I, um, er, apologize for my untimely exit. Something just overcame me."

"No apologies needed. I better get back to my table. We'll talk soon, Luke, about that after school program. The kids in this community need more people like you believing in them. And give your dad a hello for me. Nice seeing you again, Reagan."

She nodded, but before she could give her licentious actions any more thought, Luke nuzzled his lips to her neck just behind her ear and slid his hands around her waist. "Having a good time?" he asked, breath damp and moist against her neck.

"No, terrible." She turned into his arms and linked her arms around his neck. "That's my mother and sister. I'd do anything to get out of here."

Luke slid his hand over the arch of her bottom and fisted her skirt, hiking it up to mid-thigh and pulled her taut against him. The soft flannel of his shirt rubbed through her satin blouse, his denim through her skirt, sensitizing her still raw flesh. "Anything?"

Reagan dropped her head back as his mouth moved to nibble the column of her throat. Any thought of her disapproving mother and sister disappeared as he adorned her with his affections. "Hmm, yes. Anything."

He cupped the back of her head and pulled her mouth to his. He swept his tongue between her lips and fully claimed. Her fingers nipped his shoulder blades. The world beyond her sensations ceased to exist. Reagan melted into the golden delight of Luke's kiss, the texture of his body pressing against hers, the strength in which he held her.

He ended the kiss with a nip at the corner of her mouth, then he rested his forehead to hers. "Go back to your table now before I take you right here."

Reagan nodded and stepped away. She would have opened for him then and there if he'd chosen to take her. Nothing else mattered when his hands and mouth were upon her body. She returned to the table and sat before her piece of chocolate cake with melting ice cream.

She lifted a spoon and scraped off a mound of frosting, licked, and moaned. "Now, where we? Catherine said you had a busy day, Mother. Garden Club tonight, is it?"

Her mother seemed to have lost her ability to speak. She poured herself a glass of house wine from the decanter on the table, her manicured hand trembling slightly as she gulped the entire glass down. Then she proceeded to do something Reagan had never heard her do her entire life.

She belched.

Reagan turned to her sister. "Josie still enjoying preschool? I hung the watercolor she did for me on my office wall. She really has talent, don't you think?" Her sister didn't seem to hear; she was too busy stealing glances at Luke and trying not to be obvious about it. Reagan snapped her fingers in front of Catherine's face. "Hello? Josie? Preschool?"

"Oh, yeah. Um, she's doing great. Misses you. If I didn't say so before, I really appreciated your help with her this summer. The morning sickness was so terrible."

For the first time Reagan truly felt Catherine's thank you was heart felt. "You're welcome."

Catherine glanced at Luke again. "Wow. He's gorgeous. Did you really, you know?"

"Yes." She smiled. "Yes, I did. And I enjoyed every moment of it." Reagan shoveled a big slice of cake into her mouth, swiped a bit of chocolate from her bottom lip.

Mother poured another glass of wine.

Chapter Five

Reagan turned the next segment of *Good Girl Gone Bad* in before deadline and spent the rest of the week answering fan mail. Dreams achieved were so much better than she ever could have imagined.

But the fact she hadn't heard from Luke weighed heavily on her mood.

She contemplated calling him, sending him a little note, maybe stopping by his house. Only, she didn't want to seem like one of those needy women who expected the stars and moon just because the sex was out of this world.

It proved to be more difficult during the weekend. Without the distractions of the office to occupy her thoughts, she remembered over and over the way Luke had made her feel when he touched her, as if she were the center of his every focus and desire.

Like a spinster, she spent the entire weekend alone.

Back to work Monday morning, Reagan sat at her desk staring at the week's edition of *Glimmer* that held her second article. On a sigh, she planted her chin on steepled fingers. None of the excitement she'd felt just a week ago bubbled inside her. The second article made her feel a fool, an imposter. Luke said he could never get enough of her. *Hah.* That lasted all of two encounters.

Now she faced another deadline. She pushed the magazine aside and flipped to a fresh page in her note pad. Tapping the pencil against her chin, she knew her readers expected another interlude. Fine, she'd write fiction for the next segment. Besides, she couldn't rely on writing about sex with Luke for her entire career.

Michaelo said research was what she did best. Leaning back in the chair, Reagan sighed and closed her eyes. She'd definitely done some very good research with Luke. Problem was, she didn't want to end her discoveries. She knew there was so much more he could teach her. She ached for Luke's touch, physically and emotionally. Craved him like she never knew possible.

Unable to concentrate, Reagan packed up her brand new briefcase, the first purchase after receiving her bonus for *Good Girl Gone Bad*, and headed home early. She just didn't have fiction in her today.

Paxton stopped her in front of the elevators. "That column is looking like a very good possibility, Reagan."

Reagan tried to smile, failed, and simply nodded. She didn't deserve the column. She was a fraud. If anyone deserved the column, Luke did.

The elevator door dinged open and Reagan stepped inside, murmuring a soft "Thank You" to Paxton.

Curled up on the sofa, where she'd been all afternoon, Reagan let the phone ring four times before turning down the TV volume and lifting the receiver. "Michaelo, I've told you twice already, I don't want to come out and play." The last thing she wanted to do was celebrate something she was in the midst of failing.

"Michaelo, huh? Should I be jealous?"

Reagan sat up, clutching the phone to her ear. "Luke?"

"Disappointed?"

"No." Her heart skipped a beat, another. "I—I just didn't know if I'd hear from you again."

"Been out of town."

All that worrying, believing he was through with her. "I've missed you."

"Bring me there," he said, his voice low and seductive. "Tell me what you're wearing right now."

Reagan stretched out her legs and glanced down at her fuzzy pink slippers, gray sweats and white t-shirt. Maybe fiction wasn't so bad. "Umm, a sexy little red thing?" Okay, so she needed a little polishing in the impromptu department.

"Hmm, sounds nice. If I recall, there's a mirror hanging over your fireplace."

"Uh-huh."

"Go to the mirror, Reagan."

Nibbling her bottom lip a moment, she stood, stepped before her reflection. "Okay, I'm there."

"Every detail, Reagan. Tell me what you see."

She would deny him nothing, but one glance at her hair pulled back in a low pony tail, strands sticking out here and there, at her smeared makeup, and she knew further creative thinking would be required.

"Tell me how beautiful you are."

The words made her delve a little deeper, past the lingering doubts where she still believed herself to be the family's ugly duckling, to the place where she felt beautiful, the secret place of pleasures and orgiastic discoveries.

Closing her eyes, she imagined herself as she wanted to be, returned to that first night Luke came for her. She imagined him standing before her, his dark gaze lingering a caress over her body.

She pulled the band from her ponytail and lifted her hair off her shoulders. "My hair is swept up, just as you like it. There are little wisps falling down, tickling my nape with butterfly kisses."

"You have a beautiful neck, Reagan. A smooth column of softness."

She smiled, encouraged to play his game. "I've dabbed perfume behind my ears."

"I can smell it. The scent is warm and fragrant, intoxicating. Where else did you dab your perfume?"

Dropping her hair, she ran the tips of her fingers down her neck, over the front of her t-shirt, between her breasts. "Well, the negligee is cut low and there's, ah, lace edging it, white, no, black lace." She breathed in deeply, her tone dropping to a whisper. "The perfume is there, beneath a little satin rose."

"Hmmm, I can smell you, Reagan. The light mist of perfume mixing with the sweet smell of your skin, and the heat of your valley. Are you wet, Reagan?"

The begging pulse began to throb between her legs, echoing a hunger for his touch. How easily he commanded her body into want. "Oh, yes. I wish you were here."

"Tell me how the silk feels between your legs, Reagan."

She slid her hand down her belly, over her drab gray sweats to slip between her legs. Only in her fantasy, her touch didn't find cotton. She found molten heat simmering beneath silk and lace. Inhaling a deep breath, a shudder rippled through her, and she nearly dropped the phone. "It's like warm oil, slippery and smooth. Hot. I'm ready for you."

"Hmmm, not just yet," he said, his voice seemingly coming from within her dream world rather than over the line. "Sometimes the greatest pleasures come after anticipation. Tell me, Reagan, have you been wanting me?"

She glided her hand between her legs in a slow stroke. "Like I've never wanted before," she whispered, breath catching in her throat. "No matter how hard I try, I can't stop thinking of you."

"Why should you want to stop thinking of me?" Humor rode the current of his smooth, rich tones.

"Because I can't bear the thought of not being with you."

"And if I tell you I don't think I could ever get enough of you, would that satisfy you?"

Only if he told her every day for a million years. "Y-yes."

"Good. Because I want you, Reagan. I want to be inside you. Will you take me there, Reagan?"

"Yes," she breathed, untying the draw string of her sweats and slipping her hand beneath her panties, easing a finger within her swollen sex, adjusting the width of her legs to grant his wish. Her sheath begging to be filled.

"Take me there, now."

She plunged deep inside her core at his command, pressing the pad of her middle finger upward, the palm of her hand pressing hard against her nubbin. "Luke…" She sobbed his name as her sheath clenched. An orgasm exploded from her core, sucking her breath away, filling her closed eyes with tracers of light. The phone dropped to the ground as her hand fisted her hair, pulling it free of the ponytail.

Her entire body shuddered, and her eyes clamped tighter. She bit her bottom lip. Her nipples pinched into nail heads, and she imagined herself leaning back into Luke, his hard frame supporting her liquifying body. She lolled her head to the side as she imagined his kiss, warm and moist on her neck.

"Again," his voice said, the word swirling her earlobe like a mist off the warm ocean.

She opened her eyes to see hands lifting her breasts, her nipples pinched between thumbs and forefingers. Suspended in a realm of fantasy pleasure and reality, she glanced in the mirror to see Luke standing behind her, his mouth working kisses over her shoulder.

"How…" she began to ask, words dying off as a shiver slid down her spine.

"Again. Now," he demanded with a growl, releasing her breasts to push her sweat pants to the floor.

She braced a hand on the fireplace mantel and slowly withdrew her finger from deep within her core, then slid it back into her fiery sheath. "I thought you were out of town," she said, hips rotating to the rhythm of her stroke.

"I was. Now I'm back and ready to have you, Reagan. Would you like that?"

She nodded, heat and pressure building deep within her upon the aftershocks of her first release.

"Tell me." He took her hips in his hands and tilted her pelvis back. She heard the sound of his zipper as he opened his pants, his gaze on hers in the mirror.

She withdrew her hand to find her nubbin with her slick finger and played upon it with little circles and varying degrees of pressure, teasing herself as she said, "Yes. Now. Please, Luke."

"With pleasure," he said, easing his erection between her legs and pressing upward into her. Another orgasm shattered through her, her body milking him with the ebb and flow of her release. He growled, his member jutting inside her, hands clenching her hips as he held taut, waiting for her climax to ease before he pulled out and thrust inside her again and again until she screamed his name.

The next orgasm, which came upon his, was so forceful, so extreme, so powerful, she could only bow her head on her arm and sob.

Reagan's fear Luke was done with her completely disappeared over the next several days. He constantly surprised her—with intimate dinners, cruises on his yacht under the moonlight, the movies with a huge bucket of buttery popcorn, a salsa dance lesson. Intense, funny, charming, and handsome, Luke made each and every moment special and memorable.

And he stole every opportunity to continue the "lessons." Positions, places, and experiences even her research books didn't cover, and no doubt a few new moves invented along the way. The only place Luke hadn't taken her was his bed.

With all the unending adventures, nothing could have surprised Reagan more than when Luke pulled her through the heavy metal doors of the gymnasium located in a part of Seattle where she'd never go alone, even in the daylight, and onto a basketball court where at least thirty kids were hanging out.

Some were in street clothes standing in small groups back in the shadows, smoking cigarettes. Another group at the far end of the court played booming music from a portable CD player and were doing a combination of old break dance moves and new dance steps. A few girls sat on the stands, leaning back, elbows on the bench behind them, sipping soda from mini-mart cups and popping chewing gum.

The largest group of kids was dressed in worn sneakers and tattered gym clothes, shooting hoops on the scuffed gym floor, the boundary marks long worn off. At Luke and Reagan's arrival, the ball suddenly stopped bouncing.

"*Whazzup* Mister N?" a kid holding the ball under his arm asked with a jerk of his chin.

"Not much, Julio. Get that application in?"

"Last Tuesday, just like you said."

"Who's the *be-atch*?" another player asked from the back.

Julio turned and thrust the ball at the other player's chest, knocking him back several steps. "Don't you be *dissin'* Mister N's girl."

"Yeah," one of the girls from the bleachers called out, elbowing the girl beside her. "Any fool can see Mister A's got himself a classy ass bitch."

Reagan took a step back. Luke squeezed her hand. "They're just testing you," he said, voice low.

"Yo, ever shoot hoops before?" Julio asked, catching the ball on a return throw.

Luke wouldn't have brought her here if it wasn't safe. He was sharing a part of his life with her, the part that mentored trouble teens, the part that cared about his community. She realized she was not just being tested by the kids, but by Luke as well.

She released Luke's hand, took off her jacket and tossed it to the sideline, then clapped her hands for the ball. Julio tossed it to Reagan. She caught it, began to dribble, passing the ball between her legs.

"Just in case you're wondering," she said, maneuvering around a player who tried to block her. She picked up speed, jumped into the air and shot from behind the three-point line. The ball swooshed through the net as she landed with the grace of a ballerina. "White girls *can* jump."

The girls in the back stood and did a cheer.

"She's *aye-right*," Julio said, slapping Luke on the shoulder.

Later, sitting in a booth next to Luke in a all-night diner, hair limp, clothes damp from sweating through four games of hoops and one disastrous lesson in street dancing, Reagan felt exhausted. And deliriously alive.

"Where'd you learn to play like that?" Luke asked, putting an arm around her shoulder and kissing the top of her head.

She snuggled into him, reveling in the simple pleasure of being near him. "My basketball team went to state all four years I played. I wasn't the tallest on the team, but I had a lot of heart, according to my coach. Thanks for taking me with you tonight. I had a lot of fun. "

"Any time. It was good for them. They don't welcome outsiders easily."

"Them against the world?"

"Something like that, yeah."

She looked into Luke's eyes and realized being with those kids meant more to him than simply adding to a list of good deeds. "Why do you do it? What makes you care when so many don't?"

He tucked a strand of hair behind her ear, glanced over her shoulder. "Someone has to."

She leaned her head on his shoulder, his arm tightened around her, and she knew without a doubt that she loved him.

Chapter Six

"*Hmm, mmm, um.*" Michaelo held the spread of *Good Girl Gone Bad*, segment three open in front of his fiery orange satin shirt and sauntered back and forth in Reagan's cubicle. "Girl has definitely gone bad." He played his hand over the photograph of a woman kneeling before a naked Greek God type man. "Any idea who this model is? I'd love to look him up."

Reagan laughed and pulled the magazine out of his hands. "You're incorrigible. Did you really think it was as good as the first two articles?"

He fanned his face with his hand. "It's H-O-T-T, suga. You're one lucky woman."

"It's not me." And this time, Reagan told the truth. The third segment was indeed fiction. She had what it took to write a unique, sexy, interesting piece using her own skills and imagination. Thanks to Luke's lessons and her research skills.

"Uh-huh." He snagged the magazine back, opened to the article, glanced it over and back at Reagan. "Right."

"Don't you have work to do?"

"Who can work with men like this loose in the city? Tell me, is the real thing as hot?"

She tossed him an *I'll never tell* look. The phone rang and she shooed Michaelo out of her workspace.

"Oops, sorry," Michaelo said to someone outside her cubicle before he waltzed away with an imaginary partner.

Reagan shook her head and picked up the phone. "Yes. Uh-huh." *Wow.* "Well, I'm so very pleased that you enjoyed *Good Girl Gone Bad*, but I'm afraid I'm declining all public appearances." She held up *a one moment please* finger to the person giving a little rap on her cubicle wall. "Yes, well, I appreciate that, but since the subject matter is a little provocative, I feel it's in the best interest of—" She looked up as the knocker stepped inside her cubicle. The phone dropped from her hand. "Mother!"

Her mother picked up the open magazine from Reagan's desk with her thumb and forefinger in the fashion of a stinky diaper and dropped it into the trash. "This is what I put you through college for, to write trash?"

Reagan looked from the garbage and up into the face of severe disapproval. "Wh-what are you doing here?"

She pulled a hanky from her designer bag and dabbed her eyes. "I came to prove that my daughter would never shame our good family's name."

Remembering the phone, Reagan picked it off the floor and hung it up, hoping the caller hadn't heard what her mother had said.

"How could you do this to me?"

Reagan bit the inside of her cheek for a moment, but she simply could not stand to watch her mother play *poor me* once again. "Do what, Mother? Write a successful article? Gee, that's so terrible, isn't it?" She turned to her computer and began clicking on random keys.

Mother stuffed the hanky back in her purse and closed the clasp with a snap. "It is when it's nothing but smut, and the entire garden club knows it's *my* daughter who wrote it."

Her fingers halted, she whirled around. "What?" No one outside of the office knew she penned the articles, and Paxton had promised her identity would be held in the strictest confidentiality. Her emails were sent to a special folder listed in her pen name and her calls directed to a second extension.

Her mother extracted the hanky again. "Now, because of you, I won't be able to show my beautiful African Violets at the festival. Oh, Reagan, how could you?"

Reagan stood, squared her mother by the shoulders, not caring one iota about her mother's violets. "Stop being so melodramatic. Tell me what's going on."

Mother placed the back of her hand to her forehead and swooned.

"Dammit." She lowered her mother into the desk chair. Mother put her elbows on the desk, head bowed in her hands and let out an inhumane wail loud enough to cause heads to peep up over the cubicles throughout the office.

Reagan glared at her co-workers, sending them back down into their chairs. "Who knows I wrote the article, Mother?" she asked in a harsh whisper.

The older woman's shoulders shook with barely contained sobs. "The garden club met this morning. Oh! It was so terrible!"

Patience slipped another notch. "What happened at the meeting?"

Her mother lifted her head and took in a deep breath. "Pansy Wilcox brought the past three copies of *Glimmer* to the meeting, ranting and raving about some silly article she claimed would…would…" She dabbed at her eyes, soaking up dry tears. "Well, never mind what she said, it's simply too inappropriate to repeat. Imagine, a refined woman like Pansy Wilcox reading that smut."

Reagan let the smut comment slide; she expected no less from her prudish mother. "Then what happened?" she asked, gritting her teeth.

"Everyone passed around the magazines, laughing and giggling like naughty schoolgirls. What a fool I felt sitting there, knowing my daughter worked for the company responsible for publishing that trash!"

Reagan's shoulders sagged in relief. "So no one knows I wrote the articles?"

Her mother began to sob, yet again, mascara running down her face in black furrows. "Oh, they know all right! Everyone knows! The garden club met today at Mrs. Nelson's house. Do you have any idea how long we've waited for an invite to her home? Imagine her surprise to find the very incident that ruined her prized Ernest Markham Clematis vine, trained and pruned for five years to climb just perfectly up the trellis, right there in the magazine!"

Reagan closed her eyes a long moment, the name repeating her in her head, over and over. Mrs. Nelson. The Dean Nelson. She gulped. *Luke Nelson*. "Oh, god." She braced a sudden headache with the palm of her hand. Not only did she and Luke have sex at the Dean's house, but it was his parents' house as well!

Oh god, oh god, ohgodgodgod.

Regan counted to ten. "Okay, so she knows what happened to her Clematis. How does she know *who* did it and that *I* wrote the article?"

Her mother lifted her head and raised her finely plucked brows. "Because, my dear, Pansy suggested that since my daughter worked for *Glimmer,* I should ask you to investigate the Clematis killing, and then Mary Bollox—she's the one who grows those amazing orchids in her green house—she picked that very moment to remember that I had told her my daughter was dating a college professor and couldn't meet her son over Thanksgiving. Oh!" Mother plucked five tissues from the Kleenex box. "The connection was made. I denied it, of course, and came here to prove your innocence, only to be slapped in the face by, by that *filth*." She waved her hand toward the magazine in the trash. "How could you do this?"

"That's exactly what I'd like to know," Paxton said from behind Reagan. "My office, now."

Reagan heard a loud pop of her dream cloud bursting into a zillion pieces as she followed Paxton toward the end of her career.

Reagan lay with her head on Michaelo's lap as he smoothed her hair off her tear dampened cheeks. He'd shown up at her door an hour after she was fired with two half melted large DQ Banana Splits, doubled toppings.

"Thank you for being here," she said, tears finally spent.

"Anytime, *suga*. Chin up, now. It's time to start focusing on the positives instead of the negatives."

"And what would those be? My mother thinks I'm a slut and a Clematis killer. I've been fired. The man I love won't take my calls." Apparently Mrs. Nelson wasted no time in informing her son of the articles.

"Your mother will get over it, just as soon as those biddies find something better to gossip about. You have offers from other magazines, you won't be out of work long."

"The offers have been rescinded."

"As for the man," Michaelo continued, a thoughtful expression on his light shimmer-powdered face, "you're just going to have to prove to him that you're truly sorry."

"I can't prove anything to him when he won't even speak to me!"

Michaelo patted her head like a lost puppy. "If he loves you, he'll give you a chance once he's done being angry."

Her heart frowned. "That's just it, Michaelo. He's never said he loves me."

A long pause. "Then we may have a problem."

"I liked it better when you were pointing out the positives," she said, reaching for a spoon of melted ice cream, dripping it across the coffee table, carpet and Michaelo's leg to her mouth.

"Now, now. I said we may have a problem. Didn't say we can't find a way to fix it. But the first thing you need to do, Reggie, is pull yourself together, get your cute little heiny off this couch and do what you do best."

She sniffed. "Observe, research and read?"

Michaelo pushed her up and held her rag doll body by the shoulders. "No, that was the old Reagan. The new Reagan goes *va-va-varoom*. You gotta get your motor going again, baby. Ask yourself what you want, answer it honestly and then lead foot that pedal and go after it. Now, I've gotta jet, unless you need me to stay."

She shook her head. "I'm going to miss working with you."

"Anytime you need me, just stick your head out the window and call. I'll be there." He kissed her cheek, leaving a smudge of pink lipstick. "TTFN."

Reagan watched him go, then took her sorry self to bed. She just didn't have any *va-va-varoom* in her. Maybe a good night's sleep would make her feel better.

Reagan didn't sleep; instead she tossed and turned, thinking about Luke, the experiences he had shared with her. She thought about her job, about Paxton's threat that if Luke sued the magazine for being written about without permission Reagan would be blackballed in the writing community from Seattle to New York—Paxton promised to see to it personally.

Not that it'd matter much now. Word of her lack of journalistic integrity probably had already made rounds.

Just before daybreak, Reagan dragged herself from bed and went to stand before the mirror over the fireplace. She closed her eyes, asked herself what she truly wanted and answered herself honestly, as Michaelo told her to do.

When she opened her eyes, she looked in the mirror and saw herself as that woman, despite the puffy eyes and tousled hair.

She saw herself as Reagan Malone, independent woman, creative writer, beautiful and strong.

For a long time she stood there, in the daylight playing through the open windows, realizing even if Luke never forgave her for betraying his trust, she would forever be thankful to him for showing her she was the woman she wanted to be all along. She just had to stop hiding, had to be brave enough to say *"This is what I want. This is what I deserve. This is who I am."*

She had to believe in herself, in her inner beauty, strength and talent. She'd made two terrible mistakes; she'd betrayed the trust of the man she loved and the trust Paxton placed in her.

The old Reagan would have gone back to her bed and stayed there crying, believing herself a failure.

The new Reagan was going to take this lesson and learn from it, make things right, no matter what it took.

Finding her briefcase, she took out her notebook, sat down and began to write the fourth installment of *Good Girl Gone Bad.*

Chapter Seven

Reagan returned home after yet another day using the public Internet service at the library to send her résumé and clips to the magazines who'd previously contacted her with fabulous job offers.

She had yet to hear from a single one.

With the journalist equivalent of the plague, no one wanted Reagan anywhere near their office. She was a potential liability. She couldn't be trusted.

The old Reagan would have given up. The new Reagan was going to keep trying, fight like hell to keep her head above water and prove she deserved another chance.

She plunked down her briefcase and took the day's mail to the kitchen table, tossing aside the junk mail and the bills she wouldn't be able to pay for much longer. All that was left were two manila envelopes.

She opened the first and pulled out this week's edition of *Glimmer*, thinking the writer who had tumbled down the mountain sent it to twist the knife in Reagan's lost career.

She didn't need a visual reminder that she was no longer an employed writer, *thank you very much*. Ready to toss the magazine in the trash, a small headline near the bottom of the glossy cover caught her attention.

Conclusion:

Good Girl Gone Bad

Which Prevails? Pg. 52

Heart stammering, Reagan flipped to the page, ignoring the sheet of paper that fell from the magazine. She sat staring at the magazine for a long time, unable to believe Paxton actually had printed the fourth installment.

Reagan hadn't thought the last article would see the light of day since she wrote it after her termination. She simply wanted to prove she could fulfill a commitment, that she had learned from her mistakes.

And Reagan had written the article for herself. She needed to write about her discoveries, her growth, her lessons, her failures. Neither good girl nor the bad prevailed. Rather a combination of both emerged, strengths and weaknesses from both, to create a new Reagan. Wiser, stronger, confident.

She just wished Luke hadn't been hurt in the process. She owed him so much.

Picking up the sheet of paper that had fallen out of the magazine, she read:

"Reagan,

"I'm not forgiving your actions, but I cannot deny the readers' response to your work. I would like to discuss freelancing, within certain guidelines.

"Paxton."

Oh. My. God.

Setting the letter and magazine aside, Reagan tore open the second envelope, expecting a freelance contract. She pulled out a sheet of paper, scanned it and gasped.

The paper slipped from her hand. She shoved her chair back and jumped to her feet. Staring down at the paper, she slowly stepped away until she backed into the counter. Keywords and phrases from the letter popped through her mind like ugly red graffiti.

Ten o'clock tonight.

Expose.

Luke.

Be there.

Reagan swallowed thickly. The cryptic message was clear. Luke would be publicly exposed as the subject of her articles unless she met with an unknown person at ten o'clock tonight to discuss terms of keeping quiet.

She was being blackmailed.

Dear God. What had she done? What was she going to do?

She didn't have enough money to pay off a blackmailer.

Terror struck again and again, like lightening rods from the sky. She reached for the phone, then let her trembling hand drop. If she reported this to the police, she'd have to reveal Luke's identity and someone would surely leak it to the press.

"Okay," she said aloud. "No one knows the truth except Paxton, Michaelo and Mother." *And* the entire gardening club.

Reagan dropped her head on her palms and groaned. *Keep calm.*

Think this through. Who among the list of suspects would dare stoop to blackmail?

Paxton, Michaelo and Mother were immediately off the list. Paxton had offered Reagan freelance work. Michaelo was her best friend. Mother—she'd already suffered enough embarrassment-she wouldn't dare do anything to add to the shame she believed Reagan bestowed upon the family.

Which left the members of the garden club.

Reagan straightened her spine. She wasn't shy, timid Reagan Malone anymore. She could handle any one of those self-righteous, flower pruning, black-mailing women.

Following the blackmail letter's instructions, Reagan drove into the parking garage at exactly ten o'clock. Her gaze swept the dark, empty space; her hands gripped the steering wheel. Whichever garden club member was behind this would regret messing with the new, improved Reagan Malone.

Oh, she fully intended to protect Luke's identity. She had already embarrassed him personally with his family. Publicly she could cost him a whole lot more, possibly even his job. She'd take the Fifth to the end, would never admit Luke was her subject.

Reagan also fully intended to teach whatever green thumb, greedy woman behind this a couple of lessons.

One, blackmail was against the law.

Two, Reagan Malone would never back down again, would never again shy away from confrontation.

Three...well, she'd think of a third lesson when the time came.

Reagan reached into her purse and took out her cell phone, dialed her home number, then set it on the center console. Per the blackmailer's instructions, she rolled down her car window and waited.

She had made a mistake writing about Luke without his consent or knowledge. But it was *her* mistake. She refused to allow Luke pay for it more than he already had. So she'd go along with this game and make sure the woman behind the scheme never tried anything like it again.

"Close your eyes," a muffled voice said from somewhere in the dark parking garage. "And don't try anything stupid."

Reagan drew in a deep breath. "I'm sorry, I couldn't quite hear what you said." She reached for her cell phone and pressed send. She'd set her answering machine to pick up automatically and extended the record time. "Would you repeat that?"

"Close your eyes," the voice said, clearer and louder this time, "and don't try anything stupid."

She closed her eyes. "Now what?"

The sound of high heels clicked toward her. A moment later something soft landed on her lap. "Tie that over your eyes. No peeking."

Reagan slid the fabric through her fingers. It felt like a Pashmina scarf. She tied the scarf around her head, smelling the perfume lingering on the buttery soft fabric.

"Step out of the car."

"Tell me what you want first." Reagan needed to get as much incriminating conversation recorded as possible. Then all she'd have to do is threaten to go to the police and that'd be the end of it. "Tell me the terms of your blackmail request."

"Don't make me ask twice."

Whoever it was even did a great job of making her voice sound deep, almost like a man. Reagan blindly reached for the door handle and stepped out. She knew exactly how many steps away from the car she could take and still have a clear recording. She had practiced several times before coming, altering her voice to different levels. More than three steps, the recording became inaudible.

"Turn around and put your hands behind your back."

Reagan hesitated.

"Don't make this hard. I won't hurt you if you cooperate."

She turned around, hands in the small of her back. "Please, just tell me what you want. Tell me your terms."

A hand, a very large hand, suddenly grabbed both of Reagan's, squeezing them together and wrapped what felt like slim rope around her wrists. "Okay, you're taking this a bit far," Reagan said, trying to jerk her hands free, only to find them already bound.

Panic struck. The voice, the large hands. This was no woman. Reagan screamed. Another scarf was suddenly in the bite of her mouth, muffling her cry for help. The blackmailer tied a knot behind her head, securing the gag.

"Relax, and everything will be just fine." The back door opened, he folded Reagan inside. "Understand?"

She nodded. The door slammed shut, and a moment later the engine started and the car backed up. Inhaling a deep breath through her nose in an attempt at finding calm, she got a deeper smell of the perfume of the scarf.

She knew the scent.

Matter of fact, she knew who wore the scent *and* who owned a Pashmina scarf.

Anger and betrayal burned hot as Reagan sat blindfolded and bound in the back of her car as Michaelo drove to heaven knew where. Why was Michaelo doing this to her? They were best friends. She trusted him, relied on him. He knew how she felt about Luke.

Which was exactly why Michaelo was doing this, Reagan realized. Michaelo knew she'd do anything to protect Luke from being exposed. She just never thought Michaelo could be this cruel to turn her pain into profit. He'd always been so sweet and friendly and caring.

Which were probably exactly the same things Luke had thought about her. Reagan herself didn't think she'd be the type to betray a friend's trust for money and fame. She hadn't meant for it all to get so out of control. She'd just been so, so *inspired*. Luke had shown her a whole other world, possibilities and experiences she'd never dared believe possible. It didn't matter that she knew she was wrong, or that she'd learned her lesson. Luke had every right to hate her.

Michaelo's betrayal, Reagan realized, hot tears soaking the Pashmina, must be some kind of cosmic payment for realizing too late her mistakes.

The car finally stopped, and a minute later, Michaelo opened her door and took her by the elbow. He moved her forward, across what felt like pavement beneath her shoes, into what must have been an elevator by the ding of the doors and the lift, then out into a hallway by the feel of carpet. Each time she struggled to free herself, Michaelo held tighter. He knocked on a door, and whispered, "Sorry I had to do this, toots."

Do what? Reagan wondered a frantic moment before hearing the door swoosh open. "What the—" a man's voice said, then broke off.

Michaelo pushed her aside. She heard him speak in low tones that she couldn't understand, then he moved her forward and closed the door behind her. Again she was taken by the elbow, but she could tell by the grip it was someone else. Furious with Michaelo or not, she wanted him to stay with her.

"I'm going to take the gag off," a voice said, again muffled, but different, confirming a change in abductor. "First, promise not to scream. Understand?"

Reagan nodded, praying if she cooperated, this nightmare would end. It was just about money, she assured herself. Once she agreed to pay for silence, she'd be free. And Michaelo was going to be in big, big trouble.

As the gag came off, Reagan sucked in a deep breath. "What do you want?" she asked in a hoarse whisper.

"That's a very good question. Why don't we start with you telling me what you want."

"I…I," she cleared her throat, determined to be brave and strong, "I'll pay any price. I don't have much, but I'll make payments." A lump lodged in her throat. Luke was worth all the money in the world. "Whatever it takes."

"Takes to?"

Reagan stood erect, her heart hammering. "To keep Luke's name from being released. He doesn't deserve to be publicly humiliated."

"So let me get this straight. You're here to pay for silence."

"Yes."

"How much money did you bring with you?"

"None, I thought we'd discuss your, er, fee."

"Hmm. And why should you care if his name is released? You didn't care when you wrote your articles."

Reagan turned away, fresh tears hot beneath the blindfold. "Yes, I did care! I just thought—I didn't think—no one was suppose to know. I told you, he-he doesn't deserve this, and I-I love him. I'll do anything to protect him. I made a terrible mistake."

"Yes, you did. He had a right to know about the articles. But you made your biggest mistake by coming here."

Reagan swallowed, hard. "What are going to do to me?"

"Oh, I can think of plenty of things. You're blindfolded. Tied up." He ran his hand along her jaw. "But first, promise me you'll never do anything as stupid as this again," he said, no longer altering his voice.

Reagan recognized it instantly. Her knees went weak. Her heart skipped a beat. Oh. My. God. "Luke?"

Chapter Eight

Luke's fingers threaded into her hair above the blindfold. He drew her closer. "Yes, Reagan, it's me."

Reagan leaned her head into his palm. "What…how…why?"

"I was as surprised as you to open my door and find you blindfolded, gagged *and* bound."

"I don't understand what's going on."

"I think I do. Your friend, Michaelo, came to see me the other day, wanted to know why I wouldn't return your calls. Why I wouldn't give you a chance to explain what happened."

"*Oh, no.* I didn't send him, I promise. He's just—" Just her best friend in the entire world. "Would you please take this blindfold off?" She needed to see Luke, gauge his mood. Make him understand just how sorry she was, for everything.

"Hmm." Luke slipped his fingers through her hair, twined his finger around the end of a lock. "Not just yet." His voice sounded deep, low. Sensual.

Heaven, how she missed his voice. His touch.

"It's not everyday I get a visit from someone as…unique as Michaelo. So I let him speak, heard what he had to say. And then I explained how I had thought I could trust you. How I thought you trusted me."

"You can—I did. I'm sorry—"

He pressed his finger to her mouth. "*Shh.* Michaelo demanded I give you a chance to prove your trust. I wasn't sure I even wanted to see you."

So Michaelo had planned the whole blackmail scheme to prove to Luke she could be trusted. Reagan should be furious with her best friend, but knew he thought he was helping. "I-I'll go," she whispered. "If you want me to."

"The thing is, Reagan, when I opened my door and saw you standing there, I realized I never stopped needing to see you. Since the day in the bookstore, I've needed to see you. Be near you." The heat of his body closed in on her, his words soft and warm over her ear. He slid his arms around her and stroked her back, then took her bottom in his hand and squeezed, angling her hips to press against him. "Be *inside* you. Do you know why?"

Reagan bit her bottom lip and shook her head.

Luke slid his other hand beneath her blouse, tickled up her side, skimmed over her breasts and stopped over the beat of her heart. Sensation tingled in the wake of his touch. Her nipples budded, warmth stirred to swirls of heat. It was so hard for her to think when Luke touched her, so difficult to breathe.

"You react with such emotion. Give all of yourself to the moment. You feel, and you experience." He moved soft kisses along her jaw, worked his way to her mouth, one hand capturing the back of her head, over the knot of the blindfold.

"Only with you," she whispered. "You taught me, showed me… I never felt before the way you make me feel."

"Neither have I, Reagan. Which is why I wouldn't have stayed away much longer." His words were moist and warm against her mouth. "You drive me crazy when I'm near you, drive me insane when we're apart. I need to be near you, feel you. But damn you, if you ever do something like this again—what if the blackmail letter had been real?"

His words played in her heart and mind. *He wouldn't have stayed away much longer.* "I knew I was safe. I thought it was someone from the garden club."

"But it wasn't." Luke eased away and walked her across the room.

Reagan heard a door open, and he moved her inside. Completely disoriented in her blindness, she didn't know which room he had taken her into until he sat her down and eased her backward onto something soft. Her heart sang as she realized it was his bed he laid her on.

"Promise me you won't ever again do something as stupid as running off to meet with a blackmailer alone." The mattress bowed beneath the weight of him kneeling over her thighs.

She shook her head. "No, I won't promise you that. I made a mistake. I had to make it as right as possible."

He slipped his hand beneath her skirt, moved upward beneath the edge of her panties and skimmed his thumb between her legs, over her lobes, dipping into the heat of her valley to press deliciously against her nubbin.

Heat rushed from the tips of her breasts to coil low and deep from the pleasure of his touch. Her hips began to rock ever so slowly against his touch; warmth and dampness seeped deep inside her. Sprays of sensation radiated everywhere, lighting her darkness beneath the blindfold.

The bed shifted as Luke leaned down, his hand bracing beside her head. Soft and moist, he laved the tip of her breast through her blouse and the cotton fabric of her bra, suckled her already hard nipple. He buried his thumb deeper, pressure against building pressure. Her back arched and her head fell to the side, a moan escaping from her throat.

Releasing the tension of his thumb, he slid his finger into her core, ever so slowly. Reagan tucked her bottom lip under her front teeth and whimpered, her hips lifting to coax him further, needing to feel him deep inside her. "Fuck me, Luke," she breathed, needing his fullness, the length of him inside her.

"Not this time, Reagan." His mouth trailed down between her breasts, over her stomach. He tickled the hallow of her hip with his tongue. "This time I'm going to make love to you."

His words were amazing. Make love. Dreams and hopes coalesced into a moment so incredibly sweet, she wanted it to never end. Moving lower, he slid down her panties, kissed the inside of her thigh. Perhaps she was dreaming all of this. If so, Reagan never wanted to wake up.

Luke drew his tongue to the center of her, where heat and pressure and tiny throbs begged for more. Pressing open her legs with his hands on the inside of her thighs, he tortured her nubbin with the lightly rough tip of his tongue. "But not until you make that promise."

"Luke, please." Breath shallow and breaking on tiny gasps, Reagan tried to fight the intensity of her pleasure. She tried to focus, to form coherent thoughts. She couldn't take anymore of his sweet torture, couldn't not. She loved him, loved him, loved him. But she would protect him, would show him she could be trusted. "No, I—oh..."

He eased his finger from within in her, stroked back inside, pushing further, gliding along her upper wall while drawing his tongue down her wet slit, up again to suckle her nubbin. Her fragrance bloomed the air, sweet and pungent. Such slow, sweet, beguiling pleasure. Pleasure orchestrated by a master, bringing each melody of her body together to sing a licentious song. Feelings and emotions blended on the chords of crashing need.

He plunged two fingers deep inside her, held taut, her tender walls pulsing against his touch. "Promise me, Reagan."

Her hips jerked off the bed, so helpless as he held her dangling from a thread just shy of climax. "I want…I need you to know you can trust me," she managed, gulping in drinks of air, sprays of light playing behind the blindfold. She bore her hips against his hand, circling, pushing, needing.

"You've already proven your trust by coming here tonight. Your trust was proven the first time you allowed me to touch you."

It was difficult to think when all she wanted was him, inside her. "But I-I wrote about you in my articles. I've shamed you in front of your family."

He moved, his knees between her open legs, pressing her open further, slipping his fingers from within her. "Reagan, nothing I've done with you shames me." The weight of his body shifted to one side, and she sensed him reaching for something. Moments later what felt like little petals fluttered down over her belly.

She inhaled the scent of flowers as he slid his erection deep into her core ever so slowly. Her begging body took him fully. "If the whole world finds out how much I enjoy making love to you," he said, pressing even deeper inside her. "Then let them know." He pulled his hips back, then reentered her, building her desire again with slow strokes. He reached to untie the blindfold and slipped it away.

She blinked open her eyes and focused on Luke's handsome face above her. "Let them know I love you," he said, his eyes darkening as he stared deep into her eyes.

"I love you, too," she whispered, the words catching on her soul. "I promise, I won't ever do anything to betray your trust again." With him she climbed to a plateau where love and trust heightened their passion. As they came together in an orgasm more powerful than any before, her words of love flowed again and again with their release.

Afterward, lying in a tangle on Luke's bed, a place he had never brought a lover before, Reagan, finally free of the binds tying her hands, picked up a rich red Clematis petal dewed with the union of their bodies. "Oh, no. Please don't tell me this is what I think it is."

Luke plucked up another petal from Mrs. Nelson's prized Ernest Markham Clematis vine and ran it across her cheek. "Ah-uh. I've kept a bunch beside my bed to remind me of you. You wouldn't believe how hard it is to get those out of her house undetected."

Luke had stolen flowers from his mother. For her. Reagan smiled and snuggled up closer to him. "You really shouldn't have."

"Hey, it'll give our mothers something else to gossip about. And maybe something for you to write about next."

She nuzzled her nose to the underside of his chin, drew her tongue along his jaw. "Hmmm, I doubt I'll be lacking topics for a very long time."

Luke cupped the back of her head, lifted her mouth to his. "At least the next seventy years or so."

Reagan smiled against his kiss. "Hmmm, that's a lot of research."

"You know what they say, 'Do what you love.'"

"Can I quote you on that, Mr. Nelson?"

"Absolutely, Mrs. Nelson."

Reagan's heart stilled, her breath caught in her throat. She searched Luke's gaze, disbelieving the implication of his words. "Did you… Are you…?"

"Asking you to marry me?" Luke kissed her once again, softly, tenderly, deeply. "Yes, Reagan. That's exactly what I'm asking."

She cupped his beautiful face in her palm. A tear slid down her cheek. "I love you. Yes…yes…yes…I'll marry you."

About the Author:

Dominique Sinclair, who also writes romantic suspense and contemporary romance as Jewel Stone, lives in beautiful Washington State. When not writing, Dominique spends her time doing lots of research—which can be quite exciting when researching erotic fiction!

Good Girl Gone Bad *is Dominique's second erotic romance piece, a genre which she has discovered addictive. You can read her first novella,* Private Eyes, *in* ***Secrets, Volume 10****.*

To learn more about Dominique and her sensual, seductive, sinful world of erotic romance visit www.dominiquesinclair.com.

Aphrodite's Passion

by Jess Michaels

To My Reader:

When I read about the ancient cults who worshipped the goddess Aphrodite, I knew immediately that there was an erotic, romantic story there. I hope you enjoy Gavin and Selena's journey through passion, duty and ultimately, love.

For Michael, who is everything I ever wanted, and everything I never knew I needed.

Chapter One

London, Summer 1885

Rain trickled down the windows, and the muggy warmth made the dark sitting room stifling. Gavin Fletcher shifted on the hard, cushionless chair as he looked at the group of people staring at him. It was as if he'd been sent before a firing squad.

"I still don't understand why you require my assistance, Miss Kelsey," he said as he took a sip of tepid tea. It took all his willpower not to wince at its lack of flavor or heat. The drink was as bland as his surroundings, as pale and insipid as the woman who glared at him from her ramrod straight position on the settee.

"My father is dead because he saved your life, Major Fletcher." Amelia Kelsey frowned, thinning the light skin around her flat, pursed lips, her expression more sullen than it had been a moment before. "Isn't that true?"

Gavin flexed his left arm instinctively. A shadow of pain shot through both the damaged bone and his heart with her words, and the raw memories they evoked. Memories of a day in India. The day when he'd nearly been killed but for the intervention of his superior officer, Colonel David Kelsey. Fletcher had lived, but Kelsey had been gravely injured. Watching the man slowly bleed to death in the oppressive heat and filth of the field hospital had been agony itself.

"Major?"

This time it was Amelia Kelsey's younger sister, Adelaide, who snapped out his rank. She could have been her sister's twin with her flat blonde hair, watery blue eyes and pinched, pale face.

"Yes, your assessment is correct." As guilt clawed his heart, Gavin let his gaze slip to the shiny hardwood floor. It reflected the dim light of the lamps and a shadowy image of Gavin's own face. "Your father saved my life during a skirmish with Indian radicals. In the process, his own life was taken. My apologies to all of you. I wish to offer my most sincere condolences for your loss."

He forced his stare back up to the family. The two sisters wiped their eyes with matching black handkerchiefs, while their younger brother, Arthur simply appeared bored.

"Then you are beholden to him." Amelia set her handkerchief down and smiled for the first time since his arrival. To his surprise, it was even more unattractive than her scowl. "Beholden to *us*."

He drew in a sharp breath as he nodded with reluctance. "Yes. That is true."

"If you wish to repay your debt, you can help us."

Gavin's eyes narrowed as he looked from one Kelsey offspring to the next. That feeling of the room closing in on him began again, more acutely than before. "How can I be of assistance?"

"Our stepmother is missing." Amelia spat the words out with as much care as a viper for the comfort of its prey. "Her parents believe she's been taken by white slave traders, thanks to that ridiculous article in the *Pall Mall Gazette* last week."

"I'm afraid I've only been in country for a few days," Gavin said as apologetically as he could muster. He was beginning to despise this family with their cold, cruel stares and dark, dank parlor. He hadn't liked their father much either, but the man had saved his life. Only that unalterable fact kept him from storming out and never looking back.

"I thought as much." Arthur stepped forward with a folded copy of the paper.

Gavin scanned the story the young man pointed to. It was sensationalist drivel about the dangers of letting young women out on their own. It told of kidnappings and the systematic deflowering of virgins by lecherous foreigners who then forced them into the horrors of prostitution.

"And you believe your stepmother was taken by one of these ringleaders?" Gavin asked quietly, just managing to keep the disbelief from his voice. Even if the rumors of white slavery were true, it was unlikely a widow in her late twenties would be taken.

"No." Amelia snatched the paper from his fingertips and tossed it behind her on the floor in a show of violence that surprised Gavin. "I don't think that. Her minister father and mother think that. *I* believe she left on her own. I believe she's been overtaken by some kind of sexual hysteria and is off to make a spectacle of us all."

Gavin rubbed his temples. He had been polite, but his patience was coming to a swift end. "Why don't you tell me the entire story,

Miss Kelsey? And then explain what you want from me."

"Our father's wife," Amelia began, acid dripping from each and every syllable,"is the same age as I am. She was far too young for him and she only married him for his wealth and the purse he left for her in his last will and testament. Our father was miserable every moment he shared with her and couldn't wait to escape and do his duty in India."

Gavin arched an eyebrow but remained silent. The Widow Kelsey must have been unpleasant if a man would rather 'escape' to the horrors of war than stay with her in safety and comfort. Not that he was entirely convinced this shrew's version of the story was correct. "Go on."

This time Adelaide Kelsey spoke, continuing where her sister left off as if they had rehearsed the telling of this little tale. "After our dear father left the country, our stepmother went wild. She consorted publicly with questionable people and stayed out until indecent hours of the night. When we confronted her with our questions about her behavior, she treated us abominably and refused to answer."

Again, Gavin held his tongue. He could only imagine what kind of inquisition Mrs. Kelsey must have endured with these three. His dealings with them were trying enough, and it was clear the two women, at least, held their stepmother in very low regard.

"Do you know where she went?"

Amelia shook her head with a scowl. "No, though I have my suspicions. After my father died, our stepmother hardly mourned a few weeks before she returned to her lifestyle as if he meant nothing to her. Her attitude toward us grew more and more outrageous. Finally, we felt we had no choice but to have her committed. Unfortunately, she got wind of our plans before we could… could…" She paused with a malicious smile that turned Gavin's blood cold, even in the muggy heat of the parlor. "*Help* her. She disappeared nearly a fortnight ago, and we've had no word of her whereabouts since."

Leaning back in the uncomfortable chair, Gavin flexed his fingers across his thigh. A shot of pain burst through his arm, one he forced himself to ignore. Somehow he doubted the prudence of showing weakness in this snake's nest.

"I am sorry to hear your family lost your stepmother so soon after your father's untimely death," he said. "But again, I'm at a loss as to what this has to do with me."

Arthur Kelsey sighed with theatrical exasperation. "Since you are beholden to my father and our family, my sisters feel *you* should undertake the task of finding our stepmother and bringing her home." He frowned at the two women. "You see, they cannot rest until they insure our poor stepmother is 'treated' for her illness."

Gavin snapped his gaze toward the two young women who were nodding in unison. They couldn't be serious! He had only just returned home. "You want me to track your stepmother down and drag her back to London so you can institutionalize her?"

"She needs treatment," Amelia said firmly.

"Yes," Adelaide chimed in with a cruel smile. "She needs our help whether she desires it or not."

Gavin got to his feet and paced to the window. He watched the rain for a long moment as he considered his options. Though he did feel beholden to the Kelsey family for their sacrifice, the idea of tracking down some wayward widow, one who might be legitimately insane, didn't appeal to him. After months of being away, he had looked forward to spending time at home. To seeing his ailing mother. To meeting the nieces and nephews who had been born while he toiled away in service to the Queen's Army.

He certainly hadn't planned for a journey to find a strange woman.

He allowed himself a glance over his shoulder at the siblings. They were gathered in a semi-circle, staring at him like vultures aching to peck at rotting meat. He shuddered. If he refused their request, he had no doubt they would plague him until they felt some satisfaction that he had repaid his 'debt'. He didn't relish the idea of being summoned here more than this one time, yet his honor demanded he fulfill his obligation.

"Do you have any idea where your stepmother might have gone?" he asked softly.

Amelia Kelsey made no attempt to hide her triumphant grin. "Her closest friend and confidante was a woman named Isadora Glasier. She was married to an officer stationed in Greece, and after his death, she stayed on that heathen island far longer than was proper. We believe she and Mrs. Glasier returned to Greece or possibly the nearby island of Cyprus."

Gavin wrinkled his brow. "Why?"

Adelaide turned to the table behind her and opened a small box. From it, she withdrew the charred remains of a leather bound book.

"This is our stepmother's diary. She tried to burn it before she left the house, but one of our parlor maids rescued it. Though much is destroyed, what remains details her sick obsessions. In it, she often mentions Cyprus, as well as some kind of twisted group Mrs. Glasier introduced her to." She held out the diary as if it were a poisonous snake that could turn on her at any moment.

Gavin took the delicate book carefully. "And how will I know what your stepmother looks like if I do manage to discover where she's gone?"

Arthur dug into his pocket and produced two items. "This is a miniature my father had done of his wife before he left for India. And she had this photograph taken for her mother and father. They live in the country and rarely saw her after her marriage."

Gavin reached out to take the items and was surprised when the young man clenched them for a moment before he relinquished control. Gavin searched Arthur Kelsey's unlined face for a moment before he refocused his attention on the two items.

When he turned the photograph over, he could hardly contain his gasp. Mrs. Kelsey was far and away the most exquisite woman he'd ever seen. She had a heavy silken mass of dark hair with little wisps that spun around her cheeks and a curvaceous, voluptuous body that called out to be touched. Worshiped.

Though she was posed in the stiff posture required for the long photography sessions, her face and eyes were alive with personality and a dash of sensuality that reached beyond the picture and stirred desires in him that had been dormant since his injury.

"What is her name?" he choked out as he continued to stare at the photograph.

"Selena." Arthur Kelsey answered, his voice as strained as Gavin's had been. "Her name is Selena."

Gavin looked up and found himself locking gazes with the young man. A dangerous desire glittered in Kelsey's pale blue eyes, as dangerous as the need that suddenly burned within Gavin himself for this woman he had never even met.

"I shall do my best to find her and bring her back," he said quietly. "But you aren't giving me much information to work with."

"You will make do." Amelia folded her thin arms across her chest as she glared from Gavin to her brother and back again. "I can tell you some heathen goddess named Aphrodite is mentioned several times in the disgusting pages of that journal. Perhaps that is a clue you can investigate."

Gavin forced himself to put Selena Kelsey's grainy photo into his pocket. Even though the image was no longer in sight, he could still see it in his mind. Feel it in his pocket as much as if it were Selena's own hand there, teasing him. He struggled to keep the evidence of his sudden desire at bay, at least until he got out of this house and into the privacy of his rented rooms.

"Yes," he choked out. "I'll work as quickly as possible to uncover her whereabouts. I will inform you before I leave the country to begin my search." He edged toward the door. "If there is nothing else, I shall take my leave."

Amelia looked at him through narrowed eyes. "That is all. Our butler will show you to the door." Gavin held back a sigh of relief as he made for the foyer, but hadn't quite left the room when the young woman stopped him with the sound of her shrill voice. "Major Fletcher?"

"Yes?" He turned back with a false smile.

"Selena may be beautiful, but I wouldn't recommend falling under her spell." The young woman arched an accusatory eyebrow. "Our stepmother is not well, and if you aren't careful, she could drive *you* mad, too. Good day."

Gavin gave the family a last nod before he left the room. He burst out into the rain and raised an arm to hail a hackney. Once he was safely out of view from the public street, he sank back against the worn seat, then adjusted his trousers around the raging erection that had sprung up the moment he'd looked at the image of Selena Kelsey. Like a thief gazing hungrily at a hoard of treasure, he brought out her picture again and stared at the sultry woman with a shiver of need.

Perhaps his savior's widow *was* sick. Perhaps she was driven by hysterical needs and did require the institutionalization the Kelsey family seemed so anxious to impose. Gavin didn't know enough about her to answer those questions yet. What he did know was that Selena was utterly desirable, and that she was destined to haunt his dreams until the moment he found her.

Cyprus, two months later.

Selena Kelsey shuddered to think what London would be like at present. Cool and rainy, with the ever-present haze of coal smoke more oppressive than ever. She looked out her window with a deep sigh and a wide, if wavering, smile. Although fall was coming, the island of Cyprus remained bright and warm. Sunlight sparkled off the brilliant blue ocean waters in the distance, while a warm breeze stirred the sand and tropical foliage. It was paradise.

She shivered as she thought of the city she had left behind months before. Emotions swamped her with their intensity. The loneliness of her empty marriage. The anger and fear her stepchildren had inspired in her. The disappointment in her family for putting her in such a situation. The guilty relief when David Kelsey's death had been reported to her. And the horror when she realized that just because her husband was gone, didn't mean she was free. In fact, without his small protection, her life was in even more danger than before.

She shoved those awful memories aside. Drawing in a few breaths, she focused on slowing her racing heart and pounding blood. She had escaped the torment London meant to her. And as she had since she and Isadora arrived on the island a few weeks before, she gave a silent prayer of thanks for her newfound freedom.

Turning away from her window, she sighed. She was grateful, yes. But she was also lost. Confused. Afraid, though for different reasons than she had been in London. But despite her gratitude, she feared she didn't belong in Cyprus any more than she belonged in the repressive society of England. The free sexuality practiced by her friends in the hidden temple along the sandy beaches titillated Selena. She'd watched the sensual rituals and passionate matings of her friends with interest and desire. Still, she hadn't participated, even after Isadora's continued prodding. She hadn't yet chosen a partner to share in her awakening passion.

But her passion *was* awakening. Feelings she had been afraid to let loose in England were alive in Cyprus. Both her inhibitions and her shame were fading like the island flowers that wilted with the coming of fall.

Was it enough for her, though? While her fellow temple dwellers seemed content in their decadent lifestyle, often Selena was... lonely. Even more so than she'd been in her terrible marriage.

With a frown, she gazed in the mirror of her dressing table. Her dark hair was unbound and hung down to her waist. When she brushed it back over her shoulder, she could clearly see the dusty rose outline of her nipples through her thin sleeping sheath. Lower down, the shadow of her pubis pressed against the fabric. She watched in the mirror as her hands glided down her body. She flicked a thumb over one hard nipple, sucking in a breath as pleasure spiked through her blood.

Months ago, bringing herself pleasure had been a secret kept to dark nights in her lonely bed. A shame she tried to deny herself. But now, she was free to experience pleasure without recrimination or charges of hysteria. And she was far more aware of her body's wants and needs.

She concentrated on her breasts, tugging at the nipples with enough force to leave them tingling with sensation. She let her hands drift lower, never taking her eyes off her reflection as she pressed her chemise against her suddenly hot skin. Her fingers drifted over the hollow of her belly button, then finally found the soft folds of her pussy.

She blushed when she thought of that word. Isadora had insisted she learn all the terms for her body, from the bawdy to the medical. Her friend had even given her piles of books with explicit pictures and shocking words so she could learn about herself, learn about passion.

The boat trip to Cyprus had been educational to say the least, between reading the erotic books Isadora had given her, and watching her friend act out those stories from behind the thin sheet that separated their cabin.

That thought enflamed Selena even more. There had been so many nights when she had been a voyeur, watching Isadora act out what Selena was still ashamed to imagine. Images flashed through her mind as she lightly played her fingers along her own slit. With a deep breath, she let the images assault her senses.

There had been a night when Isadora had invited the most handsome of the ship's mates to their shared quarters. With a chiseled body, strong jaw and wild blond hair, the man had been a source of much giggling and coarse talk between the two women. But Selena never expected to awaken to his low, sensual voice just feet away from her bed.

She had peered between the separating sheet just in time to see Isadora drop to her knees. Her friend was already naked and yanked the man's trousers down to his ankles as she slithered to the floor to gaze up at him with an expression filled with promise and desire.

While Selena held back her unbidden moans of shock and wanton curiosity, Isadora had grasped the thick base of the man's fine cock and glided her fist from the root to the throbbing, red tip. He'd dipped his head back with a groan even as he thrust his hands into Isadora's hair and pulled her toward him.

Selena's fingers worked along her slit as she recalled the way Isadora laughed before she wrapped her lips around the round head of his erection and swiftly took the entire, massive length of him deep within her throat. Selena had seen pictures of the act before, but to see it happen, just feet away from her, had aroused her to a fever pitch. She'd been unable to keep from fingering herself, just as she was doing now, as she remembered the wet sucks of Isadora's mouth, and the way the veins in the man's neck lifted up as he strained in pleasure with every thrust.

Finally, he had grabbed Isadora's shoulders and yanked her to her feet. Before Selena could react, he had flipped her friend onto her stomach on the bed and speared his impressive member deep into her body. He thrust into her so hard Selena had feared he would hurt Isadora, but when her friend lifted her face, it was clear the screams that escaped her lips were cries of ecstasy, not agony.

Selena grew wetter with each hot memory. She pressed the fabric of her nightclothes up against herself and began to stroke in a firm, smooth motion. She let her eyes flutter shut as she pictured doing the same thing she had observed her friend doing all those hot nights ago. She imagined the hard thrust of a lover's cock, jutting proudly toward her as she looked up from her bent-kneed position on a soft bed.

Only her fantasy lover's face was blank.

Frustrated, Selena opened her eyes. She was on the brink of orgasm, but couldn't seem to take herself over the edge. She was too distracted, too filled with doubts about her place in the Cult of Aphrodite. Certainly, the Greek goddess of sensuality wouldn't approve of her standoffish ways.

She refocused her attention on the mirror, determined to take herself over the edge. And gasped. His image reflected in the mirror, a man stood in her doorway. Not some male member of their group, not a man she had ever seen before. A stranger.

For a moment, she was frozen by his sudden presence. She didn't turn, but took a long look at him in the mirror. He was tall, with dark hair and bright blue eyes that stood out even from across the room. Dressed in the garments of a middle class man from London, he should have seemed drab, but he wasn't. Even in a plain, brown suit and slightly crooked cravat, he had a presence about him. If she had passed him on a busy street, she wouldn't have been able to keep herself from staring. She certainly couldn't stop now, when he stood in her doorway, watching her pleasure herself.

He was handsome, perhaps only a few years older than she was.

But despite his apparent youth, he had a wisdom and knowledge in his eyes that told Selena he'd seen more of the world than most of the men in her acquaintance.

He also had a hefty dose of lust glittering in the blue depths of his stare. Along with an obvious erection that strained against the front of his wrinkled brown trousers.

The part of her still repressed by societal expectations told her to stop what she was doing. It warned her to cover herself decently and call for the guards this man had somehow bypassed.

But a larger, and now much louder part urged her to continue. Because seeing this man watch her, seeing his reaction to her act of self-pleasure, had taken her even closer to the brink of orgasm. Her wayward thoughts were now entirely focused on the sensual, on this man watching her. If she touched herself again while this man looked on, she would reach completion.

Their eyes locked a second time in the mirror, but he remained silent. Hands trembling, she allowed herself a long, calming breath before she let her fingers move. The stranger's lips parted as he realized she wasn't going to stop masturbating simply because he had invaded her sanctuary.

Instead of focusing on the memory of Isadora and her conquests, Selena concentrated on the stranger who watched her. She imagined his large hands on her skin, touching her as she touched herself. When his tongue darted out to wet his lips, she couldn't help but groan as she pictured that same tongue dragging against her. Her fingers moved at a faster, more purposeful speed against her clit as she imagined him spreading her legs while he revealed the hard thrust of his cock.

Her pleasure spiked, peaked and she found herself wailing out an orgasm that buckled her knees. She tipped forward as she spasmed, gripping at the ornate metal mirror frame with one hand as she bucked the other against her clit, over and over. Her hot, harsh breaths left a circle of steam on the glass as her body quivered one last time. Finally, she found some equilibrium and was able to balance on her shaky legs.

Each movement seemed to take an eternity as she turned to face the intruder who had driven her over the edge of pleasure with just his presence. Her heart slammed against her ribcage with trepidation and excitement. She had absolutely no idea what would happen once she looked at the man without the protection of a mirrored image, but she wasn't afraid. She wanted this stranger to touch her. She wanted him to take her, stroke inside her. To be the first man who brought her to orgasm with his cock or tongue or fingers.

She shivered at the thought. She looked up and let her gaze meet his. A thin sheen of sweat had broken out on his upper lip and his eyes were wide with desire.

"Selena," he whispered as he crossed the room toward her in long, purposeful steps that left little doubt to his intention once he reached her.

She started. How did he know her name? She'd never met him before, of that she was more than certain. Judging from his attire, he wasn't a new member of the cult Isadora had sent to her as a gift. Yet her name fell from his lips as if it were an answer to his every prayer.

He was only feet away now and each purposeful step made her sex clench. But before he could reach out to touch her, before she could give in to him or even ask how he knew her name, the door behind him flew open to slam against the packed mud wall of her hut.

Her intruder seemed to be in too much of a passionate fog to recognize what was happening. He didn't turn at the opening of the door, but continued to walk toward her with the same undeniable gleam in his blue eyes.

Two guards burst into the room behind him, brandishing sharp spears and yelling first in Greek and then accented English as they rushed forward to grasp the man's arms. Only then did he snap out of his haze. He winced in pain as the two men shoved him to the ground, and one of the guards pressed a spear into his back until his suit jacket creased.

"Stop!" Selena cried as she hurried toward them. An uncontrollable desire to protect this unknown man swelled within her, even though the guards had only come to protect her. Still, she ached to see him pinned to the ground, his face twisted in apparent agony as he tried to break free from the iron grip of the Greek guards.

"He is an intruder," one of the guards barked as they jerked her struggling stranger to his feet and dragged him toward the door. "And he must face the counsel."

Chapter Two

"What is your name?" The sharp, female voice spoke to him on what was barely more than a hiss.

Gavin winced as a spear pressed against his back, the blade slicing through his shirt, etching a warning on his skin.

"Take the damn spear out of my flesh and we can discuss this situation like civilized human beings," he snapped before he bit his tongue.

He couldn't afford to lose control of his emotions again. In Selena's room, he'd been so wrapped up in lust that he'd lost all sense of time, his surroundings, even approaching danger. Where had his passion gotten him? Caught before he could talk to Selena alone. And now he was paying the price.

His female captor laughed. Gritting through the pain, he forced his eyes up to look at her. Her stunning red hair was piled on her head, patterned after the ancient Greek style. Her chiton was also traditional, except for the round, firm breast it bared.

The woman seemed anything but embarrassed by her partial nudity. Even in a room filled with nearly two dozen men and women, all of whom stared openly, she didn't blush or move to cover herself. In fact, she appeared to thrive on the attention as she thrust out her breasts with a proud air.

From her accent and the descriptions Gavin had read in Selena's diary, he guessed this was Isadora Glasier.

"You want to talk to us about civility?" Isadora's laughter faded as a flash of sudden anger glittered in her dark eyes. "*You* who invaded our sanctuary? *You* who violated the purity of the temple of Aphrodite?"

Gavin stiffened. Selena had written often in her journal about Aphrodite, the Greek goddess of sex and sensuality. And about how Isadora had slowly tutored her in the ways of the goddess through books and voyeuristic adventures. The stories Selena recounted in the surviving pages of her journal were erotic and passionate. They had awakened Gavin's lust more than once as he read them during his long boat trip to Cyprus.

And now this woman who had dragged Selena away from London, was mentioning the goddess again.

"A sanctuary? A temple?" he repeated with a shake of his head. "What the hell is this place?"

For the first time, he let his attention shift from his guards and the woman who lead them and looked around. From the exterior, the building looked like an ordinary hut, but inside, it was patterned after one of the famous shrines of Greece where ancient people had worshipped gods like Zeus, Poseidon and Aphrodite.

The center of the room held a large, square pit. It had been sunk deep enough that an average man could stand upright and his head wouldn't clear the crevice's marble walls. The pit was surrounded by a marble railing. The other members of the cult clustered around, looking down on the 'trial' with interest, disdain and even hatred.

A throne sat on an elevated platform facing the railing. Above it were a series of elaborate paintings, done in an ancient style. But instead of detailing offerings to the gods or great battles, these depicted various sex acts. And the marble pillars supporting the high ceiling had been carved with lewd intent as well. A naked man with a thrusting cock, his head dipped back as he stroked the firm flesh. A woman being pleasured by two kneeling men.

Isadora used the toe of her sandal to turn his face toward hers. "My questions first, intruder. And yours later if I feel you deserve to know more. What is your name?"

He jerked away from her with a scowl. "Gavin Fletcher."

She smiled in triumph. "And what are you doing violating our temple, Mr. Fletcher? You were certainly not invited into our sanctum by any of our members."

He shook his head. There was no use lying about the purpose for his journey to Cyprus. If Isadora's lackeys searched his bags, they would find Selena's picture and diary. "No, I was not invited. I came looking for someone."

"For whom?" The woman's voice grew sharp and wary.

"For Selena Kelsey."

"What?"

This time, it wasn't Isadora Glasier who answered, but Selena herself. Although he'd only heard her voice once, it was burned in his memory like his own. He watched her push her way forward through the crowd. She struggled to the short staircase that lead to the pit and stumbled down into the area where he was being questioned.

Just as when he saw her the first time, his heart skittered to life. For two months Selena had been nothing more than an image in a photograph, one he had looked at over and over until he'd memorized everything about her, from the quirk of her eyebrow to the slight parting of her lips. She became his obsession, his torment, his desire as he sailed to Cyprus and an uncertain future.

He'd tried to convince himself that she could never live up to his fantasies once he encountered her in reality. He was right.

She far surpassed his fantasies. Her voice was more beautiful. Her scent more alluring. Her eyes more vibrant.

Now those same green eyes that had held him captive while she pleasured herself were dark with surprise and fear as she stared down at him.

"You came here for me?" she asked softly, and the sound of her words cut through him with a blast of need.

The room faded until he was barely aware of the hostile crowd of people, of the sharp press of the spear against his spine, of Isadora's pointed stare. For a moment, all that existed was Selena.

She, too, was dressed in a chiton like Isadora's. Her left breast was exposed, and he took a long, hungry look at the perfect globe of flesh. Her nipple darkened and hardened under his stare, and her lips parted in surprise. As he had in her bedroom, he wondered what her skin would taste like…what she would feel like when she arched beneath him and whispered his name in pleasure.

"Answer the question."

The sharp ache of his injured arm dragged Gavin from the fantasy when one of the guards twisted it behind his back. He tried to control the pain, to discipline his mind not to register the sharp burst that seemed to rush through every fiber of his body, but he couldn't help but cry out.

"Stop, don't hurt him." Selena rushed forward to push the guards away. Leaning down, she placed a soft hand on his painful arm. It was like a balm and the throbbing subsided a fraction. "Let him answer, for pity's sake."

She sank down beside him and looked into his face. She was so close, her body heat burned at him. And he could smell her, too. A tantalizing mix of the sharp, spicy flowers he'd discovered while looking for the temple and a womanly scent that belonged only to her. The remnants of her pleasure.

Despite the danger and unknown elements of his situation, his cock stiffened.

"Then speak," Isadora commanded, though she was staring at Selena, not him. "The lady has given you a reprieve from measures that would force your answers."

Gavin cleared his throat and kept his attention focused on Selena. "Mrs. Kelsey—"

She turned her face as if she'd been slapped, and her hand abruptly left his arm. "Selena. I have no other name in this place but Selena."

He hesitated at the pain and fear that flashed in her eyes, but went on. "Selena, I was sent here by your stepchildren. They were worried about your welfare."

She rocked back on her heels with a gasp.

"My stepchildren?"

"They wish for you to return to London." He grimaced as he thought of why the Kelseys wanted that.

"They hired you to take me back to London?" she whispered.

The absolute horror in her voice cut through him and hurt as much as his injured arm. "Yes."

For a moment, she appeared to struggle with her emotions, but then her jaw set and the glitter of fear faded from her even stare. "How much did they pay you? I shall double it if you simply go away and never tell them you found me. Tell them I'm dead, for all I care."

He reeled back. Despite his dislike of the Kelsey family, the idea of lying to them, of telling them this woman was dead when she wasn't, of breaking her parents' hearts, was utterly distasteful. And he had a duty he held to her late husband.

"They didn't pay me." He sighed. "I owe them a debt, and this is my method of repayment."

She pursed her lips in frustration. "Then tell me the amount of the debt and I'll give you that and more so you'll no longer be beholden to them."

He shook his head slowly. He wasn't sure how she would react to the truth, but he had to tell her regardless. "The debt is a life. Your late husband's life. I am the reason he's dead."

An audible gasp went through the curious crowd, but Selena didn't seem to notice it. Her eyes widened impossibly as she scrambled to her feet and backed away from him.

"*You* are why he is dead?" she repeated slowly as her hand came up to cover the mouth he had longed to kiss for months.

Gavin moved to rise but the guards stepped forward, brandishing their spears to keep him in place. "He died saving my life in India."

The color that had darkened her face slowly bled away until she was as pale as her chiton. "My God, that means you're...you're..."

"Didn't you tell me your husband died saving an officer in his regiment?" Isadora's harsh stare suddenly focused on Gavin with a sinister gleam.

"Yes," Selena whispered. Her hands trembled and her eyes sparkled with unshed tears. "Major—"

"Major Gavin Fletcher," he finished.

Isadora flinched back. "If you are an officer in the Queen's Army, we have no choice. I hate to do this to such an amazing specimen of a man." She snapped her fingers. "Guards! Kill him!"

As the two men advanced on his helpless position, spears pointed at him with deadly intent, Selena screamed.

"No!"

Isadora hauled Selena across the temple floor into one of the alcoves facing the sea. In the large open chamber, it was the only place that gave them some small measure of privacy. Selena flinched as her friend's fingers sunk into her shoulders and she gave her a hard shake.

"What are you thinking? This man is in the Army, perhaps stationed in Greece. If he knows the truth about our temple and we release him, the grounds will be swarming with officers in a matter of hours. Everyone here will be arrested. The men may be let go within a few days, but the women will be returned to abusive husbands and repressed lifestyles or even institutionalized for hysteria. We cannot risk setting him free."

Selena sank her teeth into her lower lip as she stole a glance over Isadora's shoulder toward Gavin Fletcher. He was still down on his knees, the guards holding him. Seeing such a strong man in that compromised position made her heart ache.

Everything her friend said was true, but it made no difference.

"I cannot be responsible for his death, Isadora. I can't live with that hanging over my head." She shrugged apologetically.

"Are you mad?" Isadora's voice went up a level before she controlled herself. "He came to Cyprus with the express duty of hauling you home to the fate your stepchildren have laid out for you. An institution, Selena! How can you feel any responsibility? What you do is to protect yourself and your friends. If anyone has his blood on their hands, it's the triplets."

Selena stifled a smile. Isadora always called her stepchildren the triplets because of their similar names and the drab coloring and ugly attitudes that made them all so distasteful.

"Yes, Adelaide, Amelia and Arthur do hold a lion's share for forcing this man to come here," she said slowly, again looking at the Major. Even crouched on the ground with menacing guards threatening to kill him, he looked every inch in command. Every part of him seemed calm, as if he was assessing his situation and waiting to see what would happen next before he reacted. He was the epitome of control.

Except in her chamber when she'd pleasured herself before him. His mind had definitely not been leading his actions in those moments. Despite herself, she took great pride in that fact.

"Then you understand we must be rid of him."

"No." Selena shook her head. "Major Fletcher is here under false pretences. I can only imagine the horrible lies my stepchildren told him and threats they held over his head. I won't see him dead because of them. Not when they wanted me dead or worse. I will not sacrifice his life for my freedom."

Isadora sighed heavily. "Then what do you suggest? For the sake of the temple, I cannot allow him to leave."

Selena stepped around her friend, affording herself a long, appraising glance at the man whose life was in her hands. He was even more handsome than she believed during the passionate moments in her bedchamber. His body was hard and lean, muscled from his years in the military. And his face had a sense of wisdom to it. An intelligence and experience that drew Selena in.

But those weren't the only reasons why she was drawn to him. Just his mere presence had triggered her most powerful orgasm to date. And when he'd told her he was responsible for her husband's death, she had wanted nothing more than to give herself to him as a reward for ending the life of a man who had tormented her for years. She was in debt to him, much as he believed he was in debt to her stepchildren. Because of Gavin, she was free from her husband's cruelty. She had to save his life.

"Let me keep him."

Isadora's mouth fell open. "Did I hear you correctly?"

Selena drew an unsteady breath. She was shocked to hear the words, herself. "I know you have been frustrated with me since my arrival. I haven't chosen my first man since we landed on the island. I've been living on the fringes of the group, watching, but never participating."

Her friend shrugged one shoulder. "You will choose a man when you find the one who suits you. Until you let go of all your inhibitions, I know you'll find it difficult to be with someone you aren't comfortable with."

Selena motioned toward Gavin. "What if this man is the one?"

Isadora shook her head in disbelief. "You truly want to choose *this* man for the ceremonies we perform here? For your pleasure, both in private and in the public forum? This man who wants to spirit you back to a life you loathed?"

Selena shrugged as Gavin lifted his gaze in her direction. The vivid blue of his eyes froze her in place as he gave her body a slow, sensuous sweep. Every nerve crackled with awareness as her body prepared itself for his touch. For him to take while she shivered around him.

"When he caught me in my bedroom, I was pleasuring myself in the mirror," she said softly. "But he wasn't horrified as many repressed society gentlemen would have been if they'd encountered such a scene. In fact, seeing me do that excited him."

"There are many men here who would be happy to watch you do the same," Isadora argued.

She shook her head. "But he is the first man *I* want to give myself to." She looked her friend in the eye. "I want him. My body aches for his touch. I may not be as experienced in the pleasures of the body as you are, but I know he wanted me in my room. If I touched him, he wouldn't resist. In fact, I think he would have me trembling in a moment."

Isadora looked at Gavin with an appraising tilt of her head. "He is magnificent, I must admit that. So strong and handsome. But with something more there than just his looks."

Selena refused to look at the distracting Major. She had to convince Isadora to allow Gavin to live. "Our studies of Aphrodite tell us the goddess was able to control a man with her sensuality. If what we teach here is true, I ought to be able to do the same. If I can put him under my spell, I can make him do whatever I wish. I can insure he'll never speak of this place or my presence here."

Her friend nodded. "Making a man like that bend to your will won't be easy." She smiled. "But trying would be most entertaining."

Without another word, Isadora slipped from the alcove and returned to the main temple floor. She mounted the platform and seated herself on the throne.

"Selena has chosen her first mate. This is a great honor, for this man will be her tutor as she enters the world of Aphrodite. As her sensuality awakens, he will benefit from her desires." She looked over her shoulder at Selena with a sly wink. "Selena?"

Her hands trembling, Selena took a few steps forward. She remembered watching other women choose their mates and tried to follow the ritual as well as she could. With a flick of her wrist, she unhooked the mother-of-pearl clip that held her thin chiton over her covered breast. The cotton swished down until she was naked from her waist up. Gavin's eyes widened impossibly, but he didn't move.

Fighting the urge to cover her nudity, Selena stepped closer and closer to the man who had intruded into her home and her sanctuary. She drew in a whiff of his scent, manly and clean even in the oppressive heat of the hall. Reaching out, she pressed her palm against his chest. His heart throbbed against her hand, wild with desire he didn't visibly show.

When he reached for her, the guards grabbed his arms and held him steady, forcing him to remain passive as was the way of the ritual. Here women had the power to choose, at least the first time.

She glided her hands up his chest, burned by his heat even through his white shirt. His taut muscles contracted with every stroke. She cupped his cheeks and lowered her trembling mouth to his. Just as she was about to take his kiss, he tipped his head up and claimed her mouth. His tongue speared between her lips, lapping at her like a thirsty man who could only be satisfied by her touch.

She wrapped her arms around his neck. God, how she wished his arms were free to hold her. Still, as she leaned her full weight against him, the thrust of his erection pressed into her belly, letting her know just how much he wanted her.

Her womb contracted with the feel of it, and her heart fluttered. With difficulty, she pulled back and whispered the words in Greek.

"You are mine until I choose to set you free."

To her surprise, he seemed to understand. His eyes darkened with desire. In a rough voice, he answered her in English. "Then take me."

Chapter Three

Gavin locked gazes with Selena. Her eyes were the darkest green he'd seen in all his travels, and impossibly wide with thrilling desire. Never before had a woman looked at him like that.

Genteel women hid their feelings in English society. They weren't allowed to be any one extreme or another. But Selena... Selena was different in more ways than one. She wanted him, needed him and wasn't afraid to show her desire or the myriad of other emotions that played across her face.

With her honesty, something remarkable happened. His regrets no longer tormented him as they had since David Kelsey's life bled away. Even the sting of physical pain in his injured arm faded into the background. And his sense of duty? His obligation to Kelsey's family?

All those thoughts disappeared as her bare breasts brushed the rough fabric of his shirt and her warm body molded to his. Everything in his heart, his body and his mind focused on her. He wanted her, despite being surrounded by strangers who would have him dead to protect themselves.

Strangely, having their gazes on him only inflamed his need all the more. With a shrug of his shoulders, he yanked away from the guards and freed his hands. They trembled for a brief moment before he finally did what he'd been aching to do since that afternoon in the Kelsey sitting room.

He touched Selena. She shut her eyes with a tiny sigh as he glided his fingertips up her exposed arms. Her skin was so impossibly soft, so supple. The reality of Selena Kelsey was far more than any fantasy. If he didn't have her soon, he feared he would explode with pent up emotions and unsatisfied need.

As his control wavered, he gripped her upper arms tighter. The rougher touch seemed to break the spell she was under. With a soft gasp, she pulled back, eyes glazed.

"Oh, my." Isadora's taunting voice shook him from his distraction.

"I never would have guessed it, but this looks like it will work out well." She stepped closer and ran a finger down the line of Gavin's shirt buttons. "Very, very well."

Selena stepped away. Her gaze shifted to her friend and some of the strong emotion faded. "Y-yes."

The other woman gestured for Gavin to approach her. She leaned close until her mouth was just a fraction of an inch from Gavin's ear. "When Selena has tired of you, come to me. Seeing you touch her like that has made me want you next."

When she leaned back, it was with a feline smile Gavin refused to return. Did she really think he would come to her bed when she had given the order to have him killed?

Isadora didn't seem offended by his scowl. "Take your Major back to your rooms, Selena. You can explain..." Her wicked smile was once again directed toward Gavin. "*Everything* to him. Prepare him for his first ritual tonight."

Gavin shivered at the unknown nature of her order. Ritual? Selena's journal had explained many things, but most had to do with her own burgeoning desires, not the true nature of Aphrodite's cult.

His mind spun with questions now that he was to be a participant in the group's activities. He gazed around at the crowd, their garb fashioned after ancient times. Somehow he doubted the twenty or so people who stared like he was some caged lion would explain anything to him. In fact, most continued to glare with unabashed anger, even hatred that he had intruded into their secret society. He would wait to ask his questions when he was alone with Selena.

The thought sent a fresh wave of desire and lust through him. Alone. Able to do anything he desired. He was afraid what he wanted right now was nothing more than a heated, quick coupling.

She turned to him with a smile that was surprisingly shy for a woman who was half-naked and had already passionately kissed him in front of a large group of people. She reached for him and took his hand. Sparks of desire arced from their intertwined fingers and had his cock at full attention.

"Come, Major Fletcher. I'll answer your questions when we return to my room." She glanced back over her shoulder at him with a bold look. "All your questions."

Selena paced across her chamber, lighting a few lamps and straightening her bedclothes as she went. Why was she so nervous?

Stopping, she peered over her shoulder to look at Gavin. He stood by her door, appearing much as he had when he caught her pleasuring herself. A wash of desire worked through her with the memory. *He* was why she was nervous.

He was a stranger. Sent to take her back to a life she loathed. And yet, she ached for his touch. Her desire for him went deeper than mere physical attraction, yet she couldn't explain it. Not to herself. And certainly not to him.

Now she was alone with him. She'd chosen him to be the first man she would take to her bed since her husband. This dangerous man who brought out needs she hadn't realized she had, even as she allowed her sexuality to be awakened by the teachings of the temple.

She sighed. The temple. There was no doubt this man had questions about the temple, the cult and what they did here. How could she tell him enough to soothe his fears about what would happen to him without telling him so much that he could destroy the group?

When she paced passed the mirror, she caught Gavin watching her. Her cheeks heated with embarrassment. Oh, what if she did this all wrong? What if she hurt her friends? Or worse, what if she disappointed him, proving she wasn't really a sensual being at all? Proving she belonged in the straight-laced society she hated and fled from.

"Now that you have me here," he said softly when it became more and more apparent she couldn't find words to speak. "What will you do?"

She struggled with an answer for a moment before her eyes fell on the large metal tub in the middle of her room. It had been filled, probably on Isadora's orders. Steam rose from the water.

"You must be tired from your long journey. A bath has been drawn for you. First you will wash, then we'll discuss our options." She was surprised how cool and strong her voice sounded when nerves caused her whole body to tremble.

"Very well." Still he didn't move away from the door and continued to watch her with caution. "I'll bathe if that's what you want, but why don't we talk while I do so?"

She nodded once. "Fine. Undress."

He looked around the room, then at her. "In front of you?"

She was pleased that his eyes widened. Obviously, he was as unnerved by the situation as she was. Probably even more so since he didn't understand where he was and his life had already been threatened.

She paused at that thought. No matter what Isadora wanted, Selena wasn't going to allow him to be killed.

She managed a smile. "Do you have something to hide, Major?"

Now it was his mouth that quirked up with arrogance. He reached up to the collar of his shirt and slid each button free. "Absolutely not. The only one in this room who has secrets is you."

She pursed her lips. How dare he take that taunting tone when she had saved his life not half an hour before? She opened her mouth to retort when he freed his shirt from his trouser waist and pulled it over his head. Then all words, all coherent thoughts disappeared.

Gavin Fletcher had felt good beneath her hands when she touched him. He had looked good in his fitted clothing. But it was nothing compared to the way he looked naked. His shoulders were broad and his arms rippled with muscles. The only marring element was a long scar jutting down his left arm. His chest was magnificently muscled with a peppering of dark chest hair that tapered into a V and disappeared into the waistband of his trousers.

She shivered as she pictured rubbing her breasts against that chest. Having those muscular arms hold her. Those strong, skilled hands touch her in every aching place. It was a body made for pleasure.

Hers and hers alone.

"Oh," she whispered as she tried to make herself stop staring. She was giving him power by making her needs so obvious, yet she couldn't control herself.

"I take that as a compliment," he said softly, though his voice had taken a husky timbre that resonated through her blood stream and vibrated through every sensitive part of her body.

He came further into the room and sat down on one of the simple, soft armchairs beside a window. He never broke eye contact with her as he lifted his foot to rest on his knee and began to unlace his boots.

Selena found herself gliding across the floor toward him. She sank down on her knees at his feet and whispered, "Let me help you."

He watched as she glided her fingers up the soft leather boot and finished the work he'd started. When her fingertips brushed his bare calf beneath his trousers, he shut his eyes with a moan.

"I'm glad you weren't my valet in the field," he murmured. "I would have died from distraction."

She smiled as she worked each boot from his feet. She ran her fingers to his knee and sighed. "You said I was keeping secrets." His eyes came open to meet hers, and she nearly tumbled backward at the piercing blue fire that captured her stare. "I suppose I am. And I cannot promise you I won't continue to keep secrets. But I will tell you everything I can in order to keep you safe while you're here."

"Can you really do that?" He pushed off the chair and began to unbutton his pants. Finally, he shoved his trousers and drawers around his ankles and stepped free. He was gloriously naked, not a foot in front of her.

She suddenly couldn't find enough breath to speak, let alone coherent words to answer his question. She was too mesmerized by every line of his strong body. His upper body she'd already worshipped, but his legs were no less developed. He was lean and hard. And the hardest part of all was the cock that now thrust toward her.

He was much bigger than her late husband had been. She found herself wanting to touch.

To suck.

To take deep inside her sheath, ride him until she screamed his name.

On trembling knees, she shoved to her feet and motioned to the tub. "Why don't you get into your bath, Major?"

To her surprise, he stepped toward her instead of away. Their bodies brushed just a fraction, but the tiny touch sent off explosions of lust inside her. She shuddered uncontrollably.

"Gavin," he corrected softly. "I have a feeling it's far too late for formalities, Selena."

She swallowed hard as she motioned toward the tub a second time. "Yes."

His smile warmed her heart before he followed her order and climbed into the painted metal tub. When his body hit the hot, clean water, he hissed out a sound of pleasure that rocked her body. She wanted to force that same sound from his lips when she touched him, pleasured him. Settling back and resting his arms against the tub edge, he looked at her evenly.

"So tell me."

She shook her head, trying to clear her thoughts. She was reeling from the sensual assault he was unleashing on her with his body, his deep voice, his male scent. She was supposed to be seducing him, taking *his* power away through sex, not the other way around.

"About what?"

He arched an eyebrow. That was a foolish thing to say. It was obvious what he meant. He wanted to know about the temple. About her plans to keep him safe from Isadora and her minions.

Crossing over to the tub, she sank down on her knees on the cushioned bench next to it and reached over to a silver tray which held soaps and perfumed oils. She took a bar of fragrant soap and rolled it in her hand nervously.

"I read your diary."

She gasped as the soap slipped through her fingers to hit the water with a splash. Gavin turned his face away from the splatter.

"That isn't possible," she whispered. Her voice trembled, no matter how she tried to control it. "I destroyed it."

"One of the Kelsey's maids rescued it from the fire. Your stepchildren gave it to me so I could find you." Gavin reached into the water and retrieved the missing soap. With a soft smile, he handed the wet bar back to her. "And it worked because I'm here."

She sighed. "Damn that Maude. I knew I couldn't trust her." So he knew at least part of her story. He'd read her deepest desires and about her most depraved adventures. Yet he was still here. And need was in his eyes, not judgment or censure. With care, she began to soap her hands. "If you've read the journal, than you need no explanation."

He shook his head, but he was staring at her soapy hands. His pointed, heated stare brought a new flush of desire through her. Every nerve ending seemed more focused, sensitive. Even the brush of wet soap on her fingers made her pussy clench and her nipples tingle. How did he do that with just a look?

"Yes, I do need an explanation," he rasped out. "The diary wasn't complete."

The room was growing hotter. She rolled the soap over her hands again and again. The want that crackled between them made it impossible for Selena to keep her well-practiced guard up.

"What do you know?"

"I know you felt little sadness when Colonel Kelsey died. That you already knew Isadora, but after his death she began to introduce you to a life somehow related to Aphrodite. You liked the things she—"

He cut off with a moan as Selena finally put the soap on the edge of the tub and let her fingers dance across his damp chest. She let out her own sigh of pleasure as skin touched skin. The wet slide of the soap suds left no friction, and her hands glided easily along his impossibly hot body. She wove her nails through the dusting of wiry hair and sucked in a breath at the way the rough curls rasped and bunched against her soapy palms.

She dipped lower, gliding each hand against his nipples. They hardened beneath her touch, just as her own were doing. Did his nipples tingle with maddening pleasure as much as hers?

Her fingers brushed lower, lower, moving toward the one part of him she wanted to touch most. But she only teased her hand below the water's surface, trailing her fingers against the muscles of his abdomen instead of grasping his fine cock in hand. There would be time for that later, and the anticipation was too enjoyable to cut it off so soon.

"Go on, Major." Her voice was now just as husky as his had been earlier. "Finish your story."

He swallowed as he shifted in the tub. Through the soapy water, she could see his cock. It was hard, thrusting toward her with uncontrolled need. A need her body echoed with a growing ache, an increasing wetness.

"You liked what Isadora exposed you to," he continued. He reached out as he spoke and pressed a wet hand against her covered breast. A ragged cry burst unbidden from her lips at the touch as the water made her chiton transparent. Her nipple was clearly outlined as if she were nude. "I read your stories about watching her. About watching others when they made love. Your descriptions and your reactions. They..."

He trailed off, rubbing his thumb against her wet breast in a slow rhythm that drove Selena mad with want. Her breasts tingled and sent an answering ache through her body to the slick nub of her clit. She squirmed in the hopes she could ease some of the pleasurable frustration, but could find no relief.

"They what?" she managed to whisper.

"They made me want you." He locked gazes with her and she was lost in blue. "Your diary and your picture drove me to find you, and not just because of my sense of duty to your late husband and his family."

She drew back in shock. "So you came all the way to Cyprus—?"

"Because I wanted you." His hand moved to her other breast, massaging gently and sending a burst of pleasure through Selena's body. Wetness slid down her thighs, and the ache was unbearable.

She wasn't going to deny herself any longer.

Pushing off the side of the tub, she leaned in to kiss him. He took what she offered greedily, winding his wet fingers into her hair. Its strands came down around their faces in a wave, rolling onto his soapy chest and into the water.

He caught her shoulders and pulled her even closer until her upper body molded to his. The water slapped against her skin. With a growl of frustration, she pulled away just long enough to climb into the tub and straddle his lap.

He kissed her, drawing her in deeper and deeper even as he shoved her sopping chemise up around her hips so that the thrust of his cock rubbed against her thigh. That touch of hard steel against her sensitive skin rocked her until she thought she would explode from touch alone.

He pulled back to cup her face, and the intensity in his eyes was almost too much to bear. "Later, later I'll kiss you all over. Later, we'll act out all those fantasies you wrote in your journal. But for now… now… I just want to be inside of you."

He said it almost apologetically, but she didn't want him to be sorry. She didn't need platitudes or preludes. All she wanted was to feel the iron thrust of him in the folds of her body. She wanted to grind down over him and ride him. She wanted everything.

Now.

"Yes, please, I want that, too," she groaned as she shifted over him to allow him better access to her dripping slit.

She expected him to slide his cock inside her with little pretense. In fact, she hoped he would. But when his fingers slid into her wet heat instead, she arched with unexpected pleasure.

No man had ever touched her like this. So intimate, so gentle and yet starting a fire that nothing but his cock would put out. She writhed, riding his hand as he slipped another finger inside. She was so close to coming, so close to losing control.

"It's been so long," she wailed as her head rolled back. "So long."

He nodded as he brushed his stubbly cheek against her breast. The friction was fantastic, and she rode his fingers even harder, coming ever closer to the brink.

He seemed to sense her crisis, for he withdrew his hand. She protested with a loud moan that echoed in the chamber. "Don't go," she murmured as she leaned down to kiss him.

"I'm not going anywhere," he promised as he positioned her above him.

No sooner were the words out of his mouth than he thrust up. Her body stretched to accommodate him as he filled her completely, molding with her body in every way possible. With just that one thrust, her body quivered on the edge of an amazing climax. He met her eyes and rocked out a second thrust that took her over that edge into blissful oblivion. A cry echoed around them, and she realized through a haze of explosive pleasure that it was her own.

She had experienced release by touching herself, but had never achieved orgasm through a man's touch. The difference was amazing. Her body trembled, the pleasure peaking up and down in long, powerful waves until she thought she would collapse in exhaustion. All the time, Gavin kept thrusting into her, holding her steady by her slippery hips.

The rhythm he set was far too good to just let him do all the work. She rode him, meeting his thrusts with equal passion, kissing him as deeply as he was delving into her body. Her soul.

Riding him brought her back to the trembling spasms of release so quickly that it shocked her. Gavin's face showed the strain as he tried to keep his own passion at bay. He was going to climax, just as she was. She wanted them to do it together.

"Kiss my breasts," she whispered, shocked she'd order him to do such a thing. Titillated to hear her voice say such sensual words.

He complied by taking her nipple between his lips and laving it with a rough tongue. The subsequent pleasure arced to every part of her body. It sharpened her awareness until finally she gripped his shoulders and rode out another powerful release.

"Now, Gavin," she cried out. "Now!"

Seeming to understand her order, he clenched her hips in an almost painful grip and let out a roar of pleasure as he pumped hot into her body, filled her with his essence.

With a groan, she sank forward to rest her head on his shoulder. They were both wet with sweat and bathwater, hot with exertion and long repressed desires.

She had never been so satisfied in all her life. How could she experience so much pleasure over and over again? It certainly explained why Isadora was devoted to her worship of Aphrodite. The exploration of sensual appetites was far more enjoyable than Selena had imagined, even in her most erotic dreams.

Without moving from her comfortable spot sprawled across his broad chest, she murmured, "I'm so glad you found me."

And it was true.

Chapter Four

Gavin swiped a damp lock of hair away from Selena's face as she rested her cheek against his chest. He wasn't sure how long they had been tangled together in the water. Time seemed slow and suspended, held still by his lazy, satiated state.

She didn't seem to be in any greater hurry to move than he was. When he touched her, she merely turned her face a fraction so she could smile up at him, then sighed as she snuggled back against his body.

He thought about what she'd said just after she exploded with her final orgasm.

She was so glad he found her.

It made no sense, but he mirrored that statement in his heart. Even though he knew so little about her, even though she was no more than a heated fantasy until a few hours before, he could no longer imagine his life before he knew her touch.

"Selena?"

She barely lifted her head with a sleepy, "Hmm?"

He sighed. Back to reality. One that could get him killed if he didn't regain some focus. "You never told me what this place is."

Her mouth thinned into a frown as she pushed away from his chest and sat up in the bathtub. Lukewarm water sloshed around them both, clinging to her sopping chemise as she dug around for the soap beneath their bodies. As she had been before they had made love, she went back to washing him as if nothing out of the ordinary had happened. As if his world hadn't been knocked out of its safe orbit by her touch.

"Aphrodite is the Greek goddess of sensuality and sex. I'm sure you gleaned that information from my journal," she explained as her hands glided over his skin in slick circles and sent shockwaves of awareness careening through his body.

He nodded, surprised that his need raged up again. It was as if he were a green boy of eighteen rather than a jaded man of thirty. Selena noticed his desire as well, for her eyes grew wide when her hand brushed the thickening thrust of his erection. Still, she continued her story.

"In ancient times, people worshipped her. They were called the Cult of Aphrodite, and they allowed themselves a free exploration of lust. Sensuality." She swallowed hard. "Love."

"Is that what this place is, then?" he managed to ask. What was left of his rational mind told him getting the answers that could save his life was more important than bedding Selena a second time. Still, his rational mind was fading behind the throbbing desires of his cock.

"Yes." She looked around the small room, and her eyes became distant with memory. "I met Isadora right before my husband left for India. I was both shocked by and drawn to her open personality. She has an uncommon zeal for life and for pleasure. One I envied."

Gavin looked at her sharply, surprised by this unexpected glimpse into Selena's past. It was like the pieces of the puzzle that made up this woman were coming together. She had been unhappy, not that he blamed her. He had met her stepchildren. But her unhappiness had been much deeper than simple regrets over marital choice.

"As she grew to know me better, Isadora told me more and more about her activities. Not just the scandalous tales of her bedroom escapades, but also about her beliefs. And the history of Aphrodite. But it was only after my husband died that I learned her real plans."

"And what were her real plans?" he whispered.

"To restart the cult. She wanted to bring women like me into her world. Women who were sensual. Women who wanted..."

She hesitated with a blush that made his entire body clench with need. How could a woman be so innocent and so sensual at the same time? Shifting, he let his erection rub against her leg. It was a sweet torture that nearly unmanned him.

"What did you want, Selena?" he asked without breaking eye contact.

Her eyes drifted shut with a quiet moan. "More. I wanted more."

Desire jolted through him like electricity, making him feel more alive than he had in months. He reached for her, but she avoided his touch and scrambled to her feet. In a stumbling motion, she got out of the tub. Her shift slopped water on the stone floor, but she hardly seemed to notice as she paced away to look back over her shoulder at him.

"Gavin, these men and women are serious about their lifestyle. They have taken vows which go beyond simple pleasure."

"What kind of vows?" he asked as he tried to rein in his disappointment at her departure.

"Vows to protect the temple." Her expression tightened. "At any cost. If the soldiers in Greece realize we have started a pagan temple here, they'll come for us. They'll destroy the temples. As for the people..." She broke off with a shiver, as if her words reflected her private fears. "The men will probably be only lightly punished. Society tends to forgive what they expect from what they call a man's uncontrollable desires. But the women..." Her face paled. "Women are not expected to be driven by passion. When they are, they are punished. It will be no different here. They will be returned to places from which there is no escape."

Gavin's mind slipped to Selena's stepchildren, of their plans to institutionalize her for what they claimed was her own good. Except now that he had touched her, filled her, watched her face constrict with pleasure, he was sure hysteria didn't drive this woman. If that were true, how could she pull back when he touched her? Why would she be more driven to explain her actions than to make love to him again?

Protecting Selena wasn't what the Kelsey children truly wanted. Revenge for whatever wrong they believed she had done their father was more likely. And perhaps a chance to take her inheritance they had spoken of with such contempt.

He stood up, sloshing water over the edge of the tub as he reached for a towel on the table nearby. He wrapped it around his waist and crossed the room to be closer to her. Somehow he needed proximity, needed it as much as he needed to draw breath.

"I understand your fears," he said softly. "And I know you're desperate to protect your friends, but they have made it clear they'll kill me." He motioned his head toward the door. "Guards are just outside waiting for me to make the wrong move."

Her gaze dropped. "Yes, if they feel threatened by you, they will kill you. In their minds, it's the only way."

"Do you feel the same?"

"No, of course not!" Her gaze grew painfully distant for a second time as expressions flashed over her delicate features. "I was trapped once. I was dying inside. I would *never* be the cause of that to another person."

"Aren't I trapped now?" he asked softly. He reached out to run his finger down her cheekbone, dipped it beneath the curve of her chin. With gentle pressure, he tilted her face toward his. She shivered with the touch.

"I chose you." She looked into his eyes and raw need glittered in her stare. "Unless you do something to force their hand, these people will respect that choice and won't harm you."

He drew away in a flash of anger. He hated cages, even those that were infinitely pleasurable.

"And I am to do… what? Am I supposed to just resign myself to a life of serving your sexual needs? And when you've tired of me, am I to be passed to Isadora, as she asked?"

Selena's face froze into a mask of surprise and betrayal. "Isadora asked to have you?"

Gavin examined her closer. Was that jealousy? It was. And he liked it. Liked that her time on this island of freedom and passion hadn't taken away her natural desire to have one man and one man alone. That the man she wanted was him… at least for now.

"Yes. She told me to come to her when you finished with me," he admitted. Selena held his life in her hands. He couldn't be anything but honest with her, at least about this.

"I see," she said softly as she walked passed him back to the edge on the tub.

She slipped her hands beneath her soaking chiton's straps and shoved the entire contraption around her ankles. She snatched up a towel and began to blot droplets of moisture from her skin. The sight was so mesmerizing Gavin nearly didn't hear her when she spoke again.

"If you wish to stay here, wish to be with Isadora, I certainly won't stand in your way." She let out a soft sigh. "But if you would truly like to leave this island, return to England and your life there, I have a plan."

He murmured in agreement, but his attention remained focused on the soft towel. She brushed the fabric across her breasts and her nipples stood at full attention as she pushed the towel lower, lower. It brought him to mind of watching her pleasure herself. But now he knew what that body felt like, gripping him as she found her release.

"Gavin?" Her voice was husky.

"Yes?"

"Do you want to hear my plan?"

He struggled with an answer. Here he was facing questions about his life, his very survival, and yet all he could think about was the woman who stood staring at him. Her skin flushed as he drank in the sight of her gloriously naked body gleaming in the dying light of the afternoon sun.

"I do." He nodded as he swallowed past his dry throat. It was hard to breathe now, let alone speak. "But not right now. Come here."

Her eyes widened with understanding. His wants were clear, and she returned them. Her lids drooped as she slowly crossed the room in long, sure strides.

He didn't have to tell her what to do or what he desired. The moment she reached him, she wound her slender hands into his hair and kissed him. His knees nearly went out from under him with the force of his lust.

"The bed," she murmured against his lips.

He followed her order wordlessly, guiding her back across the room until he reached the bed. It was surrounded by a filmy canopy that he shoved back with growing impatience.

The coverlet was soft and pale, cool even though the room seemed impossibly hot. His bare knees brushed satin as he laid her back against the pillows. It was a bed meant for passion, and if he had his way, it would fulfill that purpose. He could only hope this time he would sweep her away with his lovemaking. In the tub he had been too needy, too quick and heated to act out the fantasies he'd composed in his head during the months of travel to Cyprus.

Now that he had slaked his desire, he was ready to do what he'd dreamed about. Ready to fulfill Selena's deepest desires. Ready to make her moan out his name.

"Lie back," he said softly as he settled his weight lightly against her. She was like heaven beneath him, soft and warm. She rose up to meet his body with a moan most of polite society would have called wanton.

It was like music to him.

"Gavin," she murmured, as she laced her fingers through his hair. "Oh, please."

He nodded. He knew what she wanted. She wanted his touch, his mouth, his body. She wanted to tremble beneath his thrusts, to cry out as she spasmed in delight and fulfillment.

He kissed her mouth for the briefest of moments. Just long enough to fill his senses with her flavor. Honeyed sweetness. He wondered if she tasted that way everywhere. There was nothing like a journey down her body to find out.

She gasped as he dragged his lips down the column of her throat, nipping her collarbone as he massaged his fingers into her hips. She arched in encouragement, sighing as his mouth closed over one taut nipple. Her breath came shorter as he suckled her. It was almost as if she would explode if he did so much as touch her.

The temptation was too much. Sliding his hand down, he urged her legs apart and brushed a thumb across her sex. She let out a wail that filled the room, then her cries grew louder when he repeated the action and at the same time, entered her with a finger. She bucked beneath him, quivering out a release that went on and on until she begged for mercy he refused to give. When she finally relaxed against the pillows, he withdrew his hand from her warm body with reluctance and returned to his odyssey of taste.

His lips moved over her belly. Pausing only to dip his tongue into her navel, he continued. Lower and lower, ever closer to her center, ever closer to heaven. She seemed to come out of her haze just as he pressed a kiss against her inner thigh.

"Gavin?" Her voice was tense, questioning.

In the entries of her diary, Selena had written about this act. She'd read about it in the erotic stories Isadora had shared, and even seen it while she watched Isadora play her sex games. The entries were filled with such curious longing that he doubted Selena's selfish husband had ever given her such pleasure. It thrilled him to know he would be the first man to taste her so intimately.

The first stroke of his tongue elicited a surprised gasp from her lips. He didn't pause to let her become acclimated to this new invasion, but tasted her again in a long sweep. This time she arched up, gripping at the sheets with both hands.

"Please," she wailed. "It's too much."

"There's never too much when it comes to pleasure," he whispered against her, then dragged his tongue across her wet slit another time.

Her legs drooped wider naturally, opening her to him like the petals of a flower. Within the folds he found the nub of her clit and concentrated his attention on it. He teased her with his fingers, stroking her with sure touches until the little bud swelled and darkened. Finally, he dipped his head and took it between his lips. When he sucked her gently, she exploded, writhing above him with a series of uncontrolled cries.

When she shuddered one final time, she propped herself up on her elbows to look down at him. Her eyes were wild, filled with desire and other emotions he dared not label.

"Come up here," she said softly. "I want to feel you inside me."

He nodded, his cock aching as he rose up on his knees. "Turn around.

She did as he'd asked, glancing back over her shoulder with wary interest.

"You described this in your journal," he said softly as he grasped her hips and rubbed his iron cock against her backside.

"Yes," she murmured. "I saw a picture in one of Isadora's books. Later, I saw it acted out. Both here and on the ship."

"Why did you want this?"

As he spoke, he positioned himself at her cleft, nudging back the wet, heated folds with the head of his erection.

She shivered and gripped the headboard with both hands. "It's so primal. Animal. Possessive. To drive into a woman from behind is to make her yours. Really yours, not like the romantic drivel in some books."

"Then you…" He drove hard inside her. "Are mine."

Her hands tightened on the headboard as she flexed around him. "Oh yes. I'm yours."

To accentuate that promise, she leaned forward and slammed herself back, setting a hard, rough pace for their sex that drove Gavin to the edge almost immediately. He closed his eyes as her body welcomed him in, massaging him to the brink with heat and wetness.

It took effort to exert control over his raging lust. He wasn't going to make this another quick coupling like in the bathtub where the sensations rose and fell in a flurry.

He slid his hands up her hips to cup her breasts. Rolling sensitive nipples between his fingers, he eased her up until she was upright on her knees. She could no longer move forward and back without separating their bodies. Instead, he ground inside her in slow, purposeful circles while one hand found its way back to her clit. He stroked her between his thumb and forefinger as her cries grew louder and more intense.

Leaning forward, he pressed a kiss against her damp neck. "Is it everything you hoped for? Fantasized about?"

She nodded with a moan. "You are more than any fantasy. You're better than all my dreams."

On the last syllable, her spine stiffened and her body clenched around him like a vice. She shattered and he joined her, filling her with his essence as he wondered if he could truly live up to the expectations of her dreams.

Especially when those dreams could keep him trapped on this island forever.

Chapter Five

Selena draped the thin chiton over her shoulder and adjusted her naked breast. When her thumb brushed her nipple, it swelled and hardened, made ultra sensitive by Gavin's touch. In fact, her whole body hummed with anticipation and a powerful desire that didn't seem to stay satiated for more than an hour at a time. She finally understood why Isadora was so driven to fulfill her baser needs.

"You're sure this is what I have to wear?"

She turned to watch Gavin struggle with his loincloth. He looked magnificent with his bare chest and long, naked legs. Like a god from an ancient fairytale, come to Earth to bring pleasure. And she was the one lucky enough to be the recipient of that gift. At least for a little while.

The only thing that marred the perfect image was the scar that ran down his arm. How had he gotten it? Despite their passionate joining, she didn't feel close enough to delve into something so private.

"That's the traditional garb for this ceremony," she said with an apologetic shrug.

He took a glance in the mirror. "I feel ridiculous. And if there's a breeze, this isn't going to keep me covered."

"Then I'll pray for strong winds." She laughed as she looked him up and down. Seeing him so exposed made her want to touch him. More than touch. She wanted to drop to her knees and take him into her mouth. It was only the time constraints that kept her from doing just that. With a shiver, she said, "I must say, I've never seen another man wear it better."

He smiled as he walked across the room and took her into his embrace. A feeling of warmth and safety surrounded her. She hadn't felt like that for so long she barely even remembered it.

The thought was so startling she had to force herself not to shrug away from him.

He seemed to sense her tension and looked down into her face with concern. "Selena, is anything wrong?"

She forced a smile. How could she explain that in the span of a few hours, she felt closer to him than she'd felt to anyone in her entire life? She barely knew him. And he had been sent to destroy her dreams and return her to a life of repression and torment.

"I'm just—" she stammered as she searched for a good explanation for her sudden shift in emotions. "I was just thinking about how dangerous your position here is."

Now it was his turn to stiffen as he released her and turned away. Yet when he looked back at her, it was with a wicked grin. "We were *distracted* before you could tell me about your grand plan to protect me. Would you care to share that with me now?"

She couldn't help but laugh at his teasing, even though she sensed the seriousness of his question. She held the key to his fate, and he knew as little about her as she knew about him.

"Of course," she began. But before she could finish, there was a loud rap at her door. "Yes?"

The two guards who had been standing watch for the past few hours entered the room. Both men sent menacing glares in Gavin's direction before they spoke to her in Greek.

"The ceremony is beginning. You and the prisoner have been ordered to come with us to the temple."

Selena frowned. "He's not a prisoner. He is my chosen mate, and you will treat him with respect." She folded her arms and met each of the men's eyes. "Is that clear?"

"Yes, Selena," one of the men answered, his voice dark and sullen like a petulant child. "Still, Isadora asks for your presence."

"Thank you." She turned to Gavin with a smile. "They've told me—"

"That it's time to go to the ceremony," he said softly. "I know."

She started. "You speak Greek?"

"Yes." He shrugged. "I was originally to be stationed in Greece, but ended up in India instead."

Blushing, she turned away. Earlier when she had spoken her words in Greek in the temple and he had replied, she believed it was the heat and power of the moment that had helped him understand what she meant. She'd never thought he spoke the ancient language. Somehow she felt exposed because she had defended him to the guards.

He reached out to take her arm as they followed the guards down the sandy path to the temple. "Thank you," he whispered.

Just the benign touch of his hand sent shivers up her spine. "You're welcome," she murmured as they reached the temple.

It was the same building where Gavin's 'trial' had been held earlier in the day. When they stepped inside to reveal the high pillared ceiling and deep pit, he stiffened.

"Don't worry," she whispered before she was forced to walk away and prepare for her part in the ritual. "It won't be like before, I promise you."

Before he could reply, the guards motioned him to move away to be with the other men of the group. There he would be prepared and given instructions on his part in the nightly ritual. She could only hope he would understand and comply with what he was to do.

A man like him would be used to being in control. He wouldn't like taking orders from his captors. The ritual might even seem like the perfect opportunity for escape, and if he tried that… well, she shuddered to think of the consequences. Her intervention wouldn't stop his execution this time.

"My, my," Isadora said as she approached Selena to ready her for her part in the night's events. "I would have captured you an officer long ago if I had known it would be like this."

"Like what?"

Selena glared at her friend. Knowing how Isadora had offered Gavin a place in her bed sparked a curious jealousy in Selena. One that had no place here. Freedom was the mantra of the Cult of Aphrodite. Possessiveness had no place.

But it didn't erase the fact that Selena didn't want her friend anywhere near the handsome Major. Not after what they had shared.

"You actually look satiated. In fact, I've never seen you so relaxed." Isadora folded her arms and gave Selena a feline smile. "Of course a man like that would be to any woman's liking. Is his body as magnificent as it appeared to be this afternoon?"

She gritted her teeth. "The Major is everything I wished him to be."

Isadora's eyebrow arched. "No details? Very well. Does your soldier know what to do tonight?"

"It is being explained to him at present."

"What about you? Do *you* understand?"

She frowned. "Of course. I've seen this ritual many times since my arrival. I have chosen Gavin, claimed him in my bed. Now it's his turn to choose me in a reflection of the rituals of old. If he doesn't want me, he may pick another. Then the ritual starts again."

A curious ache filled her at that thought. What if she hadn't pleased Gavin the way he had fulfilled her? What if he wanted to take Isadora's offer of a more experienced bedmate? After the horrors of war, a soldier could easily wish to sink into the pleasures of sex for a while. And then Selena would be alone again and Gavin…

Gavin would be in more danger than he comprehended.

All she could hope was that he would choose her. To save his own life and for the sake of her burgeoning desires.

The shiny, metal mask constricted his nose and reduced his peripheral vision. Gavin hated it. He hated the idea he could be attacked at any moment, especially in this volatile place ruled by sex and emotion.

More than that, he hated what the mask represented. He had been told in the old days of the temple, a woman would prostitute herself to a stranger, allowing any man to choose her in the name of Aphrodite. The mask he wore now made him that stranger. It gave him the right to choose his bedmate. He could take Selena, confirm he wished to be her pick until her induction was over.

Or he could walk into the crowd and take any other woman. Including Isadora Glasier. He had no doubt the red head could destroy him if she wished, but she'd made it clear she wanted him in her bed, too. After a few weeks with her, he was sure he could find a way to make it off the island.

"Get out into the pit, you son of a bitch soldier."

The guard pushed him none too gently out of the hallway. Gavin stumbled into nearly the same place where he'd stood during his 'trial' that afternoon.

Was it only that afternoon? It seemed like a lifetime ago.

He gathered his composure and slowly walked into the center of the pit.

"The stranger approaches." Isadora's voice echoed in the darkened room. She sat high above the small crowd in her throne. He couldn't see her in the darkness, but he heard the sneer in her voice.

This evening only a few torches lit the room, and they all surrounded the spot where Selena stood waiting. She looked so beautiful bathed in torchlight. The fire danced off her tanned skin, reflected in her eyes. Yet she seemed nervous, fearful.

Unlike him, her life wasn't threatened in this strange place of sex and violence. Was she concerned about his safety? Or did she fear he wouldn't choose her as she had chosen him? That he would take his chances with another woman.

In that instant, he knew he wouldn't betray her. Not after everything they had shared. What they had experienced together was more than any other woman could offer him. And he was willing to risk personal safety for even just a few more of those stolen moments in Selena's arms.

"Choose from all the women here," Isadora said softly. "You may have the one who has picked you, or you may take any another to your bed. Aphrodite teaches us freedom is the only way."

He looked up at Isadora, seated in her throne of marble, above all others in the temple. Though the firelight was dim, he now caught the gleam in her eyes. To her, this was all some twisted game. The island. Sex. Him. Even Selena was a toy to her. One he was sure she would destroy if it suited her purpose.

He broke their stare to turn his attention to Selena. She avoided making eye contact when he tried to capture her gaze. She shifted nervously. Even when he started across the pit toward her, her body remained tense and ramrod straight.

Stopping in front of her, he briefly thought of the instructions he'd been given. He was supposed to remove her chiton, bare her body to the entire group, then stake his claim right then and there with the members of the temple looking on. His claim was to be taken with the mask on, keeping him a 'stranger' as in the old ways.

Normally, he would have gone along with the twisted ritual, if only to make his captors think he had surrendered. But he didn't want to share the wonders they experienced together in front of the others in the temple. He wouldn't treat Selena like a common whore.

He slipped his fingers into the folds of her robe but didn't pull it away from her shoulders. The rough pads of his fingertips brushed her skin, teasing over her covered breast until both her nipples puckered. Her eyes drifted shut with a soft whimper he was sure only he heard. He dipped his hand lower, teasing her stomach and then casually cupping her sex. She was already dripping wet, hot as a fire and ready for him. She arched closer with a louder moan, and his cock throbbed in response.

Just as she dipped her head back, he withdrew his hand so he was only playing with the edging of her robe. "I choose you," he whispered for her hearing alone.

Her shoulders sagged with relief, and the tension bled away from her face. "Now you're to remove my clothing and stake your claim," she prompted. It was clear her reminder had as much to do with growing desire as with the dictates of the ritual.

He shook his head, though he wanted to do as she asked as much as he wanted to take his next breath. Instead, he raised his voice and said, "I came across an ocean to find you, Selena. I chose you the moment I saw your photograph. After finally having the chance to touch you, my choice is no different. I choose you. However, I also choose not to share you. Not now, and not until you have tired of me."

Reaching back, he yanked the mask free and tossed it across the marble floor. It clattered against the stone in front of the watching crowd in their ancient garb.

A murmur of surprise worked its way around the waiting group. Selena's face, which had softened during his initial declaration, paled. Her gaze shot up above in Isadora's direction. Gavin refused to do the same, even though he wondered how the other woman was taking his speech. He was flouting her rules without regard to the consequences. It could work or it could backfire with terrible results.

To his surprise, Isadora's husky laugh came out of the darkness above. "Your soldier is bold, Selena. I expect he is no different in your bed. If he will not claim you for the crowd to enjoy, then let the nightly festivities commence for the rest of us."

Gavin gave a long exhale in relief. His gamble had paid off. He caught Selena's hand and drew her up close to him. She pressed against him and gave him a small smile.

"You didn't want to share me?" she whispered.

He shook his head. "Never."

He swept her into his arms and turned toward the door. Unfortunately, he didn't get two steps toward the staircase leading out of the pit when the guards blocked the exit, spears raised in readiness.

Selena shook her head. "Once the ritual starts, no one is allowed to enter or exit."

"The ritual?" he asked.

She laughed. "You haven't noticed?" She pointed over his shoulder.

Gavin turned and nearly dropped Selena. He had been so wrapped up in her that he hadn't notice the crowd. The dozen or so women in the group, including Isadora, had lined themselves up on one side of the pit. On the other, the same number of men watched and waited in a group. Slowly, each woman removed her chiton and stepped away. The men did the same with their loincloths.

Isadora cupped her own breasts, strumming her nipples as she looked at the now naked crowd. "I want you." She pointed to one of the men. "And you." Another stepped forward at her order.

The remaining crowd watched as the two approached their leader. As Isadora deeply kissed one, the other dropped to his knees, spread her legs and began to lick her slit. Her head dipped back as the second man went to work on her breasts.

"The rest of you," she panted, "May choose."

Immediately, the crowd of men and women came together. Without ceremony, one man bent a woman over a marble bench and thrust into her with a rough, hard rhythm, while at the same moment she took another man's cock deep into her throat.

Two women chose each other, laying head to foot as they licked each other with enthusiastic moans. Men and women lay in piles, hands stroking over skin, cocks plunging into mouths and pussies. Moans and cries echoed around Gavin and Selena as the sharp scent of sex filled the warm air.

"*This* is a nightly ritual?"

Selena nodded. "I've watched this every night for weeks." Her voice grew husky. "Aphrodite teaches us to enjoy the passions of the flesh. Without guilt or shame."

Gavin looked down at her. Her eyes were slightly glazed as she watched the group stroke and lick each other to orgasm. "But you never participated?"

She shook her head. "I wasn't allowed into the larger group until I picked my first mate. So I only watched. And pleasured myself."

Gavin groaned at the image of Selena watching and giving herself pleasure in reaction to the shocking, decadent display. He had to have her, but he didn't want to take her as part of this festival of lust.

She gave him a wicked smile and darted her tongue out to swipe along his exposed collarbone. "If you want privacy while we wait, I suggest one of the alcoves that face the sea. They're somewhat separate, though we can still be seen if someone chooses to look."

She glided her hand between them and gently caught his already hard cock. She stroked him only once before he grabbed her hand and strode toward the alcoves in the back of the temple.

There were four in all. Stone entryways that lead to a small room.

Each had a low bench below an open window that faced the sea. In the distance, the sun was setting, sending a rainbow of colors to dance off the temple walls and set off the crowd in erotic shadow.

Gavin chose the alcove farthest from the temple's center in the hopes it would give them some privacy from the moaning, gasping crowd outside. He set her down, putting his back to the others to block any potential view they might have of her.

Selena looked at him with dark eyes that told a tale of desire he couldn't ignore. Her gaze held an appealing combination of innocence and want, the same duo that had driven him across the continent to find her.

"What you did tonight, it was dangerous. You shouldn't have thwarted Isadora's instructions."

"Perhaps you're right." He crooked his finger. "Come here."

She swallowed hard, then took a long step toward him and pressed flush against him. Her naked breasts dragged across his bare chest, sending a shockwave of desire to harden his cock painfully.

"Perhaps I *should* have taken this scrap of fabric from your body." He slipped his fingers into her robe, but this time he yanked, and the flimsy contraption fluttered around her feet. "Perhaps I should have spread you open for the world to see and suckled you all over."

Her breath caught as he dipped his head to catch one pebble-hard nipple between his lips. He sucked, and she arched beneath him with a little cry that was almost lost in the sounds of the sexual frenzy going on in the room behind them.

"Gavin," she moaned as her fingers slanted through his hair and pushed his head lower.

He followed her order and glided his tongue down over her belly. He dropped to his knees and breathed in the heady fragrance of her woman's scent. Her legs trembled as he pushed them apart and licked one long stroke across her heated sex.

"Yes," she hissed out low. "I wanted you to. I wanted to feel you so much, I didn't care who watched."

He slid his tongue across her again as an answer. When her hips thrust forward, he sank his fingertips into her skin to hold her steady. He wanted to torture her before he let her come. He wanted her to beg him, to plead for release.

Focusing his attention on her clit, he rolled his tongue over her and suckled her, taking her just to the edge of release, but never letting her have it. Finally, her hands clenched into his hair and pulled his head away until he was forced to look at her.

"Please," she murmured. Her flushed face was taut with the strain of want. Need. It gave him a rush of power to know he'd taken her so far with such little effort. "Please."

When she released his hair, he immediately obliged her. He buried one finger inside her clenching, hot sheath while he suckled her clit one last time. In a burst of wailing cries, she trembled around him, bucking wildly as her body found ultimate pleasure.

When she went limp and leaned against him, he slowly stood up. The length of her body rubbed against his as he came to his feet. With the cries of passion filling the room behind him, the feel of her nearly unmanned him. Holding her against his chest, he looked down into her eyes.

"I choose you, Selena," he whispered. "By doing so, I put my life in your hands."

She nodded once before she glided her breasts across his bare chest in a tortuously slow motion. "I know. Your trust is a great gift. I treasure it and your life. I swear I won't let you down."

His breath caught in his throat, cutting off any ability to form words or even coherent thoughts. His entire focus was on Selena, on the way she touched him, on the way her gaze came up to capture his. Her smile was gentle and then crooked with a wicked gleam as she began to slide her way down his body as he had done to her not moments before.

She pushed aside the loincloth and captured his cock in one hand. If he had thought himself hard before, his body now went twice as rigid, filling her hand with his heat. She gave a little laugh, then leaned forward to blow a puff of warm air across the head of his erection.

His knees trembled as a wash of ecstasy rushed through his every nerve. Even though he'd made love to her just hours before, when she touched him now it was like the first time. The need raged out of control, and he was ready to explode with just the right touch.

Except she didn't touch. She sucked. The very moment she ended her initial torture, she took his cock between her lips and sucked.

His delved his hands into her hair and cried out softly.

"Mmmm." She leaned back to see his face. "I've wanted to do that for hours."

Before he could answer, she drew him deep into her mouth, rolling her tongue around him until he had to brace himself on the wall behind her to keep from collapsing with pleasure.

Her rhythm was constant and as intense as her stare. Forward and back, deeply in and then almost all the way out. His balls tightened, his limbs grew heavy as he fought to keep from exploding with pleasure.

"It's too much," he groaned.

She darted out her pink tongue to trace just the head of his erection. "You told me there wasn't such a thing."

He grasped her by her upper arms and yanked her to her feet for a long, hot kiss.

She murmured something against his mouth, but he didn't hear it. Instead, he pressed her naked back against the stone wall, stepped between her legs and drove into her in one smooth thrust. She wrapped her arms around his shoulders and clung to him like he was a lifeline. Her nails dug into his back as he took her fast and hard. Riding every thrust with an equal measure of passion, she reached the brink with lightening speed and thrashed around him, rocking out her pleasure. He had no choice but to join her, pumping hot before he thrust one last time and claimed her as he hadn't in the room behind them.

The cool sea breeze stirred across Selena's arms. Her eyes fluttered open, and she watched the curtains billow from her place on her bed. Her place in Gavin's warm arms. The sun was just beginning to rise in the distance, bathing the world in shades of warm purple and pink.

Hazy memories returned to her. Gavin taking her again and again in the alcove at the temple. Carrying her back to her quarters once the ritual was over, to continue there long into the hot night.

With a sigh, she snuggled closer to the man beside her and laced her fingers through his. His hands were so big, so strong. As a soldier, he had been capable of great destruction with those hands. He'd caused death. But here, sheltered from the world, he only brought pleasure. His hands were gentle tools of love and life.

"You're awake," he murmured against her hair. His breath warmed her neck, and the warmth spread through her body, filling her with a sense of peace unlike any she'd ever known.

"I am. Were you watching the sunrise?" she asked as she glanced over her shoulder at him.

"No, I was watching you." He kissed her neck. "You're more beautiful than a hundred sunrises."

She laughed as she looked back out across the sea. "The sunrises on our island might prove you wrong." They lay in companionable silence for a moment before she said, "Why were you really awake, Gavin? Because I know I wore you out last night."

"You did." He chuckled, but it ended on a sigh. "But I can't help but be restless here. I'm a prisoner no matter how pretty a cage you put me in."

She stroked her fingers back and forth against the back of his hand. "Yes, I am sorry for that."

"I don't blame you." He shifted slightly so he could wrap one arm around her hip. "But you must understand, I'm not used to having so little control over my own destiny. To being under constant threat without having tools to fight back. And I'm not accustomed to depending on someone else. Not for my life or my freedom."

Regrets chilled her. "It must be all the worse for you since we never talked about my plan to help you, as I promised you we would."

He shrugged. "I told you at the ceremony last night that I put my trust in you. I assume eventually we'll stop making love long enough for you to tell me how you plan to help me escape this place with my life and manhood intact."

She rolled on her back to look up into his face. No man had ever made her the focus of such attention before. His blue eyes pierced all the way into her soul. She feared that intensity yet was also enthralled by it. Gavin seemed not only to see her every thought and feeling, but want to explore them to their deepest level.

He wanted her secrets, her desires… he wanted everything.

She traced his lips with her tongue. "I want to tell you my plan. I want to put your mind at ease before you put my body at ease."

The eyes that had pinned her with such intensity now softened with gratitude. "Very well."

Continuing to examine every curve of his face, she said, "In one week's time, the members of Isadora's temple will begin a grand celebration. With the change in season from summer to fall, they'll hold a festival of decadence, a sensual feast to honor Aphrodite. The entire cult will be distracted. It will be the perfect time for a prisoner to make an escape. Especially with my help."

He was quiet for a time as he traced her cheekbone with the back of his hand. Finally, he whispered, "And what will I do for the next week?"

She reached up to cup the back of his head and drew his mouth down until it was a mere breath from her own. "Be careful. Be safe.

Be mine."

His head jerked back as he locked eyes with her. Slowly, he threaded his fingers through her tangled hair. "I may have chosen you last night, but I am *yours*, Selena. I have been since the moment I saw your picture."

His mouth descended, and this time he didn't hesitate to kiss her. She was stunned by his declaration, even as she was swept away by the pressure of his lips. He belonged to her? The idea made her heart soar, even while her stomach dropped. She had vowed never to let a man into her heart, never be subjected to the demands of one person ever again. Yet Gavin was a temptation she couldn't seem to resist.

One she didn't *want* to resist.

She stroked her tongue against his, and the tug of desire grew from the tips of her breasts all the way to her clit. With just a touch, he made her want. With a kiss, he melted her. And when he entered her, she forgot all about the rest of the world, and her focus shifted to him and only him.

His fingers slid down the apex of her body with lazy intent, playing over her nipples, then settling between her legs to nudge at her clit. A moan escaped her lips as that familiar spike of pleasure wracked her body.

Pulling back, he looked down into her eyes. His hand stilled, trapping her between explosive pleasure and the pain of withdrawal. "Will you come with me when I leave?"

She struggled to respond, stunned by his question. How could she answer that?

Even though he had only been on the island for a short time, the idea of his departure stung. How could she lose him when they just found each other? Pain mushroomed in her heart at the thought of never seeing him again.

But she was still unsure about his motivation. Here on the island he was willing to let her do as she pleased, but if she went with him, would his sense of duty return?

Here she was an erotic distraction, but away from this place rules and regulations might make him regret his choice of a sensual woman. Then what?

Would he take her back to London and her stepchildren? Doom her to the fate they had planned for her?

She wanted to trust him, but trust was something she gave reluctantly. She had paid a heavy price for it in the past. She didn't want to pay again.

His fingers twitched across her slit, erasing her thoughts and fears in a wave of pleasure. Before his mouth came down on hers, Selena caught a glimpse of Gavin's expression.

Disappointment hardened his features.

"Gavin—" She wanted to explain even if she didn't know the words to say.

He didn't allow her any further opportunity. His tongue delved between her lips as he rolled on top of her. His fingers continued to move inside of her with slick insistence until she arched up with a cry of release.

No sooner had she found completion then he pushed her legs open and pressed the head of his cock against her. Bracing one hand on either side of her head, he looked down at her. She rose up to kiss him, but he held back, keeping out of her reach as he slowly entered her just an inch.

She groaned, clenching him. This was punishment. He had given her pleasure, but now he was going to torture her to show her how unhappy he was that she couldn't answer his question.

"Gavin, I—"

"Shhh," he admonished and glided another inch inside. Her body stretched deliciously to accommodate his hard cock.

Her eyes fluttered shut with a soft sigh.

"Look at me," he said.

When she did as he ordered, he moved even further into her. With their eyes locked, the sensations became even more intense, more focused. Her world started to revolve around pleasure. If he didn't move all the way inside, she was sure she would disintegrate, cease to be entirely.

"Please." It was a whimper, but she didn't care.

He answered by sliding forward, but he was still a few inches from home. With a little cry, she lifted up and forced him even more. He gave a laugh, gripped her hips and ground a circle that made her explode. Her orgasm was so powerful, she forgot to breathe, forgot everything except that he was inside her and she was his, even if she hadn't told him.

She was his. And as he set a rhythm that would give her at least one more powerful release, she knew there would be a part of her that would be his for the rest of her life, whether she left the island with him or not.

Chapter Six

Gavin caught up with Selena in a few long steps and grabbed her hand. She smiled up at him as they walked down the beach in the warm late summer air. Sand slid between his toes, and the breeze stirred his hair across his forehead. For a moment he forgot his troubles completely. Cyprus was perfect.

Or it would have been if he hadn't been a prisoner.

"You look very serious for a man who continues to claim he looks silly in that loincloth," Selena teased gently before she lifted his hand to her lips and brushed a kiss across the knuckles. "Would you care to share the thoughts that trouble your mind?"

He frowned. The thoughts that kept him awake at night were so complicated, he could hardly understand them himself, let alone explain them to her.

He wanted to escape the dangerous prison of Aphrodite's temple, but when he thought of leaving the island without Selena, it pained him. In the days he had known her, she had become the most important person in his life. In the past, that kind of attachment to a woman would have driven him away. Now, the only thing that caused him real fear was the thought of losing her.

Still, each time he asked if she would escape with him when he left, she changed the subject. Or distracted him with pursuits more pleasurable than talking. That silent rejection stung him again and again.

She pursed her lips when he didn't answer. "Very well. You don't have to tell me if you don't want to. I understand why you wouldn't trust me. After all, I'm the reason you're trapped here."

Her eyes grew distant as she looked out over the crystal blue waters before them. As always, her stare held a bevy of turbulent emotions, and he doubted all of them were related to him.

"It isn't that I don't trust you, Selena," he reassured her as he came to a stop and gently turned her to face him. "I'm trusting you with my life."

Her face softened. "Yes. That's true."

"In fact, I wonder how much *you* trust me." He brushed a long strand of dark hair away from her stormy eyes. "After all, I know very little about you."

She gasped in disbelief. "Very little? Thanks to the prying of a lady's maid and my wicked stepchildren, you know my every desire, my every fantasy! You know each private thought I shared with my diary. I'm not complaining since you're adept at making those fantasies come true, but to say you don't know me…"

"Yes, I know what your body craves." He nodded. "But what about your soul?"

She stiffened and tried to pull away. "I don't know what you mean."

"Why did you turn to Isadora Glasier? What made you run from the Kelsey family with only a small portion of the fortune you'd inherited? Why didn't you tell your parents where you were going? Hell, I'd settle for why you married a bastard like David Kelsey in the first place."

With every question, Selena's face tightened and her body shifted until she held him at a full arm's length. He had no doubt if he hadn't been holding her hands, she would have run away down the beach to avoid his intrusive words. Over the time they'd spent together, he had learned Selena kept her secrets close to her heart. He doubted there was any person in the world who really knew her completely.

But damn if he didn't want to be that person who held the keys to her soul. Who knew her every wish, and even her every heartache.

"Why would you want to know those silly things?" She laughed, but it was a false, high-pitched sound. "After all, you and I could be doing things that are much more enjoyable."

To accentuate that statement, she stepped into his arms and tilted her face up for a kiss. Her lips were just inches from his, pink from the wind and copious kissing in the past few days. Her eyes glittered, reflecting the desire that grew in his own body.

But beneath her desire lay fear. And her fear kept him from taking what she offered, no matter how much he longed to plunge into her body.

Soon, but not yet.

"I want to talk to you, Selena," he whispered. "Let me know you a little. I swear I won't betray you as you've been betrayed before."

Her lip began to quiver, but this time she didn't pull away. She continued to stare into his eyes with an appraising expression that seemed to delve into his very soul. He was being tested, yet all he could do was wait and hope he would pass.

Finally, she relaxed in his arms with a long sigh. "I married David Kelsey because the time had come for me to marry. It is as simple and yet as complicated as that. I hadn't found another man who interested me, and my parents were becoming desperate to tie me to someone who could take care of me… and them, too, I suppose. David fit that description. He was wealthy, he was of a class slightly higher than theirs, and he had impeccable manners." Her face darkened. "Of course, during the negotiations for my hand, he never mentioned how he wished to deny me my right to have children, or that he often preferred the back of his hand to a meeting of the minds during a disagreement."

Gavin's fists bunched at his sides. "Kelsey struck you?"

It was amazing he could get the words out considering the tremendous rage that coursed through him.

She gave one matter-of-fact nod. "Not often, but occasionally. He was far too stupid to win an argument in a fair fashion. I learned very quickly to say what he wanted to hear and do whatever I desired the moment he wasn't looking. His children despised me, of course."

Gavin flexed his hands as he counted to ten in his head. For months, his part in David Kelsey's death had crushed down on him with growing weight, but now he wished he'd been the one to cut him down on the battlefield. To avenge the pain Kelsey had caused Selena, both to her body and her heart.

"Yes." He relaxed his clenched jaw. "That was very clear to me when they called me to their home. The girls, especially, have a strong dislike for you."

"I am the same age as David's eldest daughter." Selena paced down the beach. "I almost couldn't blame them. They hated that I'd come into their home, and their father expected them to treat me like a stepmother instead of an equal. But I would have taken a month trapped in a tiny room with Adelaide and Amelia over a few moments alone with Arthur."

Gavin cocked an eyebrow. "Why? Those two women are vipers. I would think the meek and mild Arthur Kelsey would be easy in comparison."

"Meek and mild?" She laughed, but the sound was bitter. "What would you say if I told you Arthur is the answer to all your other questions?"

He shrugged. "I don't understand what you mean."

She shook her head as she sank down on a log that had washed up on shore. Her shoulders trembled almost imperceptivity. "You asked me why I turned to Isadora, why I ran from London with so little money, and why I didn't inform my parents of my plans. I am telling you the answer to all those questions is Arthur Kelsey."

Gavin sat down next to Selena with a thunk. He had a sick feeling he knew where this story was going to go, especially when he remembered the possessive way Arthur had handled Selena's picture in London; the way the young man had said her name. Gavin saw the lingering disgust and fear in Selena's eyes when she spoke of her stepson.

"Tell me." He caught her trembling hand for what he hoped was a reassuring squeeze. "I want to know."

In the time he had known Selena, he had seen her expose herself to a crowd of strangers, make love to him where they could easily be caught, and do things that would have made prostitutes color. She had flushed with pleasure, her cheeks had turned pink from a compliment, but he had never seen her blush with embarrassment.

Until now.

"I have never told anyone these things before," she murmured, more to herself than to him. "Not even Isadora knows the whole truth. But you..." Her gaze flitted to him and softened. "I can tell you."

He nodded as a swell of pride and awe filled him. Her trust was the greatest gift she could give. "You can."

She took a deep, shaky breath. "It started a few weeks after I married David. Arthur caught me alone in my private library one afternoon. I was writing a letter home and didn't notice him standing there until he cleared his throat." She shook her head with the memory. "When I looked up, it was clear he was aroused by the sight of me. He didn't even attempt to conceal it or leave the room as a gentleman normally would in that awkward situation. In fact, he seemed proud of his desire."

Her eyes fluttered shut, and she struggled with her breathing for a moment before she continued. "I was shocked by the openly lustful way he stared. Since he wouldn't leave, I tried to escape without causing a scene. But-but he wouldn't let me. Arthur closed the door, blocked my escape. And then he—" She shivered though the breeze was warm. "He touched me."

Gavin shut his eyes. He could actually feel her fear, taste her pain as he pictured how shocked and horrified she must have been. It took every ounce of control for him not to slam his fist into the wood they sat on. "How did he touch you?"

"He pushed me up against the wall, groped my breast and made a lame attempt at kissing me." She shook her head in disgust. "I made enough noise that a servant interrupted and Arthur was forced to leave."

"What did you do?"

She shrugged. "I told my husband, of course. David was furious, not at Arthur, but at me. He accused me of doing something to cause his son to behave in such a fashion. Still, Arthur didn't approach me again, though at least three parlor maids quit without asking for references. I'm sure he took advantage of them. I settled into an uneasy peace in my own home. Until David went away to India."

"Without your husband in the house, Arthur felt free to pursue his interest in you," Gavin said softly as he watched the pain from those memories flicker across her face. He longed to take the hurt away, to erase the memories.

She nodded slowly. "Yes. He wouldn't leave me be. He trapped me in rooms; he followed me into closets. He groped me, tried to kiss me. A few times he went farther, but I was always able to fight him off. That was why I attempted to find interests outside of the house. Interests that would take me away in the evening when Arthur was home, before he went to the clubs or whoring with women who had no means to fight back. Before I could lock my door and keep him out."

"And that was what Isadora offered." He understood so much more now.

She sighed. "I met Isadora at a society meeting, but our association soon grew much closer. She told me she sensed I was a kindred spirit the moment she saw me. Isadora offered me friendship, and eventually a glimpse at freedom."

"I'm surprised you wanted anything to do with sensual experiences with a man like Arthur Kelsey molesting you at every turn."

She shook her head and finally looked at him without the glitter of shame in her eyes. "Just because Arthur wished to abuse me didn't mean I wasn't the same person. I had always been sensual, had appetites a woman wasn't supposed to feel. Before my marriage, I found guilty pleasure in touching myself in secret. I even looked forward to the lovemaking I expected to find in my husband's bed. But when my parents matched me with David, they took those dreams… and many others… away." Her voice was bitter. "Isadora told me I could get the promise of sexual fulfillment back. She allowed me to feel those desires without shame, without fear."

"And since you felt shame and fear at home, what she offered must have been even more attractive," he said softly.

Selena's face contracted in surprise. "Yes. I did crave the things Aphrodite represented. Freedom, power and a lack of fear. Isadora encouraged me, but never forced me to do anything. For the first time in a long time, I was in control, and I needed that feeling once we got the news of David's death."

She shivered again, and this time Gavin gave into his desire to comfort her. He was pleased when she allowed him to drape an arm around her shoulders. She even leaned against his chest with a little sigh.

"Arthur grew more persistent when his father died?" he prodded gently.

She nodded, and her hair tickled his bare chest to send a tingle of fresh desire through his body.

"Without the threat of his father's punishment hanging over his head, he grew bolder. One day he managed to catch me alone again. He told me I was now free to be his. That he expected me to give in finally to his demands. The bastard thought I had been resisting only because of my marriage vows. He tried to reassure me by telling me he would marry me if I came to his bed."

Gavin twisted his face in disgust. "But in the eyes of the law, you were his mother."

"Exactly right. I reminded him of that fact, but it didn't help. He flew into a terrible rage. He told me even if we couldn't be together legally, he would have me in his bed. He even wanted me to bear his children. And if I didn't…" She swallowed hard. "If I refused him, he revealed that he was aware of who I was consorting with and what I was doing when I went out at night. He said he would use his sisters' hatred of me and their desire to control their father's fortune to have me committed for hysteria. He said if I wouldn't be his whore, I would have no sexual pleasure with another man for as long as I lived."

Selena's face twisted, but she managed to continue. "I fled to Isadora that night, and she revealed her desire to return to Cyprus and introduce me to the temple she had begun here. To give me my sexual freedom and let me experience the pleasures I'd missed with my husband. I departed with her within the week."

Gavin drew in a deep breath, overwhelmed now that he had heard her troubling story from beginning to end. His emotions roiled inside him. Rage, pain, hatred… ugly emotions that made him want to return to London and give Arthur Kelsey his just rewards. But there was something more important, and it had nothing to do with vengeance.

"Selena." He tilted her face toward his. Despite her fragile appearance, she had such inner strength.

"It's an ugly story, isn't it?" She sighed. "I wouldn't blame you if you wanted to leave my bed."

How could she think he would blame *her* for all she had been through?

"You are the strongest woman I know. I admire you all the more for the strength and poise with which you handled your difficult circumstances, both with David and with Arthur Kelsey. Most women would have let their husband's cruelty and their stepson's sexual predation destroy their souls. But you not only kept your head, but found a way to escape." He dipped his chin for a gentle kiss. "If anything, I want you all the more."

She stared at him, stunned joy on her face. Then she pulled him down for a deeper, more passionate kiss. Her tongue speared between his lips, tangling with his in the mind-melting way only Selena seemed capable of. She filled his senses with her taste, her scent and the feel of her in his arms. She filled him with her, and he never wanted to be without her again.

"Selena," he whispered, his voice hoarse as she nibbled her way along the column of his throat. "What if someone sees us?"

She stood up and unhooked the clip that bound her chiton around her smooth shoulders. The gown fell around her feet with a swish, revealing every curve of her sensuous body in the warm sunlight.

She stepped forward with a swing of her hips that had Gavin's cock at full attention with painful speed. "The rest of the group is having luncheon on the hill behind the temple, and the bluff gives us protection." The tip of her tongue moistened her bottom lip. "I need you, Gavin. I don't want to wait. Please."

He pushed his loincloth aside to reveal his throbbing erection and opened his arms. With a smile, she straddled his lap, and her wet, warm pussy slid effortlessly over his cock. His eyes fluttered shut and for that moment he forgot about his anger, his feelings of being trapped, and simply enjoyed the gift she gave him. The gift of her body, and the gift of her past.

He knew all her dirty, humiliating secrets, but Gavin hadn't run away from her. In fact, as she straddled him, rubbing over his iron heat in slow sweeps, he seemed closer to her than ever.

With his head tilted back and stunning eyes shut, she drank in his every expression as she slowly eased herself down over his cock. She loved the way his mouth twitched as he struggled to suppress a groan of pleasure. The way his lips parted as he expelled one long, hot breath that stirred over her skin and had her nerves firing all at once.

Finally she took him all the way to the hilt and took a moment to enjoy the sensation of his body filling hers, stretching her, pressing her in all the right ways. They had been made to fit together, and she found herself wishing the moment could last for eternity.

Gavin's eyes fluttered open and he met her gaze with a warmth and an intensity, different than before. He tangled his fingers through hers, then pressed their intertwined hands against her hips. Slowly, he began to move inside her, using her hips as leverage to glide in and out, round and round, merciless as she reached a fever-pitch of need and pleasure. He never let her break away from his gaze, and he never let up, even when she cried out, even when she tried to break her hands away from his so she could guide the pace of their sex.

Finally, he mouthed one word, gave her the permission she yearned for. "Now."

The order was all her aching body needed. She came in a powerful explosion of pleasure. Her wails were lost within his mouth as he rose up to kiss her. He continued his slow torture of thrusts that ground his pelvis against the swollen, aching nub of her clitoris.

Her release went on and on until finally he matched her, stiffening on a last thrust. He filled her with his heat and the proof of her ultimate power over him.

As her throbbing heart slowly returned to normal, she examined his face. The angles and curves were relaxed, now that he had surrendered. Having such power over him wasn't as enjoyable as it should have been.

No, the emotion that lifted her heart and made her soul sing when she was with him went much deeper than mere sexual control and lust.

She was in love with him. With a man who had come to take away what she'd fought so hard to obtain. The man who would leave her side in just a few short days.

Of course, Gavin had asked her to accompany him, but could she do that? Could she leave this place where she had finally found acceptance and freedom? Depart with a man who might still follow his duty instead of his heart and return her to her hideous family.

She dismissed that thought. He wouldn't do that. Not after all they had shared, in the communion of both body and mind. But she didn't know if her love would be enough. The strains of society would still exist if she returned to England with him. Over time the tenderness between them would fade. The lust would lessen.

She couldn't bear losing him physically, but losing him emotionally would break her heart all the more. If Gavin eventually regretted bringing her home… tears stung her eyes with just the thought.

"Selena?" he murmured as he cupped the back of her neck and placed soft, melting kisses along her collarbone. "Did I hurt you?"

She shook her head even as her body reacted to his touch. "No, Gavin. You could never hurt me."

As he stirred inside her, and she braced herself for a second barrage of sensual warfare, she added silently, "I'll never let you."

Chapter Seven

Selena was distracted. Gavin wasn't fooled for a moment by her false smiles. And though their lovemaking had been as passionate as ever, she distanced herself from him whenever they weren't tangled in her bed.

Like now, when she insisted they come to the common area to eat with Isadora and the other followers of Aphrodite. Her need to be in a public place had more to do with hiding from him than it did with seeing her friends or keeping up some act for Isadora's benefit.

The heat of the other woman's stare burned into him, and he shifted slightly under it. Isadora Glasier made it no secret she wanted him, whether he was currently with her best friend or not. Her brazen desire upset Selena, as well. Her jaw had been set ever since they joined her friend, and she kept stealing glances from Gavin to Isadora.

Gavin could never be attracted to Isadora. She had already threatened his life and taken his freedom. He suspected she was far more dangerous than Selena wanted to admit. Control was clearly something the redhead wanted above all else, and not just in her bed.

"Selena, why don't you give me a moment with your Major?" Isadora asked with laughter thick in her voice. "You can go speak with Benedict and Reggie. Now that you are able to fully participate in the rituals of the temple, both have expressed an interest in you for the next cycle of the moon. I want you to determine if either of them strikes your fancy."

Selena was drinking when her friend began to speak and started to choke on her wine. When she was able to draw a breath again, she looked at Isadora in disbelief.

"You want me to be with Benedict or Reggie after this week?" she asked softly. Her gaze darted over to Gavin for a brief moment.

He clenched his teeth as he waited for Isadora's answer. The people on the island traded partners like most people traded gardening secrets, but he hadn't considered the prospect that Selena would turn her affections to another man. The idea of her sharing her lush body with another man had him seething, though he did his best to hide his emotions. They were far too dangerous to reveal in front of Isadora.

"Selena, you know better." Isadora clucked her tongue condescendingly. "This island is about choice. You may be with any man or woman you like. But the new moon will arrive just after the upcoming festival, and the cycle of passion will begin again. It's the perfect time for *all* of us to choose a new..." She trailed off and looked Gavin up and down. "Mate."

Selena's breath came short. "I see."

"Run along now. If you don't like either one of them, you don't have to choose them."

She waved Selena off like she was a child. With a frown, she did as she'd been told, leaving Gavin alone with Isadora. He was suddenly put to mind of the moments he'd spent in the Kelsey home before he departed for Cyprus. There he had been surrounded by snakes masquerading as ladies. When he looked at Isadora, he saw a dangerous python.

She slithered a bit closer and gave him what he assumed was meant to be a come-hither smile. "I certainly intend to choose a new mate once the festival is over."

He nodded slightly. "Since you make the rules in this place, I assume you make them to your own taste. Which means you like having a new partner in your bed each month. I'm surprised you haven't worked your way through your followers already."

Isadora looked at him evenly. "You don't like me. That's fine, Major. In fact, a good dose of hatred can make the passion all the higher. Because you see, I intend to pick you. You will be my mate for a month."

She leaned closer and trailed a painted fingernail across his lip. Just the right flick of her wrist would cut him. He had a feeling that for Isadora, the threat was as important as her touch. She was sending him a message.

"You told Selena that Aphrodite's Temple was all about choice." He stepped back from her and searched the small crowd until he found Selena.

He watched as she talked with the two men, as Isadora had instructed. They both ogled her mercilessly, leaving no doubt either one would take her gladly. Unfortunately, Gavin couldn't see her face. He had no idea if she liked their attentions or not.

"I'm sure Selena has explained some of the teachings of Aphrodite to you," Isadora replied as she took a sip of wine. "Or perhaps you've been too *busy* for study."

He turned his attention back to her with a glare. "She told me Aphrodite used her sensuality as a tool for power. That she believed in freedom in love, as well as equality when it came to the bedroom. A woman could choose who she bedded with as much right as a man. That's what you purport to teach here."

She nodded with an impressed smile. "It's good to know you've been listening."

"But just now you told me you would have me in your bed. That sounded like an order rather than a request. Don't I have the right to turn you down?"

Isadora's face twisted with anger. He had a suspicion none of her followers had ever dared refuse her advances.

Slowly, her rage faded to bored amusement. "Are you actually saying you wouldn't like to sample this body? That you wouldn't want to wash away the horrors of war and hardship with a month of pleasure between my legs?"

"A year with you wouldn't be enough time to wash away the horrors of a sprained ankle. You are cold, Isadora Glasier."

In an instant her earlier rage flashed back, more powerful than ever. She drew in a sharp, angry breath. "Is that right?"

"Yes. What you couldn't do for me in a year, Selena did in a moment. Why would I give her up?"

He snapped the question out and the moment he said it, he was struck by its truth. He didn't want to give up the healing balm of Selena's touch or the passionate release he found in her body. He didn't want to give up the emotions slowly binding them. He wanted her to come with him when he left the island, and not just for her own protection.

Most of all, he didn't want to lose her.

"You fool." Isadora laughed, and the sound chilled Gavin to his very bones. "You've fallen in love with her."

He refused to answer even though her accusation rushed through him like lightening. Love? It was something he had never sought. Something that had never touched him with another woman. But she was right. When he looked at Selena, the emotions that overwhelmed him went much further than desire. And much deeper than passion.

He loved her.

"Selena will *never* love you," she hissed as she moved in closer. "She told me long ago she will never let another man grow close enough to harm her. And she will always see you as the man her family hired to return her to hell."

"I would never harm her."

"Wouldn't you?" Isadora wound her fingers through his hair and pulled his face to hers. She thrust her tongue between his lips and kissed him hard. He yanked away to wipe his mouth on the back of his hand in disgust. "Try and convince her of that."

He heard the little gasp behind him. Without seeing her face, he was sure Selena had witnessed Isadora's false kiss, and it had hurt her. He rose to his feet and spun around. Selena's jaw was set in a rigid line and her normally full lips were a thin frown. By the time he looked into her eyes, Selena had hardened herself to him and to the woman she was foolish enough to call her friend.

"I think you're right, Isadora," she said softly, without even a waver to her voice. "Benedict and Reggie are both fine specimens. Either one would make a good choice for the next moon's cycle. I will have to review all my options fully before I choose."

Gavin wanted to strangle Isadora for forcing this ridiculous misunderstanding. If she thought she would get her way by pushing Selena aside, she was wrong. Even if she were the last woman on earth, he would want nothing to do with her cold touch.

"At any rate, I think I've had my fill for today. I'm going to return to my quarters to have a bath and change." She nodded dismissively in Gavin's direction but wouldn't meet his gaze. "I've no need for you at present, Major. Please feel free to stay as you seem to be having a fine time."

She turned on her heel and started toward the little huts in the distance. Gavin glared at Isadora over his shoulder before he strode after her.

"I always get what I want, Major." Isadora's laugh echoed behind him, taunting him. "Always."

"Not this time," he muttered as he hastened to catch up with Selena's long, angry stride. "For once, I plan to get what I want."

Selena sensed Gavin behind her, his presence growing ever closer even as she rushed to escape him and the pain he had caused her. She had just begun to let the walls around her heart down. She had trusted him enough to tell him her history with her husband and stepson. He had seemed to understand that, had pretended to feel her hurt.

But then he kissed Isadora.

The teachings of Aphrodite said freedom in lust was a virtue, but she couldn't help a pang of hatred toward the woman who had been her savior and friend. It was coupled with a stab of jealousy that stung her heart like salt in a wound. She didn't want Gavin to kiss anyone but her. She didn't want him to touch any woman but her. Not ever again.

Why had she fallen in love with him? It only complicated an already untenable situation.

"Stop running," he called out. "Please."

She froze and took an all-too-brief second to calm herself. When she turned, she hoped she wore a mask of disinterest.

"Oh, I didn't realize you were following me," she lied as she folded her arms in a protective shield around her heart. "You don't need to chase me. I told you I don't require your presence."

"Am I now a slave who can be so easily dismissed?" he asked as he strode up the path with wide, even steps. It was the gait of a man who was coming to claim what was his. Could it be that he was coming for her?

"You are whatever you want to be." She yawned. "I'm sure if you want to play slave and master games, Isadora will be happy to oblige. I'm not interested."

"You didn't like it when she kissed me," he said softly, and his eyes glittered with what looked like triumph.

"Don't be ridiculous." What was meant to come out as a strong denial was more like a squeak of derision. "That's what this place is all about. You can kiss whomever you like."

He reached out to wrap strong hands around her upper arms. With one yank, he pulled her flush against him, sliding one muscular thigh between her own and cradling her back until there wasn't even a breath between them. Then he lowered his mouth and claimed her lips. There was no mistaking the possessiveness of his touch. She became his the moment their breath mingled, the second their skin touched.

And she loved it. She loved feeling safe. Protected.

Even loved.

She started at that thought. Could this man love her? Had duty and honor and desire been eclipsed by some deeper, more tender feeling? One that could keep them together for a lifetime, no matter what they faced.

She pulled back, dizzy from emotion and lust. "What?…Why—"

"You said I could kiss whomever I wanted. I only want to kiss you." He searched her face, looking into her eyes, into her soul, seeing the deepest parts of her with only one glance.

"But…"

He covered her lips with two fingers. "I didn't come here to find freedom, Selena. I didn't come to bask in the sun or the heat of lust. I came here for you."

She stiffened at what his words forced her to remember. "To take me back to London."

"No." He smiled, and his mouth curved with tenderness. "To make you mine. From the moment I saw your picture, you were all I wanted. Duty to the Kelsey family became secondary, and now it no longer exists. My only duty is to make you happy. To make you feel safe. To wash away your torment and sorrow, as you have washed away my pains from the past with your touch, your kiss."

She touched his face as tears pricked her eyes. His confession was the sweetest thing she'd ever known. "You've already done that, Gavin. More than you'll ever know. I came looking for an escape from the repression and persecution in my life in London, looking for freedom here on the island. I searched for it in the teachings of a goddess. But I didn't find it until I touched you. I found my freedom with you. My salvation."

"Then come with me when I leave. It isn't safe for either of us here. Please."

She shook her head sadly. "What you think you desire now may not be what you want in a month or a year. I will *never* be a woman whom society accepts. I will always be too sensual, and I cannot bear to hide that part of myself as I once did. When we return to the 'real' world, you may regret taking me with you. It would break my heart if you grew to resent me over time."

His lips parted. "Do you think that would matter to me? I want *you* Selena. All aspects of you. The sensual. The innocent. The kind and compassionate woman. The lustful vixen. I don't give a damn what anyone else says about it."

He accentuated that vow with a hard, passionate kiss that set her world spinning. She clung to the hope he gave her with his statement.

She broke away. "Look into my eyes and tell me that is true."

He cupped her cheeks and locked gazes with her. "I will *never* regret taking you with me. Ever. Nothing will ever change the bond between us. I swear that to you on my life."

She stared at him and saw… truth. Her heart soared, and her eyes filled with tears. After arriving in Cyprus, she had thought of leaving a few times, but the idea of wandering the world alone had been terrifying. Now, knowing wherever she journeyed, Gavin would be at her side, was wonderful.

She no longer hesitated. "Yes. I will go with you."

His mouth came down on hers again, and she felt his joyful smile as he kissed her. Then his hands threaded into her hair and dragged down the loose binds that held it back from her face. Her hair fell in a perfumed cascade around them, shielding them from the sun and onlookers as it twined around them.

"Come back to my quarters with me," she said softly, pressing kisses along Gavin's sculpted jaw line. "I want to show you what you mean to me."

Later she would say it. Later she would tell him how much she loved him. But for now, she would follow Aphrodite's teachings and express her love physically. Not to gain power, as the goddess had. No, she would give her physical love to gain a future with this man. One where emotion and passion stretched outside the bedroom.

"Yes."

He pushed her back along the path until they were pressed flush against her hut's door. With a hot kiss, he turned the knob and they stumbled inside. Before the door was even closed, she ripped the loincloth from his hips, revealing his proudly jutting cock.

"Were you frightened the first day I came into your room?" he asked as he pulled the clips from her chiton and threw them across the room where they clattered against the ceramic floor.

"No." She pushed the chiton down around her ankles so she could step naked into his waiting arms. She hissed out in pleasure when her hot skin pressed against his. "When I saw you in my mirror, I thought you must be my fantasy come true. It gave me the most powerful orgasm of my life… until you actually touched me."

Though she was telling him intimate things most women of her class would shy away from, she didn't even blush. He had always accepted her sensual side without reproach. He was her safe place. She could tell him anything without fear of recrimination or loss of his affection.

"I want to touch you," he murmured as he guided her back toward the soft bed where they had pleased each other so often the past week.

"Yes, I want that, too. I want that more than anything."

Her breath came in short pants as he lowered her on her bed. It was like the first time making love to him, a moment filled with excitement and trepidation and pleasure. His hand came up to glide over her collarbone, cup her breast. She arched under the touch with a long sigh. This was what she wanted for the rest of her life.

His mouth came down to suckle her nipple, and all other thought was lost in a wash of sensation. Pleasure throbbed from where he sucked, pulling through her body all the way to the wet heat of her center.

"I want to prove to you that I will never regret choosing you," Gavin murmured between laps against her tingling nipples.

She smiled even as she arched up. "H-how?" she managed to murmur.

He pulled back slowly, looking down at her with such powerful feeling in his stare that tears of joy and wonder burned at her throat and eyes.

"I want you to see how beautiful you are when you make love to me. How there is no shame in your sensuality."

She stuggled up to lean on her elbows. "See it?"

Stepping away from the bed, he went to her full length mirror, the one she had been looking in when he first entered her life, and dragged the heavy metal frame across the floor to set it at the foot of the bed.

"Watch me make love to you." His eyes darkened as he crawled back up the bed to lie beside her.

She drew in a sharp breath as their eyes met.

"Watch how beautiful our joining is."

He motioned to the mirror at the bottom of the bed. She followed his movement and sucked in a harsh breath at the reflection in the mirror. Their bodies close together, his large and masculine and muscled, hers paler, smaller, softer. Yet as he wrapped his arms around her, they merged into one body, beautiful and erotic. Made for each other.

She watched, fascinated as his large, dark hand slipped down her stomach and between her legs to toy with her. He rolled his hands over her clit until she thought she would weep with pleasure, then abandoning the nub to move his fingers inside. One, then two, she watched as he stretched her, prepared her for the cock that rubbed against her thigh as she waited, breathless.

"Sit up," he murmured.

She obeyed, and he scooted around to sit behind her. She understood what he wanted to do. Moving into a crouched position she spread herself open and lowered her wet slit around his cock. From that position, she could see every thrust in the mirror, as could he. She was able to watch him move in and out of her, watch her own fingers play across her clit as she rode him closer and closer to heaven.

Which she did. With breath coming in ever-shorter bursts, she moved up and down, circling and thrusting over him, following the urgings of her aching body. Every movement brought her closer to completion, and seeing the look of bliss on his face in the mirror only urged her on. Still, she tried to hold back. Tried to prolong the release as long as she could to prolong his pleasure.

It was a battle she lost the moment he leaned forward, sank his teeth gently into her shoulder and reached around to strum a thumb over her clit.

She exploded, rocking back and forth with a cry of pleasure she couldn't have held back for all the gold in the world. She was amazed to see her expression of release and the tears of joy that finally trickled down her cheeks. The release went on and on, dancing on the edge of pleasure and pain until finally her body sagged, totally sated, against Gavin's sweaty chest. He came inside her with a groan as she quivered one last time around him, milking him dry.

"Amazing," she gasped when she could draw enough breath to speak. She stole another glance at the mirror and reveled in the sight of their intertwined bodies. Then she cast her eyes toward him. Their gazes met and she smiled. "*You* are amazing."

"Only when we're together," he whispered in the gathering darkness of her room.

"Then we'll be amazing together, forever," she said softly. "As soon as we get away from the temple."

"Tomorrow."

Chapter Eight

"I was able to retrieve your clothing from Isadora's private rooms," Selena said as she slipped back into her quarters where Gavin was preparing for their departure. "But if you are seen wearing your London garb, it will rouse suspicion, so you'll have to wait to change until we're safely away from the compound."

Gavin nodded and tried a joke to ease her tension. "Do *you* have anything else to wear?" He gestured to the chiton that left one breast exposed. "As much as the sailors on the ship will appreciate this stunning outfit, I'm not sure my arm can take too many fights to keep you all to myself.

She laughed, but there was no humor in the sound. Leaving here made her just as anxious as it did him. Perhaps even more since she had no idea what her future held. Only that she would be with him.

The knowledge that she was putting her life entirely in his hands was awe-inspiring. He couldn't let her down. Not now. Not ever.

"Isadora burned most of my clothing in a goddess ritual when we arrived on the island, but I managed to hide one regular gown from her minions." She looked around the hut that had been her lonely home. "I suppose I always knew I would leave this place. I never fit the mold Isadora created in her image."

In a few steps, Gavin gathered Selena into his arms. Her pulse pounded against his chest as she clung to him. He smoothed a hand over her hair and attempted to comfort her with the warmth and strength of his embrace. When she pulled back, it was with a shaky smile.

"I'm sorry I'm being so silly."

"No, you're not," he reassured her with a squeeze before he let her go. "Your life before you came to this island was horrible. Isadora and the people here were the first ones to give you a taste of the freedom you so craved. Now you're afraid to let that go for another life of uncertainty."

Dropping her gaze to the floor, she nodded. He cupped her chin and turned her face toward his with a gentle nudge.

"Selena, your life with me will be nothing like what you had with the Kelseys or your own family. I promise you that."

Her lower lip trembled, but she straightened her shoulders with a brave nod. "Of course, I trust you. You've put your faith in me to get you away from this place. I've put my faith in you for what happens after our escape."

He smiled. Her trust overwhelmed him and roused every protective instinct he'd ever experienced. And awoke a deeper love for her than he'd imagined was possible.

"There's no time to be afraid. I've always made decisions and never looked back. I won't look back from this one, either." She touched his face briefly, but stepped away. "I have a small part in tonight's ritual. Isadora cannot know I'll be gone long before I do my duty. I must go meet with her as planned weeks ago to keep her doubts to a minimum."

"Of course. You go and I'll complete the final arrangements. Is there anything you received here you wish to take with you when we leave? We can't take much, but I'll try to pack anything that's very important to you."

She turned in a slow circle, looking from wall to wall, trinket to trinket. A soft and loving expression crossed her face. "The only thing of value I found here was you. I want nothing more than that."

With that, she hurried out the door toward her meeting with Isadora. When the door shut behind her, Gavin sighed.

"You have me, my love. You have me forever."

Isadora's quarters were dark and sultry. The windows had been blackened so even when the sun was blazing, her bedroom had to be lit by the multitude of candles that surrounded the huge bed in the center of the room. Selena shivered when she entered, dreading this final encounter with Isadora.

"You're late."

Isadora's voice came from the darkest corner of the room, and Selena jumped before she turned to face her former friend. "I'm sorry. As you said yesterday, my choice of mates has been keeping me occupied. I lost track of the time."

Isadora strolled into the dim light with a cold smile, one that didn't quite reach her beautiful, dark eyes. "I'm glad you have enjoyed the Major. It's too bad you'll be giving him up soon."

Selena's heart leapt at the mere thought of losing Gavin, but she managed to maintain her composure. "I don't know, Isadora. I've been enjoying him so much I believe I might keep him. I was cheated by choosing him so late in the month. I think a full cycle of passion is required before I turn him loose for another to have."

Isadora didn't answer, but walked over to a large leather chair beside her bed. She sat down and crossed her legs, staring at Selena with an appraising glare.

"Indeed? You mean you would like to keep him even though you have your choice of any man in the Temple?"

Selena quivered under the coldness of her friend's voice. She'd never known Isadora to sound so threatening, yet her words were innocuous. Voices of warning sounded in her head, which she tried to push aside in an effort to remain calm.

"Or perhaps I'll change my mind and take another man or two. As you said, I have many choices," she stammered with a shrug.

Why did this situation suddenly feel so much like a trap?

Isadora surged to her feet and drew her hand back. Before Selena could dodge, her friend slapped her with enough force that Selena's head whipped around. Her cheek stung like fire as she gripped the back of the closest chair with one hand and cradled her face with the other.

"Why—"

"You ungrateful little wretch!" Isadora paced to the ornate fireplace across the room. "How could you betray me? Betray Aphrodite this way? After I freed you from the prison you lived in? After I taught you about passion?"

"I don't know what you mean!" Selena protested even though everything was becoming perfectly clear. Isadora knew. Somehow she knew.

Her friend's eyes narrowed. "You dare to lie to me? I have ears everywhere, my little fool. You're planning to run away tonight. To smuggle Gavin Fletcher from the group and leave with him. Back to London, no doubt. Back to the society you hated not so long ago. Has his cock been so good that you cannot see what he wants to steal from you? Or are you just so frigid that any cock will turn your little brains to mush?"

Selena forced away her shock. Enough of this. She would not tolerate this abuse from Isadora. From anyone. "What I feel for Gavin has nothing to do with his skills in my bed. My decision to leave with him has everything to do with emotion. Real and pure emotion. Something you have always shied away from, Isadora. Even with your friends."

"Emotion?" Isadora laughed, but it was an ugly, empty sound. "Emotion is weakness. I learned that in my marriage very quickly. Sex is power, and power is everything. I tried to teach you that. I tried to show you the glory of Aphrodite."

"No, this place isn't about Aphrodite," Selena whispered as the truth became clear. "It's about *you*. You aren't teaching the people here to worship the goddess. You're teaching them to worship you. They aren't free. They're your slaves. And I won't be your slave anymore."

"You're ridiculous." Isadora's lip trembled even as she denied what Selena said. "Aphrodite is the center of our group. She is sex, sensuality, power—"

"Freedom." Selena finished emphatically. "If you read the legends about her, what she valued above all else was freedom. Freedom in love, whether that meant choosing ten partners to play with at once, or one to love for all time. I choose Gavin. And he chooses me."

Isadora let out a scream of rage as she slammed her hand down against her mantelpiece. Sensual trinkets, sex toys and velvet ropes scattered in all directions. She drew in a few long breaths and turned to face Selena. Isadora appeared strangely serene, considering her angry outburst.

"Freedom is one virtue I cannot give you now. You betrayed me. I can't trust you won't reveal all you know to forces who would destroy everything I've built." She smiled. "And your friend, the Major, must die. Then you can continue worshipping here as you did before, with a guard by your side at all times, of course. It's for the best."

Selena gasped in shock, but before she could protest, Isadora walked away. She went to the door where a guard stood ready for her orders.

"Bring Major Fletcher to me immediately. And prepare the altar. We're going to have a sacrifice tonight to start the festival."

Selena lurched forward in horror as she realized this time Isadora would grant Gavin no reprieve. "No!"

Gavin pulled against the guards, despite the throbbing pain in his injured arm. The two men had taken great pleasure in cruelly twisting his injured arm when they had bound him. If he was being hauled away like a prisoner again, it could only mean one thing. Selena's plan for escape had been discovered.

He didn't care so much about what these people did to him. He had endured pain and could endure it again. But what about Selena? Isadora would be mad with rage when she realized Selena had betrayed her. What had they done to her? His heart raced as a thousand sexual and physical tortures filled his mind.

No, he had to remain calm, clear headed. He couldn't let his fear for Selena overcome him. Control was his only remaining defense.

At one of the huts, the guards stopped and knocked.

Isadora's cold voice answered. "Come in."

It was as he feared. Isadora was behind this. The men pushed the door open and forced him inside. It took a moment for his eyes to adjust from the fading afternoon sunlight to the darkened sensuality of Isadora's chamber.

"Unbind his hands," she said commanded. Isadora was sprawled across the bed in the center of the room, her naked body gleaming white against the darkness of the room. "And leave us."

The guards looked long and hard at her splayed legs and her exposed glistening sex, then one asked, "Are you sure, m'lady? He fought us the entire time."

"I'm sure. I only hope you didn't overly tire him," she murmured in a voice filled with sensual promise.

The guards untied his hands and shoved him inside, then they shut and locked the door behind him. He stumbled to keep from falling and winced when he caught himself on the closest chair. Pain shot up his arm.

"Hurt, Major?" she asked with a wicked smile. "Do you need any aid?"

"No." He straightened. He refused to show this woman any weakness, physical or otherwise. "I don't want anything you have to offer. Where is Selena?"

Her smile widened. "You'll know in due time. Meanwhile, why don't you sit with me on my bed? It's the most comfortable spot in the room."

He watched her slender hand slide back and forth across what looked to be Oriental silk sheets. Expensive, as were all the items in her chamber. Where had she found the money to finance this venture?

Selena had mentioned Isadora's husband had been a soldier stationed in Greece. He couldn't have had much money. A widow's pension definitely didn't stretch this far.

"If I sit, will you tell me about Selena?" he asked as he folded his arms across his chest. Surreptitiously, he rubbed his injury. Slowly, the pain faded as his muscles relaxed.

She lazily stretched one arm towards him, arching her back and thrusting out her breasts. "I'll do or be anything you want if you come to my bed."

He did not want to play Isadora's game, but did as he'd been asked, believing it would be the quickest way to discover what had happened to Selena. Once he had taken a place by her side, she draped her arms around his shoulders and placed a kiss on his collarbone.

"Mmm, delicious. No wonder she wants to run away with you."

He controlled his reaction to her words. Isadora might not know all the details of their plan. There was no need to give her any information she didn't have already.

"What are you talking about? Who wants to run away with me?"

She laughed and began to rub her bare breasts against his back. If it had been Selena doing that same thing, he would have already been putty in her hands. Instead, he was only put more on guard.

"You are a silly boy. I have spies everywhere. You were overheard yesterday when you and Selena declared your undying devotion to each other on the pathway. You really ought to be more careful about where you speak, but I imagine you were—" She reached around to cup his cock through the thin fabric of his loincloth. "Swept away by passion.

Resisting the urge to jerk away from her touch, he asked. "If you thought we were going to escape yesterday, why didn't you take us then?"

"I needed time to prepare. As I told you when you first arrived here, I cannot let you leave this island alive. You know too much. If you told the wrong people, my entire society, everything I've built, would be destroyed."

She ran another series of kisses from one shoulder blade to the other. They seemed cold in comparison to the burning heat of Selena's touch, certainly they didn't inspire his lust or any other emotion other than disgust.

"So you've brought me here to kill me?" he asked quietly. Desperation blossomed in his chest, but not for himself. He had fought in a war, seen death and caused it. He could hold his own if it came to a fight, even with a compromised arm. But Selena… she had never experienced those things. He ached to see her, to know she hadn't yet been harmed. If she was unhurt, they still had a chance.

"One of the two of you must die," Isadora's voice grew low and husky. "Either Selena for her insolence or you for your knowledge. I will offer you a trade."

He paused. "Trade?"

"Lay me back on this bed and show me what you did to Selena to make her melt at your feet," she whispered before she licked his neck. "Fuck me until I beg for mercy. If you do that, I'll let you live, and Selena will be the one to suffer for this outrage."

He looked over his shoulder at her. Isadora's eyes were glazed with a combination of passion and anger. Both were equally dangerous.

"Where is Selena?" he growled. "Tell me before I consider any offer you make."

Isadora's face twisted with indignation. "I have offered you my body, and you ask me about Selena?"

"Why did you really bring her to this island?" He shifted away from her touch. He could hardly bear her cold hands on his skin. "Was it really to free her as you've convinced her, or was there some more sinister motive? Perhaps that large inheritance which was the source of her stepchildren's hatred? Was that money she took with her part of what helped to fund this temple and the decadence you enjoy here?"

Isadora's smile returned. "You're a very intelligent man, Major Fletcher. Perhaps too intelligent for your own good. Part of why I chose Selena Kelsey as a disciple was because she would bring her funds with her, as was the reason I chose all the women here. Of course, the little fool only took a small portion of her inheritance when we left London. But it was enough to fund my project another half a year." She leaned forward until her sultry red mouth was only inches from his. "Now that I've answered your question, Major, what say we discuss the terms of my deal? I would like to tell you exactly what you'll do to me in this bed tonight.

"If you please me, as I know you will, I'll keep to keep you alive for a few more weeks while you do my every sexual bidding. Perhaps we can make another arrangement during that time."

He rose to his feet with a shake of his head. "No. I won't touch you. I am in love with Selena, and I wouldn't betray her by dallying with a woman she once thought was her friend. Or any other woman, for that matter."

Isadora's face contorted in disbelief. "You're saying you won't make love to me, even to save your own life?"

"I wouldn't make love to you for any reason."

She scrambled off the bed and darted over to the darkest corner of the room. She pulled a candle from a sconce on the wall, and when the light flared, he saw a chair covered with a thick sheet. Isadora tore the sheet aside to reveal Selena. She was bound and had a gag in her mouth, but tears streamed down her face as she locked eyes with Gavin.

"And what about to save hers? If you don't make love to me, I will choose *her* for the sacrifice I make for your sins. What do you say about my offer now?"

Selena made a muffled no, and her eyes grew wide as she shook her head back and forth. Gavin stared at her helplessly. She had been tied cruelly; her hands were beginning to turn purple from the tightness of the velvet ties binding her wrists. Her hair was bound in the knot for her gag, pulling at the roots painfully. Still, all she focused on was him, telling him without words that she would rather die than watch him pleasure Isadora.

"She called you friend!" he burst out with horror. "How can you treat her this way?"

Isadora shrugged as she glanced at Selena. "She betrayed me. If I wish to remain in control of this group, I have no choice but to dole out swift punishment. I grow tired of these arguments. Choose, Major. Now."

He dropped his gaze to avoid witnessing Selena's pain at his words and answered, "Yes. If you set Selena free, let her leave Cyprus, I will stay here as your sex slave. I'll pleasure you in every way imaginable." He was careful to conceal any expression of emotion so Isadora wouldn't see his utter disgust.

Isadora's crow of triumph couldn't drown out Selena's muffled scream of torment. He couldn't stand that Selena had to witness his betrayal with Isadora. He could only hope she would understand that he had no choice. He had to agree to keep Selena safe from harm.

"I have a vast imagination," Isadora said as she sashayed closer. "First, I want you to take that wicked tongue of yours and lick me all over. I want you to make me writhe. And I want her—" She motioned over her shoulder toward Selena. "To watch."

"Come here," Gavin murmured as he pushed back his disgust. Isadora obeyed. She wrapped her arms around his shoulders and hooked one long leg around his thigh. The heat of her throbbed against his cock, but it did not stir him. Selena quietly sobbed in the corner.

With a growl, he crushed his mouth down on Isadora's. After a moment, he trailed his fingers up to stroke her silky hair, then stroked a line down her neck. When she finally relaxed into his embrace, he pressed his thumbs down into a special pressure point as hard as he could.

Isadora stiffened beneath his hand, then went limp in his arms. With little fanfare, he dropped her unconscious form into a heap on the floor and rushed to Selena's side. Her eyes were wide as he ripped her bindings loose and rubbed her hands to get the circulation back into them.

She pulled one hand free to yank the gag down from her mouth and winced when a few strands of long, tangled hair ripped free from her scalp.

"Is she—is she dead?" she whispered.

He shook his head. "No. It's a trick of hand-to-hand combat. She'll be unconscious for a while, enough time for us to escape if we can get past the guards."

He drew her into his arms and held her tenderly. "I was so afraid she had harmed you.

"I thought I would have to watch you make love to her. I don't believe I could have borne that."

He cupped her neck and eased his face closer to hers. "Hear me, Selena. I am in love with you. I want no one else but you."

A little squeal of pleasure made him smile. "I love you, Gavin. I love you with all my heart."

She leaned up to kiss him, pouring the passion of her heart into the touch. Unlike when Isadora had embraced him, Selena's kiss inspired love and passion that had him aching all over.

"I wish I could lay you back on that bed and show you how much I love you, make you scream with pleasure," he said softly. His words had her shivering, and a surge of triumph worked through his bloodstream. "But we have no time now. Later, once we escape the compound and get to a boat leaving Cyprus, I'll have the first captain I see marry us. I will make love to you all the way to our next destination. As my wife."

Selena froze. "You want me to be your wife?"

"Yes. I never want to be apart from you. If we're married, we can return to England any time we like. Your stepchildren will have no power over another man's wife."

She wrapped her arms around his neck and hugged him so tightly he almost couldn't breathe. "Yes, yes, yes. I will marry you, Gavin."

Outside, voices sounded, drawing near, breaking up their tender moment like ice water thrown on a fire.

She released him and immediately began to untie her ankle binds. "If we don't hurry, there won't be a wedding, but a funeral."

Her bravery, her inner strength was amazing. "We need a plan to get past the guards. He surveyed the room. The hut is small; there are no back doors. And Isadora appears to have blocked all the windows even if we could use one for our escape."

She looked up at him with a smile so devious and sensual, it nearly unmanned him. "I think we ought to use the same tactic that took Isadora to her knees." She unbound her chiton to reveal her perfect breasts, her shapely hips, the dusting of feathery hair between her thighs. His body lurched in reaction. "I'll offer the guards a little candy, and you give them their just reward."

Gavin looked from the unconscious Isadora to the woman he would make his wife with a smile. "Help me move her to the bed and get those ties from the chair."

Selena took a deep breath to calm her jangled nerves, then opened the door and leaned against the frame. She could only hope she looked seductive and not terrified.

"Hello, gentlemen," she said in a low, breathy voice she'd heard Isadora use from time to time with her lovers.

She'd captured their attention with her nudity, for the guards lowered their weapons and stared at her breasts, then lower. She fought not to squirm as she thrust her breasts out further for their leering eyes.

"Isadora has decided Gavin and I aren't enough to satisfy her urges. She was hoping you two might join us." With a wink, she motioned behind her toward the bed where Isadora was currently bound, legs spread seductively. In the darkened room, the guards would not be able to see that Isadora was unconscious. Or that the bed was prepared with restraints to bind the guards along with Isadora, once they had been dealt with.

"Isadora wants us to join you in her bed?" her target asked as his weapon hit the dirt with a clatter.

"Absolutely. Please, won't you come in?"

The two guards looked at each other, then scrambled for the door.

With a wince of disgust, Selena wrapped her arms around the man she'd chosen and let him kiss her as the second man headed for the bed. When she heard the sounds of a struggle behind her, she knew Gavin had struck and rubbed her breasts against her own guard to keep his attention away from the commotion behind them. He tasted like tobacco and onions as he pushed his fat tongue between her lips. As his hands roamed around to cup her bare backside, she slammed her knee up into his groin, rendering him helpless as he rolled on the ground in apparent agony.

She pivoted to face the second man, but Gavin had already taken care of him, as he was lying on the ground in a crumbled heap. He glared down at the man who had kissed her then grabbed a handful of his shirt and dragged him upright. Gavin drew his hand back and struck him a powerful blow. The man's eyes rolled back and he went limp. Gavin caught him beneath the armpits and dragged his motionless body across the floor toward the bed.

"Very well done, my love," she said.

He shrugged as he tied the man roughly. "I would have preferred killing him after the way he was touching you, but I held back."

She laughed as she helped him move the second guard. Once both men had been securely tied and gagged, Selena let out a sigh of relief and stepped into Gavin's arms. She clung to him.

"The first part of our escape is over," he said, stroking his hands over her hair in a soothing motion. "You did marvelously well."

Selena pulled back with a shaky smile. "I'm just glad to be done with it. Now we just have to gather our things and run."

He nodded. "In just a few more moments, we'll be free."

She shimmied into her shift and grabbed his hand. As they crept along the pathway, her heart throbbed. Even though music played and torch lights glowed in the temple on the hill in the distance, she and Gavin were far from safe.

"They've started the ceremony," she whispered, as they slipped inside her hut. Their bags were within reach, and he snatched the satchels up. She flung one over her shoulder.

"How long before they'll come searching for Isadora?" he asked as he took her hand a second time and led her away from the temple toward the harbor city of Pafos where they could board a ship.

She shrugged. "It's hard to say. Often Isadora arrives at the ceremonies late. She generally indulges in pleasures of the flesh before. She told me it primes her for the erotic stimulus to come."

At the time, Isadora's explanation had seemed titillating, but now, knowing how badly she'd been betrayed and used, it made Selena sick. How could she have considered Isadora a friend? How had she been so blind and stupid?

"Then we may have just enough time."

Gavin led her away, further and further from the temple, from the compound she had called home since her escape from London. From the life she thought she wanted. Now it turned out it was all a sham.

Just as the temple lights disappeared over a bluff, Selena stopped.

"Wait. Let me look one last time." She rose up on her tiptoes and looked down at the area. With a sigh, she shook her head.

"Are you sorry?" Gavin asked quietly.

"Sorry to be leaving?" She shook her head. "No. I thought I belonged here. I thought I was a sensual spirit, a slave of Aphrodite caught in a tangled web of a society that didn't understand my needs. That was what Isadora told me."

She looked at the distant compound again. "But really, she thought I was a silly prude who had money she wanted for herself. I wasn't a disciple of Aphrodite. I was only a repressed widow after all."

Gavin grasped her shoulders and turned her to face him. With him so close, she could see his features clearly. "You think just because Isadora Glasier used you for her own devices that you aren't truly everything you believed yourself to be? You *are* sensual, the most sensual, alluring woman I've ever met.

"But, you're right. You aren't a slave to Aphrodite. You aren't anyone's slave. If anything, I am *your* slave. And I'll happily do your bidding for the rest of my life."

She smiled as a little of her confidence returned. "I don't want a slave, Gavin. I want a husband. A partner. A lover." She leaned up to place a gentle kiss on his warm lips. "Forever."

"And you'll have that with me," he whispered before he draped an arm over her shoulder. "Come, we'll reach Pafos by morning and then we'll start our new life."

"Together," she murmured as they walked down the hill and away from Aphrodite's temple. "Forever."

About the Author:

Jess Michaels has been writing since she can remember and has always loved happily-ever-afters. Of course when she discovered romance, it was the perfect fit. She also appeared in **Secrets, Volume 11** *with* Ancient Pleasures *and writes for Avon as Jenna Petersen. You can find her at* http://www.jessmichaels.com.

White Heat

by Leigh Wyndfield

To My Reader:

On an ice planet in the middle of nowhere, two loners who never should have met find each other. One has decided to stop running. The other has just started…

Chapter One

"Let me guess. It's going to snow. Now *that's* something new and different."

Raine placed her feet into the indents she'd cut in the ice wall. Pulling herself up, she straddled the top and stared off to the east. The wall didn't provide protection, since the gate had long ago blown off in a storm, but it offered a great view of the surrounding plain.

"It's going to be a big one," she said, studying the building black clouds in the distance. "White Out, for sure."

She'd long ago gotten over the fact that she now talked to herself on a regular basis after being alone for two planet rotations.

Briefly, she debated if she was finally losing her mind. She didn't think so, but perhaps she'd be the last to know if she was.

"I need to get off this planet before I *do* lose it." If she hadn't already.

There was a reason she couldn't leave. "Oh yeah, a crazed psychopath will kill me in a very unpleasant way if he catches me." She rolled her eyes.

The threat lessened the longer she stayed on this ice block. Death didn't look so bad after all, when the years stretched on before her with only the occasional big storm to keep her interested.

"Of course, I *am* rich." She grimaced. Being rich meant exactly zilch when she couldn't spend any of it. Millions of balseems scattered in hidey-holes all over the galaxies and here she was on Sector 9, one of thirteen unlucky planets in the Danthium quadrant of Galaxy Grid 219. In other words, the middle of nowhere.

The wind picked up, whipping back her hood. She let it go, scanning the horizon without the interfering fabric. Winter here lasted three quarters of a rotation, so she might as well enjoy her bare skin touching the outside air one last time before it got so cold, it would freeze her flesh off if she ventured out.

If there was one place in the whole of Creation where Malachi

Delmundo might not find her, it was right here.

And she knew he was trying, knew he would never give up until he held her beating heart in his hands after cutting it out with a blunt knife.

"Revenge," she whispered.

Three years ago, Malachi had killed her team, all six of them, and she still wasn't sure why. They'd been offered a contract to kill him, but they'd turned it down. As a rule, they didn't take contracts from cybergangs, since the money wasn't worth the risk. So why had Malachi sent his assassins after them? Now she wished they'd taken the job on and blown the bastard away.

Only she had been left alive by sundown that day, a fluke that still left her with an angry ache of guilt every time she thought about her lost friends. Malachi's men had thought she was dead, too. They were wrong.

Her vengeance had been sweet. She'd hit him where it hurt him most—his wealth. She'd taken a little under half of it and led him on a long, merry chase across the galaxies. He'd burned through more of his remaining balseems trying to run her down.

But she couldn't keep that up forever, so she'd come here.

She watched the clouds swirl in the distance. "Yep, it's going to be one hell of a storm. Early, too."

Just what she needed. Extra time locked in her icehouse.

Grasping the top of the wall, she swung herself over, somersaulting and landing on her feet. But instead of taking her customary bow to her non-existent audience, she scrambled back up the wall again.

Out of the corner of her eye on her way down, she'd caught sight of a storm building to the west as well. Her heart pounded in her chest at the thought of two blizzards clashing right above her house.

Sitting on the wall, Raine scanned the black clouds.

"Gods," she whispered.

Then she blinked and looked again.

"Not clouds. Smoke."

The only thing on this chunk of ice besides a trading station was the notorious prison, Inter-world Council Penitentiary number 569-00987, known to the people on Sector 9 as "Hell Frozen Over," or "HeFO" for short.

If it had been any other building on Sector 9, it wouldn't have burned because they were all made up of ice and rock. But HeFo was made of wood. After the first few prison breaks where the inmates managed to melt themselves out, the IWC had rebuilt the majority of the prison with imported lumber.

"And it's been drying out for weeks now, since we haven't had any snow." She whistled.

But one look at the coming storm made Raine jump down again, this time landing on her feet, then diving to execute a perfect roll.

No matter what she did, she had to keep in shape. Malachi would find her eventually. It was only a matter of time…

Walker staggered, forcing himself to move towards the relative safety of the rocks, across the slick, bare stretch of ground he'd traveled for hours. It never seemed as if he got closer.

The wind had picked up to a howl, and ice chips whipped through the air, ripping at the small patch of exposed skin on his face. Tears streamed, trying to clear the ice, which felt like grains of sand in his eyes.

His burned hands were more painful than anything he'd ever experienced. Every beat of his heart produced pain in his fingers as they throbbed with his pulse. He didn't have even a small amount of energy left to heal them.

He made his feet shuffle forward, just a few more steps. Come on, don't give up, he chided himself.

Merrium had laughed out loud when they sentenced him here. She knew he couldn't use his hidden power if he was unable to build the large amount of heat required. Being on a cold planet had cut off a piece of him as efficiently as if they'd chopped off one of his legs. Every second in HeFO had seemed like an eternity.

Or maybe she'd laughed because he was convicted of a crime he didn't commit. He couldn't provide himself with an alibi, and Merrium had known it. He'd spent the evening healing other Mixed Breeds, people like himself who looked human enough but carried alien blood in their veins. It was an automatic death sentence if the Inter-world Council found out that he or others like him had dared to bring their alien-infected blood onto IWC planets. Breeds couldn't chance going for traditional medical help, so they came to him. He'd chosen HeFO over death for himself and his patients.

Walker glanced up to find the rocks had finally gotten closer. Just a little further and he'd be there.

Raine rolled onto her back and panted at the ceiling. She could now do a hundred push-ups without pausing. Her body was in the best shape it had ever been in her life.

"Maybe it's time to go back onto the offensive."

The wind outside moaned and howled. Everything inside her screamed for her to leave Sector 9. She hated it here.

A loud bang shuddered down the ice tunnel. She sat up with a start.

"If the front entrance has collapsed again…" She didn't finish. Because if it collapsed, she'd dig herself out. What other choice did she have?

Hurrying from her main room, she ran along the entrance hallway, finally dropping to her knees to crawl to the portal at the end. The hall was set up to provide only the smallest exit possible, to keep in most of the heat.

She opened the portal slowly, shouldering the weight of the snow on the other side. She had a backup gate at the top of the hallway if she couldn't reseal this one.

Instead of the snow she expected, the portal crashed wide and a body fell on top of hers.

Malachi's assassins had finally found her!

She fought like a wild thing, punching, kicking, bucking her body below his.

The man fought harder, pinning her with his much heavier weight, his arms holding hers to her side.

Wind gusted ice and snow into her house and life-giving heat escaped. She had to do something to get the door shut.

She bought her knee up to catch him in the balls.

He moved at the last instant, deflecting most of the hit. In the unguarded moment, she managed to roll him onto his back. He tried to flip her under him again by throwing all his weight and momentum to his side. Scrambling out of his reach, she launched herself at his body. He fell onto the icy hallway, smacking his forehead hard. She wrenched his arm in a tight twist behind him.

"Who are you?" she demanded. She needed to close the door. It would take a week to build up the heat in the house if she didn't act fast. "But better to be cold than dead."

"What?" he asked and she knew she'd spoken out loud.

"Who are you?" She jerked up on his arm to add emphasis.

He groaned. "My hand."

She leaned in to growl in his ear, sliding her knife out of her belt to press it against his throat with her free hand. "Who. Are. You."

"Walker," he gasped, his body shaking from the cold. "My hand."

His eyes shut and his body went slack. He'd passed out.

At first, Raine thought he was trying to trick her. But as his body slumped, her knife nicked his neck, and blood ran onto her floor. "Nope, guess he's not faking."

Standing, she dragged his heavy body backwards as fast as she could. Which wasn't as fast as she needed. He was huge and weighed as much as a freighter in his unconscious state.

She shut the portal after one last look outside. It was a White Out and a bad one. It would be days before the snows stopped. Then the whole planet would be covered in deep mounds of powder.

Crawling into the taller part of the tunnel, she stood and tried to catch her breath. Who in the hell was this man? He moaned and it spurred her into action. She needed to tie him up before he awoke.

It took awhile, but she dragged him into the room by the shoulders of his jacket, then rolled him over. His clothing was minimal, only several thin layers of fabric, indicating he was one of the most ill-prepared assassins she'd ever encountered. Then she saw the IWC Penitentiary stamp on the jumper beneath his jacket.

"He's a prisoner," she breathed.

"What to do, what to do," she whispered, pondering. She couldn't bring herself to throw him outside.

A towel covered his face, with only a small slit in the material for him to see through. When she unwound it, the exposed flesh had the crackled appearance of snow frosting, an unpleasant and dangerous condition that could lead to death. It ran all over his skin, even where the cloth had covered it.

Something she was sure had died long ago uncurled inside her. She had to help him, for no other reason than he so desperately needed it.

She placed her hands over his cheeks. His breath hitched in pain. Even her cold fingers must feel too hot to him. His condition was more serious than she'd thought. She pulled off his boots to check for more snow frosting. No sign of that, but she wrapped his feet in Thermo-blankets just in case.

The inner lining stuck to his hands as she wrestled with his gloves. Had he gotten them wet? The first one came off and she gasped.

"Gods and Goddesses!"

His hand was black, covered in blisters and cuts.

She dragged off the other glove, then ran for her first aid kit.

"The fire. He's burned his hands."

She threw the case down and rummaged for burn cream. She knew she had it in here somewhere.

The tube wasn't as large as she wished. She spread the oily paste all over his hands. Then she slapped a bandage across the small cut on his neck. No one would say she had a great bedside manner. She had been part of an elite fighting squad before Malachi killed them all, not a healer.

"You're probably that serial murderer they caught on LackSui last year. After I go to sleep, you'll kill me and eat my eyeballs for breakfast." Even as she said it, she dismissed the idea, although she'd keep a close eye on him just in case.

From her bathroom, her only extravagance in this ice hell, she grabbed two towels and wrapped his hands in them. Then she dragged him to her bed, falling on her butt once in the process. She needed to warm him fast.

The heating system in an icehouse was such that the hot air didn't have one specific point of entry, which would cause melting. Rather, warm air circulated throughout the rooms from a series of ducts. Which meant the house was freezing since they'd had the portal open.

No way could she get him up onto her bed. Spreading a thermal tarp to prevent melting, she pulled her mattress to the floor and rolled the man onto it. He moaned when his weight came down on his hands.

"Oops, sorry," she said.

Then she piled every blanket over him that she had in the house and finished by stuffing his head into one of her bigger hats. She sat for a while, warming his cheeks with her bare hands.

For the first time, she looked at him. Before she'd jammed on the hat, she had seen that his hair had been shaved almost to his scalp in typical prison fashion. A dark blond, although it was hard to tell with it that short.

"His face isn't exactly handsome, is it?"

His mouth turned down as if he understood her words. She had to remember not to talk out loud. She didn't even realize she was doing it half the time.

Still, he was good-looking, in a rugged way. He had nice, strong features, and full, sensuous lips. A shadow of beard covered his face, making him seem mysterious.

She grinned at her musings and resisted the urge to peel one eye open to see what color they were.

Lowering her head, she placed her lips to his cheek to check the temperature. Cool but not ice cold. He was warming up fast. Faster than he should have. She realized the snow frosting had disappeared. She was sure she hadn't been mistaken, but there wasn't any sign of it now. Strange.

Suddenly, his head rolled and his lips caught hers, his arm curving around her neck to hold her down, his hand kept carefully aloft.

For a moment, she was shocked into stillness.

Her body, which hadn't felt the touch of another human for three years, exploded with fire. His lips feathered on her mouth, before his tongue slowly stroked across her lips. His arm tightened around her neck, as if he was afraid she would pull away.

But Raine didn't want to move. She had thought she'd been okay here. Annoyed maybe, but fine without companionship. With this stranger's kiss, she realized she wasn't fine. Her stomach tightened with a need so great, she didn't try to fight it.

Instead, she opened her mouth and let his tongue slip inside. Suckling lightly, his taste exploded into her mouth. Different from anything else she'd ever savored, like warm bread straight from the oven, something that brought to mind fields of grain blowing in a summer breeze.

The kiss wasn't demanding. Soft and gentle, it felt pleasant and right, as if she'd been sitting here on Sector 9 for two years just waiting for his lips to touch hers. And maybe she had, she thought, reveling in the burn of desire between her legs, making her body yearn for release.

Pulling slowly away, unsure if he'd let her go, she was careful not to jar his hands. Warm green eyes stared up from only a hand-length away. They were the color of green moss or Orchid leaves in the heart of a lush, tropical jungle.

For a brief moment, her mind showed her a picture of what they must look like heavy lidded with passion, intense before the moment of climax. Her stomach flip-flopped with desire.

Walker stared up at the woman and, with a certainty that shocked him, he understood exactly what she was.

Mate.

The word breathed through his mind, through all his reawakening senses, shaking him to the core. That he could have found the one person meant for him in all of Creation, here in this icy hell, boggled his mind. All this time, he'd thought his mixed blood had meant he wouldn't have the bonding of his father's people, that the generations of inter-mating with humans had taken this destiny from him.

But for the first time in many lunar cycles, his power stirred, even though his body temperature wasn't high enough to support it. The touch of her hands had set him on fire and increased his heat level in the way his father had told him it would if he was ever lucky enough to find his mate. His blood pounded though his veins, his senses on overload with the smell of her body, the taste of her lips, and her dancing gray eyes.

He wanted to tear off her clothes, rip away his own, and press his naked body tight against hers. The warmth would be amazing. He could heal his hands and bring her to orgasm with his touch. The way she poured heat into him during their kiss, he knew he could do it.

He forced his body to remain still. His hat had fallen off and her fingers filtered through what was left of his hair. The scalp was a great conductor of heat, and hers flowed into him, building his reserves even more. The sensation filled him with a burning need only she could fulfill.

Right now, he was almost helpless, his body exhausted by the fire and the long walk in the storm. If she kept going and kissed him a few more times, he'd have enough energy stored to heal his hands.

"Kiss me again," he said, his voice rusty from lack of use.

He could tell she was reluctant, her hands stilling.

"Please." He'd spent his whole life never begging for anything, but at this moment, he'd do whatever it took for more of her touch.

Her mouth pulled into a frown, her brows lowering, then she shrugged and dipped her head.

Pleasure ran the length of his body and back again, tightening every muscle, making his cock rock hard as she slanted her lips and slipped her tongue inside his mouth. He wanted to grab her, roll her beneath him, but instead, he kept his hands out to the side. He bent his fingers, the spike of pain reminding him to go slow with her.

He didn't know how he was going to do it, but he needed her to take off both of their clothes and press her body against his. As his mind cranked through possible scenarios, his lips enjoyed her kiss. He tried to think, even though her taste filled his mouth with warmth and pleasure exploded inside him.

Then a plan came into his mind, something he'd never considered before.

Chapter Two

Walker had spent his life concealing his power until he'd witnessed another Mixed Breed being beaten by the Council police. The man's tainted blood had been discovered when he went for medical help. In that moment, a weight of responsibility had come crashing down on his shoulders, because he knew he could provide the medical help his fellow outcasts needed.

Even though he'd used his talents to help others, he'd rarely made use of them to help himself, and he'd only once tried them during sex. Merrium had been appalled and had rejected his efforts, but even before that, he could tell his power didn't react to her. It didn't stir to life, tingling below the surface of his skin.

Not like it did now with the woman he kissed, the woman who ran her warm, magnificent hands through his hair, making his whole body throb.

He wanted to explore everything she was from the inside out, but he couldn't let her know about his skills. All Inter-world people were disgusted by Mixed Breeds. Still, he could push energy into her slowly, increase the burn between them so it felt like desire. Intense, wonderful, amazing desire.

For a moment, he struggled with his plan. His hands throbbed with every beat of his heart. If he used the energy to heal himself, he could cut his pain in half. But he would lose everything if she stopped kissing him.

Slowly, tentatively at first, he breathed power into her mouth, the act much like a mini-orgasm, relieving the growing pressure as a wave of pleasure sped through his body into hers.

He must have pushed too hard, because she jumped and pulled away. Gray eyes, the color of icy seas, stared down at him, blinking in surprise. "What was that?" she asked. "It felt like lightening racing through me. Did you feel it?"

He still had his arm around her neck but resisted the urge to drag her down. He'd seen how strong she was when he had tried to force his way into her house.

"Please," he whispered. If she was his mate, she would want him too. Badly. He could only hope the sharp bite of desire between them would overcome her resistance.

Her head cocked to the side. "It feels good, but this is probably one of your stupider ideas," she murmured.

"What?" he asked, shaking his head. He glanced around the room, but couldn't figure out who she spoke to.

"Oh," she said, a blush streaking across her face. Dropping her head, she kissed him quick, as if she tried to cover up for something.

He didn't understand and quite frankly, he could care less. This. This is what he wanted. Following the seam of her lips with his tongue, he asked for entry. She parted for him, and his tongue brushed hers. Energy poured from her body into his, making his skin break out into a sweat. How long had it been since he'd been this warm?

Unable to fight the desire to give her back some of the pleasure she gave him, he carefully returned some power to her. Just a flash of heat that would feel like a whisper of warmth filling her from the inside out.

She moaned and as she deepened the kiss, her fingers splayed across his cheeks, down his neck and buried in the top of his jumpsuit. Gods and Goddesses, if she would just strip his clothes and run her hands along his skin.

As if she could hear his thoughts, she bared the top of his chest and trailed her hands over the muscles that had built from months of hard labor in HeFo.

It felt so good. So good.

But not enough. No, he wanted more. Much more.

His energy level was high now. Hotter than he'd been in so long, he healed his hands with a thought, the flash of pain at the healing making him break the contact with her on a gasp.

She stared at him in wonder, her tongue darting out to lick over her lips in a slow, sexy glide.

"I'm Raine," she whispered.

"Walker," he said, forcing his gaze to meet her eyes instead of staring at her lips. He kicked away the blankets, too hot now to stand them.

Raine looked down the line of Walker's body and saw that she wasn't the only person totally, completely, one-hundred percent turned on. Oh no. She closed her eyes and grasped for her sanity. She didn't even know this man. He'd been in HeFO, a prison for murderers and thieves. She lowered his head to the ground, sliding her arm from beneath it.

"Raine." He allowed her to straighten, but she could tell he didn't want to. He gritted his teeth on whatever else he wanted to say.

She moved until she was sitting beside him instead of kneeling at his head. "You don't look cold anymore." Unable to resist the overwhelming urge to touch him, she rested one hand on his exposed upper chest and raised an eyebrow.

"I'm warmer than I've been in months," he murmured, his green eyes studying her intently.

Watching him for any sign that he might not want what she was about to do, she ran her hands down his bare skin.

She was sick and tired of being cold and alone on this heap of ice. If this stranger fell into her lap, she was going to make the most of it. He felt right to her, and her mind whispered that she could trust him. If something went wrong, he wasn't in any condition to hurt her. She didn't think he would do anything but bring her pleasure. And she wanted pleasure. She deserved it, dammit.

Didn't she?

A brief hesitation flitted through her and she studied his bright green eyes. He was in HeFO for a reason.

Her hands glided down to his crotch, and he groaned and closed his eyes against the feel of her brushing his rock hard erection.

"Oh yes," she might have whispered out loud. Or maybe she didn't. Who knew? Who cared? Not her. Not right now. A burn filled her body, driving her onward like nothing she'd ever felt before.

Leaning over him, she spread open his jumpsuit to study his body. Smooth muscled perfection greeted her, the sheen of sweat catching her eye. He shouldn't be this hot, should he? Maybe he had a fever.

Then the thought was swept away as he shrugged the coat and jumpsuit off his shoulders, sitting up on his own and peeling the fabric off his body in one sweep. When he lay back, he was naked.

"Oh my," she thought or said. Who knew with this man lying before her?

Every inch of him was hard perfection. What his face lacked in handsomeness, his body far, far made up for in sheer flawlessness.

Somewhere in the back of her mind, she worried about the snow frosting. Where had it gone? She hadn't imagined it, had she? She'd never gotten the condition herself. Maybe the crackling hadn't been what she'd thought it was.

She blinked and the thoughts fell away as she gazed at his shoulders. Double the width of hers, they ran down into rippled abs, that moved into slim hips, that flared back out into well muscled thighs. The curve of his leg glided gracefully down into trim, solid calves.

His erection matched the rest of him—big and hard, the head pulsing and engorged, a drop of pre-come dotting the top.

She wanted to touch so very, very badly, so she did.

She dragged her hand along the bounty of his thigh, skirting his sex and stroked across his lightly haired chest. Circling a nipple, she watched in utter fascination as it hardened with her stroke.

"Raine," he said, his breath catching with her action.

As if she was in a dream, she slowly gazed up at him.

"Kiss me." He wasn't begging anymore and he wasn't asking. His voice was all command.

Her natural rebelliousness flared to life and she narrowed her eyes. Keeping eye contact, she lowered her head in degrees until she planted a chaste kiss on his nipple.

Even that simple action made him swallow. He'd liked it, she thought, and still keeping her gaze locked to his, she ran her tongue in a circle around the hard bud, then sucked it into her mouth. The taste of his skin exploded into her mouth, spicy male and salt from the sheen of perspiration that covered his body.

He hissed in a breath, his sex jumping up to briefly touch her side where she rested across his body while she kissed him.

With a shaking hand still wrapped in the makeshift bandages she'd put on, he attempted to drag off her thermal sweater.

"No, you'll hurt your hands." She pulled out of reach. With one movement, she was out of the sweater, but immediately regretted it as the chilly air hit her breasts, tightening her nipples into painful peaks. "Oh! It's too cold."

"Come here," he growled, his gaze on her breasts. "Don't put it back on. I'll warm you."

She stretched out beside him, and he immediately rolled to cover her, supporting himself on his forearms. Their chests were pressed together and it felt so amazing, she moaned. Briefly, her mind questioned why she felt this way, how she'd never before felt so much desire that she didn't care about her safety, didn't care about anything but touching him. He was steaming hot now, able to keep them both warm in the freezing cold of the room.

"Strip off your pants," he said, nuzzling his face into her neck and biting lightly.

Now was T-minus Zero in the countdown. *Speak now or forever hold your peace, Raine.*

She felt him smile into her neck. "You talk to yourself, don't you?" he asked, and for the first time she could hear humor in his voice.

It irritated her. "Yes, dammit, I do." She pushed on him. "Back off, buster, or I can't get naked for you."

He blinked and the corners of his eyes crinkled as if he fought a smile.

She narrowed her eyes, and he frowned to stop the grin from spreading to his mouth. She could tell.

He distracted her by raising up so she could reach her belt. When her hands found the buckle, she brushed his erection and then neither of them was smiling.

"Gods, you feel like the sun on a tropical day. All lightness and wonder." His voice sounded pained.

She fumbled with the closure at her waist, then pushed down until her pants were caught at her boots. He rolled to one side to let her sit to undo the fasteners. The moment her clothes were free, he caught her and brought her beneath him, as if all he really wanted was to press his skin to hers. He sighed and it was a joyous sound.

Then his eyes opened and he kept her gaze as he worked his legs between hers. "Yes, Raine, speak now or forever hold your peace."

His voice was hoarse, but the head of his erection slid along the top of her thighs until it ran into the wetness she'd accumulated there. Then it raced down her clitoris to stop at the very edge of her opening.

For once, she was speechless. All she could do was pant and wait for this wondrous thing. Had she really been thinking about going after Malachi, who would surely kill her, when she could have *this*?

"So be it." He said the words as if he sealed her fate.

Before she could dwell on the significance, he eased his cock into her channel. Even though she was ready, she had gone a long time without someone in her bed. He stretched her to the limit, the strength of his cock expanding her so that all she could do was grasp onto the bulge in his biceps and experience the feel of him sliding into her body.

When the team had lived, she'd been lovers with Antilli, a small, wiry assassin. Gods, she had missed him after he'd died. They hadn't been in love, but he had been her friend and her confidant.

She hadn't been touched by a single other person since that day. She'd been too fragile at first, then too angry, then she'd ended up on this hunk of rock where she went months without seeing another living soul.

But Walker wasn't like Antilli in any way. Walker was all muscle and bulk. Huge.

He pulled back out and reached between them to glide his erection over her wetness. "You're tight. I don't want to hurt you," he said, his green eyes intense, his face tightened with desire.

He slowly thrust into her, this time sliding all the way in to the hilt. She hummed, feeling as if some piece of her soul was reborn, as if she had finally come home.

"Did that hurt?" he gasped, lowering his body fully onto hers.

"No."

He took a deep breath and let it out. "I'm not going to last long." Rocking forward, he seemed purposely to grind his body on her clitoris.

Raine bit her lip to stifle the scream that threatened to erupt at the intense storm building inside her.

He repeated the gesture, his whole body drenched in sweat, the light hair on his chest scraping over her already sensitized nipples. She fought to have him touch every part of her at once. All she could focus on was the feel of him filling her after being alone for so long.

"I need you to come, Raine." His voice sounded desperate, as if willpower alone kept him from climax, but she didn't open her eyes to look at his face. All she could do was experience the pleasure.

Then he kissed her and that strange, wonderful sensation breathed through her body, tightening her from the inside out. She came in a blaze of heat, the powerful release making her arch and grab his shoulders.

Walker ground himself into her and his body jumped with his own release, causing another ripple of pleasure to surge through her.

He collapsed, enveloping her body with his, his erection still connecting them in the most intimate of ways.

Chapter Three

"You're from the prison." Instead of wanting to push away from him, she kept her legs wrapped around his body to keep him close. She felt wonderful, dreamy, right.

He nodded. "The fire freed me."

His voice slid like warm honey down her spine. Everything about you is warm, she thought.

But he answered her with a nod, so she must have spoken out loud again. "I'm from the Gratermor Quadrant."

"The Outer Worlds?" She shook her head. That was on the edge of some very scary alien territory. No one lived there if they could help it.

He closed his eyes. "It's warm there." He blew out a breath. "Gods, I miss the heat."

"What were you in prison for?" She absently ran her fingers through his wheat-colored hair, wondering why she didn't move away from him. She should feel embarrassed at what had just happened between them, since she hadn't even spoken a dozen words to him before they'd jumped into bed. Or more accurately, *he* hadn't spoken that many words. She'd babbled enough for both of them without even meaning too.

But the human contact was more than she could resist. Just touching another person's skin felt like heaven. She hadn't realized how much she'd missed it.

Green eyes opened and turned hard. "Murder," he said.

She stilled, her hand on his cheek.

"I won't bother telling you I didn't do it. Why would you believe me?"

She searched his eyes. *Why indeed?*

"Yes, why indeed." His lips curled as if he was disgusted, but he didn't move away.

She tried to decide why she thought he was innocent. Or maybe not innocent, but not guilty. After all, she'd taken quite a few lives herself. Or the team had, but they couldn't have done it without her planning skills. Did it matter that the men they had killed were all killers themselves? The team had specialized in taking out the baddest of the bad—kidnappers, rapists and baby killers. But the fact that she had been the team's strategist and had contributed to the deaths of the targets her team had terminated made her a murderer too, didn't it? In the strictest sense of the word?

She'd never really thought about it before. Since she was a child, she'd known that she was born to take down the bullies of the universes. It was her mission in life, the one thing burning in her soul.

"Raine the Avenger," she heard herself whisper self-mockingly.

He narrowed his eyes. "I'm not returning to HeFO. I'll kill myself first."

She raised her eyebrows. She believed him. It was there on his face. She knew what it felt like to die for something you believed in. Only she hadn't died. Her team had.

"I took the punishment of another. I had to, or reveal something much worse, and the bastard who framed me knew it."

She shifted to get more comfortable, and he hissed in a breath, the movement of her under him making him grow hard inside her once more. Desire shot through her body, her mind flashing back to the intense orgasm they'd just shared. Her channel tightened around his erection in a pleasure-filled pulse.

She fisted her hands and battled the need to have him again. Where had her normal control gone? What had happened to her constant diligence and threat assessment? She wouldn't let herself be distracted. "Why did they frame you?"

"Because they could. What burns me is that it was nothing personal. I took the fall because I was an easy mark." For a moment, he met her gaze, then he kissed her, hard and long. It wasn't sweet like the kisses he'd given her earlier. He kissed her as if he wouldn't let her go, as if he'd fight to the death before he'd let her free.

He left her gasping, distracted by the rising need inside her body, which is why at first she didn't comprehend what she was seeing when he leaned on one elbow and stripped the bandage off one hand, then the other.

"I have to run my hands over you," he growled. He withdrew from her and sat on his knees between her legs. His fingers wandered along her stomach, drawing her gaze with the feather-light, worshiping touch. She shivered as need spiked through her again. Her reaction to him wasn't normal. Too intense, too amazing, as if he held the key to her body's pleasure.

Finally, she took two big breaths and formed a coherent sentence. Kind of. "Your hands. Burned."

He stilled with a jerk as if she'd slapped him, looking at his hands as if he'd noticed them for the first time.

Slowly, without the hammering pleasure he gave to her senses, her mind clicked back into itself. She turned one of his hands in hers.

"Perfect. Not a scratch."

He let her move him as she would. She dropped that hand to study his other with an equally close inspection.

He was silent.

"Walker," she whispered, smoothing her fingers over the perfect skin of his palm. "What happened?"

Walker watched his woman—and she *was* his, she just didn't know it yet—stare at his hand. *Yeah Walker, what happened?*

He struggled to come up with the words to tell her. The truth might cause her to run screaming from him. She couldn't do that. She was his. They were fated to be together. If he lost her, he would spend the rest of his life without the soul-redeeming closeness of a mate. They would both have a piece of themselves that would be left half formed and aching, a constant reminder of what they'd lost.

"The snow frosting." Her fingers brushed his cheek, causing him to meet her gaze. "You had it all over your face. I know you did." Her soft hands flowed across his healed skin. "I thought at first I must have been mistaken, yet now I know I wasn't."

She shivered, and he resisted the urge to pull her into his warmth, knowing she wasn't cold but unnerved.

"Your hands should have taken months to heal." She choked on a strangled laugh and pulled away the bandage on his throat. "Even your neck." She pressed on his skin. "I nicked you with the knife, and now I can't even tell where I did it."

"Raine," he said, finding his voice in the face of what looked to be impending hysteria on her part. He had to calm her, make sure she didn't leave him during this crucial bonding stage. He had to stay with her long enough to cement the fragile link he could already feel woven between them. "Listen—"

"No." She shoved away but before she could stand, he launched himself forward, pinning her with his body.

She couldn't leave him. She couldn't reject him.

"Wait," he yelled, when she started to fight.

She paused long enough for him to say, "Listen, I—I can heal—" He stumbled on the explanation, opening his mouth and closing it several times.

She snorted. "Heal what?" She thrust against his chest. "What? What?" Each word grew progressively louder.

"You," he whispered, then hummed in irritation and said, "and me. I can heal anyone." He took a deep breath. Might as well tell all of it. "And I can do other things. With my hands."

She collapsed back and closed her eyes while she shook her head. "Of course he can, Raine. What do you expect? You can't think that a normal male with this hot a body would waltz in your icehouse when you're living in the freaking middle of nowhere!" She smacked her palm on her forehead. "You freaking idiot!"

Walker cleared his throat, and her eyes flashed open. He didn't think she'd meant for him to hear all that.

"So what *are* you?" she asked, anger clear in her snapping gray eyes.

He blew out a breath. Now was when she'd go ballistic. Merrium certainly had. And then she'd betrayed him. He was a Breed, an abomination, something that had to be destroyed. His heart clenched at the thought that Raine would betray him, too. That he'd lose his mate.

Gritting his teeth, he decided he wouldn't give her the chance. He would be at her side every moment of every day until she realized she had to be with him, that the Gods had intended it. It wasn't just that his power liked her, either. Everything about her was perfect and right. The way she looked, the way she'd fought him, the way she hadn't thrown him into the storm when she'd found out he was an escaped prisoner. Beauty and strength. Courage and compassion. It was a heady mix any man would want in his woman.

"Hello." She waved a hand before his face. "Are you in there?"

Holding her in place with the weight of his body, he said, "I'm a Mixed Breed. I have magic, passed from my father's line."

Her mouth dropped open, and her gaze rolled to the ceiling. Instead of fighting him as he'd thought she would, she laughed.

Big, breathy guffaws.

She wiped the tears from her eyes. Every time she got herself under control, she went into another bout of laugher.

It annoyed him.

"Something funny?" he ground out.

"Y-y-yes," she managed.

"Care to share?"

If she didn't feel so damn good naked beneath him, he'd strangle her.

She cleared another trail of tears with the back of her hands. "What are the chances," she said, suddenly sober, "that the first person I touch in three years is a Mixed Breed? I mean, the Inter-world Council's bounty has basically brought your kind to extinction and in you stroll, having escaped HeFO." She frowned. "No way HeFO knew you were Mixed. They would have killed you, not put you in prison."

"They didn't know." He tried not to let her see that her words hurt him. On the bright side, she hadn't tried to pull away. That counted for something. A lot of somethings, actually.

"You said earlier you were framed. Whoever did it knew what you were?"

"Yes." *Touch me*, his mind begged her. *Forgive me for being who I am. Want me for me.* But he kept his face blank.

"But your accent is from the Inner Worlds."

"I've lived most of my life within the IWC, most of it on Borrus itself."

"The Capital Planet," she breathed. "I'm impressed. You blend in well." She gazed at him critically, as if trying to see his tainted blood.

"My father was a third generation Mixed Breed. Only the magic of his line is left inside me. The rest has been bred out." He kept his voice flat. The magic and the ability to mate, he knew now.

"What did you do on Borrus?"

"Heal other Mixed Breeds."

Her eyes widened. "That's your job?"

"Yes."

"There are enough Breeds for you to spend all your time healing them?" Her tone held disbelief.

"Yes."

"Gods." She seemed impressed rather than outraged.

"What do you do?" he asked, turning the tables on her. It finally occurred to him that she shouldn't be here on this planet any more than he should.

"Me?"

"Either you or the other person you speak to all the time. Either of you is welcome to answer."

She frowned at him and tapped his shoulder with one finger. "For your information, I have lived here by myself for two whole planet rotations. There wasn't anyone else to talk to and it just seemed so…" she shrugged as if she searched for a word, "lonely not to hear voices, even if I only heard my own."

His heart twisted. Holy hell. At least he'd had human contact while in HeFo.

"I'm sorry."

Her eyes widened in surprise. "For what?"

"That you were lonely."

"It's not your fault. It's my own." An impish grin flashed across her face. "I am Raine the Avenger."

"You said that earlier, but I wasn't sure who you were talking to." For the first time in his life, Walker had hope. Hope that someone would accept him for what he was. She knew and she hadn't rejected him. "Who are you avenging?"

The question made the smile fade from her lips. "My team."

He waited for her to go on. Something about the sudden sadness in her eyes made him cautious, made him want to curl around her and hold her tight.

"They were killed three years ago, and I made the bastard who was responsible pay."

"Literally?"

"Oh yeah." Mischief returned to her eyes. "I stole half his net worth and then he had to spend more to chase me." Some of the spark went out of her eyes, and she sighed. "But then my luck began to run a little low, and I had to hide out. You have to admit, this is the last place anyone would look for me."

Something in her voice made him ask, "How bad did your luck run?"

"Move off me and I'll show you."

Walker released her reluctantly. Her body felt like heaven below his, firm muscles and womanly curves. He shifted so his body pressed against hers. He almost halted her when she rolled away from him onto her stomach, because he didn't want to lose the contact.

The sight of her back stopped him. He hissed in a breath.

She craned her neck over her shoulder trying to see her back. "I haven't looked at it in awhile. Is it that bad?"

"It must have hurt," was all he could say as he stared at the scar that ran from the top of her left shoulder, down her back, and across her right buttock. In some places, the brown streak was two fingers wide. Rage that someone had done this to his woman flashed through him, the thought of her pain hitting him like a physical blow to the stomach.

"Too bad you weren't around to heal me."

Stroking along the scar, he silently agreed, although if he was honest, he'd never healed a full human before. He didn't think it made a difference, but he couldn't be completely sure.

"You must have made this person pretty mad if he's still chasing you."

"Oh, Malachi is still pissed, I'm sure." She grinned over her shoulder.

Walker's heart stopped, then started again at double-time. "Malachi who?"

Raine gave him a funny look as she sat and gathered several blankets around her. "Delmundo, why?"

Walker couldn't speak for a long moment. It was too much of a coincidence to be true.

Chapter Four

Walker finally spoke. "Malachi Delmundo framed me for the murder."

"No way." She almost laughed, but the coincidence unnerved her enough to keep her sober.

"It's true. A woman I had thought was my friend told him about my Mixed Breed status and that I worked each night at the Breed hospital."

He'd told someone about the hospital, which meant he'd trusted them very much. A weird feeling curled through her as she realized this woman must to have been his lover. "Breeds have their own hospital?"

Walker's mouth twisted with wry humor. "Of course we have a hospital."

"And it hasn't been discovered by the authorities?"

"Who would betray the only place they can go for medical treatment?"

Raine made sure she stayed silent as she thought about the fact there was always someone who would give you up, if the price was right. Someone had told Malachi where her team had been staying the night they'd all been killed.

"It was easy for him to plant evidence that I had been at the murder scene."

"Who did he murder?" she interrupted.

"As far as I can tell, he was just a citizen, although there must have been some reason Malachi wanted him dead." He pinched the bridge of his nose. "All I could say is that I was at home during the time the murder took place. I had no alibi that wouldn't end in my own death or put others in jeopardy."

Raine whistled. *Lord, that sucks.*

"That's an understatement. On this ice planet, I've not been able to generate enough heat to use my powers, essentially losing one of my senses. I lost part of who I am."

"But you healed your hands."

He wiggled his fingers, and a grin flashed across his face. "You helped my heat level immensely."

"Yeah, I guess sex will do that," she admitted, snuggling into the blankets.

He still sat without anything around him, totally naked, with his gorgeous body showing in all its perfection. Every one of those muscles curving in all the right places. She would love to run her hands over him again. Her palms itched with desire.

"Raine!" she said sharply, then silently lectured herself to stop gawking and stay on track.

When she met Walker's gaze, his eyebrows were arched in an unspoken question.

She shook her head. "So sex makes you hot enough to use your talent?"

"Not sex exactly." His hand tapped one muscled, fantastic thigh, drawing her attention. "It's hard to explain, but let's just say my power likes you."

"What in the hell does that mean?"

"Just touching you gives me energy." He knee-walked up the mattress and sat beside her. "Since I haven't touched you for a while, I'm starting to take on the room's temperature."

She slid a hand out of her warm cocoon and felt his shoulder. He wasn't hot anymore. "Wild. You want one of these blankets?" She made herself retract her hand, even though she longed to stroke him.

"I'd rather join you, if that's okay?"

She studied his face. His features were almost harsh, softened by his intense green eyes. He would look much better with some hair framing his face. Of course, the prison cut wouldn't make anyone look good. He waited, his expression blank, as if her decision to let him close didn't matter, but she thought it might.

The impact of what he'd shared hit her with a jolt. The last time he'd trusted someone with this information, he'd ended up in HeFO, but he'd told her anyway. He'd essentially trusted her with his life, since if she revealed who he was, he would be killed as soon as they could catch him. And she didn't think he was as savvy about running as she was. After all, she'd made a career of it.

Raine was humbled he had so much faith in her, although she

wasn't sure she was worthy of it. Gods knew, her team had trusted her, too.

Walker sat silent, waiting for her answer.

"If you want to raise your heat levels, we should take a bath." She wasn't ready for this to end, she realized. Her heart skipped a beat, and she wondered why she felt this strongly about this man. Maybe she *had* gone insane.

He pulled back a bit, as if her answer wasn't what he was expecting. "You want to take a bath with me?" he asked, his tone carefully neutral.

She stood, suddenly excited to show off her bathroom. She'd never had anyone to brag to before. "Come on. Come on." She skipped across the freezing floor, knowing that very soon she'd be in luxury.

When she reached the portal, she turned to find out why he hadn't followed. Her abrupt stop had him catching her shoulders to keep him from running into her.

She started in surprise. "Whoa! I didn't think you were behind me."

He tightened his hold on her and grinned. "Where else would I be? I'm not giving up the offer of having a bath with a beautiful woman."

She disengaged herself and turned to fling open the portal.

He hummed in appreciation.

"It is amazing, isn't it?" She could hear the pride in her voice, but dammit, look at it!

Tile lined the room, while the floor was covered in rugs so her bare tootsies didn't have to step on the ice floor. She'd done the whole room in a sea foam green. It looked like heaven, if she did say so herself. Walking to the bathtub, a sunken monstrosity from the Gods raised on a special platform so the heat wouldn't melt her house down, she threw the levers to fill a space big enough for four.

She turned to give him a history of her struggles to bring greatness to an ice heap in the middle of nowhere and jumped because he was once again behind her.

His hand shot out to steady her before she pitched backwards into the tub.

"You are abnormally quiet when you move," she said, huffy because he kept surprising her.

"I don't mean to be." He peered around her. "This tub is the best thing I've seen in my lifetime, except for you."

Before she could stop herself, one of her hands fluttered to her chest. It was the second time in minutes he'd said nice things to her.

It made her feel downright girlie. It had been a long time since she'd been flattered.

He climbed the two steps of the platform and sat on the rim to dip his feet in. "Oh yeah. It's scorching hot in here."

She waited until the tub was half-filled before dropping her blankets, dashing up the stairs and sinking into the water with a sigh.

Pulling her knees to her chest, she said, "How do you like my Secret Palace of Pleasure?"

He sat beside her, unnecessarily close given the size of the tub. The water rose higher. "I love it."

"The only sad thing is that you can have just one bath a week. It takes that long for the water to warm up again." She hugged her knees. "Occasionally I'll push it by taking another at day four or five." She paused, a thought coming to her, "But you know, with your weight in the tub, I bet we'll use less water to fill it."

"I'm glad I am of some use."

She laughed. "You sound offended, but honestly, I could keep you around forever if I thought I would get two baths a week in this tub."

His eyes sparkled oddly, and she wondered what he was thinking, but all he said was, "This is nice." He groaned and leaned against the side. The water had reached chest level quickly.

Raine pushed off beside him to float to the levers and shut the water off. Yes, he was handy. It hadn't taken long at all to fill it.

Keeping her body below the water's surface, she asked the question she'd been thinking about for a while now. "So when are you going after Malachi?"

Walker watched his woman float in the huge tub and forced himself to stay still when he wanted to swoop down on her like a hawk on prey.

Gods, she was beautiful. Even her back with the streak of brown scar begged for his mouth upon it.

He made himself speak. She wasn't going to figure out how much she wanted him if he didn't talk to her. Heart, body, mind, he had to win them all or he'd spend his life mourning her loss. His gut twisted with wonder—how amazing to know who you were destined to be with for your whole life. To look at that person and know that if you were with them, you'd be happy forever. He couldn't make mistakes. The price of failure would be too high, for both of them.

"I hadn't planned on going after Delmundo."

She sat up with a splash. "What? Why not?"

He shrugged. "What good would it do?"

"He harmed you, took your freedom. Took your powers." She knelt beside him. "He deserves to pay."

Walker could care less. He wasn't wasting his time and energy on that cyber-scum.

She blinked, then shook her head, and frowned. "Well, that's okay." Settling across from him, she pulled up her legs to her chest and rested her chin on her knees. "I'll take care of him for you."

Now it was his turn to say, "What?"

"After this White Out, I'm leaving Sector 9 to go on the offensive again." She grinned, and it was bloodthirsty. "I plan to hit Malachi where it hurts. It's been so long that I'm sure he's relaxed his guard. He might even think I'm dead by now."

Walker's heart constricted at the thought of Delmundo capturing Raine. He was a sadistic bastard who had framed Walker for a murder just because he was a handy victim. The thought of Delmundo's hands on Raine made Walker shiver, even though he was sitting in steaming hot water.

"Raine," he said, searching for the right words. "Haven't you gotten your revenge?"

"I will never finish punishing him until he's paid six times over." She cupped some water in her palm and let it trickle from between her fingers. "I figure he's only paid three so far."

"He might catch you. I've seen his torture victims and they weren't pretty." He tried not to panic. She was smart as a whip. She had to be to have survived Malachi's wrath for three years. He might be able to talk some sense into her.

She lifted one shoulder in a shrug. "If he does, I guess that will be that, but at least I'll have earned a gold star for effort."

Walker wanted to shake some sense into her. Then he realized he now had a perfect reason to stay by her side. "Fine, if this is how you feel—"

"I do," she interrupted.

"Then I'll come with you. Three lunar cycles ago he was still on Borrus."

"I suppose you deserve to have revenge too." She studied him for a long moment before nodding once. "Then I guess we'll be going to the Capital in a few days, if the snow isn't so bad that we can't leave. It's early for this type of storm, so we shouldn't have more than fifteen feet. We should be able to make it to the trading station."

Walker pushed off the bottom of the tub and zoomed over to her. "I guess we will," he said, and sealed their bargain with a kiss.

Walker breathed just a small push of power into her mouth, and Raine rewarded him with a moan deep in her throat. The sound heightened his pleasure almost as much as pushing his heat into her did. Usually touching another person meant nothing to him, but touching Raine was so very different. Something inside her fed power back to him. Receiving her energy felt like a sensual stroke of her hand below his skin. It was addicting in the extreme.

He pushed her knees down, encouraging her to unfold, then straddled her legs. He kept his lips on hers, eating at her gently.

Fitting his lower body close to hers, he enjoyed the surge of heat between them at the skin-on-skin contact. When he was locked up in HeFO, he had spent his time there staring at the walls, convincing himself that he would never find a mate. After all, he was three generations away from the pureness of his father's people. Part of him would then argue that his father and grandfather and great grandfather had found mates who were human, so he might too. He'd grown up learning from his father all the wonders of having a woman who not only could increase his power, but who would be his match on spiritual, mental and physical levels.

Framing her head with his hands, he explored her mouth. She'd said the storm would last days, and he planned to spend that time with her in bed. Already he could feel her body responding to his touch. From that first kiss, the strong chemical attraction they had between them had exploded into something so amazing, it still had him shaking inside. She would become as addicted to the power he fed her as he would be to the response of his talent to her touch.

He had this time and the week long journey to Borrus to sway her heart and mind, to bind those two parts of her to him and turn her from the idiocy of revenge against an evil asshole like Malachi Delmundo. That path would only lead to death.

He had a bad feeling it would be easier to bind her heart than sway her from her plans of revenge.

Cupping her neck, he let heat build in his palm, then slid it down her skin. At the intense sensation he created, she threw her head back and arched her body, thrusting her breast towards him. Following the line of her chest, Walker brushed her nipples with the power he held, enjoying the deepening of color in her areolas. Heat rebounded from her, making him shudder.

"Oh, Gods," she groaned between clenched teeth. "That feels like lightening."

"Good?" He knew the answer. He could tell by the way her lower body squirmed closer to his.

"Yes. Oh Walker."

He circled her other breast and caught her free nipple between his teeth, scraping the puckered bud. A strong urge to taste her desire, lap it from her core, leapt inside him. Her skin tasted so very good, like sunlight in the middle of the storm.

"Dammit," she said, mindless, her hands gripping his shoulders, tightening when he stroked her with his power, his heat.

His pleasure was intense just from watching her face as she came close to orgasm. Her full lips opened on another moan, her beautiful face pulled into lines of passion.

He had known he could do this, knew from the minute she touched him he could bring her with his power. What he hadn't known was how amazing it would feel to give her pleasure.

Licking her nipple, he lowered his hand, trailing along her flat stomach to press against her sex. Increasing the pressure in slow increments, he added power bit by bit. It took all his concentration, like a surgeon performing a complex operation. He wanted this to be perfect, to draw it out to bring her maximum enjoyment. He increased the heat, while rotating the heel of his hand. Capturing her nipple between his lips, he pressed warmth there as well.

She surged upwards against him and came with a wordless cry.

Water crashed over the side of the tub. Walker widened her legs to drop his knee between them, then caught her hips and impaled himself to the hilt before the water could wash away the slickness of her desire. His control snapped with the tightness of her channel.

The unexpected assault caused her pleasure to peak again and his orgasm washed through him as he lost control at the feel of her body contracting around his shaft in strong pulses.

"Raine!"

He held her as tightly as he could without crushing her in his arms.

Chapter Five

Raine carefully eased away from Walker and moved out from under the covers. It was cold as icy hell in the room, especially after sleeping cuddled tight against his always-warm body.

Throwing on a pair of pants, shirt and sweater, she dropped into a chair to put on her socks and shoes. She needed to check the weather. It had been a few days since the storm blew up.

Her body was sore and had a well-loved, heavy feel to it. As if she'd over-indulged—which she had. He'd kept her busy.

Gods, he could bring her to orgasm just by touching her. It had been all she could do to leave the bed.

But leave she must.

It was time to stop playing with Malachi and finish it once and for all.

Tugging on her parka, she strode towards the far wall. The person who'd owned the icehouse before her had put an observation nest in the ice and rock above her. Most of the time, she could open the main portal, but if the wind and snow had been as severe as she'd thought, she'd need to be elevated to see how bad things were. They might even have to exit that way, although if the snow had fallen that deep, they wouldn't be able to ride the Snow-doo into town. It was way too cold to walk.

Raine put gloves on before grabbing the first of the loops that had been inserted into the wall. Her skin had stuck to a metal object her first winter here, forcing her to peel off layers of flesh to get free.

Climbing the ladder at a fast clip, she reached the ceiling and opened the trapdoor.

She'd made every mistake in the book when she'd first come here, and the worst one had been in this room. She had opened the observation portal and enough snow had flooded in to not only briefly bury her, but cover the trapdoor. It had taken her hours to dig out by hand.

It had been unpleasant, but more than that, she'd been shaken, the accident proving just how alone she really was here.

She had learned to be more careful after that.

Pulling herself into the room, she went to what was essentially a round cutout in the rock, covered in a durable, clear plastic. In the non-winter months, it provided a beautiful view of the plain below. In the winter, frost covered it to the point she could see nothing.

The room temperature hovered below freezing, but she didn't close the trapdoor. After the last episode, she couldn't shut herself inside.

She grabbed the latch and tried to lower it so she could take a quick peek outside. It didn't budge. She put more pressure on it.

Then some more.

It must be frozen in place. That hadn't happened before.

She leaned on it a little more.

Then she hummed in irritation and jumped up to land her whole weight on the latch.

For a moment, she hung suspended.

With a snap, the window released. Raine plunged to the floor, and she had a moment to think, 'Oh shit,' before snow flooded into the room, covering her.

A loud thump told her the trapdoor had slammed shut under the onslaught.

In a panic, Raine fought her way to the surface. She gasped for breath. "Calm down, calm down, calm down," she counseled herself.

It wouldn't do to lose her cool. This had happened before, and she'd been just fine. She needed to save her strength to dig herself out.

Stumbling to her feet, she waded to the window. During the White Out, the wind had packed a large amount of snow onto the deep-set ledge.

"Architectural design flaw," she griped, as she stared out at the bright snowscape. They'd gotten perhaps ten feet of snow, maybe a little more. The good thing was she could get to town. The Snow-doo could handle the depth easily.

Shutting the view-port, she threw the latch into place.

"Idiot."

She waded back to the trapdoor and heard him.

"Raine! Raine! Where in the hell are you?" Walker's voice filtered up through the floor.

The slamming trapdoor must have woken him.

"Walker!" she yelled at the top of her lungs.

Long pause. "Raine?" Walker's voice came from far away. "Where are you?"

The echoes made his last sentence almost unrecognizable.

"The ceiling," she screamed.

She pictured him wandering around the room, looking up.

"I see the ladder."

"Don't come up!" She didn't want him wasting his energy trying to open the trapdoor. The snow would be too heavy to move. "I'm snowed in."

"Are you okay?" Even through the floor, she could hear his worry.

"Yes!"

She started digging.

An hour later, she was still burrowing her way out.

It was slow work and she'd stripped off the parka because she'd begun to sweat.

She was so caught up on her task that she didn't notice that the snow on top of the trapdoor was melting.

"It must be the heat from the room below." She picked up speed.

The ring handle appeared, and she grabbed it and yanked hard. The trapdoor thumped but didn't open. She knelt again and worked at the snow around the edges for several minutes.

When she tried again, the trapdoor lifted, and the snow on top slid off all at once. She went flying backwards.

Picking herself up, she grabbed her parka and pitched it down. Then she climbed through the hole, caught the door handle and closed the observation room with a bang.

She was on the ground again in seconds, but tripped on Walker's prone body when she turned.

"Walker!" She knelt down beside him, brushing her parka away from where it landed half covering his body. "Gods."

He lay on his back, one of his legs at an odd angle.

Green eyes blinked open, and she knew what he'd done. He'd heated the door to melt the snow. It had cut her captivity by hours, but he must have run out of energy and fallen from the top of the ladder. She couldn't believe he'd risked himself like this for her.

Blinking back tears, her heart twisting at the amazing thing he'd done for her, she asked, "How badly are you hurt?" She knew what to do now and threw off her gloves. "Your leg is broken. Anything else?"

He shook his head, only a small motion, and took shallow breaths.

"I take it you can't speak. That's bad, then." Her growing panic and pinging emotions made her furious. "This is unacceptable, Walker. I would have dug myself out eventually. It wasn't worth you getting hurt." She cupped his cheeks with her bare hands and leaned down to press her lips to his.

She had a flash of worry that he might not be able to heal himself. Then she pushed it from her mind.

Picturing a raging fire, she exhaled into his mouth. She had no idea if it would work, but figured if he could heal snow frosting and his hands the first day she met him, he could heal whatever he'd done to himself here.

He made a small noise, and she pulled back. "This working?" she asked.

Slowly, he nodded his head once. His eyes were big, and he gasped for breath. "Str…"

She leaned down, trying to decipher what he said.

"Straighten…" He took a deeper breath.

Meeting his eyes, she shook her head. "Noooo. Not your leg."

She glanced down at it, fighting nausea.

"No way," she thought or said or whatever.

"Must," he whispered on an exhale.

Raine closed her eyes and waged an internal battle, making sure she kept silent. She didn't want to freaking straighten his leg. It would hurt him and besides that, the thought was just plain creepy.

Looking down at his face again, she met his begging eyes and growled. "You are such an asshole for heating the door." She knelt by his leg and gave him begging eyes back. "Walker, love, I don't want to hurt you."

"Do," he said. "It."

She stabilized his upper thigh with one hand and caught the calf of the other. "Oh, Gods, I don't think I can."

"Must."

In one movement, she straightened the leg, making a crunching sound. She screamed along with him for several moments. "I'm sorry. I'm sorry." She laid herself across his chest.

When his breathing steadied, she stood and ran to her bed, tearing off the covers with a snap, suddenly angry at him again. "That was an idiot move, Walker." She sprinted back and dumped the covers beside him in a heap. "You were beyond dumb to use up all your energy until you fell."

From a nearby chest, she grabbed a thermal tarp, spread it next to him, threw one of the blankets over it, and rolled him on.

He groaned.

"Hurt, huh? Well, you deserve it!" She unfastened his jumpsuit to the crotch, then stripped off all her clothes. Picking up the two remaining blankets, she laid next to him and formed a cocoon. Then she framed his face in her hands. "What else is hurt? I think you need to feel as much of my skin as possible for this to work. Am I right?"

He gave her a brief nod.

"I don't want to hurt you."

She climbed over him and gently lowered her body until her chest brushed his. He hummed, and she thought it might be approval.

"This wasn't worth it," she lectured in between kisses. "I would have dug my way out in a couple hours."

For a long while, he lay passive beneath her. She settled down more fully on top of him, tentatively at first, then with more weight when he didn't protest.

"Have I told you that I think you're an idiot?" she asked again, still shaken to her core from setting his leg.

"Yes, I think you have," he said, his voice weak, but at least he could speak.

She met his gaze. His face was ashen, but his eyes were clearer.

"I'm furious at you."

"I can tell." His lips tipped up in a brief smile.

She licked across him mouth, then deepened to run her tongue across his. Warmth, she thought. Heat. Liquid fire. His tongue felt rough and soft at the same time.

He gasped.

She grinned. "I can almost feel the heat transfer, if I concentrate."

"It's amazing. I've never known anyone could do anything like this." He licked his lips as if he wanted to taste her again. "My father never said it was possible."

Underneath her body, his erection had worked its way from between the flaps of his jumpsuit.

She rubbed across it with her own sex, enjoying the silky smooth feel of the head of his cock sliding across her clitoris.

He closed his eyes and groaned.

"Am I hurting you?" she asked, concerned because the sound could mean pleasure or pain.

"No."

Raine didn't think it would be polite to experiment, but she wondered if sex would speed his healing. It seemed to the first day she'd met him.

He whispered her name as she slid down his body, pressing kisses into his flesh.

"Gods, your body is amazing." She liked him with a sheen of sweat highlighting all his muscles, but he looked pretty damn good dry.

On impulse, she bit his hip. He arched up and groaned. She filed away the response for later thought. Right now, she wanted to run her mouth along other things. She loved the feel of his skin below her lips, the taste of his body—heat and hard muscle.

Using only the tip of her tongue, she licked up his long, straight shaft, all the way to the top. A small amount of liquid pooled on the head, and she sucked it off, interested to see what he tasted like. The liquid was hot and had a salty, sharp taste that was so very different from anyone else in any universe. She ran her tongue over the tip again.

"Woman, please," Walker said, but Raine wasn't exactly sure what he was asking for, except that he didn't want her to stop.

She'd done this before to other men, of course, but everything about Walker was fresh and new. She worked her tongue into the hole at the tip of his cock to get another taste of him.

He writhed under her.

He tastes like summer. Like a beautiful summer morning, when you walk onto your porch and taste the beauty of a hot day. Crisp, fresh, with just the brief burn of heat underlying it.

He groaned, his eyes tightly shut.

She covered the head with her mouth and suckled him. Then she released and ran her tongue up his shaft once again.

Pressing a hand within his jumpsuit, she cupped the twin sacs below his erection. Rolling them gently between her fingers, she wondered why she hadn't done this before. *Because he's always been taking care of your pleasure.* The realization slammed into her and for a moment, she pulled away.

Walker whimpered at the loss, and she hastily took him into her mouth again.

In fact, he's always pleasuring you first, Raine. She'd been selfish in the extreme and hadn't even realized it.

She ran her mouth down his shaft, squeezing his balls at the same time. Using her free hand, she circled the bottom of his cock so he would feel totally covered and began a slow up and down glide.

She might have received more than she'd given in bed, but it wasn't too late to make it up to him, starting now.

Gradually, she increased the movement, flicking her gaze up to his face to judge her speed. She was careful not to touch his hurt leg.

A sheen of sweat covered his chest. Good. He'd gotten hot enough for that, at least.

She increased her speed when she tasted another drop of pre-come, watching as his thigh muscles became rock hard on either side of her. Every taste made her own desire climb that much higher.

"Raine." His whole body shuddered under her as he pumped deep inside her mouth. She drank him in, enjoying the burst of taste and the shivers of pleasure that tore through his body. Feeling powerful and pleased she could give him such pleasure, she was reluctant to move when he finished. But she knew the value of a hug after a person had climaxed. It felt like heaven to be held when your body was fulfilled.

As she curled into him, she was struck by the thought of what her life would be like once her plan for revenge on Malachi was fulfilled, and Walker would leave her.

Damn. She'd only known him for a handful of days and already it hurt to even think about losing him.

Chapter Six

"No." Walker tried to make it sound as final as possible. It had been three days since he'd broken his leg, but they had generated enough heat to heal it several times over.

His mate continued to work herself into the snowsuit.

"Raine," he growled.

"Use your head, Walker. You cannot travel to the trading station only wearing the clothes you came here with."

"I don't want you going without me." Anger raced through his bloodstream at the thought of her leaving. What if something happened to her while she was gone? He wouldn't be able to reach her. He'd be stuck here while she needed him. The thought twisted his guts into knots.

She rolled her eyes and stood up to bring the suit over her shoulders.

He crossed the room and grabbed her arms. "I'm being serious."

"You're not thinking this through."

"I'll go with you." He forced himself to sound reasonable.

"You'll freeze to death without a snowsuit."

"I didn't freeze on the way here," he pointed out, trying to gentle his voice.

"You were walking, which kept your blood circulating. I'll be sitting still in the Snow-doo." She shook her head. "I'm just going in to buy you clothes and arrange passage to Borrus for us with a freighter captain I know."

"I don't like it." He heard the snarl in his voice, made worse by the fact his teeth were clenched.

"Too bad." She smiled sweetly at him.

"I'm not letting you go."

"We have to get to Borrus."

"Forget Borrus." The words slipped out before he had a chance to stop them.

Her eyes narrowed.

He relented to cover his slip. "What if you are hurt, and I can't reach you?"

"I'm not the one who keeps getting injured," she pointed out.

She turned to walk to a nearby chest and stared at his hand when he didn't let her go. He debated the wisdom of holding her, then figured he still had a chance to talk her out of going. Finger by finger, he released her arm.

"What about when you hurt your back?"

She snorted. "Come on. That was two years ago." Opening the lid, she rummaged until she found whatever she sought.

"What if Delmundo is waiting for you at the trading station?"

She ambled back in his direction and laughed, the sound a little crazed. Grabbing her stomach with both hands, she doubled over, closing the distance between them.

"Are you all right?" He thought she seemed overly amused and tried to puzzle out this latest mood of hers.

She straightened, swept his feet right out from under him with one well placed kick and rolled him to his stomach.

It happened in seconds.

The restraints were in place by the time he tried to sit.

"You bitch!"

She *tsked* at him. "Such language," she purred, her husky alto sending tremors straight to his groin. Two pops sounded when she clamped on the leg restraints.

"You held them and pretended to laugh." When he worked his way free, he was going to tan her hide. Or screw her senseless.

"I'm going in to the trading station to buy you clothes." She turned him onto his back. "I'll return before night."

"Spend the time you're gone preparing yourself for my revenge." He tried to sit, but found it impossible with his hands shackled behind his back.

She batted her eyes at him. "I thought you didn't believe in vengeance."

He scowled at her. "I'm willing to make an exception."

"Fantastic! I love a good retaliation." She pecked his cheek quickly and stood. "I'll be back."

She had the gall to wink at him.

"You're going to be very sorry."

"I hope so," she said, jogging across the room. At the table, she stopped and laid a set of keys down. "Just in case something happens, you can let yourself out once you make it over here."

"When I get my hands on you—" He didn't finish, because she disappeared into the entrance tunnel.

"Raine!" he shouted at the top of his lungs.

Staring up at the ceiling, he took five calming breaths and then another ten. He needed to control his worry for her. Otherwise, it would be a long day.

If something happened to her while she was gone, he would find the person responsible and kill them with his bare hands.

He hadn't realized being in love would be such a pain in the ass.

Raine pulled the Snow-doo into the barn and shut off the engine. It was already dark, and she thanked the Gods it hadn't snowed again while she was gone, because she'd had to follow her own tracks for the last ten leagues of the return trip.

She was bone weary, so tired she could drop. Cutting the engine, she opened the door and hopped down. She slung her packages over her shoulder and hiked back to the house, moving slow.

Driving the Snow-doo wasn't difficult but the older model she'd been forced to buy when she'd gotten here vibrated to the point her spine jarred in agony with every bump. Her arms were jelly. She'd never gone to the trading station and back in one day before.

Sighing, she struggled through the snow to the upper entrance tunnel. She had to use the upper tunnel because of the recent snow fall, but the drift didn't quite make it all the way to the top. Opening the portal, she tossed in the packages before hauling herself up. It took her two tries to heave herself inside.

She rolled far enough in so she could close the portal, then lay back panting for a few moments.

"Hard day?" Walker's voice filtered through the dark.

Raine jumped, catching her chest with her hand. "Gods, you scared me."

He moved closer, grabbing the shoulders of her snowsuit and dragging her down most of the hallway.

"Walker!" What in the hell was he doing?

"I can't lift you until you're far enough in for me to stand."

"I don't need to be carried!"

He didn't stop pulling her. "It's frustrating when somebody does something you don't like but you can't stop them, isn't it?" His voice sounded calm. Too calm.

Oh shit, she thought. *He's mad.*

"Shit is right. You are in so much trouble, I can't even begin to describe it to you."

With one heave, he had her over his shoulder. He strode across the room and dumped her on the bed, then went back into the hall. Raine started to sit up, but then fell back, too exhausted to make the effort.

He returned with her bags, shaking the clothing she'd purchased for him out onto the floor.

"I went to buy you clothes, you ungrateful wretch." Raine figured a good defense might be a good offense right about now.

He sorted through them. "Good. This way you won't be able to leave without me again," he said absently, his attention focused on the clothes. "What's this?" He held up a suit worn by visiting dignitaries on Borrus. She'd bought it second hand and was quite proud of the purchase.

"Your disguise. It's part of my plan."

His intense, green gaze flicked away from the cloth to her face. "Let's talk about this plan."

"I've booked passage for us tomorrow. We leave right before dusk." She blinked and realized she only had to look at him and need began to build inside her.

"The plan," he said, throwing down the suit and stalking over to her.

She couldn't do very much but watch him. Her body wasn't functioning properly. She groaned when she thought about the return trip in the morning.

"What?" he asked.

"I'm not looking forward to tomorrow's trip to the trading station."

"Why?"

"My body is beaten to pieces. The Snow-doo vibrates so hard, I feel like my spine is compressed into an excruciating mass."

He squatted beside the bed. "You're in pain."

She sniffed. She wasn't going to ask him to heal her, not with his attitude. Just because she'd restrained him, he'd gotten all fussy with her. "I'm fine."

"I'll drive us into town."

"You've driven a Snow-doo before?" She wondered when he'd have a chance. Certainly not in HeFO.

"No. You're going to teach me." He grabbed her snowsuit and parted it in one motion. "I'm not very happy with you."

"I did what I had to do." She infused her tone with righteousness.

"No, Raine, you took the easy way out."

"You were being unreasonable." She could hear the defensiveness in her voice.

He lifted her shoulders so he could take off the suit. "I'm not going to Borrus with you unless you agree right here and now that all decisions are going to be joint ones."

Raine felt her eyes grow wide. "Wait a second."

"No, you wait, Raine," he snapped, tightening his hold on her arm. "Agree that everything either of us does will be decided upon by both of us, or you can go to Borrus by yourself."

"But—" She couldn't believe how angry he sounded.

"No buts!" He hauled her up until she sat. "None."

He was being unreasonable, but then she realized that there wasn't any need to fight him on this. He was her team for this mission. Teams always communicated and agreed on the plan, or everything would blow into pieces at the crucial moment.

"Fine," she said, not being very gracious about it.

"You'll consult me in everything." He dragged the snowsuit to her waist.

"Yes."

"Swear it."

"What?"

"Swear and I'll believe you." The muscle in his jaw flexed and he pushed her onto her back. One by one, he removed her boots and threw them so hard, they bounced off the far wall. He dragged down the suit and flung it away as if burned him. A thrill rode through her, tingles zinging in her veins even though his hands had just brushed her in a light sweep.

He was really worked into a snit.

"You won't take my word?" She tried to sound insulted, but it was hard around all the guilt she'd felt today. It must have been agony for him to have the cold eating into his skin while he slid across the ice floor to reach the keys on the table.

"No, I won't just take your word."

"What kind of oath are we talking about here?" They were tricky things, and she had to be careful. She didn't want to commit to something she couldn't stand by, no matter how much guilt she felt over leaving him locked up.

"Swear on your life you won't do anything without consulting me first."

She thought about her wording long and hard. "I promise on my life not to do anything without telling you first, unless it is a decision I have to make in the heat of the moment."

"Not good enough."

"It will have to be. I must be in a position to act if I need to."

"You're much too spontaneous." His face was hard.

"How do you figure that?" She dragged up a blanket from the bed, suddenly cold. She *was* too spontaneous. It was part of her charm.

"You didn't preplan locking me up."

"I needed to go and you weren't going to let me. I could tell." It was weird, fighting with him like this. As if they'd known each other so much longer than a week.

From behind his back, he pulled out her spare knife and threw it into the wall next to her.

"What in the hell are you doing!" Raine jumped to her feet, her mouth hanging open, the blanket dropping to the floor.

"That's how I feel when I deal with you, Raine." He closed the distance between them. "Like you're going to do some crazy thing any second."

For a moment, she couldn't speak, staring at the knife embedded in the wall. She just opened and closed her mouth, struggling for words. "You went through my trunks!"

He had put some serious skill behind the throw. The action had the appearance of something practiced and artfully done.

"I went through every trunk, drawer and bag in this place. You should think twice before you leave me here alone again." The satisfied gleam in his eyes showed he relished telling her that.

Her mouth dropped open. "How could you!"

"That's what I thought when you put the cuffs on me." He grinned like a space-pirate.

She closed her eyes and took a big breath. Okay, he had a right to do that, she told herself.

"Yes, I did." He narrowed his eyes and covered her hand with his. "We can talk things out, Raine."

Her eyes snapped open. "Look." She poked him in the chest. "I am sorry you forced me to lock you up, but we can't stay here for the rest of our lives, and you can't leave without clothes."

"Once I stopped fantasizing about wringing your neck for leaving me in shackles, I realized you had to go. I'm not the crazy one of our team."

Raine threw her hands in the air and walked a circle. "I didn't think you'd change your mind."

"I would have. I wouldn't have been happy, but you were right. You needed to go."

She strode to the knife and blew out a breath. It was buried half way up the blade. "Nicely thrown." She met his gaze. "You have talent."

He shrugged and seemed a little embarrassed. "Yeah, well, we're discussing your oath."

"If I give you my word, what do you give in return?"

He came to stand before her. His hand snaked into her hair, anchoring them together. "I promise to protect you with everything I have, heal you when you're hurt, and stand at your back no matter what mess you drag us into."

She blinked up at him for two heartbeats. It was the most beautiful thing anyone had ever said to her. "Then I give you my word." Her voice was hoarse around the odd lump growing her chest. How could she have known him such a short time and already feel this gut-wrenching closeness to him?

"And I give you mine."

His lips crashed onto hers, his kiss so filled with passion, it took her breath away.

Chapter Seven

Walker was as nervous as a barefoot blind man in a room full of tacks. Dressed in a uniform which would allow him to blend in on Borrus as one of the many dignitaries that congregated there, and the snowsuit Raine had purchased for him, he paced by her side, his hood keeping him hidden. She had said they would be leaving on a transport an acquaintance of hers owned, but they had to walk through the trading station to reach the launch pad.

For a brief moment, he allowed himself to take stock of where he stood with Raine. He'd taken a grave risk forcing her to swear the night before, but he'd been lucky. It had paid off. With her agreement to include him in all her decisions, he had moved one step closer to binding her mind to him. She would now need to factor him into everything she did. Her body was already locked to his. He thought he might have woven some small threads between their hearts as well. He'd caught something in her eyes that told him she cared about him, both last night and when he'd broken his leg.

Walker sighed and forced himself to concentrate on his surroundings. He had a week left before they reached Borrus to work on her.

Inter-world Council troops marched between warming huts spaced around the station. His stomach tightened as they walked past them. He didn't want to be caught now that he had found his mate. He'd reached a point during his stay in HeFO when he'd just wanted to die, but now he wanted to live. With Raine. He touched his gloved hand to Raine's waist and smiled at her when she glanced his way.

They passed through an archway and spilled out to the launch pad. Raine guided them between transports until they arrived at one in the back corner.

"Trond," she said, flipping off her hood and extending her arm.

She didn't smile, and Walker had the feeling she didn't like the man, even though they shook hands.

"I thought you weren't gonna show, Stormy Weather." The man

laughed, a huffing sound that matched his scarred and distorted face. He'd been born with one side wider than the other. Things had gone from bad to worse after that. Someone had carved him up on both cheeks, leaving raised white scars.

"We had to drive in this morning. It took longer than I had anticipated."

Raine didn't lie exactly. They had driven in, but they had also sold the Snow-doo and her icehouse. When he'd asked her why, she informed him she wasn't coming back to Sector 9. One way or another, she would live or die someplace else.

"Guess the weather held you up." He glanced at Walker. "Who you?"

"Does it matter?" Raine asked him, bringing Trond's gaze back to hers. "We leaving now?"

"Yes." He waved them into the transport. "My co-pilot is sick with a hangover, so you probably won't see him this trip."

"Hold!" A guard marched towards them. "I need to see papers if you're leaving. We're checking for escaped prisoners."

The soldier stuck out his hand to Walker first.

Walker only had fleeting moment to decide what to do. They needed to leave, and a quick glance around told him they were hidden by other transports. As a Healer, he'd sworn to use his powers only for good, but his need to protect his mate came before that vow. Raine would be sent to prison for aiding him. At all costs, he had to prevent that from happening. "Here you go," he said, and placed his own hand in the guard's. He was still reluctant to do harm, but made himself push power into the guard. Not too much, he didn't want to permanently harm him.

"What are you doing?" The guard tried to pull his hand away.

Walker tightened his fingers. From the corner of his vision, he could see Raine's mouth drop open.

He shoved heat and power through their connected hands, pushing past the gloves they both wore. The guard began to sweat profusely but was so confused, all he could ask was, "What are you doing?" over and over again.

Just a little bit more. He'd accidentally done this once before. He could cause a person to pass out by temporarily elevating their body temperature.

Sure enough, the guard's knees buckled and he fell forward.

"What is going on?" Trond demanded.

"Shut up." Raine's voice held authority. She backed him despite the fact she must be as confused as the pilot. Walker's heart warmed at the thought.

"What?" The guard slumped forward, passing out into the snow.

Walker dragged him behind the shelter of some crates, then strode back to the ship. "Let's go."

Raine closed her mouth and rounded on Trond. "You heard him. Get this heap into the atmosphere, pronto!"

"What did you do back on Sector 9?" Raine whispered to Walker. She was still reeling from what had happened and couldn't get her mind around it.

They were sitting in Trond's general room, which matched the rest of the ship's run down, ill kept interior. Since Trond had cobbled together parts from different transports, the seats were different shades of green and gray and had a sticky, grimy sheen to them. Panels on the walls stood open, exposed wiring dripping out. Raine hadn't had a lot of choices in transportation.

"Nothing," Walker mumbled, not moving from where he'd sat when they'd gotten onto the transport.

Raine snapped off her shoulder harness and went to kneel beside him. Something was wrong. She hadn't noticed it before because she was just too freaked out to concentrate on anything else but her own thoughts.

She had a sneaking suspicion she knew what the problem was. Flipping off her glove, she placed her hand onto his cheek, making him jump at the unexpected movement.

His skin was ice cold.

"That's what I thought. You're freezing."

Walker snapped his head away, but she'd only needed a brief touch to figure out what she wanted to know.

"Every time you use your talent, you end up an ice cube."

"It's that damn planet," he murmured, lowering his head into his hands. "Gods, I just wish I could live someplace swelteringly hot."

"Well, there are easy ways to build your heat level."

He spread his fingers to stare at her with one eye. "I'm listening." Although his voice sounded tired, there was a thread of humor running through it.

"A few kisses should boost you, right?"

He dropped his hand. “You were exhausted last night so I left you alone. I’m not sure I can stop with just a few kisses, Raine.”

His green eyes sparkled, and his gaze raked her from lips to breasts, narrowing as if he could see her nipples harden in reaction under her snowsuit.

“Sit back,” she said, pushing in between his legs to kneel where she could reach him. “I’ll make you warm again.” Power swelled through her, not magic, but pride mixed with desire. That she could do this for him gave her a heady rush similar to the first time she’d returned from a mission with the team and she knew she’d done brilliantly.

She grabbed the top pockets of his snowsuit and pulled him forward, surprised at how much she wanted him. She’d only gone a day without, but it felt like much longer.

Their lips met and she forgot about warming him as her own desire began to build, heat pooling deep in her belly. She moved closer, restless and wanting. Tugging open his snowsuit in one sweep, she ached with the need to touch him, stroke the hard, corded muscles of his body.

She broke away to gasp for air. “What happened to the guard, Walker?” Pulling his shirt up, she ran her fingers across his flat abs, enjoying the feel of his body. The smell of summer heat curled around her.

Walker rested his face in the crook of her neck, his hands banded around her, his warm breath whispering across her skin. “It’s one of the things I can do with my talent. I can warm to varying degrees, which can heal or hurt.”

“Is he dead?”

“Just unconscious. He should have woken in time to watch us leave, although he’ll be groggy for awhile.”

She sighed. “You freaked Trond out. I hope he doesn’t go run his mouth. I’ll have to have a conversation with him.” The pilot could turn out to be a large problem.

His lips whispered across the bare skin of her neck, making her shiver. “The situation seemed to call for fast action.” Regret filled his voice.

“I’m not upset. We just need to deal with it.” She considered the money she’d earned from the sale of the icehouse. It was enough to pay Trond off, or at least keep his mouth shut for awhile. The problem with buying silence was that people tended to get greedy and demand more.

"I don't suppose we can count on him to be discrete?"

She grinned and pressed her lips into his temple. Sometimes he was so naïve. She found it kind of cute. "No. He's an asshole of the first order, but we needed a transport and he's not one to ask questions."

"The incident with the guard may cause Sector 9 to communicate with the Council police on Borrus to warn them we're coming." He tangled his hands in her hair, raking his nails across her scalp.

She fought the urge to purr, placing a kiss onto the inside of his wrist instead. "We filed a flight plan going to Sector 12. We headed that direction until we were well out of Sector 9's tracking system, then turned. I seriously doubt they'll guess our destination."

He nodded, seeming to accept that. "What's our plan once we land?"

She'd been waiting for him to ask. "We need to talk to Rory Uslep," she murmured and licked across his pulse point.

He blinked several times, as if he struggled to keep his mind on the topic at hand. His eyelids had lowered, giving his dark green gaze the heavy, passion filled look she loved. "Who the hell is Rory Uslep?"

"One of the three representatives of Galaxy Grid 219. He's known as the man of the people. I figure he'll jump at the chance to prove your innocence, especially if he knows we'll give him all the credit, and he won't have to do any of the work."

Walker was speechless. He had no idea Raine planned to prove him innocent, only that she wanted revenge against Malachi Delmundo. He cupped her chin and studied her face. He knew she belonged to him. The way she responded to his power convinced him she was fated to be by his side. What she did to his body, heart and mind made him want to cradle her close for the rest of their lives.

On one level, there was intense desire and physical fulfillment, but underlying that was the respect he had for her courage, her discipline, and her brave heart. He enjoyed just sitting beside her, holding her hand with their fingers laced together. Earlier, when he'd thrown her knife into the wall, he'd loved it that he'd tilted her off balance, that he'd gained her admiration for his knife skills and brought her a step closer to seeing him as a mate worthy to stand by her side.

Her desire to prove his innocence made his heart constrict, even though he doubted it would be possible for her to succeed.

"Raine, I don't want you to take any risks for me. I think you're going to find that this revenge you plan isn't worth it." He had a sudden flash, a vision of her bloody and torn, lying on a floor, the red of the setting sun clashing with the pink marble under her and the blood on her chest. It made his fingers spasm on her chin.

She hissed in a breath.

"I'm sorry," he whispered and pressed a kiss on the red mark where his thumb had been. He blew a healing breath into her skin. Laving the spot with his tongue, he had the satisfaction of watching her tip her head so he could continue unimpeded down her neck.

He wanted to give her something wonderful, erase the vision he'd just seen in his mind. Pushing her back, he dropped to his knees, lowering her until she lay flat. His fingers made quick work of her snowsuit, then the blouse she wore beneath.

Resisting the temptation to use his power to bring her to orgasm, he used only his mouth in whispering touches. A lick here and suckle there, he savored the taste of his woman and the soft texture of her skin under his lips. He drew her nipple into his mouth and brushed the tip of his tongue softly across the tight bud.

"Oh, he's so good," she murmured. "Amazing. Better than anything I've ever had."

Walker grinned. He hoped she never stopped talking to herself out loud. He loved hearing her uncensored thoughts.

Nibbling down her stomach, he ran his tongue under the band to her panties. Raine arched and moaned below him.

"You make me feel like I'm going to explode inside, like the sky is twirling out of control." Her warm, wonderful hands tunneled in his hair as he eased the snowsuit off, taking her pants with it.

"Mmmm…" he hummed, always loving the look of her body. It was as if he saw it for the first time whenever he undressed her. She was slim, but totally in shape, a mixture of hard muscle and soft woman. Beautiful.

He pressed his face into her panties, nuzzling her clitoris lovingly with the tip of his tongue.

"Oh!" She started to sit up, but he pinned her down with his hands on her stomach and licked through the cloth of her underwear.

Her legs fell slack to the sides, and he took the opportunity to lie more comfortably between them. One hand traced up her body to roll a nipple with his thumb and forefinger.

He felt strong, his energy restored with only the touch of their bodies. His father had told him his mate could do this, but he was overwhelmed by the actual experience.

Keeping her panties in place, he moved his tongue over the fabric, wanting to heighten her pleasure with the rough texture of the cloth. She was soaking wet, her amazing scent wrapping about him, pulling at his own desire, but he ignored his needs.

She wanted to prove his innocence. The thought had his mind spinning in joy.

He knew she still planned to go her separate way when they finished this mission. But he was a step closer to winning her heart and mind. She cared enough to try to exonerate him.

He sucked her clit into his mouth through the white Moresung fabric. Raine almost levitated off the floor.

"Walker!" Her head tossed back and forth.

She was close. He could feel her orgasm just out of reach.

He swept aside her underwear and blew warm air on her wet sex.

She shivered and tried to close her legs at the sensation.

"Come for me, Raine," he murmured, before burying the tip of his tongue underneath the sensitive bud and fighting his way upwards.

Her hands tried to grab his hair, but it was too short for her to hang on.

"I," she said. But she didn't continue. Her orgasm shuddered through her on the word.

"Love," he whispered, gathering her limp body into his lap.

"Nice," Trond said from behind them.

Chapter Eight

Raine tried to surface up from the haze of complete satisfaction. Someone had spoken and it wasn't Walker.

Her man held her body on his lap, curling around to protect her from whomever stood in the doorway.

Her man? Well, he was kind of hers, she supposed. Certainly he wasn't anyone else's.

"Mind if we have a little privacy, Trond?" Walker's voice sounded deadly, even as his hand gently pressed her into his chest.

"I came to talk to you about that little scene on Sector 9." Trond didn't sound impressed with Walker's bravado, which didn't surprise Raine. Trond wasn't known for his brilliance.

Raine tried to put her mind in gear. Nudity had never really embarrassed her. She kept clothed because men tended to get out of hand around a naked woman. Fighting them had always been a pain in the rear.

She leaned against Walker's arm so she could sit. He didn't want to let her, but finally eased enough so he could meet her gaze.

"Let me handle him," she said, and kissed his full, masculine lips.

He hadn't lost his erection with their uninvited visitor, and the kiss caused his cock to jump under his clothes, brushing her thigh where she sat across his lap. He growled in her ear to let her know he wasn't pleased to let her up.

Her legs were shaky, but she managed to stand gracefully. This wouldn't work if she stumbled or tried to cover herself. At first, Walker's hands impeded her attempt to rise, then assisted her. She smiled, gathered her clothes in her hand and sauntered past Trond to the head. "Don't worry, Trond, we'll pay for your silence. Just don't get too greedy. I would hate to have to kill you to keep you quiet."

Trond's eyes snapped from her breasts to her face, and she could tell he believed her. It was in the frowning mouth, twitching eyelid, and narrowing eyes.

She wasn't surprised when he turned insulting. After all, in a way she'd insulted him by not caring if he saw her nude.

"You think you're man enough to kill me, Stormy Weather?" he sneered

"I don't have to be a man to kill you." As she walked past, she swept his feet out from under him and pushed his back so he fell face down on the floor. It happened so fast, he couldn't fully catch himself with his hands, and his forehead smashed into the floor with a thump.

Walker materialized beside her and rested a booted foot on Trond's shoulder. "I suggest you stay there and catch your breath. Bad things happen to people who threaten my woman."

Hmmm, Raine thought, careful to keep silent. Seems she wasn't the only one becoming a tad possessive.

Since Trond couldn't see her from his place on the floor, she put an added swing into her hips and smiled saucily at Walker as she left the room.

Trond yelled as Walker shifted his weight and leaned hard on his booted foot.

Borrus.

It was good to be back again, Walker thought. The atmosphere here was ideal for humans, the weather mild and the location centralized so that trade flowed in and out, bringing any item a man might want. It was perfect—so perfect that it was horribly crowded in certain parts of the Capital City.

He wasn't quite sure how they were going to pull off Raine's plan, even after she'd explained the whole thing through twice. But he had to admit, his woman was a mastermind at strategy. She'd casually thrown out that she had done all the planning for her team.

He'd also been impressed with the way she'd handled Trond. Just the right combination of force and negotiation had caused the pilot to accept their deal, when he clearly wanted more money. She'd been firm on the price, although she'd paid him more than Walker would have liked.

They went to one of the seediest hotels he'd ever stayed in, but Raine had told him it was in the factory district, one of the few parts of town Malachi didn't control. The air here was thick with smoke from the nearby factories, chasing away most people and making it a perfect hide out.

As they checked in, the desk clerk flirted with Raine until Walker leaned over the counter, grabbed his shirt front and pulled him forward. He smiled and said politely, "Room key, please."

The pimple-faced clerk nodded rapidly, and Walker set him down so he could follow his orders.

"El...Elevator's broken," the younger man stammered. "Gotta take the stairs." He pointed to the stairwell door.

Raine led the way, not saying anything until the door banged shut. "Nice he-man routine there, Walker."

"That imbecile deserved a scare. I think he would have flirted with you for as long as you let him."

She turned on the stair, brushing the wall with her shoulder. Peeling paint rained onto the floor. "Wait a second, you don't think I was encouraging him, do you?"

Walker laughed. He couldn't help it. Raine was so far out of the clerk's league, the thought was comical. "No, I thought you were being nice." In fact, she was way above Walker's league. But the Gods had matched them, for which he would be eternally grateful.

"Oh." She turned and climbed to the landing. "We'll need to meet with Rory at the Naked Lady tonight."

"We're going to a strip club to meet a Senator?"

"Yeah, well, he tends to hang there at night while the Senate's in session. It's kind of his home away from Galaxy Grid 219."

Walker held open the door for her to pass into the dimly lit corridor. "So it's a dive?"

She grinned. "How'd you know?"

Walker strode quickly down the hall to the room, afraid his feet might attach to the floor if he paused on the sticky carpet. "Just a guess."

Raine watched Walker close the bathroom door and stripped off her clothes as fast as she could. Time was tight but she had to have him before they left to meet Rory.

Just the thought of him inside her made her breasts heavy with desire and her panties soaking wet. She wiggled out of them, throwing her clothes onto the room's only chair.

When Walker opened the door, she stood casually posed against the dresser, half sitting on the edge. She gave him a challenging look, feeling like a temptress for the first time in her life. Every particle of her being was involved in this seduction. He had to come to her, touch her, love her. In only a few hours, their revenge would begin, and they wouldn't have time for love play.

Walker dropped a shoulder against the doorframe. "Gods, you're beautiful, Raine." His gaze wandered her body like a caress.

"I'm in the mood for you." She lowered her voice, infusing it with promise. She traced a circle around one breast, a thrill shooting through her when his eyes became heavy-lidded, his gaze following her hand.

She swept over the nipple, then squeezed it, sucking in a breath at how good it felt to see his erection strain against the front of his pants.

"Cup your breasts," he murmured.

When she did, he rewarded her by pulling off his shirt, revealing his muscled chest. He was perfectly formed, down to the swath of light brown hair that tapered into his pants.

"Brush your nipples with your thumbs."

She did as he asked, watching his reactions, and a zing ran straight to her clitoris when his hands balled into fists. She licked her lips against the physical ache to taste him.

The action made him unbutton his pants. "Sit on the dresser."

She had never known him to be so demanding before, although she'd seen flashes of this part of his personality. He might be laid back, but he certainly had moments when he could be forceful. It made her even hotter. She levered herself onto the cool metal of the dresser.

He toed off his boots and left them on the floor without taking his gaze off her. "Spread your legs so I can see how much you want me."

She widened them, cupping her breasts again. Liquid desire pooled inside her and slid past the lips of her sex.

His eyes flicked behind her, and she realized he watched in the mirror as well. For a moment, she was self-conscious about the scar on her back, but she pushed the feelings aside.

"Dip a finger inside yourself and tell me if you're ready."

Prolonging his anticipation, she pinched her nipples a second longer, then dropped a hand to meander down her stomach. She brushed the outside of her sex a few times.

"Raine," he growled.

His impatience turned her on even more. She pressed a finger inside her channel, sliding on her own wetness, then pulling out to stroke across her clit. Her gaze never left his body.

He ripped off his pants and stood trembling in the doorway. Sweat covered his skin, making her hum. She loved him hot like this, full of power and life.

Then he strode across the room, determination mixing with the lust in his eyes. "I was left unfulfilled on the ship." He grabbed her hand from between her thighs and licked across her wet fingers. "I don't want to be gentle."

She blinked at him, her brain slow and unfocused with desire. "Then don't be."

He growled low in his throat, whisking her off the dresser and turning her to face the mirror. "I'm going to take my pleasure," he rasped from between gritted teeth. "Keep up or I'll leave you behind."

She laughed at the thought, since she was on the edge of orgasm, but stopped when he bent her forward. His feet widened her stance until she stood on tiptoes, supporting herself with her hands on the dresser. He was so strong, he could easily overpower her. The thought made her hiss in a breath with need.

Keeping one hand on her back to pin her, he met her gaze in the mirror and prodded her entrance from behind. Her body shook with anticipation.

And then he was inside, penetrating with a slow glide that just kept going until he reached the top of her passage.

His eyes narrowed into slits of green, and he pulled his cock out half way. "Take all of me," he ordered, as if she hadn't on purpose.

She pushed her buttocks up and back as he came home again, slamming into her this time. A flash of painful pleasure shot through her.

"Yes," he praised, closing his eyes and tightening his hold on her hips.

Raine knew she only needed two more thrusts and she would climax. She inhaled a rough breath, his scent filling her lungs and adding to her desire.

He withdrew, then returned, picking up a rhythm that had nothing to do with her pleasure. His teeth bared in a silent growl.

It didn't matter, because she was coming.

Right.

Now.

She peaked and jerked through a soul splitting orgasm, but he continued to ride her.

Forcing her eyes open, she watched his face tighten into harsh planes and his arms bulge as his own release drew close. He was so magnificent, so absolutely male, covered in sweat and muscles, the smell of their mingled desire curling around her to clutch at her heart.

He tossed his head back, the muscles in his neck, arms and chest bunching with tension, and came on a shout. She could feel him pumping into her, and another orgasm ran through her body, catching her by surprise, making her scream his name.

Staring at her own reflection in the mirror, Raine watched her body shake uncontrollably with the after-shocks of pleasure. A painful sense of loss struck her at the thought of when they would part company. Squeezing her eyes shut against the image, her heart clenched and stuttered. She was too caught up in him, already too attached. How had this happened to her so quickly?

Chapter Nine

The owner of the Naked Lady didn't spend a lot of money on lighting. Everything was so worn down, the clientele might have turned around at the door if they had been able to see clearly. A long bar ran the length of the left wall, the seats taken by a boisterous crowd cheering the dancers on two stages. The front platform shimmied with a well-endowed blonde, the tiny silver disks adhered to her nipples blinking in the spotlights to match the patch of red, shiny fabric between her legs. The second stage held a nude redhead who spun upside down by her legs from a pole, her long hair sweeping the floor as she twirled.

Raine knew that the Naked Lady was only packed with patrons when the Senate was in Session. Since Rory used this as his home base while on Borrus, people had to wait to see him in the strip club, paying the two drink minimum.

They had been here for two hours, but Raine knew Rory would move her up to the head of the line as quickly as he could. For most of the time, he'd been speaking with a fat man who had the look of a fellow Senator. When that man had left, Rory had met her gaze, but another man ran to his table and started speaking, his words blurred but panicked.

Rory smiled at her and shrugged. She grinned back.

"You know him?" Walker had noticed the by-play.

"I did him a favor once. He owes me." She stirred her drink but didn't take a sip. She couldn't be the least bit distracted for the upcoming interview. She'd have to play her cards right to get everything she wanted.

"What kind of favor?" Walker's tone turned cold, and she focused on him.

"Are you asking if I've slept with him? Because if you are, the answer is no. The team took care of a problem for him." Was she irritated or glad at his possessiveness? Maybe a bit of both, she decided, not liking her conclusion.

He said nothing, but stared at her. Raine found it hard to concentrate on their conversation when her eyes lighted on a dancer standing between the legs of a man sitting at the next table. It appeared she planned to spend the whole evening wiggling her generous butt on his crotch.

Walker tapped her hand. "What problem?"

"I can't tell you, Walker."

"He wants you. I can feel it from here."

"You're getting a wee tad bit possessive, don't you think? First the clerk, then this." They were both getting out of control. It frightened her. They were moving too fast.

Green eyes danced in the dim lighting, capturing her as effectively as his hands did when they squeezed her wrists. Power pushed through his skin. It sizzled along her veins into her stomach, which did a crazy little flip-flop.

Raine forced herself to keep her face even.

"I am possessive, Raine, because you're mine. You might think it will be the end after this revenge of yours is over, but you won't be leaving me."

"Oh no?" Rebellion rose inside her. *Just who does he think he is, anyway?*

"Your mate, that's who."

She hummed in annoyance that she'd spoken her thoughts out loud again. "Don't try to boss me, Walker." *Mate.* She snorted.

"I'm not at all." He relaxed back into his chair and took a swallow of his drink. "I'm only telling you the truth."

Raine blinked and tried to figure out how she felt about that statement. She wasn't as angry as she should have been and if she were honest, she had been thinking similar thoughts about him only hours ago on the transport. She felt something for Walker beyond mere physical attraction, but what, she wasn't sure. The feelings were not only confusing but also overwhelming. She didn't like being out of control.

"Am I interrupting anything?" Rory Uslep sat at their table uninvited.

Raine forced herself to smile at him and focus on the business at hand, instead of dealing with her confusion. "We were debating what percentage of this place you own."

Rory barked a laugh, a free, open sound that was as fake as the rest of him. Not that Raine didn't like him. She did. When his daughter had been kidnapped, he'd spared nothing to get her back. It had been touching to see how much he loved his child.

Rory's smoothed, long, brown hair was worn in the Senator's queue, and he dressed with a polish he hadn't acquired in Galaxy Grid 219. Raine wouldn't be surprised to learn he'd moved there only because few people would run against him. After all, he just had to live in the middle of nowhere half the year. The rest of the time, he was here on Borrus.

To some, he might appear out of place in the Naked Lady, but Raine thought Rory tended to gravitate to situations where he was a diamond among pieces of coal.

"You know I don't own any of this place, Raine darling." He patted her arm as if he reassured her, but left his hand a second or two too long.

Beneath the table, Walker's foot pressed down on hers.

She removed her hand from under Rory's and picked up her drink. "I'm calling in that favor." No use messing around. Rory was a busy man, with important things pressing for his time, and all that.

"I figured you didn't show up with another man to take me up on my other offer from three years ago." Rory signaled the waitress for a drink, pointing first up in the air, then at his glass.

Raine was impressed Walker kept his face blank and, if she was completely truthful, she was impressed he'd seen Rory's desire through only a single exchange of glances. Walker was naïve about some things, not stupid.

"My friend here has been accused of a crime he didn't commit, and I need you to get him a Senate Pardon."

Rory snorted. "You don't ask for much, huh?"

Raine smiled and said sweetly, "We both know you have the juice to procure the pardon."

"I can get it. I just doubt he's innocent." He studied Walker. "You innocent?"

"Of the crime I'm accused of, yes." Walker's voice was pleasant enough, but there was something there that felt challenging and male, even to Raine.

"A comedian!" Rory barked another laugh. "What are the details?"

"I need you to send a note for me and witness the resulting discussion. When the criminal confesses, you are to have him arrested."

"Who will be your confessor?"

"Malachi Delmundo."

"Why am I not shocked?" Rory shook his head and took his drink from the waitress. "No wonder you're hanging out with this guy. You'll do anything to burn Delmundo."

"I've burned him quite a bit, but can you really have enough revenge?"

Walker shifted in disagreement.

"You most certainly cannot." Rory twirled the swizzle stick, making the liquid in his glass slosh over the side. "I'm not sure I want to get involved with Delmundo."

Raine's drink had come only half full. Rory's drinks were full and free. Looking at the waitress wiggle away, she didn't think that was all he received on the house. Raine was careful to remain silent unless she meant to speak. The last thing she needed was to have her opinions on Rory's sex life aired out loud.

"He'll jump at the chance to meet with you." Raine knew Malachi so very well.

"And then he'll hunt me down if this thing goes wrong." Rory's voice held no emotion.

"Tell him the note was forged." Raine didn't think Rory was really worried about Malachi. Killing a Senator wasn't a very smart move, especially since Rory could easily blame her if Malachi questioned him about this. Rory was trying to limit his effort as much as possible and still have the debt between them satisfied.

"This seems a little simplistic. Your plans are usually more complicated than this."

Raine nodded. He was right, they were. "The first rule in strategy is to keep it simple. The fewer moving parts, the less there is to go wrong. The most important thing is that I can't have Malachi figuring out I'm on the planet. He'll skip the meeting and hunt me down if he knows I'm on Borrus."

"What if he doesn't give the confession you're looking for?"

"Oh, he will." Raine had no doubt. Malachi's downfall would come from his uncontrollable bragging. "The minute he sees Walker and me together, he won't be able to stop himself. Anyway, what fun is sticking someone else with a crime if you can't tell anyone about it?"

"You better be right."

"Whether I am or not, your debt will be paid."

Rory shook his head. "You could have done so much more with

this favor than save a stranger with it." He raised his arm in the air and snapped his fingers while still maintaining eye contact with her.

"You know, I'm a sucker for green eyes."

"No, I didn't know that." Rory leaned towards her. "I have green eyes." He fluttered his lashes, turning the words into a joke, but Raine knew on one level he was serious.

The pressure of Walker's foot on hers increased so suddenly, Raine jumped into the table, sloshing Rory's full drink onto his suit. He sprang away from her, and the waitress appeared with napkins to brush him off.

"Sorry about that. I'm a little space-sick from the long flight here."

Rory nodded, stilling the waitress's wandering hands and patting her ass to send her on her way. One of Rory's goons arrived bearing paper and a pen as if he'd overheard them. Raine wondered if he had.

"What do you want the note to say?"

"Meet me on top of the Senate Building tomorrow at the start of the afternoon session to discuss a mutually beneficial business proposition."

Rory wrote it and signed his name. "He could kill you, you know."

"Not there."

"You'll have to leave eventually."

"Theoretically, he'll confess, and you'll have him arrested." She raised an eyebrow.

"You better hope he confesses, Raine."

"He will." Raine stood before Walker did something to piss off Rory or she said something out loud best left securely in her head.

"I'll be there tomorrow. You and I should talk afterwards." There was a promise in his words.

Raine nodded and turned to the door.

"Talk, my ass," Walker fumed as they returned to their hotel. "I was about ten seconds away from laying hands on him." He stalked beside Raine, angry on more levels than he could count.

He wanted to tear Rory Uslep into pieces. How dare the pompous ass proposition his mate when he was sitting right there at the table? And he knew Rory would try to convince her again after they finished with Delmundo. Walker could see lust coming off the other man in waves every time he touched Raine.

This was the wrong moment to have another man vying for her affection. Raine hadn't committed to him, hadn't accepted yet that she was his mate. A growl rose in his chest filled with frustration.

He'd been sure that their lovemaking at the hotel had taken them to the next level, sure that he'd stamped his brand on her. It had been the first time she'd initiated sex like that, provoking him with her sexy body, adjusting her seduction to follow the images he'd had of her in his head, as if she'd truly connected with him on every plane.

The powerful feelings she'd invoked had made him insane.

Then in the Naked Lady, it had felt as if she'd taken a giant step back from him, all but promising she'd leave him when Malachi was defeated.

Walker gritted his teeth and tried to think around his growing anger and frustration. He wouldn't lose her.

Walker sounded bloodthirsty, but Raine didn't comment. She was too busy wondering why Rory's touch had caused her skin to crawl. She'd always considered having an affair with him. The only reason she hadn't was because at first, she'd been involved with someone else, then she'd been set on getting revenge. But tonight, she'd been physically repulsed by him.

"It's because I'm so far beneath you that he thinks he can easily steal you from me," Walker growled.

Raine grabbed his arm and hauled him to a stop in front of the hotel. "You aren't beneath me." What was he talking about?

Walker's jaw worked back and forth as if he ground his teeth. "Of course I am. You're beautiful, and I look like a thug."

Raine studied the pain in his eyes, hearing his unsaid insecurities over the fact he was a Breed. She tried to lighten his mood and reassure him. "You do look better without your clothes on."

His eyebrows went up so far, they hid under his short hair. She'd been right—it was wheat-colored and as it grew longer, it did help his appearance, softening the harsh planes of his face. Several times over the last couple days, she'd caught herself thinking his body wasn't the only part of him she liked.

"You think so?" He swooped her up and spun her around, the action filled with relief, but from what, she didn't know. "Maybe I should stay naked all the time."

"Maybe you should," she agreed, unable to figure out his swinging moods.

He let her slide down his body and tipped her head so he could meet her gaze. "Tell me you don't want him."

"I don't want him." She said it with so much conviction, she surprised even herself.

For a moment, Walker grinned at her, but then dropped his hands and strode away, scraping his fingers through his hair. "I have no idea what my problem is. I feel jealous if another man even looks at you, let alone touches you." He met her gaze. "I could have ripped him to shreds, Raine. That's how possessive I feel about you right now." He threw his hands out in a helpless gesture and stared off down the street.

Raine closed the distance between them to whisper, "Do you think this has anything to do with your father's blood?"

His jaw worked for a moment before he answered. "Maybe. Most likely. He was always overly protective of my mother."

"Walker." She rested her hand on his arm and felt his muscles bunch. "I don't want Rory."

"It was all I could do not to twist his arm off." He finally met her gaze. "I should be a bigger man and tell you to be with him. He's obviously rich and successful, even if he does hang out in a strip club." He stroked her arm, then gripped her hand. "But I won't, for no other reason than I want you with every particle of my being."

"It's okay," she soothed. And it surprised her that it was. She'd always been the cool one in every relationship she'd ever had. She'd been the one totally in control. She'd never felt this raw and scared.

But when she turned the tables and thought about what she would feel if a waitress had rubbed Walker's arm as Rory had done hers, she was the one gnashing her teeth. Because she knew the other woman would touch what she did every night—bunched muscles and warm, hair-dusted skin that smelled like summer and tasted like heaven.

She stepped close to him, then did something shocking, but she couldn't stop herself. Pulling his head down, she bit his neck. Hard. So hard, she started to feel her teeth sink through his flesh but stopped herself in time before she broke the skin.

Walker growled and cradled her head in his hand, holding her tighter, instead of pushing her away as she expected.

Taking a shuddering breath, Raine tried to figure out what was going on. Her behavior since the moment she'd met him had been out of character. Walker had said they were fated to be together, but she knew that was craziness.

"What's happening to me?" she murmured into his chest. Tearing herself from him was an agony, but she had to do it, since she couldn't think clearly while she touched him. Stepping away, she rested her head in her hands.

She realized she'd turned to him for comfort when he was the very thing that confused her.

She hated this feeling. Hated it with a passion. It was as if she would soon need him just to breathe. She'd never been so out of control. "So vulnerable," she whispered.

As much as she enjoyed him in bed, she didn't want the attachment she now felt. It was stronger than even the bond she'd had with her team and it shook her.

Her mind reached overload, and her flight instinct clicked in place.

She would act out her revenge and run as fast and as far from Walker and these feelings as she could.

Chapter Ten

Raine had pulled away from him mentally as well as physically. She hadn't touched him since their conversation outside the hotel the night before. He'd tried to start her talking, but she'd told him she needed to think and had ended up sitting in the room's only chair staring out the window all night.

They were to meet Delmundo in only a few hours at the top of the Senate Building.

"We're assuming he'll show up." Walker broke the deadly silence that ruled the room.

"He'll show." Raine's voice came out flat. She stood and leaned her head against the glass, still gazing out the window.

Walker moved beside her to stare out the dirty glass. The Capital City stretched out in every direction, but the streets in this part of town were relatively unpopulated, a combination of the rain, which had started a few minutes ago and fell in sheets, and the seedy part of town. Warehouses and factories stretched in every direction, smoke pumping into the sky from forges, adding to the dreary skyline.

"Why are you so sure?" He wasn't trying to argue, just keep her talking. Walker's heart constricted in his chest, a deep ache that hurt with each beat of his pulse.

"He won't want to miss this opportunity."

"Rory or Delmundo?" He made sure he kept any inflection from his voice.

"Both. Malachi won't be able to help himself, and Rory will show to satisfy the debt he owes me."

He studied her reflection in the window. There was something sunken about her stance, as if she held a large weight on her shoulders. Her face had closed in on itself, her eyes listless, her body completely still. He wanted to reach out and cuddle her against his chest, rub her back, comfort her but he knew she wrestled with her feelings for him.

The bite she'd taken from his neck had shaken her as much as it had pleased him. It was not the right time to tell her she was acting out the mating ritual, branding him as hers. This was their destiny, but she had to come to him on her own, not because he told her it was their fate.

Without meaning to, he brushed his fingers across the bruise she'd left. Raine's eyes flicked to his in the window, and she winced.

"It's not a big deal, Raine. A love bite, nothing more."

She exploded a breath outwards, but instead of arguing as he'd expected, she said, "I was thinking that you shouldn't come with me today."

"Not a chance." He wanted to shake her and ask her what in the hell was wrong, but he kept his temper in check with effort.

She turned and leaned back against the window, hugging herself with her arms. "I don't know what Malachi might do and I'd rather you stay here."

"We both go or stay. We're not separating. You promised I got to agree to the plan before we put it into effect."

"You're not trained for these types of missions," she said, her voice reasonable.

"Fine then. We won't go." Walker crossed his arms and let his biceps bulge to emphasize his raw strength. He wasn't letting her go alone.

She narrowed her eyes. "We need to prove your innocence."

"By tricking Malachi into a confession? Come on. He won't fall for that."

"I'm telling you, he will. He's the biggest braggart in all of the Inter-worlds. He won't be able to help himself."

"He'll show up with twenty of his men and they'll simply kill us. You know that's a possibility."

"He's going to murder us on top of the Senate Building? He's not that stupid. We'll be safe, since we have to go through security before we reach the roof."

Walker sighed. "Raine, just talk to me about what's upsetting you. No matter what it is, we can work it out."

"I'm not sure we can, Walker. I don't like what I'm feeling right now."

Walker rested his hand above her head, caging her in. Maybe they needed to fight it out. She sure as hell wasn't going to tell him on her own. "Which is what?"

She gritted her teeth and stared at the wall opposite her, not meeting his gaze. "Out of control."

Walker laughed, he couldn't help it. "Of course you feel out of control. Love is like that, Raine."

She dropped her hands on her hips and stood on her tiptoes, her face turning stormy.

A knock cut their battle short. They both stared at the door in surprise.

Raine glided to one side of the portal, all signs of their fight replaced by intensity and focus. "Who is it?"

"The desk clerk. I have a message for you."

"Damn," Walker mumbled, shaking his head. At this rate, they'd never get this settled.

"Rory better not be backing out, the bastard," she snarled, but she pointed to the door for Walker to open it. Pulling a long knife from the top of her boot, she pressed herself against the wall.

Walker opened the door right as one of Malachi's men slashed the pimple-faced clerk's neck.

Raine saw the blood splatter first. It streaked across the front of Walker's shirt.

He stumbled back as if it were hot oil. "What the hell?"

She didn't have to guess who had come for a visit. Damn, how had he found out she was here?

Malachi and three men were inside their room within a heartbeat, dragging the dead clerk along with them.

"Nice, Malachi." Raine recovered as fast as she could from the shock of seeing her archenemy suddenly appear in her hotel room. "You've messed up the beautiful carpeting."

Malachi looked down at the sticky, thread-bare mess that passed for a rug. He grinned. "Oops." His brown-eyed gaze swept over her where she still stood pressed to the wall. "Close the door," he ordered one of his men without taking his eyes off her. "I received a note to meet your buddy, Uslep. I've known since you did that job for him that he was trying to jump into your pants. Took me all of five minutes to bribe one of the waitresses at the Naked Lady to find out you saw him last night." His tone took on a gloating singsong.

"You know what your problem is, Malachi?"

"Enlighten me."

"You are a braggart." She rolled her eyes. "Haven't you ever heard of mystery? Suspense?" Shrugging her shoulders to loosen the tension, she added, "Building anticipation?"

"You're insane." Malachi breathed the words as if they had just occurred to him. He blinked and seemed to force some emotion away.

If she didn't know better, she would have thought her sanity, or lack thereof, unnerved him.

Raine stared at him, taking in his stylish clothes and good looking face. Chocolate eyes and hair combined to create a breathtaking panorama. Beside him, Walker appeared coarse and unrefined.

And wonderful.

"What?" Malachi asked, his brows lowering in confusion.

Walker snorted, obviously fighting a laugh, drawing his gaze.

Shit, she'd spoken out loud. It was an annoyingly persistent habit that she was beginning to think was impossible to break.

"You," Malachi said, his lips tipping into a smile that didn't come from amusement. "Well, well, well. Look who has joined forces. The Breed and the Bitch."

"You should fit right in, since you're a Bastard." Raine made sure she gave the B a capital sound, mimicking him.

"Always sassy, even to the end, eh Raine?"

"I'm not afraid of you, Malachi." Raine thought fast. There were four of them. Walker was on the other side of the room from her. He met her gaze, arching one brow to show her he was waiting to follow her lead.

Her heart flipped. That he would trust her to make the call spoke of his respect for her planning ability. It wasn't the typical male thing to do. Most men would start fighting or try to talk their way out or do anything but follow a woman, especially one they'd slept with.

And right at that moment, with death standing only a few feet away, Raine fell totally, completely, one hundred percent in love with him.

"You should be afraid." Malachi turned to Walker. "I thought you were serving a life sentence on Sector 9?"

Walker shrugged, but didn't speak.

"Cat got your tongue, Healer?" Malachi stepped over the dead clerk towards him.

Raine controlled the urge to leap between them. She knew Malachi could be fast when it came to knife work.

"What do you want, Malachi?" Raine asked to distract him.

"I was wondering why you wanted to see me on top of the Senate building." He didn't turn around.

"I was trying to save some lives. I didn't think even you would be dumb enough to kill someone there." Raine stared at the clerk and shook her head. "You always were a bastard. Why kill this kid?"

That got his attention and he turned around. "Why not? He's nothing." He seemed genuinely confused.

"You know, you don't even understand that taking a human life is against the Gods." Raine had always pondered his ease with death. He'd had her team killed on a whim as far as she'd been able to find out. They hadn't been after him, even though he was on par with the usual scum they hunted.

"Human? An interesting word, Raine." He circled Walker, who stood in a relaxed pose, a blank look on his face. "Did you know the Healer here isn't human?"

"As far as I'm concerned he's more human than you are." Raine didn't like Malachi being this close to her man. Dammit, she wished she wasn't so far away. She glanced at the knife in her hand. She could throw it, but even if she killed Malachi, he had three guards here with him.

"Doogie, guard her with your blaster," Malachi said. "So, Walker, you escaped from the prison? I didn't think you had it in you."

"Blasters are illegal," Raine informed the man who pulled the gun.

"So's killing," the man said.

"True."

He had a point, that was for sure.

"So what's the story?" Malachi prompted. He obviously burned with curiosity, shifting from one foot to the other.

"Didn't you know that everything comes back to haunt you, Malachi?" Walker's voice was smooth and unconcerned, but his gaze flicked to the blaster, letting Raine know he was worried about it. "Even me."

If Malachi gave the word to kill her, she would throw the knife into his chest as a final goodbye. But she realized she didn't want to die. She wanted to feel the beautiful muscles of Walker's body one more time, run her hands along his amazing chest, her skin sliding in the sheen of sweat which showed her just how turned on she made him.

She knew one thing—all hell would break lose if they killed

Walker first. Death would sweep through the room, and she would wield it. They would both live or both die.

Someone tapped twice on the door.

A man who looked like Doogie's twin went to let another person in. This time it was a woman. She was stunning, wrapped in a red dress that hugged all her curves to their best advantage. Her blond hair winged away from her heart-shaped face and baby-blue eyes.

"You remember your girlfriend, Merrium, don't you?" Malachi asked Walker.

Raine felt a pang of jealousy zip through her before she saw Walker's face. He actually growled at the blonde, baring his teeth. Merrium stepped back, placing a manicured hand on her chest, and Raine realized this must be the woman Malachi had used to betray Walker.

"The car's waiting," Merrium said and retreated to stand by the door, as far away from Walker as she could go.

"I didn't expect you to be coming along, Healer."

"Are we going someplace?" Raine asked.

"I have always wanted to kill Raine and drink her blood." Malachi sauntered over to tap Raine's cheek. "While it's tempting to do so here, I want to be able to take my time."

"I hope I poison you." Raine smiled at him and tightened her grip on the knife in her hand. *Closer, just get a little closer, you bastard.* Raine bit her lip to keep from speaking the words out loud.

They absolutely could not go back to Malachi's stronghold. She'd never been able to reach him there because he kept himself surrounded by so many people. It would be impossible to escape once they were there.

"Such bitterness." He shook his head. "If you had just let the whole thing drop, I would never have had to do this. But you had to have revenge."

"Yes. I did."

"Speaking of which, what did you do with my money?" Malachi leaned closer, his breath whispering across her face.

Raine rose up onto her tiptoes and whispered, "I spent it, you rat-bastard."

Chapter Eleven

Whatever Raine whispered in his ear made Malachi slap her hard. "I'll make you pay for that." Malachi's hand shook as if he wanted to slap her again. "I knew when your team signed that contract to terminate me that the seven of you would keep coming until all of you were dead."

Walker was so angry, he almost missed Raine's movement as she whisked Malachi's knife out of the sheathe behind his back and pitched it into the wall beside Walker's head.

The blade was a little closer to his face then he would have liked, but he didn't have time to think as he grabbed it.

Doogie fired right as Raine pushed Malachi into the blast. His body flew into the far wall as if swatted by the hand of a God.

Merrium stood beside the door, screaming.

Walker threw his knife at Doogie's chest. It ended up sticking out of his throat since he was also watching Raine fighting across the room. He launched himself at Doogie's look alike. Picturing his target several inches further back for maximum impact, he rammed his fist at the bad guy's nose. Walker might not be formally trained, but his cellmate at HeFO had taught him quite a bit during the long, long hours they had nothing to do but talk about the ins and outs of the criminal lifestyle.

Doogie's twin crumpled to the floor as his nose imploded like a piece of rotten fruit under Walker's fist. He wasn't going anywhere for a while.

Turning to Raine, he watched the beauty of her body as it flowed gracefully while she fought, her foot rounding to deliver a vicious kick. The man ended up in a heap on the ground.

With the last man's fall, Merrium went eerily quiet. For the first time, Walker analyzed his feelings for her. Nothing. No anger or desire or anything at all except maybe pity. Raine had healed the scars Merrium had left on his heart, and the anger faded with the realization that the Gods had sent him to Sector 9 for a higher purpose.

"You okay?" Walker asked Raine.

She nodded and wiped her knife on the fallen man's shirt. Taking a deep breath, she crossed the room to his side and touched the blood on his shirt.

"None of it's mine," he assured her.

"Good." She let out the breath as if she'd been holding it. "Gods, I was worried."

He caught her arm and started to pull her forward. "Don't be." Everything was going to be okay. He had her. She was safe. They would move to the hottest planet in the galaxies and raise magical children and live happily ever after.

Something moved in his peripheral vision, and Walker glanced up.

"Die, you Breed bastard," Merrium said, and fired Doogie's blaster.

Raine buckled backwards and crumpled so quickly, Walker didn't even have time to catch her as she fell. Merrium flung open the door and sprinted down the hall.

He dropped to Raine's side. If his mate died, he'd hunt Merrium and scrape her heart out with his bare hands. But there was time for that later, he promised himself. *This must be what Raine felt when Malachi killed her team—the burning urge for retaliation and retribution.*

Raine lay curled around her stomach, holding herself together with her hands. He pried her hands away to assess the damage.

What he saw stopped his heart and made him dig his fingernails into the flesh of her wrists before he controlled himself. She was dying and he knew it. A noise rose from his throat, a low growl of pain and fear.

"We," she blinked away the glaze from her eyes. "Have to move." She gasped and it sounded painful. "The Council police will be here soon."

"I can't move you. You might die." *Save her, dammit. Right now.* Hadn't his father once told him it was possible to exchange his life for hers? That he could transfer his life force to save his mate from death? He wasn't sure, couldn't think, couldn't remember.

"Do it." She gave him a hard stare, frowning with pain.

Walker gazed at her torn stomach, the wound not much smaller than his palm, the edges ringed with black. He would need a large amount of time to heal this kind of damage. Time he wouldn't have if he was back in prison.

He had no choice but to move her. Gods, she could die from the shock alone.

No!

He couldn't, wouldn't think that.

Get yourself under control. NOW!

He picked her up and grabbed their pack. Sprinting from the room, he burst through the hall door and jogged down the stairs. Each movement jarred her in his arms. Small, pain-filled cries escaped with each step, ripping at his soul and tearing at his own flesh as if he was the one bleeding to death.

He ran through the emergency exit at the bottom of the stairs, setting off the alarm, which wailed into the dark, rainy day.

"I'm sorry, baby," he whispered, scanning for a place to go.

His heart hammered so hard he couldn't hear anything but the rush of his own pulse.

Liquid slithered the length of his arm, thicker than rain, a drop hanging at his elbow for a moment before it fell. He refused to picture her life draining from her here on the sidewalk, and yet he had a sudden vision of the street filling with her blood, rising up to engulf him.

Shutting his eyes, he took a breath through his mouth and whispered, "I've spent years preparing for this moment. I will save her. I can do this." Calm settled over him, like a mantle from the Gods.

When he opened his eyes, he saw a factory ahead, the fence pried up so he could duck beneath it.

He felt the heat before he saw the open bay. Checking first to make sure no one was around, he slipped into the warehouse and slid behind some crates in time to avoid a man walking out.

Raine moaned from the pain.

"Shh," he whispered.

She fell silent, breathing rapidly through her mouth, and Walker's heart constricted.

He needed to get near the heat source he felt radiating close by. It would increase his chances to heal this kind of damage. Dodging behind some crates, he stopped at the edge of an immense room, staring in awe at the mechanized casting operation that poured red hot liquid of some kind into molds. There wasn't a single person to be seen; factory work was only done with humans on the less technically advanced Outer Worlds. The Inter-world Council had long ago banned these jobs as unskilled for everyone but the specialists who did repairs on the machines.

Stepping as close to the open pit as he could without being doused with sparks, he laid Raine down. She curled into her stomach, coughing convulsively.

"Don't die," he ordered, wiping off the foamy red substance that gathered at the edges of her lips. The calm mantle was still in place, and he felt strong, in control, and steady.

She wouldn't die because he willed it to be so.

He forced her hands away so he could press his own into her wound. She moaned in pain, then screamed when he pushed power into her.

Not too much. He had to be careful. Concentrating on repairing her wounds, he dove in and started to heal her.

Painstakingly, he moved through her core, mending torn muscles and healing her body.

He had no idea how much time had elapsed before he surfaced. Maybe minutes, but most likely long hours. He was exhausted, swaying in pain, having run his energy level lower than he'd ever pushed it.

The heat had sustained his temperature, allowing him to heal for much longer than he would have normally been able to. Raine's stomach still had a hole the size of his thumb, but he couldn't completely heal it. Not without re-energizing.

A flutter at his knee attracted his attention.

"You," Raine licked her dry lips. "You look like hell."

"So do you," he said, but that wasn't entirely true. Her color had returned, and he'd stopped the blood flow and healed most of the wound. "I'm out of energy, Raine. I've got nothing else to give you." He fell forward, barely catching himself with his hands. Stretching out alongside her body, he gathered her into his arms and held her close. Fear washed over him. He had no idea what would happen to her, since he'd never left someone half healed before.

The barrier he'd built around his emotions cracked; the feelings he'd held off coursed through him. Agony seized his heart and squeezed. He cradled her, rocking slightly to comfort his woman, while fear made him pant and bite his own lip to keep the pain from ripping free.

If he lost her, he would only live long enough to kill Merrium. Gnashing his teeth, he fought the urge to scream until tears spilled from his eyes to track down his cheeks.

Raine's hand came up to capture them. "It's okay, Walker. I just need to sleep." She moved her head a fraction closer to him, and he wrapped around her with the last bit of his strength.

"I love you," she whispered.

"I've always loved you, Raine, from the moment you first touched me back on Sector 9."

Raine woke when someone kicked her leg.

"What the hell are you two doing?" a gruff voice yelled at her. "This ain't no hotel."

She blinked up at a man with a toolbox in his hand.

"You've got until the count of five to get out of here or I'll call the guard."

Raine glanced back to find Walker staring at her. "How do you feel?" he asked.

"I said move!" The man with the toolbox flushed red in the face. "I'm two seconds away from turning you two in."

She sat up. Her stomach didn't protest, and she felt oddly rested, as if she'd been sleeping for days. She ran a hand along her skin. Perfect. There wasn't time to dwell on the miracle. "We're going."

Walker staggered to his feet and helped her stand, then shrugged on the pack. Like a pair of drunks, they lurched out of the factory into the sunny day, leaning on one another for support.

"What happened to my wound? The last thing I remember is that you couldn't heal it all."

"I didn't heal it completely." He shook his head and pulled up what remained of her shirt to stare at her stomach. "Perhaps the healing continued on its own while we slept. It shouldn't have, though. But everything seems to work differently with you than it does with others."

For a moment, they stood silent, taking that in. Raine rubbed her hand across her belly and realized they were *more* together than they were apart. Better. Stronger.

Magical.

She shivered as the importance of their relationship hit her. He had healed her. He had fought for her. But more than that, he had trusted and respected her.

Love made her knees feel wobbly and her body weak. She couldn't run now even if she wanted to. The thought brought relief. She threaded her fingers through his to lock him to her.

"How long do you think we were sleeping?" she asked, shading her eyes from the sun with her other hand.

"The night for sure. It was raining when we went in and close to dark."

Walker's face was still ashen, and Raine went up on her tiptoes to kiss him.

"What was that for?"

"Just because I love you, I guess."

"Just because, huh?" He smiled and she noticed some of his color had returned.

Malachi was dead. Her revenge was complete. Her whole life stretched out before her in an endless stream.

"What happened to the woman who shot me?"

Walker shrugged. "She escaped with her life." His tone sounded bloodthirsty.

She tipped her head to stare at him, surprised at the anger in his eyes. "We'll send a note to Rory and have him pick her up. He can put her in HeFO for her part in all this. Certainly a few years freezing on Sector 9 is revenge enough." She glanced up and down the street. "So what now?"

Walker squeezed her hand and she met his gaze. "I'm still a wanted man. We never proved my innocence."

"No," she said. "Maybe I can still get a pardon from Rory." She heard the doubt in her own words.

"You think that will work without proof?"

She wanted to say yes, but couldn't. "No, and I'd rather use him to put that bitch Merrium on ice."

He blinked at her candor and humor lines spread across his face. "You're the master planner. What do you suggest?" He became serious. "I'll follow your lead, Raine, as long as we stay together."

"I want to spend the rest of my life with you, wherever we end up."

"We'll be happy as long as we're together." He made it sound like a promise.

Her heart tumbled and love filled her.

Walker mouth pulled into a sudden frown. "You know, I wonder why Malachi killed your team. That's what started this whole thing to begin with."

Raine had racked her brain for three years over the very same question. "Before Malachi died, he said he knew the team would keep coming for him when he heard we'd signed a contract to take him out." She blew out a breath. "The thing is, we turned down the contract we were offered. The team decided he was too well insulated and would be too hard to take out for the small amount of money we were offered. Malachi must not have known."

"All this death and pain and revenge over something that wasn't even true." He brought her hand up to kiss her knuckles. "I'm glad that part of your life is over."

"And a new life for both of us is beginning." She would come up with the perfect plan so they would live happily ever after. "First we find someplace to change clothes and clean up." She paused, thinking about the fact that Malachi would no longer be tracking her so she could freely spend his money. A slow smile of satisfaction spread across her face. "Then we're going to the One Bank to make a withdrawal."

"Why are you smiling?"

"We need to purchase fake papers for you, and then we're going on the trip of our lives."

"I think it will take more than fake papers to keep me free."

Her palm cupped his chin. "How do you feel about your face?"

"It's the one I was born with, so I suppose it's good enough." He pressed his lips onto her fingers. "Although I seem to remember you saying something about it not being exactly handsome."

"You heard that?" Raine felt a flush inch up her neck and cheeks.

He grinned, his green sparkling eyes telling her he was teasing.

Happiness bubbled inside her. "I've actually grown quite fond of it, but sadly it's the face of a wanted man."

"Yes."

"I was thinking we may need to change it." She gave his hair a playful yank. "And let your hair grow."

"Reorganizing my face and forged papers will take some serious balseems."

She skipped a happy circle around him, letting her hands touch his hard chest, bulging arms and sleek back.

Walker laughed. "Uh oh, you've got something up your sleeve."

"We're going to live the rest of our days spending Malachi's money, starting with buying you a new identity."

"You have that much?"

She looked at the love of her life, a slow smile spreading across her lips. "Oh, yeah." Raine flung out a hand. "Think of it, Walker. Sunsets on LackSui, taking luxury cruisers from planet to planet, staying in one of those hotels under Goda's oceans. We can go anywhere we want."

He shook his head. "If that will make you happy."

"It will."

Walker waved a hand and executed a perfect bow. "Then lead on. I'll be at your back, no matter where you take us."

She smiled because she knew he would.

About the Author:

Leigh Wyndfield spends her time away from writing reading anything she can get her hands on, watching movies, and skiing or hiking, depending on the season. Hooked on Battlestar Galactica *as a child, she often slipped away from her music lessons to sneak in the show after school. As she grew up, she realized she also loved romance novels. Unable to get her hands on romances that take place on other worlds, she started writing her own while working in the real world and obtaining her MBA from a top-tiered university. Installing software systems just didn't seem like any fun compared to writing, so she recently quit her job to create stories full time. Visit her website to learn about her other books at* www.leighwyndfield.com*!*

Summer Lightning

by Saskia Walker

To My Reader:

Picture this: you're totally alone and enjoying the summer sun on an isolated beach. What would make it even better for you—seeing a gorgeous hunk walking naked in the waves? And if he arrived at your door in the middle of a storm, offering to help you out of a fix? Well, what's a girl to do…

Chapter One

The sky roared overhead, the fluffy summer clouds fleeting across the expanse of bright blue. Sally spread her arms wide, closed her eyes and allowed her other senses to take over. Her skin warmed and prickled as the summer breeze danced over her. Against her back the solid shape of the sand dune molded her body, arching her as if offering her to the elements. The smell of ozone filled her nostrils, and the mesmerizing sound of the waves rolling up onto the shore washed over her. The sun broke through the racing clouds, and through her closed eyelids, the light dimmed and then brightened, charting its progress.

She sighed happily and rolled over onto her belly, folding her arms under her chin and exposing her back to the sun. It was idyllic; the small cove was so isolated she had pulled off her T-shirt and lay on the warm sand wearing only her shorts and deck shoes. Her nipples tightened when they made contact with the gritty sand; her skin tingled as her body responded to every stimulus that surrounded her.

It was just as she had imagined it would be—the secluded idyll fulfilling her desire to get closer to nature. Best of all, she still had another six days before she had to head home. She'd taken two weeks away from London and the office for much needed time to devote to her sculpture. She'd been busy working on a new cyber-warrior figurine when she decided to get out of the cottage and walk along the shore. Something about exposing herself to the elements made her feel closer to the clay when she returned, and this time would be no exception.

A strand of grass tickled her nose. She rubbed it away and opened her eyes, squinting, while she grew accustomed to the bright sunlight again. Much to her surprise, she saw a figure moving further down the cove.

"Damn," she whispered.

She hadn't seen another soul on the beach during the whole time that she had been there, and she snatched her T-shirt against her, lying flat against the ground. The clumps of beach grass lining the top of the dunes gave her cover, but she wanted her T-shirt nearby in case she needed it.

It was a man, and he seemed to be alone. *A very attractive man.* Perhaps she'd been away from people for too long, she thought. A few trips to the local village for supplies obviously wasn't enough contact to keep her in touch with the real world.

She smiled to herself, watching as he kicked off his sports shoes and walked barefoot towards the edge of the shore. He was tall and well built, with sun-streaked hair. He wore loud shorts and a T-shirt that was threadbare. His legs were corded with strong muscles, and she eyed them as an artist, and more, as a woman—a woman subconsciously hungry for such a sight.

He had the look of a beachcomber, but as she watched, he walked into the water and dipped a long plastic tube into the surf. He lifted it and looked at it in the light, then sealed it with a plastic cap. She wondered what he was doing.

He walked back to where he'd left his shoes and deposited the tube. Then he pulled his T-shirt over his head, giving her a look at his perfectly shaped torso as he did so.

"Wow," she whispered approvingly. If she was looking for inspiration, she had surely found it today. He was a handsome specimen all right, gorgeous looking and with a very impressive physique. The guy worked out, that much was obvious. He had amazing, powerful shoulders and a six-pack to match. He stood on the edge of the surf as if he owned it—it was as if Neptune himself had just walked out of the waves.

Sally's eyebrows shot up when she realized he wasn't stopping at the t-shirt. He was busy undoing the tie at his waistband and was about to drop his shorts. She glanced around, half expecting to see somebody else running over to accompany him. But, no, he appeared to be alone. And she was trapped there, clutching her T-shirt to her chest as she observed him, unseen. His shorts were kicked off unceremoniously and he walked, naked, towards the edge of the surf, giving her a look at his gorgeous backside. Sally was transfixed. Between her thighs a dense, humid heat rapidly built, and her sex clenched with appreciation and desire.

He waded into the water, unhindered by its temperature. She was amazed, because she knew how cold it was after a tentative paddle the week before. She had traveled up to Northumberland on the far north east of England, to get peace and solitude on this lonely coastline. The above average summer warmth was a lucky bonus, but the sea temperature was never going to get warm enough for her to consider a full-on paddle.

She watched admiringly as he waded out until the water reached half way up his powerful thighs. He ran his fingers through his hair, arching his back, his face turned upwards and his eyes closed. Sally sighed longingly. She was willing to bet that running her hands over his physique would feel pretty darned good. He turned in the water, and she got a full frontal view of his masculinity, and she was very impressed. A purr of appreciation escaped her. The sound lifted and was swept away on the breeze as she looked at his cock, hanging heavy at the junction between his thighs. It was an imposing sight. He reached down and grasped it, his hand moving expertly as it grew and rose before her eyes.

Sally couldn't believe what was happening. At first she'd been alarmed to see someone there, and now she was enthralled. The most gorgeous hunk of man had stripped, right in front of her eyes and was now touching himself, completely without self-consciousness. What an incredible sight!

She was getting a secret show from an absolute sex god, and she was getting very horny as a result. Her clit was pounding, and her sex clenched as she eyed the magnificent tool he held in his hand.

He stroked his erection lazily up and down, and Sally felt an overwhelming urge to do the same. She pushed her hand inside her shorts, her fingers quickly sliding into her damp, sticky sex folds. She stroked her clit in time with his movements, her breathing speeding, her eyes riveted to the man standing in the waves, the water lapping against him as he unashamedly indulged himself. She wriggled and reached, her body beating out its own response.

What if he saw her, what if he caught her doing this, while watching him?

The sudden unbidden question brought about a rush of embarrassment and self-awareness. She couldn't believe she was doing this, out here in the open,but she couldn't shy away from the secret session of mutual self-loving. It was like a secret pagan ritual.

It was such a turn on.

His fist was moving faster, and his body tensed. His cock reached and then jerked an impressive stream of fluid into the air. She cursed under her breath, squeezed her hand over her pussy, crushing her clit and worked hard until she too came in a sudden rush. Her breathing rasped, and she felt stunned at the unexpected, deviant desire he had caused in her and the subsequent rush of sensations.

He turned around in the water. What if he came back towards her now? How was she going to get away without being seen? But then, much to her relief, she saw him dive and swim away. Taking advantage of the situation, she grabbed her T-shirt and pulled it on as she stood up. She shot off, jogging back towards the cottage, her mind already racing with ideas for a new sculpture, something pagan and sexy.

She glanced back over her shoulder. At the far end of the cove she saw a motorbike parked. A tent had been erected nearby. He was staying over. Would she see him again? A shiver of anticipation ran through her veins as she considered the question and then she darted inside her rented cottage, smiling to herself.

Julian Keswick lifted his boot a fraction, and his motorbike began to slow down. He had almost covered the five miles from the cove to the local village when he caught sight of Tom walking at the side of the road. He drew up alongside him. The old man started, as if alarmed, and Julian pulled off his helmet to reveal his identity.

"Oh, Mr. Keswick, it's you… got me old ticker going then, so you did."

"Sorry Tom, I didn't mean to spook you. Yes, it's me, back again. Anything new since my last visit?"

Julian had warmed to the old man from the first time he had come to this stretch of coast, five years earlier. On his visits he always made time for Tom, who many of the villagers referred to as "the local idiot." Not the case. Julian had many conversations with him and quickly found that Tom had a handle on everyone in the area and knew all the latest gossip. It helped Julian out when someone would willingly shed light on any changes or anything going on in the locality that might affect the local beaches.

The year before, Tom had given him the word on an illegal red diesel scam that could have had detrimental effects on the environment if the local fisherman hadn't been made aware of what exactly they were buying. As a marine conservationist on coastal duty, Julian's responsibility was to monitor the beaches of the area. It was a job he was not only dedicated to, but enjoyed immensely.

Tom pondered the question. "Come up to the pub with me and I'll tell you all," he offered, with a wink. That was his code for "buy me a pint and I'll spill the beans."

"Will do," Julian responded, pleased, and climbed off his motorbike. "Is there someone staying at the cottage in the cove?" He had noticed a Land Rover parked outside as he headed out and, earlier, when he'd been swimming; he thought he'd caught sight of movement at the cottage. It had never been occupied on his previous visits, and he was certainly surprised, and annoyed, if that was the case now.

"Aye, young woman up from London staying there now. Old man Greg came up from Newcastle and had it done out to be rented out as one of them holiday cottages. We didn't think anyone would come, you know, with the dirt track to navigate and all." He chortled. "But we was wrong. She's the third visitor; the other lots were families."

Julian gave an inward groan. *Tourists. Damn it.*

It was only a matter of time until it had to happen, he supposed. In his mind, it was *his* place. Isolated, hard to find, perfectly beautiful. Ramblers and coastal walkers sometimes happened by, but their kind had an innate respect for the environment. He had spent many hours alone at the cove, and he cared for it. He resented the idea of sharing it. Especially with a bunch of ignorant tourists who knew nothing about how precious the place was.

"Come on, I'll buy you a pint and we'll have a proper chat." He was about to push his bike on when he realized for the first time that Tom was without his bicycle. He was rarely seen without the archaic iron horse and even if he was walking, it was usually being pushed alongside him. "Where's your bike?"

Tom's mouth turned down at the corners. "The sea, *she* took it."

Julian grinned. As well as being a font of information, Tom shared Julian's appreciation of the ocean and thought of it as a woman, a very powerful woman—just as he did.

"I left it outside me cottage one night when I was late home from the pub, and she was mighty angry with me for some reason and came right up onto the sound and took it away. I've just about forgiven her now." He shook his head at Julian, forlornly.

Julian gave him a supportive pat on the back and gestured him on to the pub, some fifty yards ahead on the hillside. He often thanked his lucky stars that he had been stationed in this part of the world. Its strangeness never ceased to fascinate him, and the scenery along this stretch of coast was awesome. In particular, the cove where he had erected his tent was one of his favorite places.

He might be a scientist but he wasn't your live-in-a-lab type scientist. He liked to get back to nature; that's why he'd opted to study environmental science, to protect and support the earth's natural resources. That's also why he worked like he did, staying on location, instead of returning to base every day as was expected. He didn't want to be cooped up.

It was with a strange, longing feeling that he realized it was the first time he'd ever had to share the place with another human soul. He also realized, reluctantly, that he ought to go and introduce himself. He didn't want to scare the visitors while he went about his business, but he didn't relish the idea of the task. *Far from it.*

Sally refilled her dousing dish, set it down on the table and dipped one hand into the water. With the other hand, she pulled off the large, damp cloth that kept the clay workable, and then ran rivulets of water over the sculpture. She'd worked late into the night and slept until noon before waking, ravenous, and realized that she hadn't even eaten supper the night before. After a hearty breakfast, she'd pulled on an old shirt and jeans and returned to the sculpture.

When it was gleaming wet, she walked around the large kitchen table that she had covered with plastic sheets to use as her workstation while she was at the cottage. The torso was about half life-size. She wished she'd had enough clay to do a full size version, but then there would be the issue of getting it home, and she was very sure that she'd want to keep this one. She ran her fingers over the sculpture, possessively. It was well underway, and she was pleased with her progress. The rough clay at the base rose up just as the sea had, buffeting the strong columns of his thighs. There, she had already worked her magic, and the strong muscles were shaped and made hard and real by her fingers. She reached forward and stroked the outline of his cock, half formed from the clay. She was savoring that part for as long as possible, because she knew she would really enjoy molding it.

His abdomen, buttocks and hips had absorbed most of her time the night before, and she could already see something special emerging from her work. The cyber figurines she spent every moment of her spare time on had become very popular. She'd been selling them over the Internet for fourteen months already, but this was something different, more classical and yet earthy. She laughed at herself. Maybe it was because she felt possessive about the model. This was certainly one way to get her hands on him.

She moved to stand behind the figure, her hands against his buttocks, wondering what would feel like to have the real man there, to have her hands on that glorious body of his. She stroked lightly around his hips to the front, where she touched the heavy, rising cock. It was only half formed—but in her mind? She remembered every glorious inch.

Smiling, she moved forward and rested against the back of the sculpture, not caring whether she stained her shirt. She always got herself into a complete mess when she worked. She sighed as she mentally planned working on the potent orbs of his testicles, and her fingers began to mark them out in the clay. This was so creative, she mused, and therapeutic, allowing herself to drift, her eyes still closed. *Very therapeutic indeed.*

When she heard the loud rap on the door, she leapt back, nearly overbalancing the table in the process, her eyes flashing open and her mouth opening in a silent exclamation. *Who the hell could that be?*

Maybe she could ignore it. When she leaned over and saw the dark shadow moving behind the glass door, she realized that it was too late and she couldn't hide. She'd probably already been seen. The only door into the cottage went straight into the kitchen, where she had set up her workstation. She cursed and took a regretful look at the torso, before stepping over and hauling the heavy door open.

She stared, in absolute horror, speechless. It was the man himself. He was right there, on her doorstep, looking gorgeous, despite the scowl on his face. He was wearing a bright, white t-shirt and blue jeans, a motorbike helmet hanging casually from one hand, his bike parked up a little way off. She gathered herself and moved quickly, edging herself into the open gap, holding the door as closed as she possibly could to block his view into the cottage.

"Well, hello," he said, his gaze traveling slowly from her face down to her bare feet and back up again. His expression morphed slowly from grumpy to friendly, and he shook his head and broke into a smile. "I've just popped over to introduce myself." He stuck out his hand. "I'm Julian Keswick, and I'm working along the coast here. I've set my tent up at the other end of the cove." He gestured over his shoulder. "Thought I'd better call by and say hello, to assure you the natives are friendly." He grinned at her again, his sensual mouth conveying so much in that simple, friendly gesture.

It was a totally gorgeous smile, warming her to the core, despite her awkwardness. Sally was transfixed, because he was even better looking close-up. He had startling green eyes, heavily fringed, and his hair was darker than she had originally thought, but sun-streaked from his time working outside. His skin was sun-kissed.

In fact, you know that he's sun-kissed all over, don't you, Sally?

She blushed at the memory, attempting to push it away. His bone structure was solid and strong, making her fingers twitch instinctively. The desire to reach out and trace the bones of his face was so great that she clutched her hands into fists.

Still standing with his hand extended, he looked down and noticed her reaction. "I'm sorry, have I caught you at a bad time?"

She felt as if she had been caught red-handed. She glanced down at herself and realized what a state she must look. She had damp patches all over her clothes, and she hadn't even combed her hair. Not only that, but she was standing there with her hands in fists as if she was about to give the poor guy a black eye because he had dared to knock on her door.

With a great deal of effort she mustered up a smile, hoping that he wouldn't see past her and into the kitchen. If he caught sight of the sculpture and recognized something about it… well, that wasn't worth thinking about. She'd simply die of embarrassment.

"Sorry," she said, rubbing her hands on her shirt and taking his offered handshake. "I'm just surprised to see anybody around here. I've been here for a few days and the isolation has been great, but here you are now." It was coming out all wrong. Instead of trying to lure the guy in and have a go at chatting him up, which is what would have been ideal, she was literally chasing him off. All because she was so bloody nonplussed by his sudden appearance at the very moment that she had been fantasizing about him.

His smile faded somewhat, a small furrow developing between his eyebrows. Despite that, he gripped her hand, and when their eyes met over the contact, something instinctive passed between them. *Something very sexy and intimate.*

"I'm really sorry, but I can't invite you in," she blurted, trying to repair the damage of her less than hospitable welcome, and then bit her lip anxiously. Whatever the hell was she going to say next? She couldn't trust her own mouth. It was true enough that she couldn't invite him in though, but she would have to give a reason, or he'd assume she had something to hide. *And I don't have something to hide*?

Heat rose in her cheeks, and she silently cursed herself for not even thinking to cover the torso before answering the door. "I'm in the middle of something; it's nothing personal, really." *And now I am fibbing, because 'personal' is surely what it is.* She attempted to paste on another smile, regret at the missed opportunity already swamping her. Damn, the guy only presented himself at her door, and she practically had to chase him off with the broomstick. "Maybe another time?" *Feeble, still sounded like a brush off.* That was the last thing she wanted to give him.

"Sure, whatever." He looked her up and down again, as if regretful. "Shame," he murmured, and then shook himself slightly, saluted her and turned his back. "You know where I am if you need anything," he shouted over his shoulder, and pointed down the cove.

"Thanks," she called after him, her spirits lifting somewhat. Her heartbeat was still erratic, her nerve endings tingling. It was as if her whole body had grown acutely aware of the perfect male specimen who had been at such close hand. She blushed at her intense, animal response. Standing on the doorstep, watching him walk away, she suddenly became aware of the rising humidity in the atmosphere. That had to be partly to blame for the way she was feeling, surely?

She turned and went back into the kitchen, hands on hips, eyeing the torso accusingly. "You," she said, "are going to have to find a new home!"

Chapter Two

Julian fidgeted restlessly. He was lying on top of his sleeping bag with his hands folded behind his head. The tent flap was open, and he stared out into the night. The sky was rumbling; a storm had been threatening for the past few hours. True to form for British weather, a few days of glorious heat was quickly followed up by humidity and sudden rainfall. The radio had reported a whammy-doozer of a storm hitting the north-east coast by midnight. He knew he ought to go check on the motorbike and secure the tent pegs. Instead, his mind kept wandering restlessly over to the woman at the cottage.

What a pleasant surprise she had turned out to be. He'd been unhappy about the visitor's presence, but his misgivings had vanished immediately when he had caught sight of her. It felt like a trick, though. A trick to make him forget his territorial attitude to the cove. He gave a wry smile at the idea of it. Perhaps Old Man Greg had put her there to distract him from his aggravation about the turn of events. Perhaps she was a gift from the sea, a symbolic gesture that would point out his ridiculous self-righteousness about the place. The sea had a way of showing Man he was but a small thing in nature's grand scheme.

Whatever it was, he couldn't shake off the woman's image. She was a sexy little thing and she'd been in his mind all day long. When she'd opened the door, she'd been embarrassed. He was convinced that he had caught her up to something—something sexy? She'd stood in the doorway, looking startled, as if he'd caught her *in flagrante delicto.* Her pupils had been dilated, her nipples hard and visible through that baggy shirt she'd been wearing. She'd been unmistakably aroused, but she was supposed to be alone. Tom had said she was staying there alone, and Tom's information had always been accurate.

He sat up and stuck his head out of the tent. On the distant horizon, the incoming storm was already visible, with flashes of lightning illuminating patches of cloud far away. Crackling electricity filled the air, and the humidity was at its most dense.

Over to the left, he could see the outline of the cottage. There was a light flickering at the window. It had to be a candle, or was he being overly symbolic and wishful? He'd certainly like to explore the resident by candlelight.

He'd definitely been without sex for too long, he decided. He used to have a relationship with a barmaid down the coast in Whitby, a nice uncomplicated sex thing, but Sandra had left for the city the year before, and since then he'd been self-sufficient. Until the woman at the cottage that morning—one look at her and his hunting instincts had instantly flared into action.

She had wild, long hair, bed-tousled and mahogany colored—the sort of hair a man could tangle his fingers in during a hot one-on-one session. He sighed. That wild hair, her dark brown eyes and the silver jewelry she wore gave her an untamed, gypsy look that was fascinating. *Untamed.*

Julian would readily admit to having a thing about wild, gypsy-looking women. The woman at the cottage was certainly that, and his imagination had been actively wondering what she looked like under that baggy shirt of hers. It was messy, like she'd just thrown it on to answer the door.

What *did* single women get up to, to satisfy their urges, he mused. Oh, he knew well enough, and it was a favorite topic to linger on. Assuming that she was single, he reasoned. She was certainly alone. He pictured her using a vibrator, and his cock instantly hardened as the image meandered through his mind, and then took up residence. Had that been what she was up to, when he had called by? *Maybe.* He could just picture her, lying back on her bed, a big silver vibrator humming in one hand, the other playing with her tits. In his mental image the vibrator slid easily in and out of her glistening pussy. He groaned, sat up, then climbed out of the tent and inhaled a deep draft of air. He really wasn't helping himself any.

Suddenly the sky cracked open, and a loud clap of thunder pealed overhead. Lightning flashed, lighting the area up as if it were daytime. Julian turned back to the tent and quickly began to check the pegs, just as the sky opened and heavy torrents of summer rain began to pour down, breaking the humidity instantly. Before he climbed back inside, he glanced at the motorbike. It would fare better than the tent, and he rather wished he'd taken off and booked into the local B&B, but something had held him there, despite the incoming storm. And Julian knew exactly what—or rather *who*—that was.

Sally jumped when her mobile phone bleeped into action. Everyone had agreed that she needed a total break from business, and so far it had only rung a couple of times. Both times it had been traders who hadn't known she was out of the office.

"Hey, Sally, how's your sanity holding up?"

"Kitty! Oh, it is good to hear your voice." Kitty was her right hand woman and her best friend to boot. "My sanity is just fine."

"Excellent news, I know we said we'd leave you alone, but I was thinking that cabin fever might have set in by now."

Sally laughed in delight. "No, not at all, besides I've been busy with my cyber guys. How are things there? Are you coping?"

"We're coping well, so you just enjoy yourself. What's it like up there? Have you happened on any local talent?"

"It's beautiful and, well, actually, there is a guy."

"Oh, do spill, is he a hunk?"

Sally could practically see Kitty's face, avid with interest.

"Like you wouldn't believe, but it's probably just one of those things, you know, ships that pass in the night."

"Hey, girl, if his ship is passing, you make sure you jump it. A single woman can't pass up an opportunity like that, and you've been single for far too long."

She was right. Sally had sacrificed a potential love life to build her company. Relaxation time was infrequent, and when it did come along, she had her art to turn to. There hadn't been a man for a long time. *Too long.*

"Maybe." Sally smiled at the picture in her mind, of jumping Julian's ship in the night, but she didn't want to talk about it any more, in case it came to nothing. Kitty would grill her for details when she got back to London, and if there were none to tell, that line of conversation would get old and tired very quickly. "Anyway, tell me what I am missing."

She listened happily to Kitty relating the week's events as she sat up in bed, keeping an eye on the night sky out of the window. The storm had been going on for over an hour, and Sally had been trying to chill out and settle down in bed with a book when her friend rang. She was far too excited to sleep, and even after they had said their goodbyes, the electric atmosphere and the spectacle of the storm continued to fascinate her. The sky kept flashing into action, rain coming in off the sea in sheets that lit through each time the electricity in the atmosphere hit, brightening even the dark distant sea on the horizon and every surface between. The wilder elements and the force of nature surrounded her. She was wired.

When the storm had first begun, she had paced back and forth through the cottage, watching the summer lightning from the various windows, occasionally wondering about the man who was so close, yet so far away in his tent on the other side of the cove. Perhaps he'd gone home, wherever home was, when the storm hit, or earlier. She kind of wished she'd brought her binoculars, then she could have…what? *Spied on him? Sally, really!*

She chastised herself for even considering it, but it was an interesting idea. After all, hadn't that been what she had been doing when she first saw him? Inadvertently, of course. *Did that make it any better, or not?* She rolled on to her side on the bed, looking once again into the restless night sky. She'd left the curtains open so that she could watch it from the bed. The sash window was propped open, and she kept catching breaths of the fresh air that followed in the wake of the storm.

She couldn't understand why some people disliked storms. She found them entrancing, and being out here on the coast sure made it more intense. In the city, everything conspired to obscure the view. The feeling of being at one with the wilder side of the elements was lost when surrounded by high-tech city living.

The storm ran pure, liquid excitement through her veins, as real as if it had been tapped into her blood directly from the thunderous skies overhead. The wind had lifted substantially, and at that very moment, she heard a distant thudding sound, moving in time with the gusts through the tree. She sat up and strained to hear it again. Something was blowing in the wind, and it sounded like a door opening and closing. *The tool shed*? The letting agent had told her there was patio furniture in there, in case she fancied a barbecue. She hadn't even looked at it, because when she was outside she wanted to be on the dunes.

She switched on the bedside lamp, and listened again. When she heard the sound once more, she got out of bed to investigate, slipping on her deck shoes and a long, baggy t-shirt. As she went through the house, she flicked on all the lights, her city-girl upbringing making her more wary in the dark hours.

When she opened the door, the sky was mottled and streaked with moonlight edging between the clouds. The storm had started to move on, leaving a mournful wind in its wake and occasional incoming sheets of rain. She squinted out into the night. Why hadn't she thought to bring a light with her? Maybe there was one in the house. She was about to turn back inside when her eyes began to adjust, and she could see what was going on.

The tool shed was indeed open. It had a barn door affair, and the two large wooden panels had got unlatched and were flapping in the wind. About three feet out from the doors, a single white plastic garden chair lay on its back, edging along the ground, as if it were being tugged out of its housing on a piece of string. If it hadn't been such a nuisance, it would have been comical.

She took a deep breath and darted out, heading towards the escapee. As she did, she noticed another chair edging out behind it. What was it with these things? Busting to get out and get some sun, or what? The flapping motion of the doors had to be creating a draught that was catching them and sucking them out. If she didn't get them back in soon, the whole set would be out and partying.

Grabbing the farthest plastic runaway, Sally felt rather like a cowboy chasing an escaped herd. She smiled, undeterred by the latest sheet of rain that swept in and splattered against her. It was rather exhilarating, being out here in the thick of it, if a little cold. She flicked back her damp hair, wrestled the two chairs together into a stack and carried them back towards the outhouse. Pushing them inside, she grabbed at the nearest door, and turned around to see how to secure the doors. Suddenly, her blood curdled. Out of nowhere, a hand had reached over hers. A scream rose in her throat.

"Hey."

She jolted round. It was the man from the cove, Julian, and he was holding the door, helping her.

"Oh, it's you," she gave a slightly hysterical laugh, relief sinking through her veins.

"Seems that I've got quite a knack for disturbing people." He looked at her, concerned. "I saw all the lights going on, and I thought you might be in some kind of trouble, with the storm and all."

"Thanks, it's just that these doors have got loose." She looked up at him. His hair was so wet that it was stuck to his head, and there was a small gash on his forehead.

"What happened to your head?"

"I had a run in with a flying tent peg. It's nothing, really." He gave her a big smile, and she melted inside. He must have gotten soaked coming across the cove in this weather. Sure enough, his t-shirt and jeans were wet through.

"Oh, my, you're drenched!"

"Um… so are you, lady." She followed the line of his eyes and gasped, astonished, when she looked down at herself. Like the prize-winner in a wet t-shirt contest, her breasts were thoroughly exposed against the utterly translucent scrap of fabric that clung to her body in a most insistent way. She wrenched her shirt further down on the thigh, peeling it away from her body in an attempt at respectability, blushing to the roots of her hair.

"Watch out."

She heard his warning, and then felt herself being snatched in against his body, his arms quickly going around her. Winded by the sudden, intense strength of his physical embrace, she shut her eyes. She felt him kick out, batting against the loose door with one booted foot. The door would have crashed into her, would have injured her for sure. Her knees suddenly turned to jelly. Was it because of the near miss, or the proximity of her rescuer?

"Are you okay?"

They were welded together, both their damp clothes and the warm flesh beneath seemingly unwilling to part. She nodded and looked up into his eyes, shaking back the wet strands of hair encroaching on her view. His brow was drawn down, giving him a fierce, hungry look. A gust of wild sea air whipped up around them, buffeting them together as if colluding with the storm to unite them.

His hands moved to her upper arms, stroking her gently, possessively. Her breasts were chaffing against the hard outline of his chest. He had to be able to feel them; she could feel every ounce of him, every hard surface, every warm beat of his body, *everything*. The alert pulse throbbing inside her sex quickly stepped up its pace, beating out a fierce, erratic rhythm.

She shivered.

He blinked. "Why don't you go back inside," he whispered, his breath warm on her cheek. "I'll sort these doors out for you."

"No…I mean, yes, but what about you? Won't you come inside too?" She didn't want him to disappear. *No way.*

"I'll head off on my bike. My tent has perished in the storm." He shrugged it off.

"Look, please come in and let me see to that." She nodded at his forehead. "Let me say thanks for the help." He hesitated, and she swallowed her rising doubts. "I have brandy," she added.

He broke into a slow smile. "Okay, I'll come for the brandy. I don't need tending though. It's really nothing."

"We'll see."

Neither of them had moved, and after several more moments enjoying the mutual proximity, they finally eased apart. Sally stepped away and watched, her arms folded across her breasts, while he latched the doors closed and threw a large rock in front of them for good measure.

Inside the house, she noticed again how tall he was. What was she doing inviting a complete stranger into the house? Doubt mingled with the desire running in her veins. She wasn't in the habit of picking up men or taking risks with people she didn't know. *But*, her sensible side intervened, if he'd had dubious intentions, he would have made himself a nuisance earlier on, instead of helping her out, wouldn't he? She glanced back at him as she gestured to the sitting room. He was simply gorgeous. Her body flared immediately. There was no turning back. She needed to find out what might transpire.

He overwhelmed the tiny sitting room. Sally smiled as she set down the brandy glasses and bottle on the table next to the overstuffed armchair he was sitting on. *What was it Kitty had said, about jumping his ship*?

"Cheers," she whispered, as she offered him a glass and lifted her own, taking a long draught for courage. "Thanks for coming to my rescue." She peeled her t-shirt off her thigh again, flapping it lightly. His right eyebrow lifted, as if he was musing on a private joke.

"What is it?" she dared to ask.

"You're standing there half undressed, offering me brandy, like a fey woodland nymph tempting me into your lair, and *you* are thanking *me*... It just seems a bit ironic, that's all."

He was direct, that was for sure. And there was that humorous quirk in his eyebrow again. He gave her another slow, sexy smile. It was *so* suggestive. Sally felt warmed right through, and it wasn't just the brandy that was causing it. This certainly looked like it might be going somewhere interesting. She smiled at his blatant commentary on her appearance, set down her glass and picked up the small first aid kit she'd dug out of her wash bag.

"No arguments," she instructed, and moved closer to clean and dress his wound. The tension between them had barely lessened, and now, as she moved in against him, leaning closer, the tension began to creep higher again.

"I really appreciate you doing this," he said, looking up at her while she tended him.

Sally's gaze lowered from the band-aid she had just applied, to look into his eyes. They were devilish in their direct appraisal. Anticipation ran heavy and hot in her veins. The room suddenly felt stifling hot. She went to step away, but he grabbed her around the wrist with one strong hand.

"I don't even know your name."

"Sally, Sally Richards. I'm sorry. I was a bit preoccupied when you called by earlier." She blushed. He still held her in his grip, strong and firm. How strong might his arms feel around her, she wondered? His shoulders looked powerful—he'd be able to lift her easily. She'd be at his mercy, if he so desired. For some reason that notion made her cream.

"Sally…" He rolled the word around his tongue. "I like that." He was looking at her with a dark, roaming expression in his eyes, and she was very aware of her state of undress.

"You're not frightened, are you?"

She was surprised, but she shook her head. "I invited you in, didn't I?" She managed to get the words out and gave him a smile.

"You did, but now you are trembling." He fixed her with a determined gaze. "Your body is giving off some very strong signals, my dear, and my guess is that it's either fear, or arousal."

Sally trembled again. His words both shocked and thrilled her.

With one finger he stroked the tender, sensitive flesh on the inside of her wrist, as if encouraging her to confess to him, confess what it was that she was feeling.

"Yes," she whispered. "Yes, I am…aroused." *Be brave.* "I didn't want you to leave."

"And now?" he demanded, his voice controlled.

"Now, I…I still don't want you to leave." Her gaze dropped from his as she breathed out the words.

He let go of her wrist, rose to his feet and rested both hands on her waist, pulling her towards him. His face was millimeters from hers. The expression in his eyes told her he wanted her as much as she wanted him. She could see it; she could feel it. Her lips parted with the desire for his kiss.

"You're sure?" His hands stroked up over her waistline and caressed the sides of her breasts through the clinging wet t-shirt.

Sally groaned, nodding. She was quite willing to beg at that moment, beg for his body against hers. "Please…" she murmured. He reached down to slide her damp t-shirt up and over her head. She dutifully lifted her arms, allowing him to take control. He murmured appreciatively when her breasts bounced free, and he stroked their sides, lifting them and molding them gently in his hands. He ran a thumb over each nipple. A thread of electricity seem to spring from his fingertips and charge through her body, straight to her core, firing the dense heat there to fever pitch. Sally whimpered with sheer pleasure. He lowered his head to kiss her neck, his tongue darting out to taste her as he went the length of her throat.

"Oh yes, you look and taste just as good as I thought you would."

Somewhere his words registered. He had been imagining her naked too. Her body writhed in his arms at the very idea of it. He grabbed her and pinned her to the wall, his hips pressed hard against hers. The rigid, jutting outline of his cock inside his jeans pressed forcefully against her belly. She was swamped with lust, sheer, rampant lust, barely contained. It crackled between them, as palpable as the summer lightning that had sliced through the night sky minutes earlier.

Her hips moved against his, begging for him to take control of them. All she could focus on was the swell of his cock through his jeans. A gush of liquid heat had fired through her body when she felt the hard bulk of his erect cock. She wanted, badly. His eyes glinted, his hips rocking against hers, and then he glanced around.

"Where's the bed? I want to see you on your back"

Sally trembled at his directness. Her heart thudded out a violent rhythm.

"This way." She took his hand and led him through the cottage, to the oak and linen furnished bedroom, where the bedside lamp and the moonlight at the open window gave the room an eerie aura, the encroaching elements filling the atmosphere with tension. The curtains at the window lifted on the night air, the room swept through with the smell of the sea, as if the place were a cave on the shore.

She turned to him once they were inside, and her hands moved to his t-shirt of their own accord, eager to feel his chest. He grabbed the material and pulled it off, revealing the torso that had filled her mind since she'd first seen him on the beach. It was hard and defined, powerful, covered with a fine coat of hair, bleached golden. His biceps flexed as he moved to touch her. He put his hands into the niche of her waist, and walked her back towards the bed, easing her down onto it, before she could say or do another thing.

"What a picture," he murmured, looking down at her naked body. His hands went to undo his belt, his fingers moving deftly on the silver buckle, his muscular arms flexing. A draft of air from the open window lifted his hair, and the lamplight cast his face in shadows as he looked down at her. The muscles of his body seemed to unfurl as he moved, powerful and sexy. Like Neptune, a sea god stepped from the waves. Sally felt another pang of longing thrumming inside her.

He eyed her possessively as he undid his jeans and kicked his boots off. Her gaze dropped as he climbed out of his jeans, and she saw the bulge of his erection. His cock reared up, long and thick, its head beautifully defined and dark with blood. Her breath sucked into her lungs, as she wanted to suck the beautiful, hard thing into her body.

He reached down and kissed her deeply, his tongue teasing against hers. Her fingers twined around his neck, drawing him closer. His hands swept between her thighs, and her legs fell open. He climbed between them and rested over her. His hips were moving against hers, pressing his erection between them, and it was driving her wild. Every move he made sent a whirlwind of awareness through her senses. His closeness, his sheer maleness overwhelmed her with a rush of sensations.

"Please, Julian," she pleaded.

His eyes flashed at her. "Patience, my dear, or I might have to teach you some lessons in *restraint*."

Sally moaned at the idea of it.

"Oh, so we're not adverse to the idea, huh?"

No, I'm not.

But she couldn't form the words to answer. She pressed her lips together, her eyes flashing at him, her need overwhelming her.

He gave a dark chuckle and bent to tease each nipple with his tongue, moving from one to the other. His face pressed into the soft skin of her cleavage, absorbing her scent. His attention was too delicious; her nipples were tight knots of desire, and her breasts ached in his hands, sending rivers of heat through her body. When he moved lower, his mouth traveling over her belly, she couldn't hold back the whimper. His fingers stroked over the soft down on her pubis, then he opened her up, and she felt his breath hot on the tender, anxious skin between her thighs. When she felt his mouth touching her there, she clutched at the sheets, her lower lip caught between her teeth. She was helpless under his assault.

He teased her with his tongue, inviting her to enjoy his caresses. In the distance, the soft crash of the waves on the shore rolled in a rhythm as mesmerizing as his mouth on her sex. She heard the pleasured murmurs rise up from her own mouth, and then felt him as he followed the sounds, his tongue retracing her most sensitive places until she blossomed into climax, sweet and sudden. She was lost to it for a few moments, until she became aware of him moving. He snatched at his jeans and pulled a condom from the pocket. And then he was there, the weight of his body between her trembling thighs, and the hard nudge of his cock made her gasp, desire opening her up to him.

He locked her eyes with his, watching her expression as he eased inside her, slowly at first, then more forcefully. When he finally drove the full length of his shaft inside her, she gave a cry of pleasure. She felt him throbbing and clasped at him with her inner muscles. Holding him close, her hands absorbed the feel of the taut muscle of his backside. Their bodies locked together to fulfill the need that had been planted in them, thrusting and reaching, urging each other on. Each thrust inside her was so powerful and devastating, the sensitive flesh of her over-aroused sex was a riot of sensation, pumping and clasping at him. He had driven her to distraction and now he was moving so in tune with her body that Sally felt as if she was about to come, each and every time his cock stroked deep inside her.

As their movements grew increasingly feverish she bucked her body up against him. A blossom of that pleasure began to burst, to seep through her and her breath caught, her body arching. His hands roved feverishly through her hair. The heat of imminent climax flared up through her body.

His brows were drawn down, a bead of sweat sliding slowly down one side of his face. His mouth opened and each quick thrust drew a harsh breath from him. Sally cried out when the heat welled inside her. She felt his whole body arch and bow against hers. His cock heaved and lurched, their bodies clutching together in the moment of mutual climax. She was powerless to do anything but enjoy—she was in ecstasy.

"Oh yes. . .yes," he murmured, his eyes afire with passion. The wave of pleasure washed over her, lifting her on its crest, and then lingered, as if on the turn of the tide, before ebbing slowly away, leaving her panting and trembling with sensation, like a castaway clinging to the shore.

Chapter Three

Sally awoke to the distant sound of humming and the wafting aroma of breakfast. She stretched luxuriously and rolled over in the bed, opening her eyes. The sunlight poured in through the window, bathing everything in warm light. The storm had lifted the torrid atmosphere; the day was bright and clear. She sighed, her mind quickly recounting what had gone on the night before. They'd made love till dawn. Each time they thought themselves replete, they had begun to explore each other some more, testing the durability of the bed with their love-making all over again. And by the sounds of it, Julian was still here.

She got up, stretching, and pulled on another baggy T-shirt from the stack that she had brought with her. Checking the mirror to make sure her hair wasn't too mussed, she pulled the shirt straight and pushed her hair back. It occurred to her that she should have brought something a bit more interesting in the clothing department. He'd said he liked the way she looked naked, but she felt the urge to impress him dressed, too. She'd thought she was going to be on her lonesome sculpting all the time, not colluding with the local beachcombing stud. She smiled. Luckily, she had brought a couple of summer dresses with her; they may well be needed.

As she walked down the hall, she felt a wave of nerves hit her. She'd gone to bed with a complete stranger in the night. It was a heat of the moment thing; there was no holding back that kind of passion, but now they had to face each other.

Peeping around the corner of the kitchen door, she was delighted to see that he was indeed cooking breakfast. He was completely naked, apart from a cook's apron that he had donned for the task. The view was so spectacular and amusing that Sally wished she had her camera handy. The apron cord hung around his neck and high on his waist, leaving his muscular back and his gorgeous buttocks on full display for her eager eyes. There wasn't a woman on earth who wouldn't be pleased to find a sight like that in her kitchen first thing in the morning. And it put all thoughts of nervousness out of her head.

"Good morning, sexy," he said, when she entered the space, grabbing her into one arm for a slow, lingering kiss. The pulse point in the pit of her belly leapt into life. She would have to try to stay focused on rational behavior, at least for some of the time, or she'd be reduced to a puddle of lust every time he touched her. She sidled out of his arms, nonchalantly, pretending to be more interested in what he was cooking. She was hungry and her stomach was growling, but still she had to drag her gaze away from him to look at the food.

"I raided the fridge. I hope you don't mind."

"Of course not," she answered, looking up from the delicious meal he'd managed to conjure up with the few items she'd had in the fridge. The variety of flavors and textures made her mouth water. He clearly had more talents than the obvious ones that she had already discovered, and he was darned good at those. Apparently, he could cook as well.

"All this hot sex works up quite an appetite," he added, smiling a slow smile and winking at her.

She sat down, and he put a plate down in front of her. He'd made a fresh omelet, accompanied by strips of bacon that looked like he'd griddled them until crispy, then sautéed in butter with juicy cherry tomatoes and shallots. From somewhere he'd found what looked like fresh herbs. She took a mouthful of the succulent omelet, which he had mixed to the most amazing consistency, and it melted in her mouth. There were definitely chives in there, chives and fresh parsley.

"Where did you get the herbs?" she asked when he put a plate of warm bagels and a coffee pot on the table and then joined her, settling easily into the chair opposite her.

"There's a small herb patch in the back garden."

There is?

"It's gone wild because the house has been empty for years. But it's in a sheltered spot and some of them have survived."

"You know a lot about the place." She watched him butter a bagel and take a hearty bite. He nodded, wielding his fork over his portion of omelet. Everything he did only seemed to emphasize his strength and agility. He was like a prowling creature, always watchful, sleek and predatory.

"I approached the owner about buying the cottage, a year or so ago. It was his mother's house, and it had been empty since she passed on. I wondered what he had in mind for the place, but all has now become clear." He gestured around the recently refurbished kitchen. "Not bad, but I had better plans for it than letting it to a never ending stream of tourists." The last words were ejected with feeling, and it was grim.

Tourists? Is that how he saw her? An annoying tourist on his patch?

He gave her a quick, reassuring smile when he noticed the growing tension in her expression.

"I'm sorry, I don't mean you. You're a very welcome sight." He winked. "I just worry about the area getting overpopulated, you know."

His smile was still tight, she noticed. She had begun to wonder if he had been upset about her presence in the property, which he obviously had a hankering for. But it seemed more than that; it was the cove itself. She could have guessed that, she realized, if she'd thought back to her first sighting of him. She frowned, wondering where she stood in all this. And how would he feel if he knew the agent had advertised the property as if the cove was the exclusive domain of the tenant? When she'd read about it, she knew it was just a sales pitch. The beaches were national property. But what would other visitors make of it? And more importantly, what would Julian make of it? That kind of news might be better coming from her than anyone else. She mentally shelved the task. She'd get to it later on; why spoil the current mood any further than it had been already?

"Don't worry," he added. "I got over it. I have a flat I use as a base instead, down the coast in Hull. It's close to the waterside and to the conservation unit, my HQ. I have to go back there at the end of every week to report anyway…" His voice drifted off as he tucked into the food.

"What is it that you do?"

"Beach patrol, conservation, up and down the coast from Hull to the border of Scotland. I cover a lot of miles so I camp out when the weather's good."

That explained the test tube. It was part of his work.

"And if you get caught out by the weather, you can take advantage of the local *tourists*?" she teased, trying to lighten the underlying attitude she felt to her presence.

"Only if they're attractive brunettes with come-to-bed eyes."

Well parried, she reflected, smiling at his remark.

"And what is it that you do? Something to do with these guys?" He nodded over at her latest cyber warrior, who stood by on the far work surface.

Thank God she had tidied everything away after his last impromptu visit. The new piece that he had inspired was safely hidden in the broom cupboard. "Yes and no. That's more of a personal project, but I have sold a few. I'm an importer, figurines too, but oriental mass-market stuff. I studied sculpture at art college, and I felt I knew enough about it to become a buyer. At first I worked for a major fancy goods importer, then my dad encouraged me to start my own business and things went from there."

"Corporate lady, are you?" He eyed her up and down.

"Not really. It's a specialist market, and I mostly supply hotel chains. I've been in the business for five years, and it's gotten easier as I've gotten more experience. Things are changing for me all the time. When I started out, I had to go over to Singapore to shop for samples. Now, because so many companies worldwide are selling their goods over the net, I don't really have to leave my office, except if I'm looking for new outlets. My reputation is built to the extent I don't have to do as much of that. In fact it's ticking over so well that I was able to take my first proper holiday and take time for my own sculpture." She gestured over at the cyber figurine.

He nodded, looking thoughtful. "Do you have staff?"

"Yes, all part timers, working mothers mostly. It's me doing my bit for womankind."

"The politically-correct city girl, huh?"

"I guess I try to be, although I don't label myself that way." She stuck her tongue out at him.

"And is there a partner knocking about?" He looked a bit awkward, and a hint of color rose on his angular cheekbones. The man was almost blushing.

"No partner, business or otherwise." She smiled, showing him she wasn't concerned by his question.

He nodded. "Do you have to wear a suit and high heels and all that?"

He looked perturbed as he asked. That amused her greatly. He was such a man of the shore, so unlike any man she'd ever met before. Was that why she was so attracted to him? Because he was so unlike all the stuffed suits and smart-mouthed city lads she met in London?

"Sometimes. Why, does it bother you?"

"It doesn't bother me. I was just trying to picture it."

His hot stare made her feel restless, and she wriggled on her seat, and then set down her knife and fork. She picked up her coffee cup to distract herself. She glanced out of the window, away from his sexy expression. Could she stop thinking about sex at all with him around?

"I'll have to head to Morpeth, the nearest big town, to pick up a new tent." He smiled across at her.

"It might sound selfish, but I'm kind of glad you didn't have a tent to go back to last night."

"I couldn't wish for better hospitality, but I'll be out of your hair soon."

An instant objection to his words rose up inside her. She quelled it, trying to stay cool. *Why not, though?* He was the perfect companion, the perfect man for a wild holiday affair. "You're welcome to stay in the cottage, with me." Her gaze lifted to meet his. "For the rest of the week. I'm here until Friday." She could see he was interested.

"Well, if you're sure I wouldn't get under your feet..."

Nothing could be further from the truth. "There may be some sort of forfeit... sexual of course." *Did I really say that?*

He laughed. "Of, course. I'll take you up on your offer, but if you change your mind, just say. I have to be back in Hull on Friday anyway. I can pick up a new tent then."

"Good, that's sorted." *Bliss, three more days of hot sex*! "What do you have to do today?"

"I need to survey two beaches about twenty miles up the coast, take samples, check the wildlife numbers and make notes on any changes. When I'm in this neighborhood, I usually stay here on the cove all week and use it as a base. Both spots are within easy reach. One's a cliff edge shore; the other is a small harbor beach, both terrific places. You should check them out while you're up here."

"Well, I need to get out, so if you're up for it, we could go in my Land Rover. I haven't seen enough of the coast. You could be my guide."

He nodded, smiling that sexy smile. "Sure, it's a great idea." He reached for his coffee cup and took a sip, still looking at her over the rim. His hands were strong—she felt the urge to sketch them. He put the cup down and frowned. "Do you have any sugar?"

"No, sorry, I don't take sugar so I didn't bring any with me, although there might be some in a cupboard somewhere."

Sally rested back in her seat and watched him moving along the cupboards, quickly glancing in each. He was so nonchalant about the fact he was naked, all but for an apron! How could she not love that? In fact, he seemed totally unaware of his body, completely lacking in self-consciousness. He was certainly unaware of the effect he had on her. She crossed her legs, savoring the rhythmic, ticking sensation deep between her thighs. She'd never met a man so at ease with himself. He was every artist's dream model. She wondered if he would model for her during his stay. Just as the question permeated through her consciousness, he crossed the kitchen towards the far work surface, glancing approvingly at the cyber figurine as he went past.

"He's cool, I like the little man."

"Thank you."

She got the words out and then the smile on her face froze and she watched, horror struck, when his hand reached for the handle on the broom cupboard. She clapped her hand over her mouth. She'd completely forgotten about the torso when he'd started hunting through the cupboards on his quest for sugar.

"Hello, what have we here?"

She prayed he was talking about the broom. The dustpan and brush? *Let it be the feather duster, please.* But, no, he was bending into the cupboard, looking at what had to be her latest sculpture.

"This looks interesting."

Maybe he wouldn't recognize it.

He squatted down on his haunches and slid out the thin chipboard plinth it was resting on to get a better look. "Why have you got it hidden away in the cupboard?" he asked, and turned back to her before she had a chance to do anything about composing her features.

She dropped the hand from her mouth, and laughed, nervously.

His brow furrowed, a half-smile still hovering. He glanced from her to the sculpture and back, a curious expression on his face. He turned the plinth slowly, looking at the clay.

She was speechless. What could she say? All she could do was hope that he wouldn't realize the sculpture was of him. Maybe the floor would open up and swallow her.

"This is me, isn't it?" he said, still puzzled, but fascinated too.

Damn. She couldn't bring herself to deny it.

"But you certainly didn't have time to get up and do this between dawn and breakfast…so, when…?" He turned the plinth again, and looked at the hand, which rested on the rising cock, the thumb obviously working against it.

Oh no! That was such a huge clue.

He stared at it for what seemed an age and then pushed it back into its hidey-hole in the cupboard. She realized she was holding her breath, and her lungs were about to burst.

He shook his head, and stood up, closing the cupboard, and turned to her. His expression was dark but controlled, and his eyebrows were drawn down as he considered her.

She bit her lip. *How upset was he going to be?* How would she feel, if the tables were turned? She had intruded on his privacy, and she shouldn't have worked on the model without his permission. What had she been thinking of?

"You were watching me on the beach the other day, weren't you?" His tone was stern, and he folded his arms across his chest while he contemplated her.

She felt like a naughty schoolgirl. "I couldn't help it." *That sounded so lame.* She'd made a conscious choice here. "I'm sorry, I just…well, you inspired me." She adopted what she hoped was an imploring expression. He took a step closer, his fingers tapping against his folded arms, his mouth tight. She'd blown it with him already. He was upset with her. She stood up as he approached.

She swallowed. "I'm really sorry," she added.

"That's not good enough." He frowned. "You'll have to be punished."

"Punished?" Her voice faltered. What had she got herself into here?

He grabbed at her wrist, drawing her in close against him. His eyes were gleaming, his hand strong and controlling on her wrist.

"Yes, punished."

She stared up at him, in disbelief. Then she saw it. Despite his deadpan features, she caught a glimpse of the dark, expectant twinkle in his eyes. His mouth twitched to one side in a sardonic smile.

"Your face is a picture," he commented, and then broke into a laugh, the timbre deeply amused and satisfied. But he didn't let her go.

"You devil!" She gave a nervous laugh, her eyes wide with incredulity. He was teasing her!

"That's as may be, but you've still got to be punished."

She stared at him, disbelief spiraling inside her. Whatever did he mean by it, to punish her? Then, somewhere inside her an instinctive pang of anticipation suggested an answer to the question: did he mean to have her, for her naughtiness? On his terms, whatever they might be. Her heart began to race. He was having fun with her, but he also seemed intent on following it through.

He eyed her up and down with deliberation, as if the idea of it was very appealing to him. Clasping her waist, he drew her whole body up against him. If she had any doubt about his sheer physical strength before, it was all erased. She was easily captured in his grasp. For some reason it made her legs tremble, and she felt the heat building between her thighs. He ran his hands over the outline of her breast, where her nipple jutted hard through the fabric of her t-shirt.

"I'll give you a thirty second head start, but I have to warn you, I'm fast on my feet."

As he said the words, he set her aside. He flexed his arms and knotted his fingers in a stretch, as if preparing to work her over. He nodded at the door.

She stared at him. *He couldn't be serious*!

"Thirty…twenty-nine… you're wasting time. Anyone would think you wanted to be punished!" And then he smiled again, and the urge to spar rose up alongside the flood of anticipation inside her.

"*If* you can catch me. I'm pretty fast on my feet too," she retorted. She turned and headed for the door.

"Twenty-eight!"

She heard his voice as she bolted out across the grass bank that linked the cottage grounds to the edge of the cove. The grass was deep and springy beneath her bare feet, damp and lush from the overnight rain. Where she was headed, she didn't know; she just wanted to make space between them, to outrun him, to show him she was game as much as he was.

Punish her indeed.

She glanced back over her shoulder, to see him nonchalantly leaning up against the doorframe, watching her with that smile on his face. He was an absolute devil, taunting her like that! She turned back to her path and ran as fast as her feet would carry her, her breath catching in her lungs, her emotions flying somewhere between elation and trepidation. She squinted into the distance where she could make out the outline of his motorbike on the far end of the cove. If she could make it that far…she'd have proved a point. She dug deeper and found more resources, moving faster than she thought she could. Behind her, she heard him shouting after her.

He was on his way.

She didn't pause to look back, but noted that the grass beneath her feet had first become thicker and heavier, and now it was sparser, where the earth turned to sand at the edge of the cove. She had a good start on him.

But not good enough.

She heard him thundering up behind her and couldn't resist taking a glance. That was fatal. The sight of a gorgeous hunk ripping off an apron as he ran after her put a massive obstacle in front of her determination.

"Damn!" She'd tripped and landed with a thud on the first sand dune she'd had to mount. Struggling to her knees, she pulled her t-shirt down over her exposed bottom, suddenly realizing she was in as much of a state as him. What if someone saw the pair of them running around half naked?

"Perfect," he declared, as he descended to his knees beside her, and grabbed her into his arms. She struggled hopelessly, wriggling in his arms in an effort to get free. He lifted her easily, flipping her over onto her hands and knees.

"You have the sexiest bottom I've ever seen. You can't expect a man to watch you running around like that and not have the urge to give you a good seeing to."

Sally giggled, her head hanging down as he pushed her t-shirt up over her hips and shoulders, letting it to drop down her arms and pool on the sand in front of her. She was totally naked, out here in the bright sunshine. It felt strange, but somehow right.

He rested his hand around the curve of her buttock. She leaned into his touch, quickly forgetting her attempt at escape. He moved his hand, stroking her gently in circular motions. It felt deliciously naughty, his movements warming the surface of her bare bottom. Her pussy was flooded with arousal and her entire nether region tingled with sensation.

"Are you ready to accept your punishment?"

Her head swung around just as he lifted his hand away from her bottom and held it aloft. When she realized he was serious, her amusement faded. Her mouth opened and she attempted to move, but he had her in a firm grip. He didn't keep her contemplating the situation for long, his hand quickly slapping down onto each of her buttocks in turn, making quick bursts of contact on her buttocks. The sting and the sudden shock of it made her gasp, but very soon a warm, tingling glow spread from the point of contact and quickly keyed into her body, as if each slap was triggered to make contact with the pounding pulse raging inside her. She wriggled, rubbing her thighs together and arching her back, quickly becoming addicted to the beautiful mixture of pain and pleasure he was arousing.

"You're enjoying this, aren't you, you naughty girl," Julian said, and gave a dark chuckle.

She felt her cheeks color but she nodded her head, unable to deny it. She'd never been spanked before, and she was shocked at the hot, tingling sensation it brought about. Her hair trailed on the sand as her head hung down. He was spanking her naked bottom, here, out in the open on the beach. Pleasure, pain and shame engulfed her. He gave her another round of slaps. The heat spread quickly from her backside, heightening the points of arousal in her body, each sting quickly interacting with the need for some overt, sexual activity that her body desired. Her breasts swung down, swaying with every movement of her body, her nipples sticking out like totems of lust. Her sex was creaming; she could smell her own desire mounting all around them. Her whole body was on fire and trembling from the quick fire contact on her buttocks, and she was aching for more.

As if he knew what she was thinking he paused, and thrust his hand lower, sliding his fingers along the folds of her sex. Sally's head lifted and she bit her lip to stop herself from crying out. She watched the sea moving, rhythmic and strong, making its way surely into the cove, as surely as the liquid signs of her arousal were spilling down her inner thighs and over his inquisitive fingers.

"Oh yes, you are so wet, you little sexpot." He shoved his thumb inside her, drawing a sudden gasp from her. He flexed his hand, rocking it so that his index finger caressed her clit, and his thumb rubbed inside the entrance to her sex, where her sensitive flesh swelled and throbbed under his touch. Within seconds she was teetering on the edge of climax. She cried out and thrust her hips back onto his hand in the moment of her release.

She panted for several long moments, her eyes shut, trying to regain her equilibrium. Then she swung her head around to look at the man who had mastered her senses so thoroughly. He was kneeling beside her, looking down at her body with a satisfied half smile. Self-assured and totally lacking in self-awareness, he was fisting his cock in one strong hand, riding the stiff shaft hard, its head gleaming with a creamy drop of his semen. She stared, transfixed, absorbed by the experience, her responses instinctive.

"You want it, don't you?"

She nodded and crawled nearer to him, her body burning up with arousal. She had never been overtly submissive before. Sometimes in her fantasies, yes, but she'd never met anyone like Julian before. It was only him that made her feel this way, like it was right and she didn't have to hide it. His total male virility and his prowess as a lover overwhelmed her. And she was so goddamn hot as a result!

He smelt delicious, and she breathed him in, running her nose against his thigh. She opened her mouth, her tongue licking up the underside of his cock.

"Oh yes, that's good. Do it, Sally, suck me."

His cock was long and dark, fit to burst. Her fingers closed on its girth, and she stroked its velvety smooth surface. She leaned into him, her tongue tracing the crown of his cock. He groaned, his body taut with restraint. She licked the length of him, reveling in the taste of his body and the effect it had on her, sending wild frissons of delight through her entire body. She looked up at him from below as her mouth closed over the crown of his cock.

"Yes, yes, let me see it sliding into your pretty mouth." His eyes were glazed, his lips parted as he watched her moving on him. "That looks so hot," he groaned. "I'll remember that image forever."

Under her tongue and hands she could feel his tension building. She began to move faster, sensing his need. His hands moved through her hair and stroked at the back of her neck, cupping her then letting her slip away again when she took him deep. Suddenly she could taste him, the first salty offerings of his climax. His cock reached, seemingly growing even larger. He panted loudly, his voice hoarse. Then his head went back, and he bellowed at the sky. Under her fingers his balls contracted. A moment later, he was spilling into her mouth.

His body shuddered. She glanced down at the spilled drops on her breasts, slowly rubbing them into her skin. There was something very pagan and earthy about doing that, which left her unable to resist.

"You are one sexy woman," he said, when he caught sight of her massaging her breasts with his come.

She didn't know what she liked best, seeing him roaring at the sky like a beast unleashed, or when, afterwards, he grinned and grappled her into his arms, rolling her across the sand, laughing and kissing her face while singing her praises.

She hadn't had so much pleasure and so much fun since…well,

ever. No, she admitted to herself, purring as he came in for another kiss, she'd never had so much fun. Ever. He kissed her tenderly, and then he gave a deep sigh.

"You have the most gorgeous bottom I have ever seen, but I think you enjoyed your punishment far too much. You were on fire, you little harlot."

"Should I apologize?"

"No," he commented, smiling. "I'll just have to keep thinking of ways to get even with you."

"I can't wait to see what you come up with," she replied, teasingly.

"The tide is coming in," he commented, as he lifted her easily into his arms and began to walk away from the spot where they had been nestled for some time.

She gazed up at him, spellbound. She was convinced she was dreaming. At any moment she would wake, and it would be the night of the storm, but she'd be alone. Or, worse still, she'd be at home in her South Kensington apartment, alone. She shunned the idea but prayed that she wouldn't wake up, not yet.

"This might help," he murmured, his face in shadow, the sun fanning out behind his head.

"What?" She smiled up at him, idly, and then she felt the lap of water around her dangling toes. She jumped. *What on earth*?

"You got so hot when I was trying to give you a spanking, I think you need a bit of a cooling off. This will surely do it."

She gasped, snapped back into reality, and looked around to see where they were. He'd waded out into the water, and she hadn't even realized. She'd been so enamored with him, so lost in her reverie that she hadn't even noticed where he'd been headed. The water was rising up around her legs, icy cold and getting deeper all the time. His grip slackened. She knotted her fingers around his neck, shaking her head at him, emphatically, but he grinned and peeled them off easily and swung her in his arms, hoisting her out into the water.

"But Julian.. I ..."

It was too late. *I can't swim.* Sally gasped and cried out, her heart leaping as the icy water enveloped her.

Chapter Four

Julian froze.

What the hell have I done?

"...I can't swim." He caught the words just as he saw her slip under the water, her expression filled with fear.

Within a heartbeat, he ducked down under the water to lift her back out, easily capturing her arms as they thrashed against the water. She gasped and coughed when he stood up, lifting her out of the water.

"Sorry, sweetheart, sorry," he soothed, holding her close to him.

"Silly," she gulped. "It's silly of me, I know. It's only shallow water, but it's just that I had a bad experience as a kid and I...panic."

"Shh, don't say anything. There's no need to explain. I should have thought about it before I pulled the prank. I shouldn't have assumed you'd be okay with it."

He carried her back towards the shore and frowned when she began shivering in his arms. It was stupid of him—he hated himself for being so ignorant.

Setting her down against the first dune they reached, he dropped down beside her and began to rub some heat back into her body. It was mostly fright and she snuggled up in his arms, taking the comfort he offered.

"What a pity you aren't going to be here long enough for me to teach you to swim." Already he felt annoyed that their time was limited. He was enjoying her company. *In so many ways.*

"I ought to learn," she replied, vaguely.

He pushed her wet hair back and wrapped himself around her back, positioning her between his thighs to maximize the shared warmth.

"God, that feels good," she murmured, when he started to massage her shoulders, releasing the tension knotted there.

"Pleased to be of service."

Her shoulders and the delicate beauty of her spine were exquisite, and he traced them with his fingers, gently massaging her. Just when she seemed to be totally at ease in his arms, she stiffened again. He stopped rubbing her and followed her gaze. She was looking out into the bay.

"Oh my god, there's someone out there. They must have seen us!"

He looked over where she was pointing, at the figure on the horizon, just visible on the edge of the next cove. Julian wasn't concerned; he knew that it was most likely to be Tom, collecting his shrimps. He shielded his eyes to get a better look.

Sally tried to hide herself under him.

"That's Tom from the village, and he's very short sighted, so your honor is safe, Missy." He turned back to her. "Although…as you were such a bad girl earlier… maybe I should call him over for a second opinion on whether I've punished you enough."

Her mouth opened, her eyes widening. He growled at her and dipped down to nibble on her collarbone, tickling her with his warm breath.

"No," she wailed, giggling and squirming against him.

He lifted his head. "So, I have to take care of it all by myself. A man's life is hard one."

There was a beatific smile on her face. He looked down at her, shaking his head, but he was smiling too. It felt good; it felt easy and comfortable, being around her. She responded so well to his teasing ways. And she was a wildcat in the sex department.

She reached over and ran her fingers through his hair. "So you're not really upset about the sculpture? That I saw you..? I mean, it wasn't my fault you were frolicking around naked in my cove."

"*Your* cove..?!"

"Sorry, I meant…" She blushed.

"It's okay, I know what you meant," he said. "It makes you feel that way when you're here alone, doesn't it?" She nodded and something deeply intimate passed between them, like a silent acknowledgement about the place and its special aura. "And, no, I'm not upset about the sculpture."

"In that case, would you be prepared to model for me again?"

"Again? I wasn't aware that I had ever modeled for you before."

She pouted up at him. "I mean, would you please model for me…for the first time?"

"Yeah, why not? I'll give it go, but if I feel you're taking artistic license with me, I may have to punish you again."

Her eyes brightened with interest. Whatever this was that had been triggered between them, he liked it. *A lot.*

"I'll try to remember to behave appropriately," she murmured, as his mouth descended to hers, and he kissed her with a possessive, consuming force that swept everything away, leaving just the two of them, clinging together in the sand, as hungry for each other as they were for life itself.

Julian couldn't keep his eyes off her when she stepped down from her Land Rover that evening. She looked like a dream date, and she was his for the night and for the rest of the week. That felt good, really good.

Her hair tumbled past her shoulders in a burnished, sable curtain. She was wearing a gauzy summer dress that looked as if it might slip off her shoulders at any moment, and she seemed to float rather than walk. It had been hard to get his job done that day, with her along, but luckily she had wandered off occasionally and given him a minute here and there to compose his thoughts, take his samples and make notes. Even then, thoughts of their escapade on the beach that morning came to mind far too readily.

She smiled when she saw him watching her tuck her keys into her bag, and her eyes were glowing with the hidden secrets they shared. He couldn't help thinking what a treat the inhabitants of the village pub were in for.

He stopped her just as he was about to open the door and usher her inside. "Are you ready for this?"

"Ready for what?"

He loved that look she gave him. There was an openness about her expression that he found entrancing. Especially when it revealed to him how hot she was for him. That had him wanting to capture her into his arms—and keep her there.

"The Lobster Pot." He nodded up at the sign over the pub. "The social hotbed of a small village pub. You'll be the focus of everyone's attention. I've seen others backing out of the door because of the scrutiny they received in this place."

She lifted one eyebrow at him.

"Have you ever seen that film, *An American Werewolf in London*, where they go to the pub on the moors?"

She gave a nervous laugh. "Stop it! You're teasing me again!"

"Wait and see." He shrugged her comment off.

"Actually, they did rather give me the once over at the shop." She nodded across the street. The one and only convenience store slash post office was stationed right opposite the pub on the main street, two vital lifelines for the village close at hand. The pub also doubled up as the local eatery, and the store was stocked with everything from fishing tackle to frozen food, and stamps to stationery.

"I just thought the shopkeeper was a bit odd, you know."

"No, believe me; the whole village will be enthralled." He nodded at the pub. "And there will be a fair few of them in here right now." He was looking forward to it. He loved observing the locals and it was going to be fun watching them with an out-of-towner in their midst, especially one who was such a beautiful, gypsy-looking woman.

Sure enough, when they stepped inside, a sudden silence descended over the interior of the pub. The bar was lined with six stools upon which the usual six customers sat, a group of men of varying age groups who did little but argue over the course of their evenings spent together. At the far end of the room a mixed group were playing snooker. When Sally walked through the door, all heads turned to silently observe her. The only movement was a lone snooker ball rolling across the table.

Julian rested his hand around her shoulders and led her towards the near end of the bar.

"What would you like to drink?"

"I'll try the local ale, whatever you recommend." She smiled up at him in the most disarming way. There was a twinkle in her eyes, and he knew that she was acknowledging his previous remarks. She coped with it well, he noticed. But then he supposed that being an international importer who had to present herself and her wares at business meetings meant that she would have to have the requisite confidence.

The pub slowly began to revert back into its usual hum of conversation, but Sally continued to be the subject of speculative glances and whispered conversations throughout their visit.

Brenda, the motherly, friendly landlady, took their order with a smile and winked. "Just you ignore them ones that stare, sweetheart." Brenda offered conspiratorially.

"We're going to eat, so I'll take a menu over to the snug." He indicated a cozy booth nested into a bay window overlooking the street outside. Brenda nodded and deposited their ale on the bar.

"I have to ask," Sally said, after they had put in their order and reflected on the day's visits. "Why do you call him Old Man Greg?"

"You'll find that everyone gets a nickname around here and they really stick. When he was a young man, I understand that he was called that because of his build and posture." Julian sipped his beer, wondering what a city girl would make of it all.

"I see." Her eyebrows had lifted, but she didn't comment further. "And what do they call you?"

He shuffled his feet under the table. He was beginning to regret the line of conversation.

"I guess you'll find out anyway…they call me Double O Beach-patrol, you know, like 007."

As one would expect, she burst out laughing. "That would be because you are spying on behalf of the government?"

He nodded.

"I'd love to know what they might call me if I were a regular." She had such a naughty smile, Julian couldn't hold back his grin.

"I can think of a suggestion or two, very flattering, of course."

She idly studied the various boat related objects and fishing tackle that decorated the walls of the pub. "Where are you from, originally?" she asked.

"Well, much as I hate to admit it, I'm sort of a city boy, much like yourself." Her eyebrows went up again. He knew she'd be surprised. He tried not to be too self-righteous about the difference between the city and countryside because the spotlight usually ended up on him as a result.

"So, let me get this right. You teased me about being a city girl, when you're 'sort of' a city boy yourself?"

"Yes, I suppose you've got a point there."

It was she that tutted at him then.

"I was brought up in Surrey, just outside Guildford. Home Counties stock. My dad is a high-court judge, my mum runs the local Women's Institute." He wasn't surprised when she giggled. People often did because it didn't hold with the image he had carved for himself.

The food arrived but he carried on. "Let me get this over with. The whole family are city dwellers. I have two older brothers who are lawyers and one who is a schoolteacher. I used to take my younger sister off to the coast rambling and collecting pebbles and shells when we were kids, but to no avail. She's a DJ and a part time psychology student."

"So you're like the black sheep or the *wild* sheep or something?"

"That's exactly it. The whole family thought I was mad. On weekends they'd head to the theatre, museums and concerts while I'd head the other way to the coastline."

"Do you have to do the family thing and visit at Christmas time?" She was biting her lip, trying not to giggle. "I mean, it must really be difficult for you having to go to there."

"You can tease all you like, Madame, but as it happens I don't have to go down at Christmas time because the family have always traditionally rented a cottage in the Lake District, and I meet up with them there. In fact I blame that yearly event for the way I have turned out." He gave a smug smile.

"Well, I guess that is some sort of reason." She pouted mockingly. "Shame I won't see you down in London at Christmas time though."

Julian hitched up on taking a mouthful of his fish pie. He was so surprised, he grabbed his pint to give himself a moment to compose a suitably open-ended answer. He realized he certainly wouldn't mind seeing her again, if he did happen that way.

"You never know, things might change," he offered. With her there, the city was looking a whole lot more inviting.

She smiled and continued with her meal, but he could tell she had another question in mind.

"Go on, what else did you want to ask? I can see you're busting to ask another question."

"I was just thinking about the fact that you are so attached to this place, to the cove."

"It's always felt like home to me. I don't know why, it just does. Can you understand that?"

She nodded, but he noticed that she had grown serious.

"You feel very strongly about the cottage drawing tourists, don't you?"

"I feel strongly about the fact it has brought you, so much so that I had to act."

She smiled but the concerned look didn't disappear. "You're avoiding the issue."

"I am. Okay…I can't say I am pleased about it." He knew he was being self-righteous, but he wasn't in the habit of lying. Besides, he had already made his feelings known earlier that day. She was a clever lady, and he was worried above all that he had offended her. All he could do was hope to explain. "It's nothing personal. It's just that I've seen other places suffer simply because people don't follow the rules and show no respect."

She nodded, again looking very thoughtful. "Julian, there is something you should know. The cottage is being advertised as having a private beach nearby."

What the hell? It was as if someone had tripped a switch in his head.

"They've got no right." His volume control was quickly flying up and several curious stares came in his direction. He attempted to drop his voice a notch. "I bet that's Old Man Greg cashing in. Why should he care? He doesn't live here any more. But he should have more sense. It won't be worth it in the long run."

"I doubt he had anything to do with it. It's just an advertising slant," Sally reasoned. "It will be whoever is marketing it."

"Damn them. It is *not* a private beach…although I wish it bloody well was!" Through his indignation, he realized he was taking out his concerns for the cove on her.

Thankfully someone put money into the jukebox and the atmosphere between them began to ease up. "I'm sorry," he said and reached out for her hand.

She gave him a weak smile. "Did we have just have our first disagreement?"

"I guess so. Forgive me, please?"

"Yes, of course. I understand, I just thought you should know."

"You were right. I need to lighten up and do something positive about it. I'll look into getting the place signposted with local information and arrange refuse collection and all the rest."

Just then he felt a tap on his shoulder. Glancing round he saw that it was Tom, and he was pointing over at Sally's plate.

"The shrimps are good. Did you like the shrimps?"

Sally looked up at him and smiled. "Oh yes, of course. The shrimp was delicious."

"I caught them fresh this morning." Tom beamed. "You must be the lady staying at the cottage, the one that he was asking about."

"This is Tom," Julian interrupted. "A font of knowledge on all things local."

Sally looked at Julian with an accusing expression. "Well, I don't feel so bad about spying on you now, Mr. Double O Beachpatrol, since you were busy asking about me," she commented when Tom finally ambled off.

"Guilty as charged. I saw your car and did some snooping."

"I'm glad you did..." She gave him a smile that recalled last night's lovemaking. This morning's. Just looking into her eyes made him hard.

"So am I."

"Let's forget about the tourist thing," she said decisively. "I want us to enjoy our time together. Let's just go with the flow," she added, suggestively.

"I'm not arguing."

"Besides, you promised to model for me."

Why did that sound like it was going to be a difficult task, Julian wondered? *Because she gets you going every time she looks at you with those curious, sexy eyes, idiot.*

"Hmm, so I did," he eventually replied, wondering what he was letting himself in for. Every time she looked at him with those sexy gypsy eyes, he got aroused. Would he be able to rein in his natural urges and cope with the scrutiny?

Chapter Five

Sally pulled the curtains shut in the kitchen window and turned back to her subject. *Oh boy, her subject.* Julian was standing in the middle of the rustic kitchen, looking possibly the most self-aware that she'd ever seen him, awaiting her instructions. She'd changed into her work gear, a tank top and jeans, and had brought in a couple of lamps from the sitting room to spotlight him.

"Right. I've got my sketchbook, so if you'd like to..." She indicated his clothes. "Undress."

She could tell that he tried not to look amused or surprised, but both reactions were there in his expression.

"This is purely work for you, isn't it? I mean I'm not going to be treated like some sort of sex object?"

How did he manage to make that question sound more like a suggestion? She chuckled. "Would it bother you if I was thinking about sex while I measured you?"

There was a moment's hesitation before he came right back at her. "Well, you were the one who first mentioned forfeits of a sexual nature in return for your hospitality, and as I'm your guest, I aim to fulfill my obligation."

He winked at her and began to undress, not once breaking eye contact with her, as if daring her to look down at his body instead.

She realized she ought to distance herself from him, but she couldn't help herself. Apart from the little disagreement that they'd had back at the pub, the teasing, sexy atmosphere between them hadn't really let up since their first morning together. If anything, it had increased as the moments passed, just waiting to peak into something much more specific and physical when the time was right.

She busied herself setting the lamps up on either side of him, taking care to throw his body in relief, casting shadows into the areas that fascinated her artist's eye the most—the dips in his buttocks, the curve of his lower back, the chiseled plane where his abdomen veered into his groin.

"I'm all yours," he said, arms outstretched.

She flexed her fingers. "May I get more closely acquainted with my subject matter?"

He nodded and watched quietly, letting her do as she wished with him. Stepping closer, she gave a sigh of pleasure and ran one finger down the muscle between his neck and shoulder. She stroked the back of her hand down his chest. The sensation of skin against skin only seemed more electric through the fine covering of hair on his pecs.

With her hands on his shoulders, she moved slowly down to trace the powerful line of his biceps, memorizing them in three dimensions with her inner eye, storing away the information for future use. She glanced over at the torso that she had set nearby for comparison. One thing was for sure; she would be reworking it in a life size version when she got home.

"Do I measure up to your satisfaction?" he asked, flexing. He gave her a half smile, as if he was amused by her attentions.

She only nodded in response. She was trying to ignore her body's signals, but it was futile. She had quickly bypassed simmering and was well on her way to boiling point. *Must concentrate.* At least for a little while. She had to show him she had some iota of self-control.

Her hands trailed around his hipbone and across his back as she walked around him. She splayed her palms over his shoulder blades, noting the shape and strength of each part of him, memorizing each bone and the way it was sheathed in muscle. Her hand slipped down into the dip of muscle on his buttock. She smiled to herself when she remembered that just a couple of days earlier, when she had molded him in clay, she'd wished then that he were real. She closed her eyes when she recalled the wish, and thanked the goddess of wishes, who must surely be looking over her.

With curious fingers, she caressed his fit backside. It was so bloody sexy! She'd never understood the obsession some women had with the male posterior—until now. Now it all made perfect sense. Instinctively, her body told her that muscle was what drove him hard inside her during lovemaking. Feeling the muscle flex under her hand was almost too much. Her sex was alive with sensation. She sighed again and ran her hands down the back of his taut thighs, bending to get the measure of him with her hands.

She turned away and picked up her sketchbook, attempting to make some quick charcoal images. His physical reality was soon too much of a distraction. She meandered up and down around him, considering him from all angles, the sketchbook dangling in her hand. There really wasn't much hope of getting any serious work done here. Maybe in time she could relax around him enough to concentrate on his body as purely art subject, but right now, all this was doing was sending her hormones into overdrive.

"You're not drawing." He had an amused look on his face.

"No, I am finding it hard to concentrate, but…" She tried to look professional. "My visual memory is being stoked." She dropped the sketchbook on the table and briefly pressed her arm across her breasts, quelling their need for contact.

He gave her a slow grin that teased and taunted.

She blushed furiously. *Am I that obvious?*

The tension between them was ratcheting up. Stepping in front of him, she looked pointedly at his hips.

"Besides, for the purposes of this session, you are supposed to be in a state of *partial* arousal…" She eyed his upright cock with a mocking smile.

Not only was he as hard as steel, but his gaze was so hot that she began to feel restless with tension. The atmosphere between them crackled with anticipation.

"What do you expect," he murmured. "You were touching me…and I enjoyed it"

He suddenly reached over and grabbed her by the neckline of her tank top, pulling her closer to him. With the fabric fisted in one hand, he ripped it right down the middle with the other.

She gasped, astounded and yet wickedly thrilled by his unexpected, outrageous action. His eyes were on her breasts as they bounced free of the tight fabric.

"I'll buy you a new one," he said. "I couldn't resist." With one finger, he pushed open the torn material and circled the dark areole of one nipple. "Your nipples were digging through the material, I had to see them. You've been tormenting me, Sally; everything about you is made to torment me. Even this little top you're wearing was designed to get me hot and bothered."

"I couldn't help being aroused, with you so…" she swallowed, "hard."

"You're complaining about my physical state and yet it's all… your…fault."

He bent and circled her breast with his hand, caressing it then taking the nipple that he had teased into his mouth, tonguing it, then grazing it with his teeth. Sally felt weak at the knees; her head was spinning. He turned his attention to the other breast. She felt his cock brushing against her leg.

After he'd all but reduced her to a puddle of lust on the floor, he pushed her toward the nearest wall, running his hands all over her body, pressing the crease of her jeans into her hot niche. Her clit was crushed, pounding and swollen. Then he flipped her round and spread-eagled her against the wall, his foot pushing her legs apart. He explored her, urgent and demanding, molding and stroking her breasts from behind, his cock hard against her.

"I think you've been a very naughty girl," he murmured against her ear, one hand reaching down to rub her pussy through her jeans while he rocked his entire body against her back. "And you know there can only be one outcome in a situation like this. You'll have to be shown what a bad girl you've been. I'll have to demonstrate it to you…physically."

Sally's fingers clutched at the surface of the wall. Her heart was thudding, her body weak and her mind running feverishly. *Does he mean to spank me again?*

He lifted her and carried her into the bedroom. He could manhandle her so easily. She was like a doll to him, something he could toy with at will. And that notion sent her into overdrive!

"Take off your jeans," he said. "Then kneel on the bed."

She did as he instructed, pulling open her belt and zipper with trembling fingers. She crawled onto the bed, the tug of war between fear and desire making her both willing, and ashamed for wanting it so much. She was learning about the delights of submission, and there was so much more to discover.

Even though she knew what was coming, she flinched when she felt his hand against her bottom. But he slid his hand easily between her thighs and tisked when he felt the moisture that oozed from inside her.

"You are so bad."

"Yes, I am." Admitting it aloud sent a shudder through her body, as if she'd opened herself up to him even more, somehow.

He gave a dark chuckle. "I believe that you knew what you were doing to me in there," he added. His hands were soothing her buttocks, warning her, readying her.

No, I can't possibly enjoy what is to come, a voice in her head interjected. He gave a single slap on each cheek and let the fire spread through her, before returning to deliver a quick burst of short, sharp shocks across her buttocks. The sting was almost too much; she whimpered. Then the delicate strands of pleasure began to weave amongst the pain, and her cries soon became much more pleasured in nature. She bit her lip and hung her head. Yes, she did enjoy this beautiful, strange punishment. Her whole nether region was throbbing, and her core was on fire. She arched her back and pushed her bottom upward, exposing more of her pussy, and as she did, the palm of his hand slapped up against her swollen sex folds. Sheer ecstasy flooded her body and she was close to coming when he suddenly lifted her and rolled her over on the bed.

"Sally…Sally…you are enjoying that far too much. I'm going to have to think of some other way to punish you."

The linen cover on the bed felt rough against her buttocks, sending an after tremor of pleasurable pain through her.

"Oh no, I'm not done with you yet," he said, when she reached up for him. "In fact your new punishment is that you're going to have to wait, my dear. You are such a randy little sexpot, I can't think of a better way to make you suffer. I think I will have to teach you some self-restraint. *Forcibly.*"

He grabbed both her wrists into one strong hand and then snatched up the belt from her abandoned jeans on the bedside chair with the other. He quickly tethered her to the oak struts on the headboard.

It made her feel even more aroused. *Did he know that it would?* It was as if he knew instinctively what would drive her wild in bed, and Sally inwardly cursed the overwrought feeling that realization brought about.

"Please, Julian, I beg you. Don't make me wait…"

That just made him smile.

She writhed within the constraints. She was on fire. Her lust was fast becoming primitive, animalistic. She struggled against the belt. She wanted to free herself and force him to take her. Hard.

Julian stood running his hand up and down the length of his cock, an almost lazy stroke, while he watched her futile struggle. "I could look at you all evening. It suits you to be displayed like that." He nodded at her body, the way her breasts rolled and jiggled as she struggled against the restraints.

With his free hand, he leaned over and squeezed and molded the flesh of her breasts. Each touch caused her to moan aloud and tremble. He ran his hand lower and pushed her legs apart. Her legs were completely splayed, her ankles out toward the edge of the bed. Cool air ran over her burning pussy. Sally felt her face coloring. Somehow being displayed so thoroughly made her feel so exposed. And aroused. Even though he'd seen it all before, it was so blatant. She had so little control. He could do whatever he wanted to her. That was at the core of her lust, and she was becoming more desperate for him as each moment passed.

He walked to the end of the bed, and stared at her, while he continued to pump his cock.

"Your pussy is beautiful."

He was a master of torment. She knew that her clit was swollen and pounding, her sex gaping. She began to wonder if she would come without even being touched, just from being exposed under his devilish, watchful eyes while he continued his manly display.

The sensation of his gaze lingering on her breasts, her beaded nipples and the folds of her sex, brought her arousal to a fevered pitch. Yet still he did not touch her, did not bring her relief. He kept her waiting for so long, craving him and the thrust of him between her thighs. And when he finally rose up over her, she wanted him so badly that her juices were dribbling down between her buttocks. She couldn't stop herself lifting her hips and opening herself up to him.

"Please, I beg you, Julian, please."

He cursed under his breath, as if her comment had shredded his final bit of self-control. He reached for the bedside table, snatching up a condom and ripping it open. Kneeling over her, he rolled it on quickly and rammed his erect cock deep inside her, claiming her to the core and beyond.

She cried out. Tears of relief blurred her vision.

He started to thrust hard and fast, knocking up against the core of her, sending deep spasms of pleasure through her body. She moaned aloud. Even though she bit her lip to try and hold back, it was too much. Her whole body had been tenderized and made ready for this and now that he was inside her, she couldn't help shouting her joy.

"Yes, Sweetheart, you can let go now," he said, with a wicked smile.

"You bastard," she accused and thrust up against him, laughing with delight when his face contorted with pleasure. She held him deep inside her and squeezed his cock hard with her inner muscles.

"God…you're…so hot!" he said, between gritted teeth, and he

sounded as if the words had been wrenched from his lungs.

"You better believe it," she replied and rammed hard onto him again, using the struts on the bed head to gain more purchase.

She felt wild, as if being tethered up and at his mercy had unleashed some primitive urge to do combat. The truth was she'd never been this keyed up before. She had never been so close to coming, nor held off for so long.

They went at each other hard and fast, and when she finally came, her whole body jerked with the force of it. He groaned and spilled, his cock spurting inside her. She bit his shoulder, moaning loudly as ripple after ripple of pleasure soared through her, arresting her every nerve ending in the experience and making her body shudder, seize and, finally, grow limp and sanguine.

Chapter Six

Sally climbed up the bluff at the end of the cove and turned to look back at the view. Breathtaking. The day was blustery, the coolest since she arrived, and the breeze whipped through her hair, dancing amongst the skirts of her dress before it swept on. It was her last day with Julian. *The last day.* They'd shared such wonderful days, and nights…*oh, the nights.*

But all good things must come to an end, she supposed, especially holiday romances.

She had spent the morning alone, letting him go about his business while she brooded over her sculpture and wondered about the fact that she was becoming so attached to him. She finally decided she'd better be alone for a few hours, or it would be a complete shock to her system when they had to part the next day.

The relationship had been so highly sexually charged, and when she tried to think with a level head the best she could do was question her capability to analyze her own emotions at all. How could she have grown so attached to him so quickly? It had happened far too fast, and it was frightening her to death. He had keyed into a sexual side of her that she hadn't known existed. But that wasn't all; the distinction between lust and love had become a whole lot more fuzzy over the past few days. She just knew that she was going to pine for him when she got back to London, like some dreadful, lovesick teenager just back from a holiday romance. *I am a grown woman, for goodness sakes!*

She sighed and pushed her hands into the deep pockets on her dress. Just as she did her mobile phone started to vibrate, and she lifted it out of her pocket. It was Julian.

"I thought you were supposed to be back by now."

"I'm nearly there; I had to stop for petrol, so I thought I'd give you another quick call."

"You just want to keep me crazy with anticipation for your return, don't you?" She couldn't keep the stupid grin off her face, despite her attempt at levelheaded thinking just moments before.

"Oh, yes, I want you to be ready for me when I arrive back, because I'm hungry for you." There was a deeply suggestive tone to his words, and Sally gave a delighted laugh. He'd phoned her at least once an hour, and it was very easy to flirt back when his warm, deep voice tickled her every nerve ending. She turned her back on the breeze and stepped along the bluff.

"Oh, don't you worry. I am absolutely dripping with anticipation…" She let that one sink in and was gratified to hear him give a low groan. "It's been a constant and inevitable state when you're around. Besides, I want to make the most of our last night together."

She noticed the hesitant pause at the other end of the line. Their last night together was important to him, too. That much had been obvious this morning when he'd had a hard time leaving for his daily duties. She tried to redirect the conversation, secretly vowing not to mention the fact that it was their last night again.

"In fact, I was getting so hot with anticipation over the thought of your return, that I had to take a walk over to the bluff." She lifted her chin and looked up the coast, wondering how far away he was. As she did a movement caught her eye, a figure out in the bay. "Hey… it looks like that fisherman is busy again. Tom?"

"Probably, I imagine he'll be working on the turn of the tide," Julian commented.

She noticed that the figure was waving. She lifted her hand to return the greeting and chuckled into the phone. "There you go, Mr. Keswick, you were wrong when you said that we couldn't be seen on the cove. Your friend is busy waving at me as I speak." She chuckled again.

The sound of the engine revving up at the other of the phone dropped off.

"You sure? If it is Tom, he's short sighted, so even if you're standing on his side of the bluff, I doubt he could see you."

Sally looked back towards the figure in the water. It was then that she realized that he was waving with both hands, and he had begun to look as if he was distressed. "Oh my God, Julian, I think he's in trouble. In fact, the tide is coming in fast now and he's not moving. He's waving for help!"

As she spoke, the wind lifted again, weaving her hair across her face. She pulled it back and looked at the froth on the incoming tide with wide eyes. The surf was up.

"I thought it didn't sound right," Julian commented, then she heard the motorbike revving up again, and his voice was all but drowned out.

"What should I do?" she shouted into the phone.

"Call the police and tell them to alert the Coastguard. Be sure to tell them the tide is on the turn. I'll be there in a matter of minutes."

With that, the line went dead. Sally punched 999 into the phone and followed his instructions, moving down the other side of the bluff as she did so, her breath catching in her lungs. Her body started to tremble. As she got closer to the shore edge she could see all too clearly that he was floundering, but seemed unable to move. He had to be trapped in some way. She described the location as best as she could to the police operative, and kept waving to the figure in the hope that he would see her and know that help was on its way.

It was the longest five minutes of Sally's life. She felt completely useless and once again rued her inability to swim. By the time she heard Julian's bike roaring along the dirt track behind her, she was knee deep in the freezing cold water. She kept shouting to Tom, trying to encourage him. The tide had come in rapidly, and it scared her the way the wind whipped up the waves. She turned to watch as Julian clambered off the bike and threw off his helmet and jacket. She became aware of another noise and saw the Coastguard's boat roaring along the coast towards them.

"He's in no man's land," Julian shouted, as he shoved off his boots.

"What do you mean?"

He ran into the water. "It's too shallow for the boat to come in. I'll have to go get him."

Julian.

Her stomach knotted with fear. She watched as he dove into the water, his muscular shoulders quickly whipping into action as his arms cleaved through the waves.

Julian!

Whatever it was that had trapped Tom might endanger Julian as well. Her heart beat hard in her chest, her voice trapped in her throat. One hand covered her mouth. What if he got injured too? What could she do to help? She reached into the pocket of her skirt and punched in 999 again. She updated the police operator on what was happening and then watched as the Coastguard's boat drifted to a halt some twenty yards out from where Tom's head was visible in the water. The surf was up his chin now and his head kept bobbing down beneath the water as if he was weakening. His hands had long since stopped waving.

"Julian, be careful!"

She got the plaintive cry out but the sound was whipped away on the wind. The two men were barely visible in the water. She could see that the Coastguard was leaning over the side of the launch, shouting instructions. She watched as Julian finally reached the man struggling in the water. He exchanged a few words. Sally gasped when she saw him flip under the water and dive. She barely registered that she was wading in the water and it was up to her hips. A smattering of relief hit her when she saw that Julian's head had emerged from the water again and within seconds he had maneuvered Tom into the life-saving position and had begun to slowly swim back towards the shore.

When they got closer to her, she assisted Julian, helping to bring Tom the last few yards to the shore's edge. He was wearing a threadbare sweater that was water logged, and his trousers were rolled up to knee level, as if he'd only been that deep to begin with.

"Oh my God," Sally cried, when she saw the trail of blood on the sand. On one foot Tom was wearing a thin, worn, sports shoes. The other foot was bare; it was swollen and bleeding

"Got me foot stuck in the rocks, lost me shoe. Bastards got me on the way back in," mumbled Tom, in between chattering teeth as he dropped to the ground.

"Stay quiet," Julian insisted and bent down to examine the wounds. "Weaver fish," he mumbled beneath his breath.

"What's happened to him?" Sally asked.

"If you're shrimping, you have to protect your feet because it stirs up other fish along the way, fish that are less easy to handle. The weaver fish have got him. See there?" He indicated the bare foot that was bleeding.

She leaned over and saw a nasty looking object embedded in the Tom's foot.

"Weavers have spines on their backs. Their spines get stuck in and break off, poisoning the local area. It's not overly dangerous but it is very painful," he added, looking back at Tom, whose eyes were closed, his expression frozen and his complexion pale. "The foot then swells up with the incoming tide."

Sally stared in horror at the poor man. She dropped to her knees and stroked his forehead, offering encouragement.

"I tried to ask the Coastguard if he'd called an ambulance," Julian added. "But I don't know if they heard me."

"The police are sending one," she answered. "I phoned them again when I realized the boat couldn't get in."

"Good girl." Julian muttered the reply but he was focused on tracing the number of wounds.

Sure enough, a few minutes later the ambulance arrived and Tom was soon wrapped in a silver foil sheet and lifted onto a stretcher. Sally was shivering but relief began to surface when she saw the paramedics taking charge.

It was short lived.

Julian leaned over to say his good byes to Tom, and she saw the old man mumble something to him. Julian laughed loudly and gave the man an encouraging pat on the hand. The stretcher went into the ambulance, and the doors were slammed shut. Julian jogged back to the spot where she was standing. He peeled off his wet T-shirt and hauled the belt from his jeans. His nipples were nut-hard from cold, his upper arms covered in goose bumps. A shiver shook her entire body when she noticed.

"Will he be okay?"

He nodded, dropping the heavy belt to the ground. "I'm going back in."

"You're doing *what*?" She stared at him, aghast. *He can't be serious*!

"His shrimping gear is still out there. It's his livelihood." He broke into a grin when he saw her worried expression and leaned over to kiss her, briefly but passionately, on the mouth.

"Don't worry, gorgeous. It will only take a couple of minutes and it will mean a lot to Tom. I promise my feet won't touch the bottom if you promise you'll warm me up when I get back." He flickered his eyebrows at her and then slapped her on the behind.

How dare he be so nonchalant?

"I'll warm you up with a good tongue-lashing for going back in there, is what I'll do!" She was fuming at him for taking another risk.

He grinned at her and ran off, quickly cutting a path through the waves and disappearing towards the deeper water.

He was a liability, that man!

Even though he had promised her he wouldn't set foot down, her heart rate had notched up a number of levels. She knew that if she hadn't been so bloody cold, she'd have broken out in a sweat. Hadn't he seen Tom's injuries? How dare he take risks like that? The ambulance was a good quarter of a mile away, and her phone was probably dead or waterlogged by now.

She was scared to death in case anything would happen to him. She stretched her arms up in the air in an effort to relieve the tension coursing through her body, and put both hands on her head, biting her lip and trying to reason through his words. He shouldn't need to set foot down. He was right. He was strong. She couldn't help herself though.

I'll just die if anything happens to the man!

That's when it hit her. She was in love with him!

The water ran torrents over him and with his eyes closed he looked like a classical sculpture in the rain, mighty and powerful but still. The steam from the shower was building and she moved closer, her hands roaming up his chest, soaping him as she went, working heat back into both their bodies. She pushed back her wet hair and moved slowly, edging around him in the cubicle as best she could, adoring the feeling of him safe and warm again.

God he felt good. She wanted to keep her hands on him, always. A possessive streak had taken hold of her and she was struggling to make sense of that, and all the other thoughts and feelings tumbling through her mind. She gripped his arms and looked up at him. "I was so worried about you," she murmured.

"No need, but I appreciate it." He reached down for her hand, drew her fingers up to his lips and kissed them gently, watching her as he did so. He wasn't teasing this time and the connection between them had intensified.

"You crazy man."

"Yeah, crazy," he replied, his stare direct but deeply thoughtful, his eyes on her mouth. He bent his head to kiss her, moving her under the stream of water, forcing her to close her eyes and blinding her to his intense stare. His tongue probed into her mouth, his hands going to the tiles behind her head.

She felt his cock grow hard against her hip and reached for it. The possessive streak reared up again inside her and she pumped him hard in her soapy hand, moaning against his mouth while he kissed her with fire, with passion and urgency. She rode his cock hard with her fist, her other hand reaching down to grasp his balls, already high and tight against his body. She wanted him, she needed him, she loved him.

He hauled his head back and exclaimed loudly, letting out a great beast of a shout, his hips reaching each time as she slid her hand up and down his length. "I'm crazy for this, for you," he blurted, between gritted teeth, his eyes wild.

"And me for you, I want more, I want more of you, Julian. Let me see you come."

"Oh, you will," he replied with a hoarse laugh, shaking his head in disbelief, "any second now."

She looked down at his cock reaching in her hand. Her body clenched inside, but she wanted to see him come and worked him harder, ignoring his mumbled pleas for time. The head of his cock was dark with blood and oozing, each splash of water sending a jerk through him. He gave another shout, fierce and primal, and then she felt him rising in her hand. She held her breath. He spurted quick and hard, powerful to the last.

A moment later she felt his hand go around her neck, one thumb pushing her chin up so he could look into her eyes.

"Why do you have to feel so...perfect?" he mumbled, leaning into her, his mouth against her hair, his arm drawing her close and locked in against him.

"Why do you?" she replied.

"Here you go."

Sally glanced around, she was miles away and was surprised to hear his voice. She'd left him, gone out into the garden and hadn't realized that time had gone by quite so much. He had brought out two mugs of hot tea and set them down on the garden wall, then clambered up beside her. She crossed her legs, smoothing her jeans down, before picking up the mug by her side.

"Thanks, I couldn't resist watching the sunset." The sky was molten golds and reds. The wind had streaked amber threads through the atmosphere, bathing the cottage in the glorious light unique to that time of day. Despite the nip in the air, the light reflected warmly off the old stones of the house and she sighed deeply, wrapping her hands round the cup for comfort.

"Are you warm enough? Can I get you a sweater?"

"No, thanks." She smiled over at him and noticed how much warmer and relaxed he looked after the hot shower. "Are you feeling better now?"

"Yes. It didn't bother you did it, today?" He reached out to stroke her back through the soft fabric of her shirt. His expression was marked with concern.

She took a moment to allow his features to etch on her memory, to notice the way his hair lifted on the breeze and how the color of his eyes became luminescent in the outside light. "It was just a bit of a shock, and I'm still worrying about Tom." She forced a smile. She was feeling emotional after the events of the day, but that wasn't all.

"I phoned the hospital. He's fine. Mostly suffering from the effects of the cold but he'll be fine." Julian looked out at the sea. "And he'll be back out there shrimping again as soon as he can."

"Couldn't he do something else, something…safer?" She frowned and looked down into her tea before sipping at it.

"He could, but he won't. The sea is his challenge, and it's also a part of him, kind of like his wife, you know?" He smiled at her. "The nagging wife he has to pacify. It's in his blood, and I think even for people like us, who aren't born and bred here, it gets that way a bit too."

She nodded; she understood what he meant.

"It didn't put you off visiting again did it? I mean…I assumed you might want to visit again?" The question was cautiously asked.

"Yes, I want to visit again and, no, it didn't put me off. There are dangers in city life, too. It's just different here and being so close to nature, well, it's got problems as well as joys, just as anything in life. Part of what is special about the place is learning its ways and dealing with them."

"I couldn't have put it better myself." He leaned over and kissed her cheek, sliding his arm further around her. "I'll miss you," he added quietly a moment later. "I'll have to leave early in the morning."

"I know."

"I want to stop off at the hospital in Morpeth to visit Tom as I pass by, and I need to be back in my office in Hull by midday." He looked reluctant. "I could stay later but I'd agreed to have a report on the director's desk by three."

"Julian," she said and rested one hand on his chest, looking up at him with an earnest expression. "Please don't say another word. I understand. I have to go, too. I have to leave and…I have to get on with my life." It was true. It was the unavoidable truth of the matter. Her idyll was coming to an end and that brought such a sense of loss.

Julian gazed at her for a moment and then he winked and grabbed her against him possessively.

"I should keep you with me, take you back to my flat and tie you up so you can't escape." He kissed the top of her head and held her close.

He had said it in a light, joking way, but she felt the tension in him and wondered if he was putting the suggestion forward to check out her reaction.

"There are laws against that sort of thing," she retorted, but she was smiling.

"They can send me down. It would be worth it to keep you with me for a while longer." His arm was possessive around her shoulders.

Her heart gave a funny flip and she closed her eyes for a moment. This was a holiday romance, she reminded herself, but she didn't want it to end.

"If I could stay longer, I would." She opened her eyes and raised her head to look at him. *Oh yes*, he looked hopeful too. Her spirits were lifting by the moment.

"You promise to visit the cove again?"

She nodded. She didn't want it to be just a fling. And now it felt as if he didn't want that either. Could she dare to believe it could be more?

"Yes, I will, of course I will. And in the meantime…would you like to come down to visit with me, sometime?" she asked, tentatively.

"In the big city?" His sudden, warm smile told her she hadn't been wrong to ask.

"Do you think you can bear it?"

"To be with you, yes. I'd travel to the depths of hell for an hour in your company."

That made her heart soar. Knowing that he wanted to be with her again simply filled her with joy. And she believed he meant it. He was willing to endure the city just to see her again. She could no longer fight it; she had to admit just how much he had come to mean to her, so much more than a holiday romance. In her relief, the emotion that had welled in her heart finally spilled over and she was flooded with it. "As soon as you can then?"

"The summer is our busy time, but late September should be a good time to work in some leave."

Nearly three months. "I'll count the days."

"Me too."

"And can I call you when I need to?" She winked at him, suggestively.

"Oh, yes. I'll be expecting regular doses of phone sex to keep me from going mad. You know, I think I'm addicted to you."

And then he kissed her, hungrily, deeply, and passionately. He cupped her face, his fingers meshing in her hair. She melted against him, her body liquid with desire and with the need to be close to him. Their tongues rasped, their bodies acknowledging the mutual draw and the image of a possible future that had all their barriers melting.

He drew back, pushing strands of her hair back from her face and looking at her with bright eyes. "Right, now that's settled, and I know I'm going to see you again sometime soon, I can relax…" He paused to watch her reaction and she smiled, an echo of heat, pleasure and recognition running through her. "So, I'm going to take you to the village for dinner at The Lobster Pot. That's if you think you can stand the extra attention?"

"*Extra* attention?"

"It will be much worse than last time, I assure you, because by now the whole village will know that you alerted the authorities about Tom. You were simply a curiosity before. Now you're a heroine. I reckon you'll be there for at least the next ten years, maybe longer if no one else beats your record."

"Oh, Julian, it wasn't me. It was you. You're the hero." She nudged him away, smiling, and blushing too. She was flattered by his remarks, but she would always remember his courage and bravery when he rescued Tom.

"Nope, you're the one who spotted him. You're the one who took action, so you're going to have to carry the responsibility of being the superstar." He lifted his hands, as if it was nothing to do with him, then winked and hauled her closer again. "Okay, I promise I'll act like a good bodyguard and fight off your adoring fans if it gets to be too much for you."

How could she not adore that humor and that generosity of spirit?

"Thank you. You're a true hero," she mocked and rested her head on his shoulder.

And how could she not adore the feeling of bliss that his very proximity gave her?

That night they made love slow and gentle. Julian wanted to savor every moment. He couldn't get enough of her. In his imagination she was the wandering gypsy woman who'd taken up residence in his special place, but in his heart he knew that she was a city girl, a woman with a vibrant career pulling her back, a woman with friends and a life outside of this. What they had was magic, but soon it would be gone until the distant day when they might see each other again. The thought had gnawed at him insistently and he tried to lay it to rest so that they could have one last night to remember, but there was a knot in his chest that he just couldn't ignore. A knot of hard, raw emotion.

He led her to the bedroom and undressed her slowly, taking time to observe her beautiful, lush femininity. He savored her responsiveness, the building anticipation that was so evident in her expression. She seemed happy to let him undress her but she wasn't submissive tonight. No, they weren't playing that game. Tonight they expressed themselves as equals in their naked, physical union.

Her eyes sparkled, and she stroked his face, whispering affectionate words when he lifted her into his arms, carrying her to the bed. He rested her down against the covers, marveling at her curves, her warm, inviting body.

In the soft light from the bedroom lamp her skin seemed pale, almost delicate. It belied the athletic little tyke that he had witnessed running naked across the beach the other day. It also belied the tensile strength and determination he had witnessed earlier today when she had helped to haul Tom from the ocean. She was a chameleon, at once soft and feminine, yet strong and resilient. The contrast was one of the many aspects of her that fascinated him.

He touched one finger against her collarbone and drew it down between her breasts, noticing how she trembled in response. The knowledge that he could affect her that way made his blood roar. He wanted to crush her with his body; he wanted to thrust himself inside her until relief came. He ran his fingers lower, over the gentle curve of her belly. When she whimpered and her legs parted, he could only feast his eyes on her. Patches of color marked her cheekbones. She lifted an arm over her head, her breasts rolling in the most languid way. Everything about her was so feminine; she called to every atom of his being. His cock had never felt so engorged, so rigid and hot for contact. But he wanted to savor each and every inch of her body, every flavor, every texture.

He undressed. She leaned back against the pillows, watching, her gaze sweeping over him and coming to rest on his cock. Her eyes were wide and dark, her lips parted. He sat next to her, and when his hand touched between her thighs, she grabbed his hand and guided him deeper, a muffled plea in her voice. He didn't resist. His fingers stroked the soft down of her mons and then slipped easily into the damp channel below. Liquid heat trickled from her pussy. His pulse beat like a drum inside his head. Her skin there was so soft, wet and inviting, that he had to pause, close his eyes for a second, and swallow down the urge to rush.

She arched against him, and when his finger dipped into the slippery niche of her sex, his cock bounced against his belly, eager and demanding for her. She leaned up against him, her breasts rubbing against his skin. Her nipples were so hard they grazed against his bare skin. Each touch threatened to squander his self-control. He dropped down and lapped hungrily at the salty folds of her sex and when the taste and her scent washed over him, he shuddered with pleasure.

Sally, beautiful, luscious Sally.

He ran his tongue back and forth over her clit. She gave a strange, tortured cry, and her fingers tugged on his hair, pulling him up. It had to be soon. He pulled on a condom and her hand followed his, moving quickly to the base of his cock. He groaned with feral pleasure. She was begging for him to be inside her. And he wanted that above all else.

Easing the crown of his cock inside her, he let out a low growl, his thighs trembling with the effort to restrain himself. Easing slowly deeper, he felt her clutching at him with her sweetness and her moisture slid down around his balls. Her legs latched around his hips and her nails scraped over his back, sharp and possessive. They began to move in unison, reaching for the prize.

The tension built, thundering hooves of intense pleasure building speed in the base of his cock each time he rode high and tight inside her lush body. Each slow thrust of their bodies was bringing him on, the clutch of her body on him, milking him until finally he couldn't hold back any longer. His whole body reached, his back arching, every muscle in his arms cording with tension. His cock jerked, the climax roaring through him, flooding his every sense. For a moment he lost touch with reality. Dazzling white light blazed through his mind. And then her name: *Sally.*

He felt her hands clutching at him and her body was shuddering in release. Her head pushed back in the pillows, her lips parted, her eyes slits of darkness. Pleasure speared through him all over again as he watched her climax.

"Sally, yes love. Oh, yes."

Chapter Seven

Julian stomped through his lab and into the office space he shared with George MacIntyre, his lab-based colleague, and shifted a stack of papers so that he could dump his briefcase on his desk.

George stared at the shiny new leather object Julian had deposited on the desk. His glance slowly lifted to focus inquiringly on his colleague.

Julian tugged at the already skewed knot on his tie and undid the top button of his crisp, new linen shirt. "Come on then, say it. Get it over with," he said, beckoning to George with one hand while he fiddled with the shirt collar.

George smiled silently.

"Look, I'm making an effort. What's the problem?"

George shrugged. "I'm not saying there is a problem. I just haven't seen you in a suit before. How do you expect me to react?" He grinned. "She's had quite an effect on you, this Sally woman, hasn't she?"

Julian harrumphed loudly and dropped into his chair, pushing his fingers through his hair in a distracted gesture, undoing what efforts he'd made there in the process. "No. Well, yes. Actually, I have to give my termly talk to the pollution research students over at the University," he commented, vaguely. "I just thought I'd play the part, for a change."

There *was* more to it than that. But he was finding it hard to verbalize, even to George, who'd been a close friend for many years since back when they were matched up on the North-East coast workload.

"I can't wait to see Jeffrey's face," George commented.

Jeffrey, the director of their conservation unit, lived in designer suits but had long since given up trying to impose some regulation smartness on either George—who lived in a scruffy lab coat—or Julian, whose best efforts were usually jeans and a short sleeved, open neck shirt. "When is it you are off to London?" George added, glancing at the wall planner.

Julian looked back to his friend. Perhaps George knew him better than he had thought; he didn't seem overly surprised by what was a significant change in behavior. And he wasn't shying away from the cause, either. Julian had sworn he'd be in a coffin before he'd ever be seen dead in a suit and had threatened to have it written into his will that should not be the case, even then. But if he were to fit into Sally's world, change would be necessary.

"Not for another month. The wait is killing me, but I had to work it into the summer schedule." He shook his head. Yes, he had it bad. In fact he'd gone beyond that. Now he was trying to think of ways to make this long-distance relationship thing work. He'd spent restless nights going through his options, of which there weren't many.

"When you met Catherine," he said, and drummed his fingers on the desk, fighting the urge to leave the room or change the topic of conversation to the latest football results. "How did you know that she was the one? You know, the one you wanted to spend the rest of your life with?"

George sat back into his chair. "Well, it had to happen to you eventually, Mister free and easy," he said. "But the fact that you're even asking me that question…" he looked at Julian meaningfully, "tells me that she probably is 'the one.'"

Julian was about to declare the uselessness of his advice when the message began to sink in. Yes, the fact that he was asking himself that question had to be significant in itself. He'd certainly never considered the notion before.

"So what are you going to do about it?"

"Damned if I know." That was the knee-jerk response. He'd been thinking, and he'd been thinking hard. The only feasible option would have to be discussed with George anyway, because it might affect him. Why not now, Julian asked himself? The conversation was going down that road, and he'd had more than enough lonely contemplation.

"Do you remember Tony Foster?"

George chortled and leaned over to tickle the mouse on his computer so that his beloved seascape screensaver wouldn't black out. Then the smile began to disappear from his face and his head snapped back to look at Julian. His eyebrows shot up. "Ah, I see."

Tony had transferred to a post in the south the year before, much to the amusement of the whole division. He had sacrificed duties along one of the most interesting estuaries in England for somewhat more stressful work overseeing the team who dealt with the Thames area. Last they heard, Tony was engaged to a Swedish au pair and expecting twins.

Julian had wondered how George would react. To distract himself from the ominous silence coming across the desk, he opened his briefcase, lifted out the notes he was working on for his talk at the University, and the carefully bubble-wrapped package he had brought with him. Setting it on his desk, he unwrapped the cyber warrior Sally had sent to keep him company. He was a cute little guy with a cheeky grin, a harpoon and a bullet belt filled with test tubes hanging low on his hips. He was like some futuristic beach warrior and she had to know he'd love it. He set it up next to his computer and looked at it thoughtfully.

"Right," George said, eyeing the sculpture and giving a deep, heartfelt sigh. He turned back to his computer and clicked on the government home page. "We'd better take a look at the transfer possibilities, hadn't we?"

When Julian looked at him, he found George's smile wasn't, as he might have expected, mocking. Instead, it was marked with a kind of resigned sadness.

Sally drummed her fingers on her desk and wedged the phone between her shoulder and jaw so she that could continue stuffing envelopes with the latest catalogue during the phone conversation.

"Believe me, I'm in business myself, and I am well aware that you are contravening the Trades Description Act with both the information on your web site and in the brochure. The beach is *not* the exclusive domain of the cottage or its tenants."

At the other end of the phone the agent muttered on about wording and how the public could read too much into the description of the cottage.

"Excuse me, I have more to do with my valuable time than to debate wording and interpretation. It's quite obvious to me and anyone else who might read it what you are trying to do, and it's wrong. If you don't change the information immediately, I will get in touch with the Advertising Standards Agency and then you'll not only be forced to change it, but you'll have to deal with them as well."

When the agent grunted relinquishment down the phone, Sally offered her good byes and triumphantly hung up. She looked at Kitty, who had been standing watching her for the past two minutes.

"What?"

Kitty walked over to the desk and collected the stack of mail from the post tray. "I was just recognizing the signals, the pattern that is emerging."

"What pattern?" Sally asked, a creeping sense of unease rising up inside her. Kitty often second-guessed her, and she didn't know if she was ready to share her thoughts yet.

"When you start complaining about things and getting on your high-horse, it usually means you are in one of your action phases. And the last time that happened, we had a major reshuffle in the working practices here. I want to know if we have to expect something like that again, or is this just about you and the fact that you're missing your hunk?"

Sally stared at her friend, mouth open. Kitty really did have a handle on her. She knew she'd been talking about Julian incessantly since she got back, because Kitty kept pointing it out. But Kitty's analysis of her behavior was too uncanny.

"It's not just about him," she retorted, "It's the place, the cottage and the cove. It's special and I miss the place."

"You're only saying that because you don't know for sure if Julian feels the same as you do. It's displacement theory in action. You are focusing on the cove and acting on it, because if you get sidelined by him, you still have the cove to fixate on, to help you through."

"Kitty, do you have to be right about everything?"

Kitty grinned, proud of her deductions, and tucked the stack of mail under one arm.

"Well, I don't think you have to worry about your beach hunk, because he calls you so often he's obviously just as infatuated as you are. Besides, if it was the place that meant so much to you, you'd be telling me my job is at risk, and you're going to pack up and do a runner to the north."

Sally stared down at her desk, color climbing into her cheeks. "Your job isn't at risk," she replied.

Silence followed. She forced herself to look up. Kitty was staring at her, her expression somewhat more subdued.

"I see. Is it too soon to ask what your action phase might involve this time around?"

"It is too soon, because I haven't decided on anything definite yet, but, trust me, your job is safe and so are those of the rest of the girls.

I promise you that."

Kitty shuffled the mail from arm to arm and shook her head. When she turned to leave the room, Sally shouted after.

"And you're wrong about the cove. I do love the place."

I love the place and I love Julian. Desperately.

Julian stood at the edge of the cove, his arms folded across his chest, scowling at the sea. His mood was just about as grumpy as it could get. Being back at the cove only served to remind him that he'd had heaven for a few days and, more importantly, that he didn't have it any more. It didn't help that a god-awful brat pack had taken up residence in the cottage the last time he had passed through. They had left signs of their presence not only at the cottage but also on the beach itself. He'd had to collect their barbecue debris and their environmentally unfriendly litter. He'd have to remember to order in some friendly environment reminder signposts, which had never been needed here before. It seemed such an atrocity to him, and no matter how he reasoned it out in his mind he couldn't come to terms with it. He daren't even look over at the cottage this time, in case some similar atrocity was going on. The only person he wanted to see there was Sally. Sally whose presence had felt right there.

Sally, who had felt right in every way.

He was counting the moments until they could be together again, just living for those two weeks they had promised each other in London. It was only days away now. He loved her far too much to be apart like this. Long distance was simply not going to work. He had decided to talk seriously to her, and, if she felt the same way, he would definitely try to transfer to a location nearer her. He'd do anything, even live in the city for her—he'd decided it was the only way. He'd been happy with his life before, but it was never going to feel right again, not without her. He felt as if he'd had part of himself taken away, and it hurt, bad. *Really bad.*

He was just about to pitch his tent when his mobile bleeped at him from the pocket of his leather jacket.

"Julian?"

"Sally!" Some elemental force inside him leapt with pride and longing. Just hearing her voice brought such a rise of emotion in him; there wasn't any denying it.

"I know you're busy, and I know I called you this morning, but I had to dash for a flight, and I really wanted to tell you something."

Flight? Where was she going, and with whom?

There was a deep breath being drawn in at the other end of the line and for a split second Julian wondered if she was going to cancel his trip down, if she was going to dump him.

"What is it…?"

"Julian, I love you."

"Oh." Relief swamped him. "Thank goodness for that," he blurted. He laughed.

She laughed too. "Um, what is so funny?"

"Nothing, I'm just relieved. I love you too." They'd been so close to saying it, so many times. It was always there, silent but palpable between them. And he was so godamn relieved that it was out now. "In fact, I love you so much that I can't wait until I have you in my arms, so that I can tell you—and show you—in the flesh."

She purred into the phone. "Well, it won't be long now."

"No, and just as well."

"Are you sitting down?" she quizzed.

"No, I'm standing on the edge of the cove, looking over at our old love nest."

She chuckled. It was a gorgeous sound and it did strange, tormenting things inside his chest.

"That's even better. I've got a surprise for you. Are you looking at the cottage?"

"Yes."

"Well, I wanted you to know that I bought it."

What? She had to be kidding. "Sally, are you crazy? Stop kidding me. Old man Greg would never sell. You know that I tried to buy the cottage from him."

"I gave him an offer he couldn't refuse."

"Sally…" Both doubt and hope trickled inside him. Was this a joke, or a daydream?

"Darling, I'm loaded. I never told you, but the oriental figurine market went mad just after I got into it, and I'm the top British importer. I tracked him down and…well, he accepted my offer. I've got heaps to sort out, and the move will have to be spread over the next year or maybe more. I'll have to keep going up and down but eventually I'm going to do the majority of my work from the cottage. The actual mechanics of the business will still be based in London, but I can do all the paperwork at a distance and fly down from Newcastle when I need to."

She burbled on enthusiastically while Julian tried to make sense of it all.

"I've looked into getting planning permission for an office outbuilding, and I've been sorting it all out over the past few weeks. I'll need your help because it has to be designed to fit in with the landscape, and the stone has to be right, but it looks like it's all going to go through."

"Sally, slow down!" He couldn't keep up with her stream of enthusiasm because he was so thrown by the whole thing.

"Okay, I know it's a lot to take in. I just didn't want to tell you about it until I knew I could pull it off."

"You really own the cottage?" That much had just about sunk in.

"Yes, you don't mind do you? I mean…I wanted it so that it would be our place."

"Ours?" The doubt that he'd felt had withered away, and hope had lodged itself inside his heart. Her words were slowly sinking in, but he still couldn't come to terms with it. He'd been lecturing himself on staying focused on visiting her in London, and now she was talking about owning the cottage? Living here? Even if it was only part-time…what bliss it would be. His beautiful sexy, clever Sally, here, close by when he needed her? And he did need her.

"Yes, darling, *ours*, although I want you to be friendly to any other visitors to the area. No growling or scaring them off. I'll be around to make sure of that." She laughed again. "And I want you to help me convert the attic into a studio for me, so I can see the cove… and watch Double O Beachpatrol frolic in the waves while I sculpt." She gave another delighted chuckle.

"I can't believe you're saying this, I can't believe it's true."

"I'll prove it's true for you. Tell me, can you still see the cottage?" Her voice had grown somehow more intimate.

"Yes, and it's so beautiful, I wish you could see it now, in the sunset."

He looked over at it, the old stone walls warm and mellow, so inviting in the light of the setting sun. A movement caught his eye. The door opened. Standing in the doorway was Sally, wearing a floating purple dress. And she was beckoning to him, like a gypsy woman calling her wandering man home for the night.

Julian whooped. She giggled in the phone.

"Sally, you are in *big* trouble for tricking me like this," he said.

"So you better start running now, because when I catch you…!" And with that he dropped the phone and began to run down the cove towards her.

But Sally didn't run. She switched her phone off and stayed put, and when he arrived at her door, she walked into his arms, forever.

About the Author:

Saskia is British and lives on the edge of the Yorkshire moors, close to the home of the famous romance writing sisters, the Bronte's. There's heaps of inspiration in the beautiful windswept countryside nearby, and in her most wildly romantic moments, Saskia swears she can feel the spirits of Cathy and Heathcliff out there on the moors!

Saskia has had short fiction published on both sides of the pond and is thrilled to be the first British author writing for **Secrets**. *Visitors are welcome at* www.saskiawalker.co.uk *and she loves to hear from readers, so send her an email at* saskia@saskiawalker.co.uk.

If you enjoyed *Secrets Volume 12* but haven't read other volumes, you should see what you're missing!

Secrets Volume 1:

In ***A Lady's Quest***, author Bonnie Hamre brings you a London historical where Lady Antonia Blair-Sutworth searches for a lover in a most shocking and pleasing way.

Alice Gaines' ***The Spinner's Dream*** weaves a seductive fantasy that will leave every woman wishing for her own private love slave, desperate and running for his life.

Ivy Landon takes you for a wild ride. ***The Proposal*** will taunt you, tease you, even shock you. A contemporary erotica for the adventurous woman's ultimate fantasy.

With ***The Gift*** by Jeanie LeGendre, you're immersed in the historic tale of exotic seduction and bondage. Read about a concubine's delicious surrender to her Sultan.

Secrets Volume 2:

Surrogate Lover, by Doreen DeSalvo, is a contemporary tale of lust and love in the 90's. A surrogate sex therapist thought he had all the answers until he met Sarah.

Bonnie Hamre's regency tale ***Snowbound*** delights as the Earl of Howden is teased and tortured by his own desires—finally a woman who equals his overpowering sensuality.

In ***Roarke's Prisoner***, by Angela Knight, starship captain Elise remembers the eager animal submission she'd known before at her captor's hands and refuses to be his toy again.

Susan Paul's ***Savage Garden*** tells the story of Raine's capture by a mysterious revolutionary in Mexico. She quickly finds lush erotic nights in her captor's arms.

Secrets Volume 3:

In Jeanie Cesarini's ***The Spy Who Loved Me***, FBI agents Paige Ellison and Christopher Sharp discover excitement and passion in some unusual undercover work.

Warning: This story is only for the most adventurous of readers. Ann Jacobs tells the story of ***The Barbarian***. Giles has a sexual arsenal designed to break down proud Lady Brianna's defenses — erotic pleasures learned in a harem.

Wild, sexual hunger is unleashed in this futuristic vampire tale with a twist. In Angela Knight's ***Blood and Kisses***, find out just who is seducing whom?

B.J. McCall takes you into the erotic world of strip joints in ***Love Undercover***. On assignment, Lt. Amanda Forbes and Det. "Cowboy" Cooper find temptation hard to resist.

Secrets Volume 4:

An Act of Love is Jeanie Cesarini's sequel. Shelby's terrified of sex. Film star Jason Gage must coach her in the ways of love. He wants her to feel true passion in his arms.

The Love Slave, by Emma Holly, is a woman's ultimate fantasy. For one year, Princess Lily will be attended to by three delicious men. She delights in playing with the first two, but it's the reluctant Grae that stirs her desires.

Lady Crystal is in turmoil in ***Enslaved***, by Desirée Lindsey. Lord Nicholas' dark passions and irresistible charm have brought her long-hidden desires to the surface.

Betsy Morgan and Susan Paul bring you Kaki York's story in ***The Bodyguard***. Watching the wild, erotic romps of her client's sexual conquests on the security cameras is getting to her—and her partner, the ruggedly handsome James Kulick.

Secrets Volume 5:

B.J. McCall is back with ***Alias Smith and Jones***. Meredith Collins is stranded overnight at the airport. A handsome stranger named Smith offers her sanctuary for the evening—how can she resist those mesmerizing green-flecked eyes?

Strictly Business, by Shannon Hollis, tells of Elizabeth Forrester's desire to climb the corporate ladder on her merits, not her looks. But the gorgeous Garrett Hill has come along and stirred her wildest fantasies.

Chevon Gael's ***Insatiable*** is the tale of a man's obsession. After corporate exec Ashlyn Fraser's glamour shot session, photographer Marcus Remington can't get her off his mind. Forget the beautiful models, he must have her —but where did she go?

Sandy Fraser's ***Beneath Two Moons*** is a futuristic wild ride. Conor is rough and tough like frontiermen of old, and he's on the prowl for a new conquest. Dr. Eva Kelsey got away once before, but this time he'll make sure she begs for more.

Secrets Volume 6:

Sandy Fraser is back with ***Flint's Fuse***. Dana Madison's father has her "kidnapped" for her own safety. Flint, the tall, dark and dangerousmercenary, is hired for the job. But just which one is the prisoner—Dana will try *anything* to get away.

In ***Love's Prisoner***, by MaryJanice Davidson, Jeannie Lawrence experienced unwilling rapture at Michael Windham's hands. She never expected the devilishly handsome man to show back up in her life—or turn out to be a werewolf!

Alice Gaines' ***The Education of Miss Felicity Wells*** finds a pupil needing to learn how to satisfy her soon-to-be husband. Dr. Marcus Slade, an experienced lover, agrees to take her on as a student, but can he stop short of taking her completely?

Angela Knight tells about reporter Dana Ivory stumbling onto a secret—a sexy, secret agent who happens to be a vampire.She wants her story but Gabriel Archer believes she's ***A Candidate for the Kiss***.

Secrets Volume 7:

In ***Amelia's Innocence*** by Julia Welles, Amelia didn't know her father bet her in a card game with Captain Quentin Hawke, so honor demands a compromise—three days of erotic foreplay, leaving her virginity and future intact.

Jade Lawless brings ***The Woman of His Dreams*** to life. Artist Gray Avonaco moved in next door to Joanna Morgan and now is plagued by provocative dreams. Is it unrequited lust or Gray's chance to be with the woman he loves?

Surrender by Kathryn Anne Dubois tells of Lady Johanna. She wants no part of the binding strictures of marriage to the powerful Duke. But she doesn't realize he wants sensual adventure, and sexual satisfaction.

Angela Knight's ***Kissing the Hunter*** finds Navy Seal Logan McLean hunting the vampires who murdered his wife. Virginia Hart is a sexy vampire searching for her lost soul-mate only to find him in a man determined to kill her.

Secrets Volume 8:

In Jeanie Cesarini's latest tale, we meet Kathryn Roman as she inherits a legal brothel. She refuses to trade her Manhattan high-powered career for a life in the wild west. But the town of Love, Nevada has recruited Trey Holliday, one very dominant cowboy, with ***Taming Kate***.

In ***Jared's Wolf*** by MaryJanice Davidson, Jared Rocke will do anything to avenge his sister's death, but he wasn't expecting to fall for Moira Wolfbauer, the she-wolf sworn to protect her werewolf pack. The two enemies must stop a killer while learning that love defies all boundaries.

My Champion, My Love, by Alice Gaines, tells the tale of Celeste Broder, a woman committed for a sexy appetite that is tolerated in men, but not women. Mayor Robert Albright may be her salvation—*if* she can convince him her freedom will mean a chance to indulge their appetites together.

Liz Maverick takes you to a post-apocalyptic world in ***Kiss or Kill***. Camille Kazinsky's military career rides on her decision—whether the robo called Meat should live or die. Meat's future depends on proving he's human enough to live, *man* enough, to make her feel like a woman.

Secrets Volume 9:

Kimberly Dean brings you ***Wanted***. FBI Special Agent Jeff Reno wants Danielle Carver. There's her body, brains—and that charge of treason on her head. Dani goes on the run, but the sexy Fed is hot on her trail. What will he do once he catches her? And why is the idea so tempting?

In ***Wild for You***. by Kathryn Anne Dubois, college intern Georgie gets lost and captured by a wildman of the Congo. She soon discovers this terrifying specimen of male virility has never seen a woman. The research possibilities are endless! Until he shows her he has research ideas of his own.

Bonnie Hamre is back with ***Flights of Fantasy***. Chloe taught others to see the realities of life but she's never shared the intimate world of her sensual yearnings. Given the chance, will she be woman enough to fulfill her most secret erotic fantasy?

In Lisa Marie Rice's story, ***Secluded***, Nicholas Lee had to claw his way to the top. His wealth and power come with a price—his enemies will kill anyone he loves. When Isabelle Summerby steals his heart, Nicholas secludes her in his underground palace to live a lifetime of desire in only a few days.

Secrets Volume 10:

In Dominique Sinclair's ***Private Eyes***, top private investigator Niccola Black is used to tracking down adulterous spouses, but when a mystery man captures her absolute attention during a stakeout, she discovers her "no seduction" rule is bending under the pressure of the long denied passion.

Bonnie Hamre's ***The Ruination of Lady Jane*** brings you Lady Jane Ponsonby-Maitland's story. With an upcoming marriage to a man more than twice her age, she disappears. Havyn Attercliffe was sent to retrieve his brother's ward, but when she begs him to ruin her rather than turn her over to her odious fiancé, how can he refuse?

Jeanie Cesarini is back with ***Code Name: Kiss***. Agent Lily Justiss would do anything to defend her country against terrorists, including giving her virginity away on an undercover mission as a sex slave. But even as her master takes possession, it's fantasies of her commanding officer, Seth Blackthorn, that fuels her desire.

Kathryn Anne Dubois' ***The Sacrifice*** tells about Lady Anastasia Bedovier who's about to take her vows as a nun, but decadent, sensual dreams force her to consider that her sacrifice of chastity might mean little until she has experienced the passion she will deny. She goes to Count Maxwell and, in one erotic night, learns the heights of sensual pleasure. Maxwell thought he was immune from love, but the nameless novice that warmed his bed has proved his undoing, and despite his desperate search, he can't reach her.

Secrets Volume 11:

Jennifer Probst brings us *Masquerade*. Hailey Ashton is determined to free herself from her sexual restrictions. Four nights of erotic pleasures without revealing her identity. A chance to explore her secret desires without the fear of unmasking.

Jess Michaels's *Ancient Pleasures* tells of Isabella Winslow who is obsessed with finding out what caused her late husband's death, but trapped in an Egyptian concubine's tomb with a sexy American raider, succumbing to the mummy's sensual curse takes over.

Manhunt by Kimberly Deanis about Michael Tucker. Framed for murder, he takes Taryn Swanson hostage—the one woman who can clear him. Despite the evidence against him, the attraction between them is strong. Tucker resorts to unconventional, yet effective methods of persuasion to change the sexy ADA's mind.

Angela Knight returns with *Wake Me*. Chloe Hart received a sexy painting of a sleeping knight. Radolf of Varik has been trapped for centuries in the painting. His only hope is to visit the dreams of women and make one of them fall in love with him so she can free him with a kiss.

Secrets Volume 13:

Out of Control by Rachelle Chase introduces you to Astrid's world, which revolves around her business. She's hoping to pick up wealthy Erik Santos as a client. Only he's hoping to pick up something entirely different. Will she give in to the seductive pull of his proposition?

Amber Green's *Hawkmoor* is about shape-shifters who answer to Darien as he acts in the name of the long-missing Lady Hawkmoor, their hereditary ruler. When she unexpectedly surfaces, Darien must deal with a scrappy individual whose wary eyes hold the other half of his soul, but who has the power to destroy his world.

Charlotte Featherstone offeres *Lessons in Pleasure*, where a wicked bargain has Lily vowing never to yield to the demands of the rake she once loved and lost. Unfortunately, Damian, the Earl of St. Croix, or Saint as he is infamously known, will not take 'no' for an answer.

In the Heat of the Night by Calista Fox tells of Molina, who's haunted by a century-old curse and fears she won't live to see her thirtieth birthday. Nick, her former bodyguard, is hired back into service to protect her from the fatal accidents that plague her family. But *In the Heat of the Night*, will his passion and love for her be enough to convince Molina they have a future together?

Secrets, Volume 1

Listen to what reviewers say:

"These stories take you beyond romance into the realm of erotica. I found ***Secrets*** absolutely delicious."

—Virginia Henley,
New York Times Best Selling Author

"***Secrets*** is a collection of novellas for the daring, adventurous woman who's not afraid to give her fantasies free reign."

—Kathe Robin, *Romantic Times* Magazine

"...In fact, the men featured in all the stories are terrific, they all want to please and pleasure their women. If you like erotic romance you will love ***Secrets***."

—*Romantic Readers* Review

In ***Secrets, Volume 1*** you'll find:

A Lady's Quest by Bonnie Hamre

Widowed Lady Antonia Blair-Sutworth searches for a lover to save her from the handsome Duke of Sutherland. The "auditions" may be shocking but utterly tantalizing.

The Spinner's Dream by Alice Gaines

A seductive fantasy that leaves every woman wishing for her own private love slave, desperate and running for his life.

The Proposal by Ivy Landon

This tale is a walk on the wild side of love. *The Proposal* will taunt you, tease you, and shock you. A contemporary erotica for the adventurous woman.

The Gift by Jeanie LeGendre

Immerse yourself in this historic tale of exotic seduction, bondage and a concubine's surrender to the Sultan's desire. Can Alessandra live the life and give the gift the Sultan demands of her?

Secrets, Volume 2

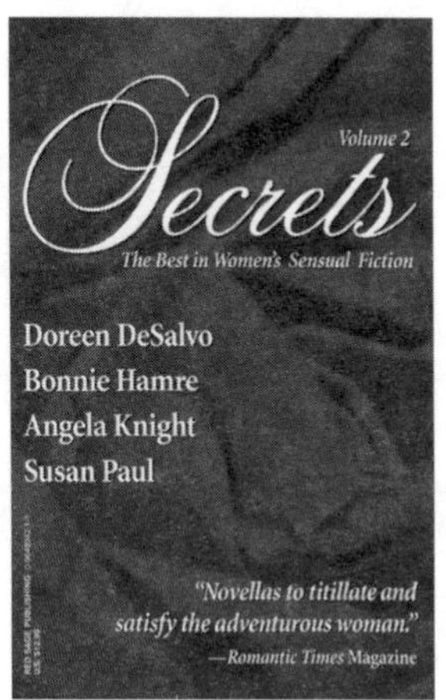

Listen to what reviewers say:

"***Secrets*** offers four novellas of sensual delight; each beautifully written with intense feeling and dedication to character development. For those seeking stories with heightened intimacy, look no further."

—Kathee Card, *Romancing the Web*

"Such a welcome diversity in styles and genres. Rich characterization in sensual tales. An exciting read that's sure to titillate the senses."

—Cheryl Ann Porter

"***Secrets 2*** left me breathless. Sensual satisfaction guaranteed…times four!"

—Virginia Henley, *New York Times* Best Selling Author

In ***Secrets, Volume 2*** you'll find:

Surrogate Lover by Doreen DeSalvo

Adrian Ross is a surrogate sex therapist who has all the answers and control. He thought he'd seen and done it all, but he'd never met Sarah.

Snowbound by Bonnie Hamre

A delicious, sensuous regency tale. The marriage-shy Earl of Howden is teased and tortured by his own desires and finds there is a woman who can equal his overpowering sensuality.

Roarke's Prisoner by Angela Knight

Elise, a starship captain, remembers the eager animal submission she'd known before at her captor's hands and refuses to become his toy again. However, she has no idea of the delights he's planned for her this time.

Savage Garden by Susan Paul

Raine's been captured by a mysterious and dangerous revolutionary leader in Mexico. At first her only concern is survival, but she quickly finds lush erotic nights in her captor's arms.

Winner of the Fallot Literary Award for Fiction!

Secrets, Volume 3

Listen to what reviewers say:

"***Secrets, Volume 3***, leaves the reader breathless. A delicious confection of sensuous treats awaits the reader on each turn of the page!"

—Kathee Card, *Romancing the Web*

"From the FBI to Police Dectective to Vampires to a Medieval Warlord home from the Crusade—***Secrets 3*** is simply the best!"

—Susan Paul, award winning author

"An unabashed celebration of sex. Highly arousing! Highly recommended!"

—Virginia Henley, *New York Times* Best Selling Author

In ***Secrets, Volume 3*** you'll find:

The Spy Who Loved Me by Jeanie Cesarini

Undercover FBI agent Paige Ellison's sexual appetites rise to new levels when she works with leading man Christopher Sharp, the cunning agent who uses all his training to capture her body and heart.

The Barbarian by Ann Jacobs

Lady Brianna vows not to surrender to the barbaric Giles, Earl of Harrow. He must use sexual arts learned in the infidels' harem to conquer his bride. A word of caution—this is not for the faint of heart.

Blood and Kisses by Angela Knight

A vampire assassin is after Beryl St. Cloud. Her only hope lies with Decker, another vampire and ex-mercenary. Broke, she offers herself as payment for his services. Will his seductive powers take her very soul?

Love Undercover by B.J. McCall

Amanda Forbes is the bait in a strip joint sting operation. While she performs, fellow detective "Cowboy" Cooper gets to watch. Though he excites her, she must fight the temptation to surrender to the passion.

Winner of the 1997 Under the Covers Readers Favorite Award

Secrets, Volume 4

Listen to what reviewers say:

"Provocative...seductive...a must read!"

—*Romantic Times* Magazine

"These are the kind of stories that romance readers that 'want a little more' have been looking for all their lives...."

—*Affaire de Coeur* Magazine

"***Secrets, Volume 4***, has something to satisfy every erotic fantasy... simply sexational!"

—Virginia Henley, *New York Times* Best Selling Author

In ***Secrets, Volume 4*** you'll find:

An Act of Love by Jeanie Cesarini

Shelby Moran's past left her terrified of sex. International film star Jason Gage must gently coach the young starlet in the ways of love. He wants more than an act—he wants Shelby to feel true passion in his arms.

Enslaved by Desirée Lindsey

Lord Nicholas Summer's air of danger, dark passions, and irresistible charm have brought Lady Crystal's long-hidden desires to the surface. Will he be able to give her the one thing she desires before it's too late?

The Bodyguard by Betsy Morgan and Susan Paul

Kaki York is a bodyguard, but watching the wild, erotic romps of her client's sexual conquests on the security cameras is getting to her—and her partner, the ruggedly handsome James Kulick. Can she resist his insistent desire to have her?

The Love Slave by Emma Holly

A woman's ultimate fantasy. For one year, Princess Lily will be attended to by three delicious men of her choice. While she delights in playing with the first two, it's the reluctant Grae, with his powerful chest, black eyes and hair, that stirs her desires.

Secrets, Volume 5

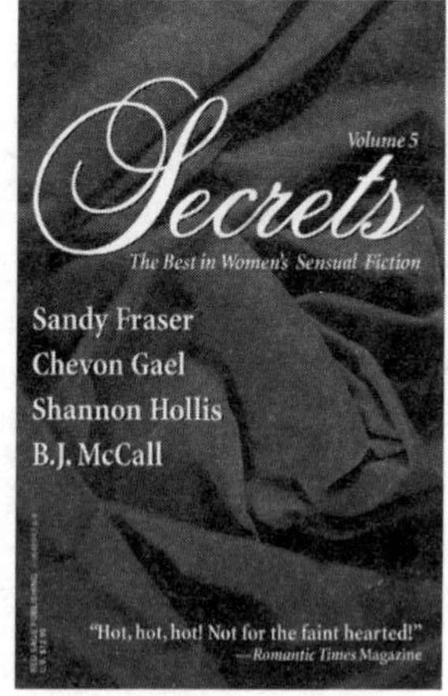

Listen to what reviewers say:

"Hot, hot, hot! Not for the faint-hearted!"

—*Romantic Times* Magazine

"As you make your way through the stories, you will find yourself becoming hotter and hotter. ***Secrets*** just keeps getting better and better."

—*Affaire de Coeur* Magazine

"***Secrets 5*** is a collage of lucious sensuality. Any woman who reads ***Secrets*** is in for an awakening!"

—Virginia Henley, *New York Times* Best Selling Author

In ***Secrets, Volume 5*** you'll find:

Beneath Two Moons by Sandy Fraser

Ready for a very wild romp? Step into the future and find Conor, rough and masculine like frontiermen of old, on the prowl for a new conquest. In his sights, Dr. Eva Kelsey. She got away once before, but this time Conor makes sure she begs for more.

Insatiable by Chevon Gael

Marcus Remington photographs beautiful models for a living, but it's Ashlyn Fraser, a young corporate exec having some glamour shots done, who has stolen his heart. It's up to Marcus to help her discover her inner sexual self.

Strictly Business by Shannon Hollis

Elizabeth Forrester knows it's tough enough for a woman to make it to the top in the corporate world. Garrett Hill, the most beautiful man in Silicon Valley, has to come along to stir up her wildest fantasies. Dare she give in to both their desires?

Alias Smith and Jones by B.J. McCall

Meredith Collins finds herself stranded overnight at the airport. A handsome stranger by the name of Smith offers her sanctuaty for the evening and she finds those mesmerizing, green-flecked eyes hard to resist. Are they to be just two ships passing in the night?

Secrets, Volume 6

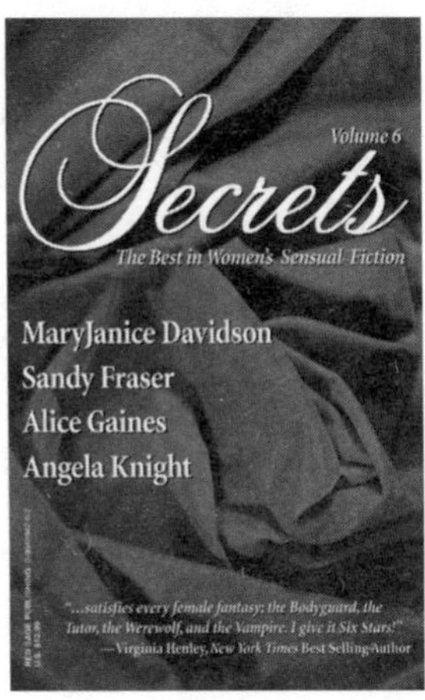

Listen to what reviewers say:

"Red Sage was the first and remains the leader of Women's Erotic Romance Fiction Collections!"

—*Romantic Times* Magazine

"***Secrets*, *Volume 6***, is the best of ***Secrets*** yet. …four of the most erotic stories in one volume than this reader has yet to see anywhere else. …These stories are full of erotica at its best and you'll definitely want to keep it handy for lots of re-reading!"

—*Affaire de Coeur* Magazine

"***Secrets 6*** satisfies every female fantasy: the Bodyguard, the Tutor, the Werewolf, and the Vampire. I give it Six Stars!"

—Virginia Henley, *New York Times* Best Selling Author

In ***Secrets, Volume 6*** you'll find:

Flint's Fuse by Sandy Fraser

Dana Madison's father has her "kidnapped" for her own safety. Flint, the tall, dark and dangerous mercenary, is hired for the job. But just which one is the prisoner—Dana will try *anything* to get away.

Love's Prisoner by MaryJanice Davidson

Trapped in an elevator, Jeannie Lawrence experienced unwilling rapture at Michael Windham's hands. She never expected the devilishly handsome man to show back up in her life—or turn out to be a werewolf!

The Education of Miss Felicity Wells by Alice Gaines

Felicity Wells wants to be sure she'll satisfy her soon-to-be husband but she needs a teacher. Dr. Marcus Slade, an experienced lover, agrees to take her on as a student, but can he stop short of taking her completely?

A Candidate for the Kiss by Angela Knight

Working on a story, reporter Dana Ivory stumbles onto a more amazing one—a sexy, secret agent who happens to be a vampire.She wants her story but Gabriel Archer wants more from her than just sex and blood.

Secrets, Volume 7

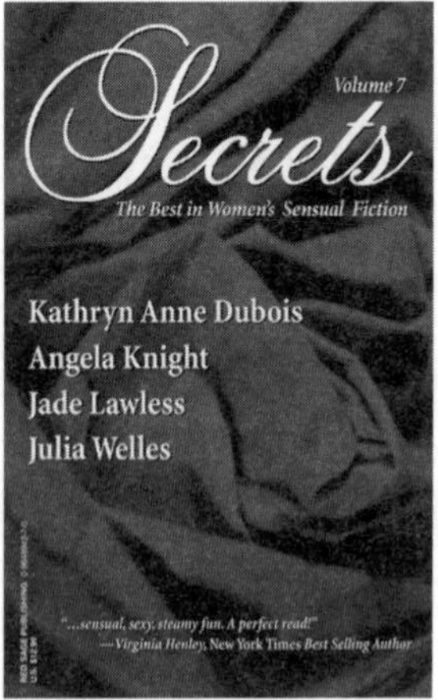

Listen to what reviewers say:

"Get out your asbestos gloves — ***Secrets Volume 7*** is…extremely hot, true erotic romance…passionate and titillating. There's nothing quite like baring your secrets!"

—*Romantic Times* Magazine

"…sensual, sexy, steamy fun. A perfect read!"

—Virginia Henley,
New York Times Best Selling Author

"Intensely provocative and disarmingly romantic, ***Secrets, Volume 7***, is a romance reader's paradise that will take you beyond your wildest dreams!"

—Ballston Book House Review

In ***Secrets, Volume 7*** you'll find:

Amelia's Innocence by Julia Welles

Amelia didn't know her father bet her in a card game with Captain Quentin Hawke, so honor demands a compromise—three days of erotic foreplay, leaving her virginity and future intact.

The Woman of His Dreams by Jade Lawless

From the day artist Gray Avonaco moves in next door, Joanna Morgan is plagued by provocative dreams. But what she believes is unrequited lust, Gray sees as another chance to be with the woman he loves. He must persuade her that even death can't stop true love.

Surrender by Kathryn Anne Dubois

Free-spirited Lady Johanna wants no part of the binding strictures society imposes with her marriage to the powerful Duke. She doesn't know the dark Duke wants sensual adventure, and sexual satisfaction.

Kissing the Hunter by Angela Knight

Navy Seal Logan McLean hunts the vampires who murdered his wife. Virginia Hart is a sexy vampire searching for her lost soul-mate only to find him in a man determined to kill her. She must convince him all vampires aren't created equally.

**Winner of the Venus Book Club
Best Book of the Year**

Secrets, Volume 8

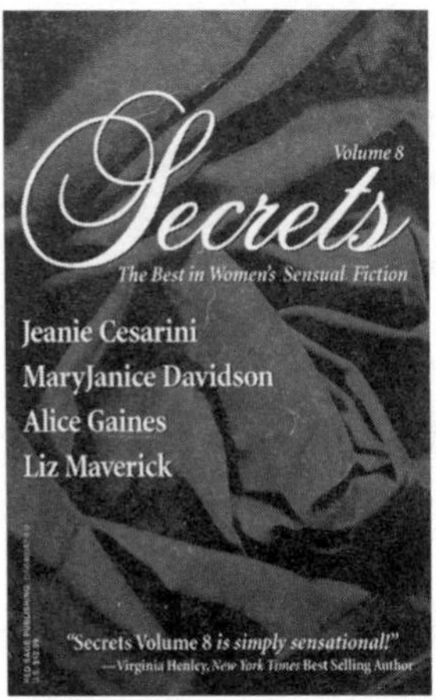

Listen to what reviewers say:

"***Secrets**, **Volume 8***, is an amazing compilation of sexy stories covering a wide range of subjects, all designed to titillate the senses. …you'll find something for everybody in this latest version of ***Secrets***."

—*Affaire de Coeur* Magazine

"***Secrets Volume 8***, is simply sensational!"

—Virginia Henley, *New York Times* Best Selling Author

"These delectable stories will have you turning the pages long into the night. Passionate, provocative and perfect for setting the mood…."

—*Escape to Romance* Reviews

In ***Secrets, Volume 8*** you'll find:

Taming Kate by Jeanie Cesarini

Kathryn Roman inherits a legal brothel. Little does this city girl know the town of Love, Nevada wants her to be their new madam so they've charged Trey Holliday, one very dominant cowboy, with taming her.

Jared's Wolf by MaryJanice Davidson

Jared Rocke will do anything to avenge his sister's death, but ends up attracted to Moira Wolfbauer, the she-wolf sworn to protect her pack. Joining forces to stop a killer, they learn love defies all boundaries.

My Champion, My Lover by Alice Gaines

Celeste Broder is a woman committed for having a sexy appetite. Mayor Robert Albright may be her champion—if she can convince him her freedom will mean a chance to indulge their appetites together.

Kiss or Kill by Liz Maverick

In this post-apocalyptic world, Camille Kazinsky's military career rides on her ability to make a choice—whether the robo called Meat should live or die. Meat's future depends on proving he's human enough to live, man enough…to makes her feel like a woman.

**Winner of the Venus Book Club
Best Book of the Year**

Secrets, Volume 9

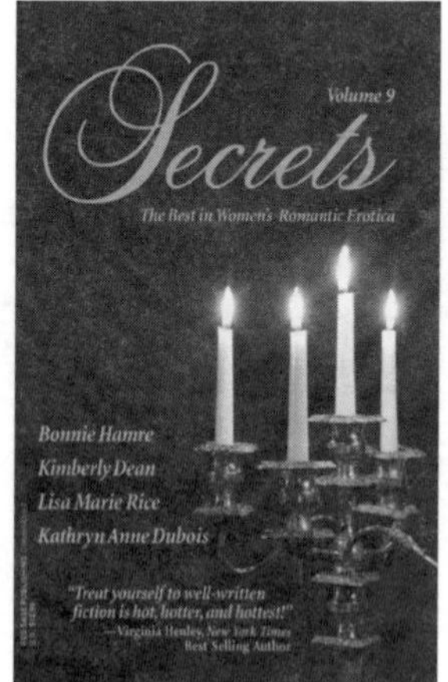

Listen to what reviewers say:

"Everyone should expect only the most erotic stories in a ***Secrets*** book. ...if you like your stories full of hot sexual scenes, then this is for you!"

—Donna Doyle Romance Reviews

"***SECRETS 9***...is sinfully delicious, highly arousing, and hotter than hot as the pages practically burn up as you turn them."

—Suzanne Coleburn, Reader To Reader Reviews/Belles & Beaux of Romance

"Treat yourself to well-written fictionthat's hot, hotter, and hottest!"

—Virginia Henley, *New York Times* Best Selling Author

In ***Secrets, Volume 9*** you'll find:

Wild For You by Kathryn Anne Dubois

When college intern, Georgie, gets captured by a Congo wildman, she discovers this specimen of male virility has never seen a woman. The research possibilities are endless!

Wanted by Kimberly Dean

FBI Special Agent Jeff Reno wants Danielle Carver. There's her body, brains—and that charge of treason on her head. Dani goes on the run, but the sexy Fed is hot on her trail.

Secluded by Lisa Marie Rice

Nicholas Lee's wealth and power came with a price—his enemies will kill anyone he loves. When Isabelle steals his heart, Nicholas secludes her in his palace for a lifetime of desire in only a few days.

Flights of Fantasy by Bonnie Hamre

Chloe taught others to see the realities of life but she's never shared the intimate world of her sensual yearnings. Given the chance, will she be woman enough to fulfill her most secret erotic fantasy?

Secrets, Volume 10

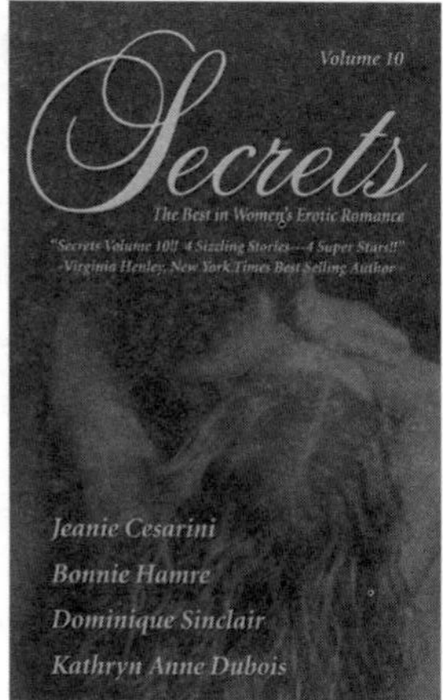

Listen to what reviewers say:

"***Secrets Volume 10***, an erotic dance through medieval castles, sultan's palaces, the English countryside and expensive hotel suites, explodes with passion-filled pages."

—*Romantic Times BOOKclub*

"Having read the previous nine volumes, this one fulfills the expectations of what is expected in a ***Secrets*** book: romance and eroticism at its best!!"

—*Fallen Angel Reviews*

"All are hot steamy romances so if you enjoy erotica romance, you are sure to enjoy ***Secrets, Volume 10***. All this reviewer can say is WOW!!"

—*The Best Reviews*

In ***Secrets, Volume 10*** you'll find:

Private Eyes by Dominique Sinclair

When a mystery man captivates P.I. Nicolla Black during a stakeout, she discovers her no-seduction rule bending under the pressure of long denied passion. She agrees to the seduction, but he demands her total surrender.

The Ruination of Lady Jane by Bonnie Hamre

To avoid her upcoming marriage, Lady Jane Ponsonby-Maitland flees into the arms of Havyn Attercliffe. She begs him to ruin her rather than turn her over to her odious fiancé.

Code Name: Kiss by Jeanie Cesarini

Agent Lily Justiss is on a mission to defend her country against terrorists that requires giving up her virginity as a sex slave. As her master takes her body, desire for her commanding officer Seth Blackthorn fuels her mind.

The Sacrifice by Kathryn Anne Dubois

Lady Anastasia Bedovier is days from taking her vows as a Nun. Before she denies her sensuality forever, she wants to experience pleasure. Count Maxwell is the perfect man to initiate her into erotic delight.

Secrets, Volume 11

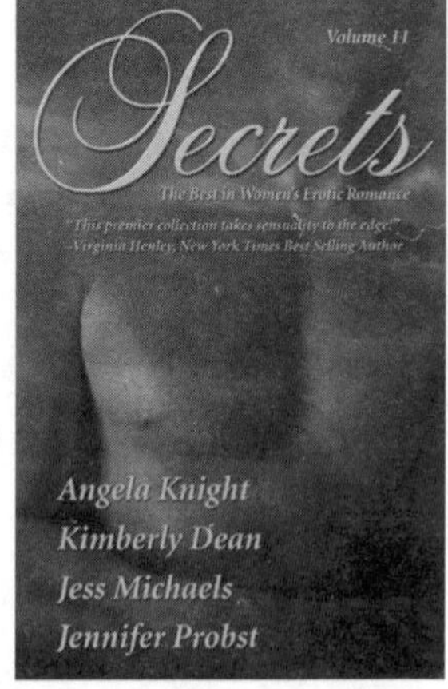

Listen to what reviewers say:

"***Secrets Volume 11*** delivers once again with storylines that include erotic masquerades, ancient curses, modern-day betrayal and a prince charming looking for a kiss." **4 Stars**

—Romantic Times BOOKclub

"Indulge yourself with this erotic treat and join the thousands of readers who just can't get enough. Be forewarned that ***Secrets 11*** will wet your appetite for more, but will offer you the ultimate in pleasurable erotic literature."

—Ballston Book House Review

"***Secrets 11*** quite honestly is my favorite anthology from Red Sage so far."

—The Best Reviews

In ***Secrets, Volume 11*** you'll find:

Masquerade by Jennifer Probst

Hailey Ashton is determined to free herself from her sexual restrictions. Four nights of erotic pleasures without revealing her identity. A chance to explore her secret desires without the fear of unmasking.

Ancient Pleasures by Jess Michaels

Isabella Winslow is obsessed with finding out what caused her late husband's death, but trapped in an Egyptian concubine's tomb with a sexy American raider, succumbing to the mummy's sensual curse takes over.

Manhunt by Kimberly Dean

Framed for murder, Michael Tucker takes Taryn Swanson hostage—the one woman who can clear him. Despite the evidence against him, the attraction between them is strong. Tucker resorts to unconventional, yet effective methods of persuasion to change the sexy ADA's mind.

Wake Me by Angela Knight

Chloe Hart received a sexy painting of a sleeping knight. Radolf of Varik has been trapped for centuries in the painting since, cursed by a witch. His only hope is to visit the dreams of women and make one of them fall in love with him so she can free him with a kiss.

Secrets, Volume 12

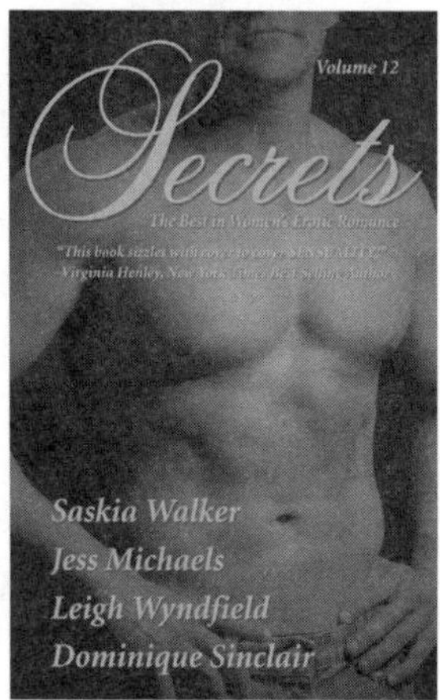

Listen to what reviewers say:

"*Secrets Volume 12*, turns on the heat with a seductive encounter inside a bookstore, a temple of naughty and sensual delight, a galactic inferno that thaws ice, and a lightening storm that lights up the English shoreline. Tales of looking for love in all the right places with a heat rating out the charts." **4½ Stars**

—Romantic Times BOOKclub

"I really liked these stories.You want great escapism? Read ***Secrets, Volume 12***."

—Romance Reviews

In ***Secrets, Volume 12*** you'll find:

Good Girl Gone Bad by Dominique Sinclair

Reagan's dreams are finally within reach. Setting out to do research for an article, nothing could have prepared her for Luke, or his offer to teach her everything she needs to know about sex. Licentious pleasures, forbidden desires… inspiring the best writing she's ever done.

Aphrodite's Passion by Jess Michaels

When Selena flees Victorian London before her evil stepchildren can institutionalize her for hysteria, Gavin is asked to bring her back home. But when he finds her living on the island of Cyprus, his need to have her begins to block out every other impulse.

White Heat by Leigh Wyndfield

Raine is hiding in an icehouse in the middle of nowhere from one of the scariest men in the universes. Walker escaped from a burning prison. Imagine their surprise when they find out they have the same man to blame for their miseries. Passion, revenge and love are in their future.

Summer Lightning by Saskia Walker

Sculptress Sally is enjoying an idyllic getaway on a secluded cove when she spots a gorgeous man walking naked on the beach. When Julian finds an attractive woman shacked up in his cove, he has to check her out. But what will he do when he finds she's secretly been using him as a model?

Secrets, Volume 13

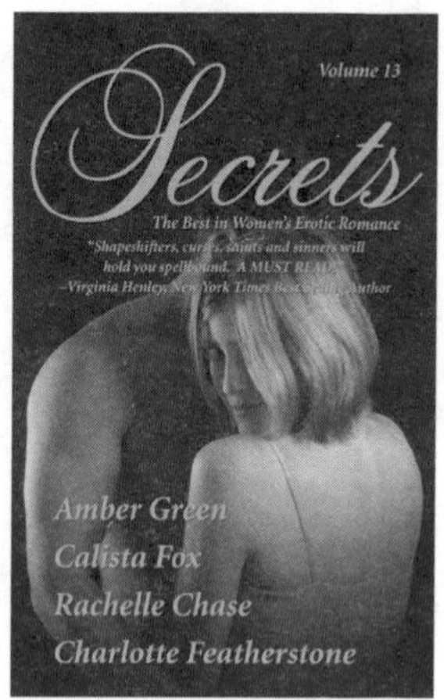

Listen to what reviewers say:

"In ***Secrets Volume 13***, the temperature gets turned up a few notches with a mistaken personal ad, shape-shifters destined to love, a hot Regency lord and his lady, as well as a bodyguard protecting his woman. Emotions and flames blaze high in Red Sage's latest foray into the sensual and delightful art of love." **4½ Stars**

—*Romantic Times BOOKclub*

"The sex is still so hot the pages nearly ignite! Read ***Secrets, Volume 13***!

—*Romance Reviews*

In ***Secrets, Volume 13*** you'll find:

Out of Control by Rachelle Chase

Astrid's world revolves around her business and she's hoping to pick up wealthy Erik Santos as a client. Only he's hoping to pick up something entirely different. Will she give in to the seductive pull of his proposition?

Hawkmoor by Amber Green

Shape-shifters answer to Darien as he acts in the name of the long-missing Lady Hawkmoor, their hereditary ruler. When she unexpectedly surfaces, Darien must deal with a scrappy individual whose wary eyes hold the other half of his soul, but who has the power to destroy his world.

Lessons in Pleasure by Charlotte Featherstone

A wicked bargain has Lily vowing never to yield to the demands of the rake she once loved and lost. Unfortunately, Damian, the Earl of St. Croix, or Saint as he is infamously known, will not take 'no' for an answer.

In the Heat of the Night by Calista Fox

Haunted by a century-old curse, Molina fears she won't live to see her thirtieth birthday. Nick, her former bodyguard, is hired back into service to protect her from the fatal accidents that plague her family. But *In the Heat of the Night*, will his passion and love for her be enough to convince Molina they have a future together?

The Forever Kiss
by Angela Knight

Listen to what reviewers say:

"***The Forever Kiss*** flows well with good characters and an interesting plot. … If you enjoy vampires and a lot of hot sex, you are sure to enjoy ***The Forever Kiss***."

—*The Best Reviews*

"Battling vampires, a protective ghost and the ever present battle of good and evil keep excellent pace with the erotic delights in Angela Knight's ***The Forever Kiss***—a book that absolutely bites with refreshing paranormal humor." **4½ Stars, Top Pick**

—*Romantic Times BOOKclub*

"I found ***The Forever Kiss*** to be an exceptionally written, refreshing book. … I really enjoyed this book by Angela Knight. … 5 angels!"

—*Fallen Angel Reviews*

"***The Forever Kiss*** is the first single title released from Red Sage and if this is any indication of what we can expect, it won't be the last. … The love scenes are hot enough to give a vampire a sunburn and the fight scenes will have you cheering for the good guys."

—*Really Bad Barb Reviews*

In ***The Forever Kiss***:

For years, Valerie Chase has been haunted by dreams of a Texas Ranger she knows only as "Cowboy." As a child, he rescued her from the nightmare vampires who murdered her parents. As an adult, she still dreams of him—but now he's her seductive lover in nights of erotic pleasure.

Yet "Cowboy" is more than a dream—he's the real Cade McKinnon—and a vampire! For years, he's protected Valerie from Edward Ridgemont, the sadistic vampire who turned him. Now, Ridgmont wants Valerie for his own and Cade is the only one who can protect her.

When Val finds herself abducted by her handsome dream man, she's appalled to discover he's one of the vampires she fears. Now, caught in a web of fear and passion, she and Cade must learn to trust each other, even as an immortal monster stalks their every move.

Their only hope of survival is…***The Forever Kiss***.

Angela Knight is the 3rd Place winner in Paranormal Romace for ***The Forever Kiss***

Finally, the men you've been dreaming about!

Give the Gift of Spicy Romantic Fiction

Don't want to wait? You can place a retail price ($12.99) order for any of the *Secrets* volumes from the following:

① **Waldenbooks and Borders Stores**

② **Amazon.com** or **BarnesandNoble.com**

③ **Book Clearinghouse (800-431-1579)**

④ **Romantic Times Magazine**
Books by Mail (718-237-1097)

⑤ Special order at other bookstores.
Bookstores: Please contact Baker & Taylor Distributors or Red Sage Publishing for bookstore sales.

Order by title or ISBN #:

Vol. 1: 0-9648942-0-3
Vol. 2: 0-9648942-1-1
Vol. 3: 0-9648942-2-X
Vol. 4: 0-9648942-4-6
Vol. 5: 0-9648942-5-4
Vol. 6: 0-9648942-6-2
Vol. 7: 0-9648942-7-0
Vol. 8: 0-9648942-8-9
Vol. 9: 0-9648942-9-7
Vol. 10: 0-9754516-0-X
Vol. 11: 0-9754516-1-8
Vol. 12: 0-9754516-2-6
Vol. 13: 0-9754516-3-4

The Forever Kiss: 0-9648942-3-8 ($14.00)

Red Sage Publishing Mail Order Form:

(Orders shipped in two to three days of receipt.)

	Quantity	Mail Order Price	Total
Secrets Volume 1 *(Retail $12.99)*	________	$ 9.99	________
Secrets Volume 2 *(Retail $12.99)*	________	$ 9.99	________
Secrets Volume 3 *(Retail $12.99)*	________	$ 9.99	________
Secrets Volume 4 *(Retail $12.99)*	________	$ 9.99	________
Secrets Volume 5 *(Retail $12.99)*	________	$ 9.99	________
Secrets Volume 6 *(Retail $12.99)*	________	$ 9.99	________
Secrets Volume 7 *(Retail $12.99)*	________	$ 9.99	________
Secrets Volume 8 *(Retail $12.99)*	________	$ 9.99	________
Secrets Volume 9 *(Retail $12.99)*	________	$ 9.99	________
Secrets Volume 10 *(Retail $12.99)*	________	$ 9.99	________
Secrets Volume 11 *(Retail $12.99)*	________	$ 9.99	________
Secrets Volume 12 *(Retail $12.99)*	________	$ 9.99	________
Secrets Volume 13 *(Retail $12.99)*	________	$ 9.99	________
The Forever Kiss *(Retail $14.00)*	________	$11.00	________

Shipping & handling (in the U.S.)

US Priority Mail:		UPS insured:	
1–2 books	$ 5.50	1–4 books	$16.00
3–5 books	$11.50	5–9 books	$25.00
6–9 books	$14.50	10–11 books	$29.00
10–11 books	$19.00		

____

SUBTOTAL ________

Florida 6% sales tax (if delivered in FL) ________

TOTAL AMOUNT ENCLOSED ________

Your personal information is kept private and not shared with anyone.

Name: (please print) ________________________

Address: (no P.O. Boxes) ________________________

City/State/Zip: ________________________

Phone or email: (only regarding order if necessary) ________________________

Please make check payable to **Red Sage Publishing**. Check must be drawn on a U.S. bank in U.S. dollars. Mail your check and order form to:

Red Sage Publishing, Inc. Department S12 P.O. Box 4844 Seminole, FL 33775

***Or use the order form on our website:* www.redsagepub.com**

It's not just reviewers raving about *Secrets*. See what readers have to say:

"When are you coming out with a new Volume? I want a new one next month!" via email from a reader.

"I loved the hot, wet sex without vulgar words being used to make it exciting." after ***Volume 1***

"I loved the blend of sensuality and sexual intensity—HOT!" after ***Volume 2***

"The best thing about ***Secrets*** is they're hot and brief! The least thing is you do not have enough of them!" after ***Volume 3***

"I have been extreamly satisfied with ***Secrets***, keep up the good writing." after ***Volume 4***

"Stories have plot and characters to support the erotica. They would be good strong stories without the heat." after ***Volume 5***

"***Secrets*** really knows how to push the envelop better than anyone else." after ***Volume 6***

"These are the best sensual stories I have ever read!" after ***Volume 7***

"I love, love, love the ***Secrets*** stories. I now have all of them, please have more books come out each year." after ***Volume 8***

"These are the perfect sensual romance stories!" after ***Volume 9***

"What I love about ***Secrets Volume 10*** is how I couldn't put it down!" after ***Volume 10***

"All of the ***Secrets*** volumes are terrific! I have read all of them up to ***Secrets Volume 11***. Please keep them coming! I will read every one you make!" after ***Volume 11***